W.F. CARLI

STONE TOTEM

SHOOTING STAR PUBLISHING

Friday Harbor

Published by Shooting Star Publishing
Friday Harbor, WA 98250
Copyright © 2009 by W. F. Carli

ISBN: 978-0-9787311-1-3
Library of Congress Control Number: 2009904387

10 9 8 7 6 5 4 3 2 1

Cover design by A. Shull Design, Friday Harbor, WA
Cover art by Robert Warren, Friday Harbor, WA
Book design by www.FreelanceBookDesign.com

Printed in the U.S.A.

This book is dedicated to Alden and Stella

STONE TOTEM

Prologue

I am more than life. I am spirit as well. I taste, I see, and I learn in ways that you cannot understand. I am rooted deep into the earth and my arms stretch high to the heavens. Now, for the first time in a thousand years I fear, for I can hear you coming.

* * *

It was the season of heat and long days, when the rain from heaven shuts off, and the earth becomes parched tinder. How long I lay dormant, I have no idea. We are cast forth to live or to die, with no help. Only through death and destruction can come birth. I know that to live, one must be born, but I cannot remember mine. I also know that in the time of great heat and no rain the earth fears fire. All life fears her, for she comes with no mercy, no regard for what she takes. She is all that I have ever feared, until now.

It was close to dusk, the air was still and the earth groaned under another heated day. In the west the sky grew dark, not from the setting sun but from the rising storm, a summer lightning storm. The earth seemed to take a deep breath collectively, as if all could wish this coming storm away. Large and small, those that could flee and those that must stand and face whatever comes, all held their breath. From the sea the storm came with increasing winds that strengthened by the minute. The clouds raised their heads and touched the heavens. They grew darker as they billowed forth, heavy with the promise of rain and the curse of fire.

The first lightning bolt hit far from where I lay. If I could see above the rest, maybe I could have seen the smoke. It would have been

1

so small at first, a slight touch of gray upon the wind. All that were near the lightning strike could smell it, could taste it, and they all feared it. With one crack from the heavens a bolt of lightning hotter than the surface of the sun exploded into the dry mountainside. A mighty Douglas fir, two hundred feet tall and over three hundred years old took the lightning's blast directly. The top of the tree blew into a thousand shards of burning embers all cascading down onto the dry earth. The power of the lightning descended through the tree and all that was near it instantly ignited into a huge circle of flames. The earth was dry, and fire was hungry; it didn't take her long to turn her appetite outward.

It took three weeks for the flames to reach me as I lay dormant in my cocoon of hardened shell. The fire raged consuming all that was above ground, except for the mighty cedars and huge Douglas firs, all life that could not flee died. The hemlock burst into flames and became dust. The madrona shrieked in agony as its beautiful red bark burned and its branches and dry leaves curled into an inferno before dying. I was buried under much earth and debris. I felt no fear. I felt no heat. I was not yet born.

It took days for the fire to burn past where I lay. It continued its attack upon the earth, unchecked for another month before the rains came and ended its appetite. It was the rain that gave me life. The flames awakened my inner being, but the water brought me forth. By now the season of heat was gone. It was the beginning of winter, the time when our mother the earth goes inside herself, becomes still, and looks only to her own needs after a season of heat and growth and new life. The first thing I remembered was the cold, a wet cold as the rain made its way down into the earth and seemed to wake me from a deep slumber. I awoke already knowing that my struggle for life had begun. I burst forth from the earth into a strange world. My journey started with energy and a desperate attempt to reach upward and away from the cold earth into the warmth and life of the light. The mighty red cedar that had survived the fire was the closest thing to me, and it was over seventy-five feet away. The alder, hemlock, and madrona that would have covered the land were gone. The forest floor was but ash after fire had her way. Day after day, year after year I reached ever higher toward the light.

I will always remember the old man who entered into my domain. I could sense his every step. He was a kind, wise man, I could tell. He walked with the help of a wooden stick to give his body support. I knew he was on a mission, a holy quest, for he had purpose in his stride, and his mind was sharp, focused, he was searching. He stopped and looked at me, spent ten minutes in silence, as if in prayer, before he turned and walked to the mighty red cedar. Kneeling in front of my friend, he started to sing in a soft voice. I couldn't hear his words, he was too far away, but I knew their meaning. He was praying, asking permission to take its life.

The old Indian was named Shakiawaii, which means *he who sings to the wind*. He was the spiritual leader of the village that lived by the sea two miles away. Shakiawaii had spent three days in solitude, confined to a small cedar house set apart from the village. He had eaten no food and had little water. He simply spent his time in prayer asking his gods to give him wisdom, to guide his feet to the tree that would become the next totem for the village. He sought a holy tree, chosen not by man but by the heavens, a tree blessed by his gods. Only a tree such as this could stand before the sea as the village totem. The old man had walked for two days once he left his solitude. Now, as he stood at the base of my friend, he had found what he desired. I know all of this because I have wisdom beyond what mortal men can understand.

Shakiawaii built a small fire carefully surrounded by stones. As night started to fall he gathered more wood and continued to pray. All through the night he kept the fire going. He often stood and walked around my friend, looking up as if studying every small detail. I wondered if he could imagine in the darkness the totem already completed. The next morning he departed as the sun rose. I knew that he would return soon and he would not come alone. So did the cedar. It knew that the humans would take it. Its time was coming to an end but it did not grieve. It feared the pain of death, but it looked forward to becoming a new creation, one revered by so many.

The entire village came when Shakiawaii returned. Over three hundred gathered around my friend. The reverence that these people offered the huge red cedar brought emotions to us that we didn't know we were capable of. The village prayed through the entire night, a small fire casting comforting shadows for all who were there. In the morning Shakiawaii said more words as his people stood in silent respect. Once he had finished, he reached into his leather bag and took out a black stone of razor sharp obsidian, and made one small cut at the base of the tree. Once he had completed his cut, he handed the stone to the village chief, who made his. Then he passed the stone on until every member of the village had held it and had placed a small cut into my friend.

The village left and all was quiet, but we both knew, not for long. In a few days six men returned, set up a camp, and started to cut the cedar down. They used sharpened rocks on long wooden handles. It took four days before the mighty giant fell to the earth. It took another five weeks before the totem was roughly carved and carried down to the village by over a hundred men from three different villages. My friend is gone, and now I am the great red cedar of the forest.

Time has no meaning to me. I only watch as things change. I saw the village people grow and prosper, surely from the blessing of my friend. They lived in harmony with all that was around them. The salmon came and fed them when they were hungry, the deer and the plants as well. All of nature did a delicate dance with man. Life flourished and all felt blessed.

Then I saw the white man come. He treated all things that lived without any reverence, and I knew that wolves had descended upon us. I watched in horror as the village was destroyed by a disease that caused the people to wither and die, their bodies covered by sickening white scabs and pus. It caused the people to drop dead in such great numbers that it reminded me of autumn leaves falling to the ground. I saw the building of towns and then cities, of roads and then highways. I can now taste how poisoned the air and the water have become.

It was in the springtime, when life unfolds for another season, that I started to fear. I hadn't feared anything in over a thousand years, but now, once again, I know fear. I know the scream of your chainsaws, and the tears of my friends that you have destroyed, they still echo in my soul. I am the giant red cedar of the forest, the tree given to the people by the gods in heaven. I rule all that I see, and now I am terrified. Yes, I can hear you coming.

Chapter 1

A cold wind whipped through the morning sky, and dark clouds threatened rain at any moment. Captain Mondo sat in the small outside courtyard of the Grey Heron restaurant, coffee in hand, overlooking the inner harbor of Victoria, British Columbia, and he felt chilled to the bone. He knew he should get up and move inside, but it was too much effort. Taking another gulp of lukewarm coffee, he slumped back in his chair and let out a deep sigh, feeling some of the emotions he had been fighting leave him.

A few raindrops splattered on his table as he stared over the marina and watched Smokin' Joe, his forty-four-foot sailboat, tugging at her mooring lines. Looking at his beloved yacht, he let his mind wander, taking his thoughts back to some of the wonderful places he had sailed her. Beautiful tropical islands with swaying palm trees, crystal blue water and white sandy beaches, he could remember them all. Living aboard Smokin' Joe and sailing the oceans of the world was the perfect life. This cookie-cutter world that most people tolerated just didn't work for him and he knew it.

Still staring over the harbor, daydreaming between the raindrops, he thought about his last voyage, the ultimate sailing experience, the South Pacific.

He had sailed from Panama, after transiting the canal, heading west, the fabled Galapagos Islands his first destination. On board as crew was Tim, one of his best friends. The normal light winds in this area quickly turned into twenty-knot trades, creating a fast downwind sail to the first of their South Sea destination. The stark, natural beauty of this enchanted archipelago exceeded anything he

5

had been able to imagine. The sweet smell of tropical air, desolate bays and rugged landscapes, the abundance of life, life that knew no fear of man, set the mood for a trip that was to be the adventure of a lifetime.

From the Galapagos they headed south, sailing over twenty-five hundred miles, non-stop, until they reached Easter Island. This tiny island, with its huge carved stone statues, is over two thousand miles away from South America. This tiny speck of land in the middle of the Pacific Ocean holds an ancient mystery. Who created these gigantic stone statues, and how did they do it? Their sheer size and weight, some weighing over eighty tons and standing thirty feet tall, would make it all but impossible for a primitive people to have accomplished such a feat. After seeing the statues with his own eyes, Mondo couldn't imagine. From Easter Island it was on to Pitcairn Island, where all of the inhabitants could trace their ancestry back to one man, John Adams, the last remaining male survivor of the mutiny on the Bounty. From Pitcairn it was on to Tahiti, where he met Tim's sister Naomi for the first time.

"Damn . . . beautiful Naomi," he said softly as he took a swallow of cold coffee, his thoughts crashing back to the present. He stood up, dug his wallet out and paid the bill, then he walked across the street to the seaplane dock located to the right of the marina. Five minutes later a seaplane appeared over the ocean-side condos, took a steep dive and landed in a small corner of the bay. The plane slowly made its way up to a special dock and turned off its large single engine. Mondo was standing thirty feet back, looking through the tinted windows, trying to see both of them.

This long weekend getaway was Tim's idea. He had emailed Mondo a month ago and told him he was off for a two-year stint with the Peace Corps, and he would love for them to get together before he left. Mondo jumped at the chance and told him they could meet in Victoria. They emailed back and forth, got the dates and times all figured out, then last week Tim emailed and said Naomi wanted to come along. Mondo didn't know what to think. Did he really want to see her again? He almost emailed back and said no, but then he realized he really didn't have much of a choice. Sure, he emailed, bring her along. Now as he watched the seaplane door open and the pilot jump out onto the floating dock, he wasn't sure it was such a wise decision.

The pilot secured the plane, then walked back to the passenger door and pulled it down. An older couple exited first, followed by Naomi and Tim.

They both looked exactly as he remembered them; neither seemed to have aged a bit. Tim carried two small bags as he and Naomi walked up to Mondo. Naomi truly was as beautiful as he remembered.

"It's good to see you both, it really is," Mondo said.

"Likewise," Tim replied, giving him a hug.

Naomi wrapped her arms around him, and kissed his cheek, dragging up a wave of emotions from the past.

"You still look good, Captain Monod," she said with a smile as she pulled away from his hug. For a second they stood in an awkward silence, before all three of them burst into laughter.

"This way," Mondo said, still laughing.

They walked up from the seaplane dock, around the large visitor/tourist information center, and then across the stone inner-harbor causeway that led to the boat docks and Smokin' Joe.

"Permission to come aboard?" Naomi asked.

"I never remember you asking permission before."

"Well, so . . ."

Mondo bowed at the waist, sweeping his left arm out toward the boarding ladder as he reached for her right hand and helped her aboard.

"I don't need any help, thank you, captain," Tim said, shaking his head, with a laugh.

Tim climbed down the companionway steps, dropped the two bags he was carrying on the galley floor, and sat down on the settee. Naomi hesitated once on board. She took a few steps to her right and let Mondo walk past her before he climbed down below. Naomi stood on deck looking around, feeling a flood of emotions sweep over her.

"She looks good. For all the miles you've sailed her, Smokin' Joe doesn't look bad. You look pretty good too," Tim said, as Mondo sat next to him.

"I was hoping we could get out of here, go sailing for a day or so, but the weather looks bad. We might have to just hang around Victoria. ”

"Sounds good, it's just great to be here."

Naomi carefully climbed down the companionway steps, walked over and sat down next to Mondo. All three of them were wedged tight, enjoying the magic of the moment, each reliving his or her version of the past.

"We could go to the museum if you want," Mondo said with a smile, looking at Naomi.

"I was reading about the museum. Do you know it has one of the largest original totem pole collections in the world? I'd love to go . . . that is if you guys want to," she replied.

"Well, the weather looks lousy, I'm into it," Mondo said.

"Sounds good to me," Tim agreed.

They hung around for an hour, nobody in a hurry to move, just enjoying each others company, Mondo and Tim telling sailing stories, Naomi listening and every once in a while throwing in a few comments. All three of them were feeling so comfortable, enjoying the closeness of being squeezed around the small teak table. It felt like the tensions that had torn him and Naomi apart no longer existed, and Mondo prayed it would stay that way.

A cold rain still fell when they finally they climbed out of Smokin' Joe and made their way across the street to the Royal Provincial Museum. They walked into the lobby and stood in a long line to buy their tickets. While waiting, Mondo could see three tall totem poles to his right. After he bought his ticket he walked over and looked at the closest one. It had a small plaque at the base, stating that this totem was from an Indian village with a name that he could never pronounce and it was carved around 1823. Glancing back and seeing Naomi and Tim still waiting to buy their tickets, he walked over and looked at the other two totems. One was carved around 1830 and the last one was carved, according to another small plaque, around 1780.

"Look at this," Mondo said as they walked over to him after paying.

"Two of these totem poles are over a hundred and fifty years old and this one," he said as he pointed, "is over two hundred years old."

"It's amazing," Naomi said, "do you know that the totem pole was the spiritual and historical guardian of these people? They had no written language but the totem spoke for the village history and the gods that they worshipped. I think it is fascinating that they could have carved them such a long time ago and they are still standing."

Mondo was surprised at her enthusiasm.

"I didn't realize that you knew so much about totems."

"I did an article on totems a while ago, tried to sell it to the mainstream magazines, but no takers. So . . . I wasted three weeks in research but it sure was interesting."

They walked over to the escalator and rode it up to the second floor where the exhibits started. Every room they entered held beautiful displays of a way of life now lost. One room had an entire wall covered with beautifully carved masks. Each mask had a small brass plaque attached to the wall just below it with the approximate date that they were created and where they were from. All three wandered, and time slipped away. Mondo marveled at an original ocean-going canoe that the native people once took out to harpoon whales. It was unbelievably small. He couldn't imagine the nerve that it must have taken to launch a harpoon into a mighty whale from such a small boat.

They continued exploring, walking next through an exhibit of native clothing and rope, and then he and Naomi entered into a model of a native longhouse. Mondo was surprised as he realized that almost everything that he had seen so far was made one way or another from the red cedar tree.

"Naomi, were all of the totems made from red cedar? It seems that just about everything they had was from that tree; their canoes, their houses, even some of their clothing was woven from its bark."

"According to my research they thanked their gods for the red cedar above all other trees. It gave them so much of what they needed. It lasts for centuries, and all the totems that I've ever read about were carved from it."

Mondo and Naomi stood in silence for a few minutes, looking around the inside of the huge longhouse. Suddenly they saw Tim stick his head inside the small round opening that was used as the main door.

"Mondo, Naomi, come here, I want you to see something."

They walked out of the longhouse and followed him down a flight of stairs into a large room with an extremely high ceiling. It was a room full of totems. They walked from one to the other in awestruck silence. At least twenty-five original totem poles were in this room. So much symbolism, Mondo thought. They walked in silence for a good ten minutes before Naomi realized that Tim was nowhere to be seen.

"Where's Tim?" she whispered.

Naomi's question brought Mondo's attention from the totems back into the room and he looked around for him.

"Tim," he said softly.

"Over here," Tim's voice was coming from behind a wall that led to another exhibit.

They walked around the corner and there he was, standing at the base of a small totem about twelve feet high. Naomi glanced at her brother, and was going to keep walking, when she looked at Mondo. He had stopped in his tracks. He didn't even look at her when she softly called his name. What Mondo saw took his breath away, made all of his thoughts about the other exhibits flee from his mind as he stood in front of this totem. He knew instantly why Tim was captivated by it. Mondo was staring at a totem that was not like any other he had seen in the museum. Not like any totem he had ever seen in the Pacific Northwest. What made his mind spin out of control was that he had seen this carving before! This manmade image was almost the perfect replica of a statue he had spent hours studying. It was the same solemn figure, but the last time he had seen it, it was made of stone and it was over five thousand miles away on Easter Island.

Chapter 2

Time stood still for Mondo as he stared at the totem, his thoughts rushing back to Easter Island. After a few minutes he glanced down and read a little identifying brass plaque. The plaque said this totem came from a village called Neskiwaii and that it was carved around 1820.

"That's amazing," Tim said.

"I know, actually it seems impossible," Mondo replied.

"Sorry, guys, but I don't get it. What's so special about this totem?" Naomi asked.

"Your brother and I have seen this carving before."

"Okay, so?" she said anxiously, like she was the only person who didn't get the joke.

"Well, we saw this carving over five thousand miles away from here on Easter Island," Mondo replied.

Naomi tried to get it, but she knew she was missing something.

"So you saw this on Easter Island. Look, this was carved in 1820, plenty of time for some sailing ship to have visited Easter Island and then sail here. Don't you think? I mean . . . probably some artist drew a picture on Easter Island and then showed it to some native people here in the Pacific Northwest."

Mondo shrugged his shoulders.

"Maybe, but just think if this totem was older. What if it was carved before the first explorers ever reached the Pacific Northwest? Then you would have quite the mystery on your hands." Tim said.

"Like how did the native North American people meet somebody from Easter Island?" Naomi smiled as it all suddenly sank in.

"Yeah, something like that," Mondo said with a smile.

"Wow," was all she could say.

"You know, I'm really curious about this. Let's find the office and ask somebody about it. I'm sure we're not the first inquisitive minds around here," Mondo said looking at his friends.

They walked out of the totem room and into a hallway that led them back to the ticket area on the first floor. They entered the main lobby, and walked up to an older, gray-haired, impeccably dressed man wearing a small plastic tag attached to his jacket that said Museum Assistant.

"Excuse me, sir, we have a question," Naomi said.

"Yes."

"There is a totem pole in there," she said excitedly as she pointed back toward the room they had just come from, "and it looks like it came from Easter Island."

The man laughed softly. "I know, a few people have mentioned it in the past. It is rather peculiar, I must admit. I don't know much about it. I only volunteer here two days a week and that is only part time. However, if you take the elevator to the third floor and go left you will see Jonathan Beckwith's office down the hall on your right. He is the one to ask."

"Can we disturb him?" Tim asked.

"Oh yes. He is quite passionate about this subject. Most here in the museum think his . . . um . . . well . . . ," he laughed, "some here find his thinking a little off base. He teaches at the University of Victoria, teaches Northwest Cultural Anthropology. He really is quite brilliant. I think you would find him an interesting chap. I know he is in his office. I saw him enter the museum this morning."

"You don't think we would be bothering him?" Mondo repeated Tim's question.

"I think not."

The three of them walked to the elevator and pushed the third floor button. Once inside, they started laughing, looking at each other making crazy faces.

"This seems stupid, if you ask me," Mondo said.

"So, it's a rainy day, might as well meet him. It's pretty interesting that the totem resembles the Easter Island stone carving," Naomi said.

The elevator door opened onto a deserted third floor. They looked around the empty hallway, and then started walking to their left. Each closed door had a person's name engraved on a small plaque attached at eye level. They found Mr. Beckwith's door and Tim knocked.

"Just a minute, hold on," they heard from inside the office.

They heard some commotion and a small crash then Jonathan Beckwith stood there holding the door part way open. He was a tall, lean man, in his mid-forties. He wore large thick glasses and a rumpled dark suit with a bow tie. He looked surprised standing there, as if it were very unusual to have anybody knock on his door.

"Hello, can I help you?"

He stood there with a look on his face that made all three of them wonder what they were doing.

"Mr. Beckwith, a nice gentleman said we should come and talk to you. We have a question about a totem pole we saw downstairs. Hope we're not bothering you," Naomi said in a soft feminine voice that seemed to disarm him a bit.

"Please come in. I have a few minutes." he smiled as he opened the door and they followed him into his small office.

"Please close the door, thank you," he said then knelt down and picked up four large hardcover books off the floor and put them on a cluttered bookshelf, before sitting down, leaving the three of them standing. There were no other chairs in his small office.

"Your knock startled me. I was just going to put a few books away, so what's your question? I'm sorry for the lack of chairs," he said as he raised his palms up, and shrugged his shoulders.

As he stood there it seemed to Mondo that they would have about thirty more seconds of Mr. Beckwith's time before he would come up with some reason for them to leave. Oh well, he thought.

"We saw a totem downstairs in the main totem room. We've seen the design before, on Easter Island," Tim said.

Mr. Beckwith lit up the moment Easter Island was mentioned.

"Very interesting, isn't it?" he replied.

"Yes, it is. How did it get here? How did the native people know to carve that design so long ago?" Naomi asked, her excitement evident to all in the room.

Mr. Beckwith slumped back in his chair, stretched his arms up high, and then interlocked his fingers on the back of his head. He smiled again and puffed out a short laugh.

"That my dear, is a damned good question. Please, I seldom have guests here, follow me," he said then stood up and walked to a door in the corner of his office. He opened it, reached inside and flipped a light on, then turned back to them, "come in, please," he said.

The three of them followed him into a small room with a table and four chairs around it. It looked like an oversize storage room that had been converted into an office. There were a few pictures on the wall, and Naomi realized that most were of the Easter Island totem that they had seen downstairs. Next to the totem photos were three pictures, held to the wall with bright push pins of the stone carvings on Easter Island.

"Welcome to my holy grail room, if you like . . . So, you are curious? Good, tell me, what do you think?" he asked, looking at Naomi then glancing at Mondo and Tim.

They all sat down around the table and Naomi picked up the conversation.

"It's pretty strange. That totem, it doesn't fit with any that I have ever seen."

"Have you seen many?" he asked, his hands once again locked on the back of his head as he sat looking very relaxed.

"No," Naomi laughed, "but I've seen lots of pictures."

Mr. Beckwith glanced at Tim and then at Mondo.

"What do you think, why is this of interest to you?"

"We've been to Easter Island, we've seen the stone carvings with our own eyes," Mondo said.

"You have!" he said excitedly.

"Yes, we both have," Tim said.

"My, I have always wanted to go there and see those stone statues myself. Tell me, did you fly from Tahiti? I understand that is the best way to get there."

"No, we sailed from the Galapagos," Mondo replied.

Mr. Beckwith, about to say something else, stopped.

"You sailed there, from the Galapagos, how?"

Mondo laughed, "On Smokin' Joe, my sailboat."

Mr. Beckwith sat up in his chair and brought his hands down from the top of his head. He leaned his forearms on the table and absentmindedly stuck his right thumbnail between his teeth. He was lost in thought while the three of them sat there for over a minute, just watching. Finally, he pulled his nail out from in between his teeth.

"Well," he said as he gave Naomi a slight nod and a smile, "that is how the native people learned of the design, from early contact."

"When?" Mondo asked.

"That is the million dollar question, isn't it? The totem was supposedly carved around 1820 and if it's true then it's not much of a mystery. Explorers had already reached the Pacific Northwest and they could easily have brought the design with them. However, I believe that totem is much older, older than . . . " he paused, as if trying to pick the right date.

"Can't they test the totem to see how old it is, carbon testing or something?" Naomi interjected in the momentary silence, her investigative journalist skills showing by the minute.

"Of course they can, but nobody around here seems very interested. Why, I suggested it myself. I was laughed at. Can you believe it? Well, anyway, I don't think anyone wants to open up a can of worms by scientifically addressing the age of that totem." Jonathan paused again, as if thinking something else, before he said. "There are just so many coincidences."

"What other coincidences?" Naomi asked.

Mr. Beckwith laughed. "Take your pick. How about the pyramids of Egypt and the pyramids of South America? Think about it. Two peoples, separated by thousands of miles of ocean, and they build damn near the same design. That is impossible without contact."

None of them said a word.

"Okay, let's take the potato," he continued. "We think of Ireland, right? The Irish people surviving for centuries on the lowly potato, well, guess what? The potato is a South American tuber. How did it get to Europe centuries before Columbus? I could go on and on and on."

His excitement permeated the room.

"There is only one way . . . people would have had to be sailing the oceans of the world thousands of years ago," Mondo said, his voice very soft.

"You're right, there is no other way. Do you realize that all of the great cultures, the marvels of engineering and commerce in the ancient world, all came from civilizations that bordered the ocean? What if . . ." he let his words hang, as if teaching a class at the University trying to get the main point across.

"What if an advanced society was able to sail across the oceans of the world thousands of years before Christ? What if these people were traders, merchants, and explorers? Think of the wealth they could amass. Not by plunder, not by force, but by sharing what they knew with other societies that they met. The more they were able to share of their advanced culture, the more they taught those they encountered, the more riches they would be able to acquire. Although . . . I don't think these people did what they did for wealth."

"Why then?" Naomi asked.

"Why?" Mr. Beckwith seemed to be drifting off, following his own train of thought somewhere, "why, because it is the humanly right thing to do, especially if you are intelligent enough to realize that we are all the same, that more than likely we all come from a common ancestry."

"What does that say about us today?" Mondo asked.

"Not much. We can go to the moon, but we can't feed our people. My God, man, we could feed every child on the planet for what we spend on weapons!"

Jonathan slumped back in his chair, his demeanor suddenly changed. It seemed as if a tangible sadness came over him as he sat there. He looked at the three of them and didn't say a word, just slightly shook his head back and forth. The room went quiet, everybody reflecting on what he had just said. A spell had descended and nobody knew how to break it. It felt like hours, but it was only a few minutes before he spoke again.

"I'm sorry for my outburst. I am just so saddened when I think of the whole damn mess we find ourselves in. Where are the wise leaders that this world so desperately needs?"

"You're absolutely right," Tim said.

"Yes, you are," Mondo and Naomi said quietly at the same time.

"I don't know how that totem came to be carved," Mr. Beckwith said a few moments later, "the village is long gone. It was on the west coast of Vancouver Island, pretty far north. It's part of a great land trust given to the native people of British Columbia over a hundred and fifty years ago. Nobody wanted it back then, it was too far away and nobody thought about the value of all that timber, but now it is worth millions. Those trees are about all that's left of an ancient rainforest that covered most of the west coast from Alaska to California. You know I am afraid that it is only a matter of time before it will all be logged."

"What about the native people, don't they control their own lands?" Naomi asked.

"Maybe, supposedly, but we know what controls this world. Money controls this world, greed controls this world. I know that big money wants to cut every damn one of those trees down. If the huge corporations want those trees, then all they have to do is buy the politicians and they can get them. I have no doubt that they can find some way to force the native people to agree. Somehow, some way, money always wins."

"I just got depressed," Naomi said with a little laugh, but she was speaking for all of them.

Mr. Beckwith stood up. Their meeting was over.

"Why don't you come to my place for dinner tonight? I'm a lousy cook and a worse housekeeper, but I have so much to tell you."

"Sounds good to me, I doubt your housekeeping or cooking skills are any worse than mine," Mondo said with a laugh.

They followed him out of the small room into his office. He opened his desk drawer, pulled out a business card, and scribbled his address on the back.

"Here, it's not too far away. Come by around seven-thirty. Be real hungry, that way my cooking will taste better," he said, handing them his card.

"What can we bring?" Naomi asked.

It made Mondo think he should have asked that question. Leave it to a woman, he thought.

Mr. Beckwith paused, scrunched his face and lifted his shoulders slightly. He didn't know what to say.

"I'll tell you what," he said a moment later, "you can bring two things, a large bottle of wine and an open mind."

Chapter 3

A pedal-powered rickshaw pulled up to a small apartment complex ten blocks from the waterfront at seven-forty-five. The three of them climbed out, paid the young driver, who told them he was from New Zealand and had been pedaling tourists around Victoria for the last two months, then walked up to Jonathan's front door.

"Hello, welcome, please come in," he said.

They walked into a confirmed bachelor's pad. An orange shag carpet was the first thing that assaulted their eyes. The walls had a few dated paintings hung in baroque gold frames that didn't match the two plaid arm chairs and an old leather couch that took up most of the small living room. Mondo noticed right away there was no television; that was a plus. Naomi handed Jonathan a bag containing two bottles of wine (it was her suggestion to get an extra bottle) and they followed him into a small kitchen. It was open to a dining room not much bigger than the one on Smokin' Joe. Mondo liked this little dysfunctional apartment, but he still wasn't sure what to think of Jonathan Beckwith.

Jonathan put the two bottles of wine on the counter, looked at them both, then chose a California red and opened it. He smelled the cork with a fleeting pass under his nose, and poured four glasses.

"Let's sit down, please, dinner is in the oven."

He handed each of them a glass, then they walked into the living room.

Naomi and Tim sat on the couch, Jonathan and Mondo sat in the two chairs that looked like they came from different planets.

"To our health," Tim said.

"Cheers," they replied.

After the toast, there was an awkward moment of silence.

"Another toast, I guess," Jonathan said, raising his glass one more time, before he continued, "you know, I couldn't stop thinking of your question today. I didn't get a thing done after you left. You brought up a topic that is very dear to my heart, and one that needs to be addressed by the scientific community. You asked about Easter Island, and we can start there if you like, although it would be just as easy to begin with Stonehenge or ancient Egypt. Or maybe we should discuss Mesopotamia, the Bronze Age, or what about the Standing Stones of Calanais? We could talk about the many mysteries of South America if you like? You see, there is much to consider when one starts asking questions."

He paused, took another drink from his wine glass and looked at them.

"I know I talk too much. I do get carried away at times. When I lecture, some students say it is hard to follow my train of thought. If you have a question or don't follow, just ask."

They all nodded, each aware that there was no stopping Jonathan at the moment.

"Well, a few more things to think about, like Carla in Peru," he said with a slight shoulder shrug and a little smile.

"I see you never heard of it. That's fine, most people haven't. What about the ancient Mayan calendar, or King Solomon's Mines, and while we are at it let us not forget the . . ."

"Wait, wait, wait," Mondo cut him off, "I see why your students have a hard time following your train of thought! You just mentioned about ten different topics that all have to do with our ancient past. What do any of these have to do with Easter Island?"

"Everything," he said, finishing his glass of wine.

"Everything?" Naomi asked.

Tim got up, grabbed the second bottle, opened it and filled everybody's glass.

Jonathan continued, "You can't isolate Easter Island and look at it by itself. There are no answers that way. It must be looked at in the context of early mankind and his ability to travel. Mondo, you were right when you said there was only one way that the people of Easter Island could have had contact with the native population of British Columbia. But what if it wasn't the people of Easter Island who made that sea voyage? What if a nation of seafarers, who were able to sail the world thousands of years earlier than ever believed, what if they made that fateful voyage?"

He paused and looked at them, giving them a moment to respond before he continued.

"You think it's crazy, but you shouldn't. It is the only answer that is even plausible regarding most of the ancient mysteries of our known world.

"Okay, let's get back to Easter Island if you like. How did these people get there in the first place? I doubt a boatload of castaways with enough women on board floated haphazardly around the Pacific Ocean and miraculously discovered Easter Island and bred themselves into a people. That is not what happened. So who were the first people to discover Easter Island? The Pacific Ocean is too immense in size, talk about a needle in a haystack. So if you want to look at Easter Island, the first thing to think about is how did they get there? Not only once, but it is proven through archeological records that there were many different migrations of people. It's a known fact that there were established trade routes between the people of Easter Island and the people of Chile and Peru. How could they possibly continue to find it again and again?"

"Damn good questions," Naomi said.

Jonathan stood up, put his wine glass down on the kitchen table and started walking around the room. The three of them sat in silence, not wanting to interrupt his monologue. All three were starting to realize that there was more to Jonathan Beckwith than they had first thought.

"I'm sure you know that Easter Island was discovered on Easter Sunday, which is how it got its name, in 1722 by the Dutch explorer Jacob Roggeven. He reports that there were three distinct peoples on the island. Not separate groups, not different families, but three distinct ethnic backgrounds. The majority was to be expected, dark-skinned native people similar to most Polynesians, no surprises there. Then there was a second group, they were light-skinned, probably not from a Polynesian background, kind of weird, right? So what about the last group that Jacob Roggeven wrote about?"

He looked at them, letting his words hang in the air for a moment before he continued.

"It is written in his log book, the actual account of his encounter with the Easter Island natives. This is not hearsay, not second or third hand information. The third group were very fair skinned, had red hair and red beards. Tell me, where in the entire Pacific Ocean Basin do you find people like that? You don't."

The three of them sat spellbound.

"Where do you find red-haired, red-bearded, light-skinned sea-faring people? How about Phoenicians?"

"That's impossible," Tim said.

"Oh . . . is it?"

He walked back into the kitchen, grabbed his wine glass, and sat down. All thought of dinner had disappeared.

"It's only possible, realistically, if the Phoenicians were able to sail there," Mondo said a few moments later.

"That's right and it's wrong. You know that the ancient Greek word Phoinos means red, pretty damn close to the word Phoenician. Anyway, let's stretch this back a few thousand years. What if these red-haired people on Easter Island were the last of a dying breed? What if they were the last remnant of a sea-faring people who had sailed from ancient Europe thousands of years earlier? What if the stone carvings on Easter Island were built by them as a testimony to their very existence?"

"Wow," Naomi said softly, interrupting him, her voice almost a whisper.

"You three came to my office today and asked me a question that has been ignored for centuries by mainstream science. Why has this question been ignored? I'll tell you."

They knew he would; Jonathan wasn't slowing down a bit.

"It has been ignored because it opens a completely different concept of early mankind, and his abilities to travel. I believe that people have been sailing across oceans for at least five thousand years."

"Five thousand years," Mondo said, although it sounded more like a question.

"As best as my research can tell, yes," he said, smiling at the look on their faces.

"Think about this very carefully, please. When does time begin? I am serious. This is not some esoteric question. When does the Mayan calendar start?"

None of them could answer.

"The Mayans, who were extremely knowledgeable in astronomy, who devised a calendar almost as accurate as we can calculate today, started their calendar in 3113 B.C. Why? Who was around then to figure that out?

"What else started around 3000 B.C.? How about Mesopotamia or the great pyramids of Egypt? Take Stonehenge, it was started around 3000 B.C. Not what we think of as Stonehenge today, not with the monolith stones, but with fifty-six holes called the Aubrey holes that held wooden poles. Let's take the Standing Stones of Calanais, again about 5000 years old. Also it is amazing that these stones were built at the absolute end of the world on the Outer Hebrides Islands of Scotland. My God, who was there then?"

Jonathan stopped and finished his wine.

"Shall I continue or shall we eat?" he asked.

"Continue, please," Naomi said as Mondo and Tim just shook their heads in amazement.

Jonathan smiled, "Okay, I want you to understand that these mysteries are all connected. That is very important. There are so many unexplained events that revolve around this time. Do any of you know what was the first city ever created in the Americas, and where it was?"

Mondo felt like he was in school, and he thought he knew this answer.

"Fort Augustine in Florida, built by the Spaniards," he said.

"Wrong, as a matter of fact you couldn't get much further from being correct. Anybody else want to try?" he said with a laugh.

Neither Naomi nor Tim said a word.

"All right then, this and one more important thought, the oldest known city in North, South or Central America, anywhere on the whole continent, is Carla. It was discovered north of Lima, Peru and carbon dated back to at least 3000 B.C. This city was over one hundred and sixty acres, and had an estimated population of over three thousand people. It's thought that people lived there for at least a thousand years. Now Carla is fifteen miles inland from the ocean in a fertile valley called the Supe River Valley. The Andes Mountains stand right behind it. How did this unlikely spot become the first city ever built in the Americas? You sure can't say that it is easy to get to if you had to climb the Andes to reach it, but suppose you arrived by sea?" He let his words trail off, turning his last statement into a question.

"That would make a difference, wouldn't it?" he continued. "Okay, now my last little food for thought, but first more wine."

He stood up, walked into the kitchen, and a moment later came back out with a box of cheap red wine and filled each of their glasses, then set the wine box down on the table.

"Interesting so far, isn't it? Well, listen to this friends, this is the most important thought of the evening, at least I think so. As you know, the Old World can be divided into different times. The Stone Age, the Bronze Age, the Iron Age and up to the present. Let's look at the Bronze Age, shall we?

"The Bronze Age is a proven historical time. There is no question about its existence. It is a fact that bronze was used in ancient Greece by 3000 B.C. Let's just for the sake of our conversation use that date as the beginning of the Bronze Age, although it is actually much older than that. The Bronze Age flourished for almost two thousand years. But there is one big problem that science has refused to address, because there are no answers to be found that fit in with their little preconceived world. So think about this, to have a Bronze Age you must have bronze. Right, with me so far?"

He took another swallow of his cheap wine and continued.

"So to have a Bronze Age you must have bronze," he repeated himself, "and to have bronze you must have copper. About 90 percent of bronze is copper and the remaining 10 percent is tin, or some other metal. Well . . . guess what, there was never enough copper in Europe to even come close to the amount needed to create a Bronze Age that lasted two thousand years. So where did the copper come from?"

He looked at them and started laughing. It might have been the wine or it could have been the look on their faces, each of them were completely mesmerized by what he was saying.

"The vast majority of copper that was used to create the Bronze Age was mined in North America. Mines found on Isle Royale in upper Michigan have been dated back to 4000 B.C. Over four thousand mines have been discovered in this area alone and over five hundred thousand tons of material was excavated from them. So, tell me, did the native North American Indians have a Bronze Age? No? Okay, so where did it all go? It went to the Old World! Over five thousand years ago, traders, merchants and seamen were plying the waters of the Atlantic in trade and exploration and in shared discoveries."

"Why hasn't this been told?" Mondo asked.

"Same damn reason nobody says anything about three different types of people on Easter Island. What does this new perception of mankind do to our way of thinking? What does it do to the superior human ego of white Anglo-Saxon-Protestant science? It throws us and all of our lofty thoughts in the garbage."

Mondo slumped back in his chair and said, "I really can't believe it, Jonathan. Do you know what you just spelled out, a complete rewrite of ancient history?"

"There is even more, because we can't forget about tin for the Bronze Age. Where are some of the largest tin deposits in the world? How about Chile and Peru? Funny, but that's pretty close to Carla. What a coincidence, right?

"Now we're getting into speculation on my part and I will be the first to admit it. But I think that these early traders sailed to America utilizing the major ocean currents. Mondo, you're a sailor, you must have studied pilot charts. You know they are an accurate representation of the ocean currents, as well as general wind strengths and direction. Have you ever looked at the Atlantic Ocean pilot chart? It's there printed in black and white for all to see. Once our ancient mariners sailed out through the Strait of Gibraltar they would almost instantly find the Canary current, which would take them southward down the west coast of Africa. I imagine these early sailors stopped at the Canary Islands for supplies before pushing off and catching the north Equatorial current, which brings them across the Atlantic Ocean into the Caribbean. This current then becomes what we know as the Gulf Stream, and it runs up the east coast of Central America, northward along Florida and our eastern shores, before passing Nova Scotia and Newfoundland and heading back out to sea. The Gulf Stream runs at over five knots in some places! Five knots, that's faster than a lot of sailboats can sail. Once it heads out into the Atlantic it's called the North Atlantic Drift. Guess where the North Atlantic Drift ends?"

None of them said a word.

"This current would deposit a vessel near the Outer Hebrides Islands, right where the Standing Stones of Calanais were built over five thousand years ago.

"Now I have one last bit of information for you to think about. The copper mines of northern Wisconsin and Michigan came to an abrupt stop around 1200 B.C. It seems from the archeological records that one day they all just went home, whoever they were, simply went somewhere else, abandoned all of the mines, leaving tools and materials where they lay. What else do you think happened around 1200 B.C.?"

He looked at them and smiled.

"I have no idea," Naomi whispered.

"Well, I will tell you. The end of the Bronze Age in the Old World, that's what happened. Around 1200 B.C. the Bronze Age was left behind by the beginning of the Iron Age, my, but another coincidence," he laughed.

Chapter 4

t was after midnight when they finally climbed aboard Smokin'
Joe. The night's conversation at Jonathan's had been non-stop,
and they never even ate dinner. So many mysteries that Mondo
had thought about for years suddenly made sense if only he could
believe in early man's ability to sail the oceans of the world. It all
boiled down to three questions, he thought. Who were they, these
mysterious sea voyagers, and second, how were they able to sail
across the oceans of the world at least three thousand years before
Columbus, and lastly whatever happened to them?

One part of his tired brain just wanted to let the whole riddle
go. Let some scientist figure it out. What could he do that some
person with a PhD couldn't? It was foolishness on his part to waste
anymore time thinking about it, yet as hard as he tried he couldn't
turn his mind off.

He reached over, grabbed his watch and hit the glow button; it
was three-forty-five. The last time he had looked it was one-fifty.
He wasn't getting any sleep tonight.

His thoughts drifted to Naomi sleeping in the front V berth, and
of their time together in the South Pacific.

She had arrived in Tahiti on a Friday afternoon, after a long flight
from Los Angeles. Naomi was tired, but upbeat when she finally
made her way through customs and into their warm embraces. They
grabbed her few bags and left the airport as fast as they could, back
to the peaceful lagoon that Smokin' Joe was anchored in. The beauty
of Tahiti was more than she could ever imagine.

Tim had decided to start a simple engine repair two days before his sister arrived. Mondo remembered thinking it was a bad idea but Tim promised it was an easy half day project. Well, as usual it turned into a much bigger endeavor and Tim couldn't get it finished in time. The project was put on hold for a few days to enjoy Naomi's arrival, but before they could sail anywhere it had to get fixed. Finally, Tim finally asked him if he could take Naomi under his wing until he finished the repair. He didn't have to ask twice, and they spent the next few days exploring the beauty of Tahiti together. They cruised along beautiful deserted shorelines in his dingy. The two of them rode in an open bus to the market and came back with a bonanza of fresh tropical fruits and vegetables. They took walks on empty footpaths that led to distant beaches that held no sign of human habitation, and as they spent those precious days exploring, laughing, and enjoying life a shared closeness grew between them.

Tim finally got the engine fixed and after a few more days of playing they pulled up the anchor and sailed to Bora Bora. It was there, anchored under the islands towering mountain spires that things became complicated.

The three of them had decided to get up early the next morning after their arrival and hike to the waterfalls. Tim ended up spending a late night on a neighboring sailboat and dragged himself aboard about two a.m. and he wasn't going anywhere early.

He and Naomi still awoke before dawn wanting to see the beginning of a new day. The two of them sat in the cockpit drinking coffee, sharing the moment as one of the most beautiful sunrises either of them had ever seen appeared on the eastern horizon. He couldn't help but wonder if this incredible display of nature was a taste of magic yet to unfold. After sitting in silent appreciation and finishing their last cup of coffee they ate a small breakfast and rowed ashore, pulling the dingy up past the towering coconut trees that lined the beach, and started to hike the three miles to the lower waterfall.

They talked continually as they walked. Naomi was so full of enthusiasm. She was interested in so many things. She was trying to get her writing career going and doing free lance was hard she had told him. If it was just about the money she would have taken a job with the Los Angeles Herald. It paid well and was steady, but it wasn't just about the money. It was about doing what she felt was important. Being a free lance journalist gave her the opportunity to pick whatever interested her, but it also held no promise of getting a paycheck. That scared her, but it also excited her, it made it all a little more real, she had said.

She told him a lot about herself as they hiked. She had an honesty that surprised him. Maybe she was a little to honest about some things but as they walked through that tropical forest it all seemed so real and sincere.

He told her that he had bought Smokin' Joe at auction in the Caribbean, how he felt so blessed every time he looked at his boat and realized that he didn't owe a penny on her. He told Naomi that at times he wished he could settle down, find some place to call home besides his boat, but then in the next breath he laughed and said maybe he really didn't want to.

The conversation flowed so freely between them. It felt like they had no secrets to keep from each other. They both sensed a real honesty as they walked and it touched each of them.

Naomi told him she was twenty-six. Then with a laugh said that once she had been old for being young, but now she was young for being old. It was his turn to laugh. She looked absolutely beautiful.

Her strawberry blonde hair was tied back in a ponytail. She was wearing a Smokin' Joe baseball cap and her blue eyes were covered by a pair of expensive sunglasses. She was wearing a pair of ragged cut-offs, tennis shoes with no socks and a long sleeve, flowery, light weight shirt with the shirttails tied in a knot exposing her tan mid-section. A few times as they walked his mind suddenly wandered, making him lose his train of thought as he looked at her and felt a sudden weakness in his knees. They soon reached the creek that flowed down from the falls. The trail was becoming slippery in places, the earth turning to mud by the splashing of water. They held hands helping each other through the muddy places, helping each other climb around the many large boulders that lay in their path.

"Look, ripe mangos," he had said as he glanced to his left and saw a huge towering mango tree with ripe fruit within reach.

He stopped, grabbed five of them and put them in his backpack, then flung his pack over his right shoulder and they continued. Soon the sound of cascading water could be heard through the stillness of the morning.

They walked another ten minutes before coming around a large group of boulders and seeing the falls. They looked up to see water rushing over a large rock outcropping, then down through a forest of towering trees, before falling into a pool of crystal clear water. The pool was twenty feet wide and about thirty feet long, the falls landing with a loud rumble at the far end. The water looked deep in the middle, and around its edges was a shallow, gradual beach of small polished stones. A small cleft of a beach, filled with the same small stones lay to the left of the falls, surrounded by greenery.

The air held a tropical smell that invited them both to breathe deep, invited their senses to reach out and taste it, to feel it, with all of their being. The trees were full of birds shrieking and cawing, calling out in the dense forest. There was no sign of people, or any sign that a single human being had ever been here. Naomi walked over to the pool and sat on a rock near the edge and dangled her feet in the water. She took her sunglasses off and set them by her side then she looked at him and smiled.

"I feel like Eve in the garden," she said softly as if somehow her voice would disturb the setting.

"Eve didn't look as beautiful as you Naomi." the words came out before he really had time to think about what he was saying.

She didn't say anything, just smiled.

After a moment that hung longer than either felt comfortable with he said, "Mangos" and swung his backpack off and zipped it opened.

He pulled a few out, set them on a rock and sat down beside her. He chose the ripest looking one and held it up for her to admire, its skin red and golden, looking like the forbidden fruit of old.

"I've never eaten mango," she said.

"What, oh you will love it."

Taking his pocket knife out of his pack he cut four slices in the rough outer skin. Then he knocked the top off and peeled it back. The fresh juices dribbled down his fingers and past his wrist, running down toward his elbow.

"The messy ones are the best," he said as he handed her a piece.

She brought the fruit to her lips, looked at him and laughed, then in a beautiful soft voice she whispered, "I thought Eve gave the fruit to Adam."

He smiled, shook his head slightly, and fell completely in love with her right then.

Soon they had eaten three mangos, and were covered with the sweet sticky juice even his pants had juice stains on them. He stood up, took his pants off and put them next to her sunglasses. Then he took his shirt off and walked into the water up to his knees. He was wearing only his thin nylon swimsuit, his feet protected by a pair of plastic flip-flops that wanted to float free with every step he took. He turned and looked at her with eyes he hoped didn't betray how he felt.

She pulled her baseball cap off, shook out her ponytail and set the hat on the rock. Reaching down she cupped a handful of water and brought it toward her face, flinging the cool water up, savoring its chill, tasting its freshness.

"This is the most beautiful place I have ever seen. I feel like we are the only two people on the planet. If we're not Adam and Eve then maybe we're Tarzan and Jane," she said as she looked at him standing there in his thin nylon bathing suit, smiling.

"You look like Tarzan you know, the outfit's a little wrong, but you definitely could do a stand in job for him."

He looked at her and felt that nervousness starting to resurface, and suddenly he became painfully aware of a swelling that his small bathing suit couldn't hide. Giving her an awkward smile he dove into the water, swimming underneath pulling himself with his strong breaststroke, his eyes opened looking at the bottom of a crystal clear tropical pool. Holding his breath he reached the gentle gravel beach next to the falls and pulled himself onto it. This little beach was sur-rounded by flowering bushes, hibiscus and gardenia. It seemed the entire forest was shedding a fragrance that overwhelmed him with a beautiful earthy smell.

He lay on the beach letting the water slightly ripple over his back for a moment before he turned and looked at her. Naomi was already standing, kicking out of her shorts, her blouse untied and lying near his backpack. She looked at him then dove into the pool, her nakedness in this paradise the most beautiful thing he had ever seen. She swam up next to him, smiled shyly, then gently brought her hands to his face and drew his lips to hers. Her kiss was like heaven. He felt every fiber of his being explode with passion, all of him reacting to her surprise kiss.

They drifted together in the shallows, arms and bodies entwined.

"Naomi, you are the most beaut . . ." she brought her lips down hard on his cutting off his words in mid-sentence.

"It's just you and me, Mondo, the world doesn't exist. It's just us. The birds, the trees, it's just you and me and it's just right now."

He lost himself in another of her kisses as he arched his back and kicked his swim suit off. Then he pulled her on top of him and not even the cascading falls could drown out their cries of passion and ecstasy.

Chapter 5

Flick Shagwell was nervous. He smashed his fourth cigarette butt in the dirty ashtray and stared out the window. He didn't like the whole arrangement. It sounded too simple, too easy, way too easy. The phone call had told him where and when to show up. All he had to do was babysit some guy for a few days and make a grand a day. It didn't add up and he knew it, but he also knew he needed the money. Somehow, it was always the easy jobs that turned to shit, he thought.

The wind was blowing sideways and the rain was coming down so hard it was difficult to see across the street to the Madison Hotel. He was sitting inside Lou's Italian Eatery on 23rd Street, trying to get a handle on the bad feelings he had. A grand a day to babysit some guy, just keep him so drugged up he can't move and don't ask any questions. It could be easy, he thought, as he focused on the money, but somewhere in the back of his mind he knew it wouldn't be.

The Madison was a low-life sleaze joint that had rooms for twelve dollars a night. Just the kind of claptrap place he feared he would end up in if he didn't take the money. God, it's always about the money.

Two girls who worked the area should be entering the Madison soon, along with the mark that he had to babysit. Ten minutes after the three of them entered the hotel he was to walk across the street, go to the third floor to room 304. The girls would have the guy handcuffed to the bed post by then and he would wreck his night by showing up. Why somebody was paying this kind of money, he had no idea, and he was too afraid to ask.

He glanced at his watch. It was ten-thirty, and they were late.

There could be trouble with the girls, trouble with the mark, could be a lot of different troubles and it could all end up in his lap. Oh well, crime was like that, he knew.

At almost eleven he watched a taxi pull up to the Madison and the two hookers and a man climbed out. Flick could tell instantly that the guy was drunk. That was good, it made the whole thing that much easier. Ten minutes later he crushed out another cigarette, swearing he was going to quit, and walked out into the wind and rain. He ran across the empty street into the lobby, slamming the door behind him, and looked around. He saw an old gray-haired man sitting behind the registration desk, protected by a large glass panel with a small opening for paper work. The guy didn't smile a bit.

"Seeing some friends," Flick said.

The old man looked at him, then hacked up a cough and spit down into what Flick hoped was a garbage can or something. The way this place looked, the guy could have spit on the floor for all he knew.

Flick hated elevators, especially in cheap hotels like this one. He doubted it had ever been serviced and he wondered if a fire marshal had ever been inside this place. He walked up to the third floor, found room 304 and stopped.

Slowly he reached down and ever so slightly turned the door handle. It was unlocked. He put his ear to the door and faintly heard a girl laughing and another one saying something like just a minute honey. Flick reached behind him and felt the knife tucked into his back pocket. He knew he wouldn't need it, but it was reassuring to know it was there. He took a deep breath, opened the door and walked in.

The thirteen story office building located in downtown Vancouver had a beautiful view over the city. The entire top floor was occupied by Mountain Resources. Michael R. Jensen sat in his office with his feet perched on a large redwood table, his cowboy boots slid underneath. Michael wasn't even forty years old and already he was worth millions. Many of his business associates described him as a shark in a three-piece suit and he liked the analogy. He had a gift for seeing what others missed, for seeing pathways when others just saw road blocks. Analyzing the limits of possibilities and legalities was what he loved doing, and he was very good at doing what he loved. He made every effort to keep his business dealings legal, but still at times it was necessary to go over the line.

Michael had become vice-president of Mountain Resources in two short years, even though he had been hired as an accountant. It hadn't taken management long to realize his potential. One of his first decisions as vice-president had worked so well that the company had the best revenues in ten years. In one single transaction, he had increased gross sales by eighteen million dollars. But even that example of his brilliance was soon overshadowed by his next bold move. Despite reluctance from the board, he was able to create a complete external makeover for the company. He even changed the name from Pascal & Pascal Logging to Mountain Resources. There was no doubt in his mind which name was more powerful.

One year before he had been hired by Pascal & Pascal, it looked as if the company was going to be forced into bankruptcy and foreclosure. They had become just another floundering logging company, devastated by the fact that almost all of the marketable timber in British Columbia was already harvested. The ancient forests that covered almost the entire province had been logged, except for two places, and both seemed untouchable. The biggest landholders were the Federal and Provincial governments, and most of their holdings were in wilderness or recreational areas. It would be political suicide for any politician to suggest that they open these areas up for logging. The other group that holds ownership of ancient old growth forests are the First Nation Native People. The native tribes of British Columbia owned millions of hectares of virgin forest and they would never allow logging. Yet there was a third option, Michael knew of and it was the marketable timber that was tied up in the courts in disputed land ownership rights. These ownership cases, many going back decades, were between the Government and First Nation People, and these cases would likely stay locked in the courts for years. Many of these native tribes that claimed ownership rights were no longer even recognized by the government. Millions of dollars of marketable timber were protected by hundred and fifty year old treaties and native people who thought the forest was alive and talked to them.

Michael instinctively knew that these lands could be opened for logging, it was all about who you knew, and if you had enough power and Michael knew everybody, and he was very powerful.

Joseph Yazzi knew he was in trouble the moment he looked up and saw the man closing the door behind him. He looked at the two hookers, who started laughing at him. His right wrist was hand-cuffed to the metal bed post and he was filled with drunken anger and fear. He lashed his left hand out, hitting one of the girls across the face, sending her crashing to the floor.

"You bitches!" he screamed, trying to bring himself up to his knees but the cheap mattress gave him little support. Flick walked over and hit him with a right hand that snapped his head back, crashing him into the metal bed frame, and the lights went out for the drunken Indian. Flick reached for the handcuff dangling from the bed frame and flipped it over Joseph's left wrist. He wasn't going anywhere.

"You all right, Gloria?" he asked tenderly.

"Jesus, that hurts," she said through a steady stream of tears, holding her face.

"Sorry, there's another hundred for you, call it hazardous duty pay. You two get your things and split. I got this guy now," he said, as he thought how young the two hookers looked.

Flick sat down in the only chair in the room, grabbed the remote and started watching all-star wrestling. Shit, he thought to himself, the things he had to do to make a grand a day.

The call came later than Michael had expected. It was close to mid-night when the phone finally rang in his office.

"Thunderbird is home safe and sound," a male voice said, before hanging up.

Michael walked over to the bar, poured himself a glass of Scotch on the rocks and looked out the window. The city lights of Vancouver were glimmering in the darkness, reflecting shadows against a distant horizon of steel, glass and fluorescence.

With that phone call he was now one hundred percent committed to his next great business venture. He had started a journey and there was no turning back. Commitment was such a powerful tool, he knew. It made a man stronger in resolve when there was no way to back out. It was life lived on the line, with a bottom line of millions. As he sipped his Scotch he thought about what he would do with the money he would make. That was the funny part; it was all about the money, but in a way it wasn't. What did he need another million or two for he asked himself, then laughed when he realized it really isn't about the money at all. It's about taking the money away from somebody else. It's all about greed, he thought without a moment of self doubt.

He continued to stare over the city. The Scotch warmed him, burning slightly, leaving that smoky taste that he loved so much. Bringing his gaze from the skyline to the street below, he stood there wondering about all the little people he could see scurrying about below him. He wondered who was happy, who was in love, who was full of hate, who would die before the morning. So many people living like little rats in a big maze, he thought, and they're all just trying to find salvation for their screwed-up lives. He hated to admit it, but the only salvation that he had ever found was making money. There would never be enough. Money created power and that was the most precious commodity of all, and soon it would be time to start using some of his political power. He knew he might need political help to crush any protest that this plan might create if it ever became public knowledge. There was the serious threat that public outcry could force people together to form a broad base coalition that would struggle against Mountain Resources as they opened up disputed tribal lands for logging. That was the reason he needed to keep the people of Salmon Creek quiet, especially now at the beginning. Once logging started, it would be very difficult for anyone to make him stop. As long as trees were being cut, he didn't care how long he had to talk to all those damn environmentalists and protesters. The hell with them anyway, he thought, just a bunch of low-life, pot-smoking tree huggers with nothing else to do with their miserable lives.

Once logging started there would be ribbon-cutting ceremonies and plenty of opportunities for him to be photographed with his supporters. He would hold out the promise of better paying jobs, and a better future for the First Nation people and their children. Promising much, he would deliver less and less as time dragged on and logging continued. But if necessary, he would stand before the people that opposed him and tell them that he was doing what the government promised but failed to achieve. It was his vision that held the hope of the native people. It was the perfect solution to the financial disaster they had to live with. He would find it easy to blame the government, blame the courts, and even blame greedy corporations for their plight. He would shoot down his critics and demand from them how they would deal with these important issues. Once public pressure started to dissolve, once his project became old news and his name was run through the press so many times that people quit caring, then he would turn the worm, as he liked to say. He would give back a pittance, reap a bonanza and if he played his cards right, Mountain Resources might have enough timber to cut for at least the next ten years.

As he swirled the ice in his glass, he knew there was yet another alternative, one that would allow Mountain Resources to reap profits beyond any board member's wildest dreams. With this plan, there would be no need to give back a dime to the First Nation people if he didn't want to. There would be no need to defend his company or its actions. It would be one hundred percent legal, and it was so simple. All that had to happen was for the entire disputed land issue to be taken out of the courts and placed back in the hands of the politicians. Why, for Christ's sake, he thought, should he try to buy the rights to logging when he could get the government to steal it for him for free?

Chapter 6

t seemed incredibly early to Mondo when he heard Naomi stir-ring in the forward cabin. The last time he had looked at his watch it was four-thirty and his mind was still going a thousand miles an hour. He rolled over, pulled the covers over his head, and tried to go back to sleep, but he knew he couldn't. After laying there for a few minutes thinking about his restless night and his wonderful lucid dream he knew his lack of sleep was going to haunt him all day.

Finally he pulled the covers down and looked at the clock on the main bulkhead. It was eight-forty-five. Naomi was in the bathroom and it was time for him to get up. He kicked his feet out from under the covers and forced himself to move. Coffee his body and mind cried out as he threw a pair of pants on and walked over to the stove. Soon the smell of coffee filled the small cabin.

He made a cup for her with a taste of cream, just how she liked it and knocked on the bathroom door. Naomi poked her head out, saw the coffee and said, "Mondo, you're such a prince," she gave him a little kiss on his cheek before grabbing her coffee and closing the door behind her.

Mondo shuffled to the aft cabin and took a peek at Tim who was still sound asleep. He poured a cup for himself and climbed out the hatch and sat in the cockpit. This was his favorite place to greet the day. Even though they were moored in the heart of Victoria it was still so quiet. A few minutes later he heard the companionway hatch slide behind him, he turned and watched as Naomi climbed out and sat down next to him.

"Good morning, Captain Mondo. Did you have good dreams?" she said with a smile in her voice.

"Not bad, what I can remember, how about you?"

"I sleep so good on Smokin' Joe."

Mondo laughed to himself as he wondered what she would have thought about his dreams.

"What are we going to do today?" she asked.

"I don't know. What do you want to do, go shopping?"

"Go shopping! I can do that at home. I can't stop thinking about the totem. I'd like to go to a book store and see if we can find any information on the village where it came from."

"Sounds great to me."

It was close to nine-thirty when Mondo walked into the aft cabin, gave Tim a good shake and left a steaming cup of coffee on the bathroom counter for him.

Soon the three of them were sitting in a small restaurant waiting for breakfast.

"Naomi wants to find out more about the village that the totem came from," Mondo said as he looked at Tim.

"How do we do that?"

"We can start by going to a book store," she said.

"Good, you know I couldn't stop thinking about Jonathan. I sure was wrong about him. I thought he was some geeky weirdo when we first met him in the museum, but that guy is smarter than he looks," Tim said between gulps of coffee.

"I liked him. He sure wasn't pretentious, although I could have done a better job than his interior designer," Naomi said with a laugh.

"Amen," Mondo replied.

After breakfast they walked up Front Street five blocks to Othello's Books. The place was huge. It was located in the old part of town which was mostly filled with bars and restaurants. It seemed like an unlikely place for a book store. As they entered Mondo saw a small plaque to the right of the front door that said Othello's Books established 1953. It seemed Othello's had been here a lot longer than most of the surrounding businesses.

As soon as he was inside Mondo knew that he could get lost here.

Some book stores just have a feeling about them when you walk in the door. An unseen richness that just invites a soul to wander the aisles with an open mind, to get lost and see what treasures can be discovered.

Naomi walked to the front counter and started talking to a young lady. Mondo was standing off to the right just taking it all in. He felt like he needed a map to make it through all the aisles and rooms that he saw.

"Native history is upstairs to the right, that's where I'm heading," Naomi said to Mondo after her short conversation at the front desk.

"I'm going to try and find a book that I've been looking for," Tim said as he wondered off. Mondo followed her up the stairs to a huge section of Native First Nation books. The upstairs was large with isles of books branching off in every direction. In the middle of the room was a comfortable sitting area with six large overstuffed chairs and a big sofa. What a great place to spend a day, he thought.

Naomi cruised up and down the aisles like she was on a mission. Mondo was having such a good time watching her, but it also pulled at his heart. He had mixed emotions about seeing her, but he stuffed them, and tried to ignore them.

"Look at this book on totems," she said as she handed him a large photo book with a beautiful cover depicting an old First Nation village with many totems standing between the village and the sea. A small hand written note at the bottom of the picture was dated 1912.

"I'll grab a couple other books and we can sit down over there," she said as she pointed to the chairs with her head.

Mondo grabbed the book and walked to one of the comfortable overstuffed chairs and plopped down. Naomi sat next to him putting a few books at her feet.

"What was the name of the village?" she asked.

"I wrote it down, just a second," he said reaching for his wallet and digging out a small piece of paper, "it's called Neskiwaii," he said, then put his wallet back before turning to the back of the book. Searching the index, he was surprised when he realized that he couldn't find a thing about the village.

"It's not listed in this book," he said.

They thumbed through the pile of books that she had on the floor but not one of them had a thing about the Neskiwaii. Naomi got up, walked over and randomly grabbed eight more books from the shelf and brought them back.

"Look through a few of these Mondo."

After they had gone through the entire stack of books they still hadn't found one reference to the village.

"That's odd don't you think?" she asked him.

"The mystery deepens."

Tim came up the stairs with a book in his hand and sat down next to them.

"Any luck?" he asked.

"No, as a matter of fact the village where the totem came from isn't listed in any of these books. I can't image why?" his sister replied.

"Oh well," was the only thing Tim could think to say.

"Listen, we know that there was a village called Neskiwaii, or else the museum doesn't have its facts straight, which I doubt, so why isn't it in any of these books?" Naomi asked.

"Damn good question," Mondo said.

"Why don't you go downstairs and ask that lady at the desk to look in their computer base. If anybody ever wrote a book that mentioned the village they probably can cross reference it for you."

"Good idea Mondo," Naomi said as she stood up and walked downstairs.

As soon as she left Tim looked over at Mondo but didn't say a word. Mondo knew him good enough to know that something was spinning around inside that brain of his.

"What?" Mondo said with a hint of suspicion in his voice.

Tim laughed, "What do you mean what?"

"Just what I said."

"I was just wondering what its like to have us back on board. What it's like for you to see Naomi?"

"Oh man," Mondo exhaled, "I don't care if its ten years, seeing you will always be great. I really appreciate you coming. As far as Naomi, well . . . honestly, there's still something there."

"I thought so."

"I sure as hell don't want any complications. This is just a short visit for both of you, and I can't go back there, not now anyway."

Tim laughed again, "Okay, sure whatever you say. I was just curious."

"Well don't be. You have one more day, then its back to the big city, let's not . . . I don't know . . . lets just not screw things up okay."

"No problem."

They spent the next ten minutes looking through the pile of books that were scattered on the floor around them. It was so fascinating, all the history of the Native Peoples, the complex societies that they developed. Mondo was consumed by it all. He was especially captivated by their red cedar canoes.

"Look at this," he said as he handed Tim a large photo book.

He held the page open to an old picture of a very large canoe with twelve paddlers sitting in it. One person was standing in the bow dressed in an unbelievable costume. A note along side the photo said the man standing was a shaman, a holy man. In the back of the canoe was a helmsman standing and steering with a large wooden oar trailing off the back of the canoe.

"You know this picture is different from any that I have seen of their canoes. I've never seen one where they had a helmsman at the back steering with an oar, but I've seen it some place else," Mondo said.

Tim studied it then gave it back to him saying, "So have I."

"Yeah, where?" a hint of friendly rivalry in Mondo's voice.

"The reed boats of ancient Egypt."

"That's right, wow . . . this is starting to get more interesting by the minute."

Soon Naomi appeared at the head of the stairs, walked over to them and sat down.

"I found one book that had a reference to the village. It's an old book and it's out of print and they don't have a copy of it here. The lady downstairs made a few calls for me and found it in a used bookstore not to far away. I asked her to tell the owner to hold it for me and we would be right over."

"Sounds good, let's go," Mondo said.

They got up and walked downstairs. Tim bought his book and they walked out of Othello's.

"We have to walk three blocks until we find the government

liquor store. Then we go left and it's on the right a few more blocks. Its called John's Used Books," she said.

"I wonder if John will be there," Tim laughed, then seemed to apologize by saying, "that was dumb," a moment later.

They had no trouble finding the used book store. The door jingled when they entered, a small brass bell hanging on the inside of the door handle. This book store was the complete opposite from Othello's. It was small and the front counter was stacked high with books. Books lined the isles making it difficult to walk without keeping one eye on the floor. The more Mondo looked around the more he saw used books everywhere.

A long haired, old hippy walked out from behind a beaded curtain, smiled at them and said good morning.

"Hi," Naomi said, "the lady from Othello's called for me."

"Right, I have it here," he said as he reached behind him and grabbed a small hardbound book off of the shelf that lined his back wall.

"This is it. You won't find much about Neskiwaii anywhere," he said.

"Why?" Naomi asked.

"Why," he replied with a tone in his voice that made it seem like a stupid question.

"Well, because the village was wiped out."

"Wiped out, what do you mean?" she asked.

"It's in the book, it's sad, just read it for yourself, seems people been massacring each other for one hell of a long time," he said.

Mondo paid for the book and they walked outside, and stood for a few seconds before seeing a small park a block away. They crossed the street, walked to the park and sat down on a bench. Tim and Mondo sat on each side of Naomi as she opened the book. She flipped to the back, looked in the index and found a reference to the village. She started turning pages until she found the one that she wanted. Mondo and Tim both leaned over her shoulder as she held the book open for them all to read.

It was a short chapter. As they read it became obvious to each of them why it was so difficult to find any information on this village. It described how just a few years before Captain Cook arrived in the Pacific Northwest, a large band of warriors from the Queen Charlotte Islands attacked the village. The book said that the attack was in revenge for a defeat that the Northern natives had suffered at the hands of the village people years earlier. Almost the entire population was either killed or taken as slaves. The village was burned to the ground and to this day it is considered a place of sorrow and nobody lives there.

"Wow," Naomi said as she continued to read.

"The whole village was destroyed, Jesus Christ," Tim said.

"Okay, if the village was destroyed over three hundred years ago, how can the totem in the museum be from around 1860, like the plaque said?" Mondo asked.

Naomi and Tim both looked at him as if a little light had just turned on in their heads.

"It can't," she said softly.

The impact of Mondo's question sank deep into all of their minds.

On the last page of the short chapter on Neskiwaii was a map showing approximately where the village had been, and a small town called Salmon Creek. The map also had a hand drawn scale of miles on the bottom. Just to the south of Salmon Creek was a very large shaded area called the Killiatt Wilderness. Mondo quickly calculated that Salmon Creek was about eight miles from the destroyed village. Where Salmon Creek was in relationship to the outside of Vancouver Island he didn't have a clue, but he knew he would find it. When Tim and Naomi left he was going to sail there. This mystery had just gotten too big for him to turn his back on it now.

Chapter 7

The next day was a whirlwind. They went to all the book stores in Victoria, even took a city bus up to Sidney to look at a used book store, but they couldn't find any other reference to Neskiwaii. It was as if the village had been erased from history, a chapter too painful to recall.

On their last night together they went to Paparocia's for a fabulous Italian dinner. Then it was off to Jake's for drinks and live music. They spent a few hours listening to an Irish three man band before they made it back to Smokin' Joe late. By then they all were in love with life and having a great time.

Mondo put some mellow tunes on, lit the hurricane lamp over the dining table and said, "One more round, I've been saving the best for last."

He dug behind his dry storage cabinet and brought out a bottle of Mac Doven Scotch. He grabbed three glasses, filled them with ice and poured each glass a quarter full and passed them around.

"Cheers," he said as he sat back down and they toasted.

All three were sitting around the table, the hurricane lamp casting long shadows throughout Smokin' Joe, listening to soft jazz, feeling the magic of being on board. Each one of them let their minds drift back to the time that they had shared in the South Pacific.

"I don't want to go home," Naomi said with a laugh.

"Go home? I'm moving back on board. I'm quitting the Peace Corps, and I will have no forwarding address." Tim said, slurring his words.

They all laughed and laughed. The Mac Dove's went around the

46

room one more time before it suddenly all caught up with Tim. He took one long sip, put his glass down and staggered off to the back cabin without a word.

Mondo and Naomi suddenly felt an awkward silence hanging between them. All the innocent and jovial fun of the last few days seemed to stop the moment Tim wasn't there. They both knew there was a lot to say to each other and the time was getting short. Neither felt comfortable in the silence. Mondo was thinking that he should just go to bed and not even try to have a serious talk with her. He had no idea what to say and he had promised himself that he wasn't going to open old wounds on her short visit.

The hurricane lamp continued to cast its shadows then suddenly the music came to an abrupt end making the silence between them unbearable.

"Mondo," she whispered with a sense of sadness in her voice that he hadn't heard in a very long time.

She was hesitant to continue, her thoughts seemed to have trouble trying to form the right words.

"Mondo . . . I really have enjoyed this weekend. I've really enjoyed seeing you."

More silence hung between them, and he didn't know what to say.

She sat there for a minute looking at him expecting a reply and he didn't have one to give her.

Finally she stood up, put her glass on the counter and started to walk to her cabin forcing herself not to look back at him.

"Naomi," he said but then nothing else came out.

She paused, turned and looked down at him. Her heart had so much to tell him but her mind thought it best to just keep walking. Finally her heart won, seeing a man she once loved so much sitting in the soft glow. She sat down next to him and wrapped her hands around his.

"You know Mondo, I'm sad the way things worked out. No matter what, I want you to know that the time we shared was one of the most beautiful experiences of my life."

She brought her lips to his and gave him a soft kiss then stood up and walked to her cabin.

He sat there for another ten minutes in the silence and shadows thinking there was so much to tell her and yet he couldn't for the life of him think of the first few words to start with.

The next morning was frantic. All three could feel that they had a little too much fun last night. After a quick breakfast they were standing at the seaplane dock. Mondo couldn't help feeling it seemed like a month ago that he was here waiting for them. He wasn't sure what it meant but time seemed to have stood still while they were here. Ten minutes later the seaplane landed and they started walking toward the float. Tim climbed on board but Naomi didn't. She wished now that she hadn't walked away from him last night, wished that she had told him how much she still cared.

She turned and looked at Mondo and she could read that a lot was going on behind his dark blue eyes. Her emotions seemed to lose control, tears started to form and she couldn't stop them.

Mondo walked to her, brought his right hand behind her head and gently drew her face to his. He looked deep into her eyes and kissed her.

"Naomi, I will always care about you. I will always cherish what we shared together."

She didn't say a word, she just reached out and grabbed his hands, stood on her toes and brought her lips to his with a short kiss then she turned and walked to the plane.

He watched as the seaplane roared across the harbor, broke its grip with the water and soared over the high rise condos before turning east and disappearing from sight. He stood there for a few minutes thinking about the weekend, feeling the flood of emotions that had surfaced in the last few days. He had been afraid of them.

There was no way he wanted to go back to Smokin' Joe, not yet. He walked away from the waterfront up to Government Street, turned left and continued strolling until he found Vancouver Ocean Supplies. It was the largest marine store on Vancouver Island. Once inside he looked around, then walked over to the chart area and found a cruising guide for the outside of Vancouver Island. It was thirty-eight dollars, but he decided to buy it anyway. He also grabbed a chart kit that had strip charts from Victoria to Cape Scott, the northern point of land on Vancouver Island. He spent fifteen minutes searching before he found Salmon Creek. Looking over the chart he finally found the bay that once held Neskiwaii. There was nothing to indicate that the village had ever been there.

He spent close to one hundred dollars buying books and charts for his next trip. He knew this wasn't an easy area to sail, especially heading north. Smokin' Joe would be beating directly into strong currents and the prevailing northerly winds that blew along the outer coast, but it didn't matter, he would get there one way or the other.

Nootka Sound was shrouded in fog and it was very hard for Mondo to figure out just where he was. Even with his radar going and his GPS reading out latitude and longitude he was nervous about all the rocks and reefs he would have to dodge before getting into a safe anchorage, and the sun was setting fast. He wished he had bought one of those fancy high tech GPS units that showed his boat as a little arrow over an electronic chart. He always thought they were for lazy navigators but right now he would have paid triple what they normally cost.

It had been a hard trip. The simple two hundred and fifty miles took over four days. He was plagued by fog or when the fog disappeared the wind was blowing a steady thirty knots right on the nose of Smokin' Joe. He had anchored each evening just before dark and was up and going at daybreak. Finally, once he passed Estevan Point he knew the hard part was over. Leaving that prominent landmass behind allowed him to turn east and into the semi-sheltered waters of Nootka Sound.

This is where Captain Cook first landed in the Pacific Northwest and found the native people so peaceful he named this entire area Friendly Cove. Even here so far removed from the known world Captain Cook was greeted as a white god, returning as he had promised so long ago. Mondo couldn't get the word "returning" out of his mind. Who was returning, and where were they returning from?

The peaceful co-existence between native people and the whites was short lived. The absolute savagery of the early explorers amounted to genocide. The brutality that they inflicted upon the First Nation People would be considered war crimes by today's standards. The sea otter trade was the beginning of the exploitation.

Russian sailors descended upon the native populations from Alaska moving south, killing those who opposed them and wiping out the sea otters in less than eight years. Still, in the beginning Captain Cook and his crew seemed to be the fulfillment of an ancient prophecy, one that told of loving white skinned gods who one day would return to the people.

There was no way Smokin' Joe could get to Neskiwaii by dark. Mondo continued to thread his way through narrow channels and reefs before he found a good anchorage and tucked himself behind Bird's Point. As the anchor set, the fog lifted and he could finally relax after four and a half days of hard sailing that made him wonder why he kept sailing at all. He opened a beer, grabbed his fishing pole and soon a delicious ling cod was frying on the outside stern rail barbeque. All the tension of the trip seemed to ease out of him as he sat in his cockpit eating his freshly caught fish, drinking his second beer and feeling like he was the only person on the planet. The pristine beauty of this place took his breath away.

Three hours after leaving Bird Point the next morning he was just about to his destination. In less than two miles he would turn to his right, and make his way through North Pass. Then he would slowly wind his way through more shallow and rocky areas and finally be in Swartz Bay.

The morning air was still crisp, the strong rays of the sun caused large areas of the forest to give off a steaming halo of misty fog, swirling, cascading through the tree tops, suspended between heaven and earth before disappearing skyward. The area was completely empty of any human contamination. Pristine forest ran right to the waters edge. He had seen so many eagles this morning that he stopped counting after eighteen. There were playful river otters swimming around and seals seemed to be every fifty feet or so as he motored along. With careful navigation he made his way through North Pass and turned the corner into Swartz bay. What he saw as he slowly entered the bay literally took his breath away. His knee's almost buckled under him at the shocking sight that greeted him. He put Smokin' Joe in neutral as he slowly glided toward a huge barge. It was anchored close to shore in the north corner of the bay, held in place by many long lines running to the shore and some long chains running out to anchors set deep in the bay. It looked so out of place that he couldn't believe it. He saw a few people walking around but soon he realized that every person on the barge had stopped what they were doing and were now staring right at him. To find this monstrosity anchored in such a beautiful bay, so far removed from any signs of civilization was beyond his comprehension. The barge must have been at least two hundred feet long. He saw three or four small work boats tied off to one side and then he noticed a small dock built on shore. That surprised him because according to the charts this was all First Nation Land.

This ugly barge was the last thing he had ever expected to see here. It was an abomination upon the natural beauty that he had taken so for granted. It was completely out of place and it made no sense to him as he put Smokin' Joe back in gear and headed for the south end of the bay so he could anchor. He took his gaze from the barge and studied the low lying area where the village must have been. There was a long crescent shaped beach with soft white sand. Behind the beach was an area of tall, gangly, scrubby bushes and small trees. Then an immense forest rose up and continued on as far as he could see. The earth gradually climbed until it reached the distant mountains, the forest covered everywhere he looked.

He picked a spot just south of the beach and dropped the anchor in twenty-five feet of water. Mondo backed down hard setting the anchor good then he put Smokin' Joe in neutral and turned the engine off. He just couldn't believe the barge that was anchored here. It was a faded yellow and covered with long dirty streaks of rust that ran down to the waterline before disappearing. In bright red letters painted on the bow was the name of this monster, BELWOLF IV. Mondo went below, got his binoculars and came back on deck and studied the barge. A huge crane over a hundred and twenty feet tall stood in the middle supported by thick guide wires. The crane had a large steel cable wound on a huge drum at its base. There were at least ten men still standing at the rail, all eyes focused on him. This was one welcoming committee that sent a cold shiver down his spine.

The magic of this place was gone, disappeared the moment he turned the corner and saw the barge. He sat there for the next ten minutes trying to figure out what the hell it could possibly be doing here. His mind was drifting with potential answers, none of which made any sense, when he heard the distant sound of a helicopter. Soon it came flying low from the north just above the tree line. It hovered over the barge as if to land then swung out and made a close inspection of him, circling Smokin' Joe twice before returning and landing on the barge. Mondo grabbed his binoculars and watched as three people climbed out. The three were greeted by a man on the barge and they walked out of sight.

Michael Jensen was surprised as hell to see a sailboat anchored in the bay. Nobody had notified him that anybody was in the area and he sure didn't want any complication. Even before he landed he decided that he would send a few of the boys over and tell that sailboat it was time to find another anchorage.

Chapter 8

Mondo dug the old book out that he had bought at the second-hand bookstore and held it in front of him studying the shoreline. According to the hand-drawn map he was looking right at Neskiwaii. Not a trace of the old village could be seen. He sat in the cockpit thinking that it was about time to launch his inflatable and head for the beach, when in the distance he heard an outboard engine start up. He turned, looked toward the barge and saw a small boat speeding towards him. It was coming in fast and before he could do anything the old rusty boat gave Smokin' Joe a glancing blow before turning around and coming to stop along side of her.

"Goddamn it, watch it!" Mondo shouted as he jumped to his feet.

The three men sitting in the boat were taken back by his outburst but they quickly regained their composure, each one of them weighed over two hundred and fifty pounds.

"Listen asshole," one of them said as he stood up, "this is private property, and we own it, so it's time you pull up your anchor and find a new home, got it?"

"This is First Nation property, so I doubt you own shit around here," Mondo spit back.

The man grabbed Smokin' Joe's rail and started to pull himself aboard. Instantly Mondo was there looking down at him holding his fish smacking Billy club. The man looked deep in Mondo's eyes and sat back down.

"You've been warned."

"Listen I can't go anywhere right now, my engine overheated. I have to put in a new thermostat, so give me a break and I'll be out of here by tomorrow," Mondo said trying to keep his anger in check.

"Okay, you got till tomorrow."

He watched as the speed boat pulled away and raced back to the barge. God he thought, none of this is making any sense. His fast thinking bought him a day but what could he accomplish with it?

Untying his inflatable dinghy from the cabin top, he lowered it overboard and led it aft where he dropped his eight horsepower outboard motor on the transom and headed for shore. He kicked along the white sandy beach, but he couldn't find a thing that indicated the village had ever been there. He sat on the beach for a while before he decided to hike back into the cool dark forest. He was amazed at the size of the trees and the abundance of life that sprouted everywhere. It was like one huge garden, he thought, as he walked slowly taking it all in. Time flew by and it was after two when he made it back to Smokin' Joe.

Now what, he thought? Something was going on around here and it wasn't good. That barge simply didn't belong. All of the heavy equipment on board looked like it was ready for a huge construction project, or he suddenly realized with a sickening feeling, a huge logging operation. The thought that somebody was going to cut down this pristine forest made him sick. No wonder his welcoming committee wanted him gone. These guys were going to log on First Nation land, but that was impossible, wasn't it? He grabbed the strip chart that showed where he was and then found Salmon Creek. Still holding the chart he jumped into his dinghy, started the engine and raced past BELWOLF 1V. If there were any answers to be found he would find them in Salmon Creek.

The village elders sat in Charles Yazzi's living room. Twelve of them sat in silence as they listened to their chief. He was an old man, weathered by his years and burdened with the cares that he had been forced to carry for his people. He was a wise old man and the entire village loved him and looked upon him with respect. Little thought was given to the sadness that everyone knew filled their chief's heart. His son, Joseph, born to follow his father's footsteps had been lost to the outside world. The last that anybody had heard Joseph Yazzi was just another drunken Indian living on the streets of Vancouver.

The elders sat and thought about the counsel that their chief had given them and they all agreed except for two. Those two would do whatever they could to influence the council not to fight against the white man's proposal. That was what they had been paid for.

Chief Yazzi knew all of the white man's promises sounded good. After two hundred years of exploitation, of lies and corruption, native people had grown very leery of the white man's word. Even though this offer came with the supposed support and backing of the Provincial government, it was still all lies and Chief Yazzi knew it.

"How can we allow any cutting of our forest? Can one open a river to let a little water out then close it back? I fear not."

The elders continued to sit in silence for another five minutes waiting for any one to respond, but all remained silent. Even the two who had been paid knew this wasn't the time to disrespect their chief.

"I can see only harm coming from this" Chief Yazzi continued, "if we take the money we will grow to want more. If we allow a tree to be cut they will not stop until our forests look like most of our ancient land, dead, scarred, raped and left behind. I fear that."

Many different times Chief Yazzi had been faced with hard decisions. Many times he had walked the run down streets of Salmon Creek in the middle of the night, wrestling with the choices that he had to make for his people, for their land, for their future. The land was all that they had anymore. Everything else was gone, or rapidly disappearing before him. Most of the salmon were gone, the bears and cougar long gone. The old ways were dying and he knew it. Even his only son had been deceived and lost, and every day that thought tore at his heart.

The words from Mountain Resources sounded good. They had mentioned all of the benefits that the money could be used for. They could build schools, and hospitals, new roads, but Chief Yazzi knew that the best of poisons were also the sweetest. This was the beginning of the end for his people if they allowed one tree to be cut from their land. This offer was death to everything that he had ever held dear to him for over eighty-five years.

"I suggest that we respond through our attorneys in Victoria and tell them we need more time to decide. That should hold them at bay for a little while. Mountain Resources will not go away. I am old but I will fight for what is ours, for what we have left, for our people and for our land."

Then he stood and the twelve knew the meeting was over.

Mondo pulled the inflatable up to the run down fuel dock that ran out from Salmon Creek. There was only one boat tied up to it, one that he remembered seeing earlier at the barge. He turned the engine off, climbed out onto the shaky dock and walked his dingy close to shore, then tied it off. He saw a few battered cars drive by as he started walking. A pack of dark-skinned children stopped and stared, not saying a word, before they ran and disappeared between buildings. Nothing about this little town looked promising to him. The sidewalks were built of wood and stood a foot off of the street which had more ruts and deep holes than it had asphalt. The main street was about five blocks long, with store fronts on each side. There was a large empty field off to the left behind town. A scattering of houses sat randomly here and there with no sense of order behind the buildings on his right. He walked down the wooden walkway and into a corner grocery store. A Native American woman, old and overweight sat behind a counter with the television blaring some ridiculous game show. She looked up at him, seemed to be taken back for a second before she turned her attention back to her show. He bought a coke, went back outside and continued walking. As he walked he peeked in different shops but everything was closed. This town had a feeling about it like it was from the Twilight Zone and it didn't sit well with him. He stopped and looked around and realized that he couldn't see one person anywhere. It was like the whole town headed for the hills the moment he stepped off the dock.

After crossing the street, he kept looking in windows until he stopped in front of a bar with some country music escaping through a partially opened door. Pushing the door open he walked into a dimly lit room with no customers except for two big white guys sitting with their backs to him at the bar. A native man was standing off to the corner behind the counter. It looked to Mondo like he was trying to keep his distance from his only customers. The two men turned around when he entered. One of them was from the boat that had hit Smokin' Joe earlier. Both sat in their seats looking at him with a mean hard look that meant trouble.

"Look it's our little yacht friend, coming for a drink maybe," the man said that had been in the boat earlier today.

Mondo almost turned and walked out, but instead he walked to the far corner of the bar and sat down as far away from the two white guys as he could.

"Seems down right unfriendly George," he heard one of them say.

The bartender came over and he ordered a beer. He sipped it slowly, thinking, trying to get a handle on what had happened since he arrived in Swartz Bay. One look around this town told him that these people were afraid of something, and he had a damn good idea it was the barge and the crew that was with it. What that helicopter was doing here was another story. It took somebody with big bucks to fly around out here in the wilderness.

Mondo was half way finished with his beer when George stood up, walked over and sat down next to him. Mondo glanced over, looked him in the eye but didn't say a word as he went back to his beer.

"You're sure one unfriendly guy, asshole."

"I don't like people crashing into my boat for starters."

"Sorry," he dragged the words out in a mocking tone, and Mondo knew this was going to come to blows real fast.

"Did we scratch your little yacht?" he laughed as he looked over at his friend sitting at the other end of the bar.

Mondo finished his beer, put the glass down, stood up and looked at him.

George stood up as well, he weighed at least thirty more pounds than Mondo.

"You don't want to go where you're headed mister," Mondo told him, keeping his eyes locked on the big man's face.

Something must have momentarily registered with George. His look betrayed his fear then he called out to his friend.

"We got a tough guy here Bud."

Mondo could hear the nervousness in his voice.

"Don't bother me George, I'm drinking."

Mondo's years of Martial Art's training was going to come down to a minute of mayhem if this guy pushed it. Mondo stood and stared never taking his eyes from George's face.

"I'm about ready to leave this bar, and like I just told you, you don't want to go where you're headin'," Mondo said, with no hint of fear in his voice.

The apprehension on George's face was easy to read. Mondo didn't take his eyes off of him as Bud stood up and started walking toward them, cussing under his breath. When he was ten feet away Mondo knew it was all coming down.

Mondo lashed out with his right foot and caught George just above his right knee cap, slamming his leg backwards, tearing ligaments and cartilage. The big man started to drop. Before he hit the ground Mondo slammed him with a right hand to the midsection that doubled him over and sent him crashing to the floor. Bud charged and caught Mondo with a wild round house punch to the side of his head. It sent shock waves through him as he was flung backwards and bounced off the bar. Bud came in for another punch, but was met by a kick that caught him in the face, smashing his nose, and sending him to the floor. George was up and he grabbed Mondo in a bear hug and slammed him back into the edge of the bar again. Mondo pulled both of his arms in tight to his chest and shot his hands up high, hitting George under the chin forcing his head back and causing him to lose his grip. Then he dropped to his knees and slid out from underneath George's huge grasp. The next second he shot up bringing a knee into George's groin that sent the big man gasping for air as he stumbled backwards then fell to the ground. Bud grabbed a chair and came at Mondo. In the last possible second he ducked down as the chair smashed into the bar behind him. Mondo swung low with a sweeping kick that took out Bud's right foot. Mondo's momentum carried him and he spun completely around before landing a powerful kick to the side of Bud's head that sent him flying into a table and chairs. George was trying to get up when Mondo hit him with a strong upper cut right under his chin, snapping his head back and he was out before hitting the floor. Bud struggled up from the broken table, his head down racing to tackle Mondo. Three feet away Mondo whipped his right leg forward in his most powerful front kick that hit directly on Bud's face, breaking his nose and sending him down to the ground for good. In forty seconds the whole fight was over. Mondo felt the pain in his back and the welts on his face. He was completely out of breath and he felt like a wild animal. His years of training had turned into complete instinct.

He turned and looked at the bartender who was already on the phone talking a million miles an hour, he couldn't understand a word.

George and Bud were both out cold, and it was probably time for him to head out of town and out of the anchorage as fast as he could.

Mondo straightened himself up, shook his head and headed for the door. Once outside he looked around, then took off at a fast pace. Just as he reached the foot of the dock, out from a side street came a police car with its lights flashing. Before he had a chance to make a run for his dinghy the police car pulled up next to him in a whirlwind of dust, and screeched to a halt. The driver jumped out carrying a shot-gun and wearing a badge. He stared at Mondo with a look that made him stop in his tracks. Then the passenger door opened and slowly out climbed an old man. Mondo watched as he started walking in his direction. He seemed not in the least bit of a hurry. When the old man was five feet away from him he stopped.

The young man with the shotgun just stood by the car not saying a word.

After what seemed like a very long time the old man took a few more steps, smiled, and extended his hand out in a handshake.

"I am Charles Yazzi, let's talk."

Chapter 9

s Mondo stood staring at Charles Yazzi a thousand different thoughts ran through his mind, and he didn't know what to do. One part of him wanted to head for the dinghy, the hell with the policeman and his shotgun, just get out of Salmon Creek and the anchorage before round two started.

The old man smiled at him again, then he turned and started walking down the street. Mondo let out a deep sigh, shook his head slightly and even though he wasn't sure why, he started walking after him. A minute later the police car slowly drove past them and stopped in front of the bar. As it sat there with its engine idling, the driver jumped out and ran inside. By the time Mondo and the old man reached the car, the door to the bar swung open and out walked George and Bud escorted by three armed Indians. Both George and Bud gave Mondo a scowl that told him this was far from over as they climbed into the back seat. One of the Indians jumped into the driver's seat, the other opened the passenger door and climbed in. The third, still carrying the shotgun climbed on the back of the trunk and gave it a slap with his right hand. He looked at the old man and slightly nodded his head as the old ford started to pull away, its dusty red globe still flashing. The car drove for two blocks before it turned left and disappeared.

Mondo looked at Chief Yazzi who just smiled at him and continued walking.

As they walked Mondo thought the silence awkward. Yet it gave him time to clear his head. He started thinking about the totem and why he had come here in the first place. Maybe this old man could answer some of his questions.

They walked a block past the bar, then turned right down a short deadend street, past a few junk cars and dying lawns and up to a small single story house. The place looked like it had seen little maintenance in the last decade, its siding showing scars of bare wood underneath sheets of peeling paint. There were faded curtains in the windows and two old rusty bicycles were leaning up against a front porch that looked like it would collapse, except that it was still connected to the house.

At the front door Charles turned and smiled, "please be my guest," he said as he opened the door.

The house was a pleasant surprise on the inside. It was clean and neat with an orderly sense to it.

"Please sit down, may I get you anything?"

"An aspirin or two," Mondo replied, feeling the pain from the fight growing with every minute.

The old man laughed, then walked out of the room and came back a minute later with two aspirin and a glass of water. Mondo thanked him, sat down on the sofa and swallowed them.

Chief Yazzi sat on a chair across from Mondo and studied him for a few minutes creating another uncomfortable silence.

"Why are you here?" he finally asked.

"I'm curious about Neskiwaii."

A smile grew on the chief's face.

"I thought maybe that was why you are here, although, I think there may be another reason that you are not aware of."

Mondo didn't know what to say and another minute of silence passed between them before the chief spoke again. His words came out slowly as if he was searching for just the right meaning.

"I think many things have brought you to us. Neskiwaii is in the past my friend, although the past does speak to the present. But I think it is the future that has brought you here today."

"What do you mean?"

"We, my people and I . . . we are facing troubles, and we have asked our spirit world for help. I think they have sent you."

Mondo laughed softly.

"Chief I respect your ways and your beliefs, but I came here because of a totem pole that I saw in Victoria."

"Yes, I know that totem."

"You do?"

"Yes, there is only one totem in the museum that is from Neskiwaii. It is very old and very sacred. Why has that totem brought you here?" he asked never taking his eyes from Mondo's.

"I'm here because I've seen that same carving before, only it was made from solid stone, and it was over five thousand miles away."

"Yes, I know of Easter Island."

Mondo was completely taken back by the casual tone in the old man's voice. It was like he knew all about the similarities between the totem and the stone carvings.

"Why has that brought you here?"

"Because I can't believe how similar they are. If that totem is old like you say it is then how was it created in Neskiwaii?"

The old man smiled and didn't say another word for a few minutes. Mondo was finally getting used to the silence. For whatever reason he found himself sitting in this old man's living room, he knew enough to shut up and listen.

Finally as if settling something, the old man gave a big grin, showing dark stained teeth, then he laughed, "I know why you are here. Our totem has called you. I could tell you much, answer many of your questions, and maybe I will, but I want to ask you something first. I want you to think about this. The totem that you speak of has stood in the museum in Victoria for the last eighteen years, yet you are the first white man to ever come here and ask about it. Why do you think that is?"

Mondo hadn't a clue.

More silence between them, yet it seemed now that even though no words were being spoken, somehow this old man was communicating with him. He was gaining an insight, seeing deep into the very essence that made Mondo who he was. Suddenly Mondo understood that in this silence time was not being wasted.

"That totem that you speak of," Chief Yazzi continued," is the most powerful totem in the museum, maybe in all of British Columbia. It is old, reaching back far into our people's past. It has stood in the museum with its power visible for all to see and yet no white man could see it, no white man has ever felt its call, or answered its call until you. That totem has brought you here, called your spirit to us because my people need your help. We are dying and without help we will be no more."

Mondo's mind was spinning, trying to take it all in. He felt in a daze sitting on the sofa, felt a pressure that seemed to descend on his entire being, making it hard for him to catch his breath, he suddenly felt physically sick. He could feel his pulse racing wildly as small beads of sweat started to form on his brow. He felt like he was going to faint. Closing his eyes, he took a few deep breaths trying to focus. What could have put him over the edge like this, a five minute conversation with a crazy old man? No that wasn't it he realized. He suddenly understood that everything this old man had just told him might be true and if so, that thought scared the hell out of him.

"I see you believe some of my words, even though they seem impossible to your rational mind. Maybe you need to discard your mind, open up your soul, look and see with new eyes, with a new insight. I have spoken the truth and you have received it even though you struggle. The question now is what are you going to do with it? What are you going to do now Captain Mondo?"

The shock of hearing his name snapped him back to the present.

"How did you know my name?"

The chief laughed in a loud voice.

"I could tell you the spirit world told me but that would not be true. One of my people saw your boat anchored at Bird's Point. It's very easy to identify a boat by its registration numbers. Finding the owners name is a simple next step. It is very easy using the internet."

He laughed again as he watched Mondo's expression when he mentioned the internet.

"We use what is useful. The internet can be most helpful. We are very interested in any boat that ventures our way. You have seen the barge, you have met the people that come to do us great harm. They are just the beginning of a flood of whites that will soon descend upon us. They will take our forest. Take all that we have left. They will take from us the last thing that makes us a people."

There was no hesitation in Mondo's mind, not anymore.

"What can I do?" he asked softly, his senses so tuned to this old man before him.

"That I do not know, but I will ask something of you. I will ask it from my heart, from my soul, I ask it for my people. Do not turn away from what has brought you here, please listen to it. Bring your sailboat to Salmon Creek, it will be safe here. Then I think we must sit in the sweat lodge as my people have for centuries. We will invite the spirit world to make known its wishes for us. That is all I have to say," then he stood up and Mondo knew their meeting was over.

Ten minutes later Mondo was at his dinghy, still trying to understand what had just happened. He fired up the outboard, untied, spun the boat around and headed back to Smokin' Joe. The natural beauty that he had so admired earlier was now lost to him. His mind was racing, thinking about the crazy events of the day. From the first moment he arrived in Swartz Bay nothing made sense. The huge barge, the helicopter, the welcoming committee that dropped by, he knew those guys meant every word they said. Then there was the hostility of Bud and George and the fight in the bar. All of these things mattered little, compared to the feelings that he carried with him as he left the old man's house.

Something powerful had pulled him to Neskiwaii and Salmon Creek, something that he understood less and less each minute as he thought about it. This was all beyond his mental ability to grasp. It was like nothing he could ever have imagined.

As he raced back to Smokin' Joe, he wondered if he should pull into Salmon Creek or just head out and back to Victoria. A part of him wanted to get the hell out of here as fast as he could. Yet, he realized that he had come this far for answers, and now suddenly he had somehow become entwined in a people's future that he knew nothing about. Could he really, possibly have been called by a spirit world, a world that he had no understanding of? A world he didn't believe in and yet at this moment somehow seemed so real to him. It was all too much to grasp, but he knew that if he returned to Salmon Creek, he would be entering into a world far beyond what his rational mind could understand. What the future would hold for him he had no idea, but he knew without a doubt he would be venturing into territory that he had never glimpsed before.

Chapter 10

J ust before nightfall, Smokin' Joe carefully made her way to the dock at Salmon Creek. Once along side Mondo jumped off and started to tie her up. He had been worried about leaving Swartz Bay. He feared that maybe the crew on the barge had heard about the fight and wouldn't let him leave without another round, but nobody seemed to give him a second glance as he motored out of the anchorage.

He couldn't stop thinking about what he had heard from Chief Yazzi. Had the spirit of a totem really called him to this town? That was stupid he knew. He didn't believe in superstition. His rational mind knew these thoughts were crazy, yet somehow he couldn't get rid of them. He remembered the last words the old man had said to him as he stood at the doorway ready to leave his small house.

"You must look into your heart. You will know which way to go. The white man in you will leave the anchorage and flee from us, flee from what your spirit wants you to do. I do not know what voice you will listen to."

With that, Chuck Yazzi had reached his right hand out and gently placed it on Mondo's shoulder. He had held it there for a second then with a smile he had turned and gently closed the door behind him. Mondo had stood there for a few minutes trying to figure something out that seemed just beyond his understanding, before he gave up and started walking back to the dock.

Somewhere while racing the dinghy back to Smokin' Joe Mondo knew he would return to Salmon Creek and that realization scared him. Whose voice was he listening to? How could he believe in something so foreign to his way of thinking, something that he knew made no sense and yet seemed so right at the same time? There were no answers he suddenly realized, not yet anyway. He would have to trust his instincts and believe in mysteries that were getting harder to believe all the time.

He was kneeling down, inspecting a cleat after he had tied Smokin' Joe to the dock when he heard something behind him. He glanced up and watched as two young men walked toward him. One of them he had seen earlier today when they arrested Bud & George. Mondo stood up and waited for them to reach him. When they got to where he was standing they stopped, but just for a moment before one of them smiled, grabbed the life line of Smokin' Joe and then gracefully swung himself aboard and disappeared below. Mondo was so surprised that he just stared at the other man.

"It's okay, we are here to keep your boat safe, do not worry," he said then he climbed aboard and followed his friend down the companionway steps.

Mondo stood there for a few seconds before he shrugged his shoulders, shook his head letting out a deep sigh that was almost a laugh, and started walking down the dock. He couldn't believe that they just jumped on board without even asking permission. Stranger was the fact that he knew it was alright, he knew that Smokin' Joe was going to be very carefully looked after. Soon he was once again at the chief's front door.

"It is good that you have returned, I am glad," the old man said with a broad grin, as he welcomed Mondo back into his home.

Mondo dropped down in the old oversized chair and smiled slightly. He felt like he was on a ride in an amusement park, the course was unknown, what was around the next bend was unknown, why he was even here was unknown.

The chief brought out some smoked salmon and bread, and a strange yellow soup in a large coffee cup with small chunks of something floating in it. He handed Mondo a mug and put the salmon and bread on the table in front of them.

They ate mostly in silence. The few times they talked it was Chief Yazzi asking questions about Easter Island. It soon dawned on

Mondo that the chief was much more interested in the stone statues of Easter Island than he had first let on.

As they ate Mondo kept noticing the old man looking at him, studying him, then whenever their eyes met Chief Yazzi would smile that little smile of his and go back to his meal. There had been something in his eyes from the first time he had met him. There was wisdom there and Mondo realized sadness as well. Those dark penetrating eyes seemed to go right to his very core. He was glad he had no secrets to hide from this old Indian chief. Mondo told himself over and over that this whole thing was crazy but deep inside he knew it wasn't.

The two finished dinner and the chief cleaned the table putting the dishes in the sink. Then he walked back and sat down across from Mondo on the old sofa.

"I have prepared the sweat lodge. I want you to join us. It is a holy place. It is sacred to my people."

"Okay," Mondo said reluctantly. Not that sitting is a sweat lodge sounded bad to him, it was just that everything was starting to seem so surreal.

"I want to show you some pictures of my people, in happier times," the old man said as he stood up and walked to a small closet and opened the door. He brought out a large stack of photo books and sat down next to Mondo. For the next hour they looked at the past together, the chief losing himself in pictures of happier times, and Mondo sensing himself being drawn more and more into these people's lives.

A car horn broke the spell and Mondo was surprised as he looked up to see that it was dark outside. They both stood, walked out the door and climbed into another old battered car. The driver greeted them, then they drove away. They headed out of town, down a tree lined dirt road, the headlights peering into the darkness. Not a word was spoken. The car made a few turns and Mondo knew he could never find his way back. Fear tried to climb into his mind, he was at their mercy and he knew it, but he forced it away. He had already made his mind up. Somewhere on his way back to Salmon Creek he had committed to trust this old man. He would have to live with that decision, right or wrong.

Twenty minutes later the car pulled into a clearing and the driver turned the engine and headlights off. There was a small fire burning and in its glow Mondo could see two men standing idly around it. After they climbed out of the car the driver started it up and slowly pulled out onto the dirt road and drove off. Mondo was surprised at the quiet of the evening. Except for the small crackle of the fire not a sound could be heard. It was almost eerie to him, and he suddenly realized just how much constant noise he lived with everyday. He followed the chief up to the fire and they joined the two other men. Mondo was surprised again at their behavior, there were no introductions, no hello's, no how are you. It was as if the holiness of this place made any extra conversation superficial.

Finally Chief Yazzi spoke, his voice a quiet whisper.

"As you know I have asked our friend to share this night with us. Let us clear our minds and souls. Let us come together tonight as brothers, for our spirits are already one."

After a few minutes of standing in front of the fire, one of the men walked a few feet into the shadows and came back with a large gallon jug. He took a long drink then passed it to his right. Mondo thought maybe it was some sacred medicine to go with the sweat lodge.

"It is only water, drink plenty of it you will get very dehydrated tonight," the man said as he handed him the jug.

Once the jug was finished and put down they stared back into the dying embers. More silence, it was a deep silence that in the stillness and darkness of the night seemed so powerful that Mondo could almost taste it. After five minutes the old man turned and started walking into the darkness. The two men also started walking and Mondo figured he might as well follow them. They walked for a few minutes until they came to a small hut, built low to the ground. The chief stood waiting.

"We will purify ourselves. There is nothing to fear. Please remove your clothes and we will enter," he said looking at all three of them but Mondo was sure he said it for his benefit.

Mondo followed the others as they stripped, set their clothes on a small wooden bench and then crouching low climbed through a heavy cloth doorway into the sweat lodge. The heat instantly struck him, it sucked his breath dry, his eyes watered and his skin instantly started to develop small beads of perspiration.

The men sat down on woolen blankets, facing inward toward a group of red hot stones. A small pile of brush and twigs sat off to one side near the chief. The heat was overbearing. Mondo tried to make himself comfortable as he started exhaling deep breaths. It soon became harder and harder to maintain his focus. The longer he sat there the more his mind seemed to start running in a direction of its own, and very quickly he lost all sense of time. His thoughts continued to drift and he started to think about the natural beauty and sense of harmony that he had experienced since he brought Smokin' Joe into this area and how it had touched him so deeply. Then his thoughts switched and he started reliving the very moment that he turned into Swartz Bay and saw the barge. Not only could he see it in his mind but he started to feel the emotions of that moment as well. The complete shock, turning to anger at seeing that man-made monstrosity anchored there.

As he sat in the heat and darkness he could feel the power of this place reaching out to him. He became aware of the intense silence, a growing silence that seemed to pull him toward the heat and red glow. Only the other men's breathing could he hear, a background noise that seemed to set a tempo which his mind started to follow. The silence soon became an overpowering wave, engulfing his senses, flooding him with thoughts and emotions, with feelings that seemed to rush through his mind and then just as quickly disappear into some great void that was just beyond his mental grasp. The deeper the silence, the more he started to feel his surroundings with new senses that were so foreign to him. His mind seemed to slowly detach itself from his being as he felt his spirit rise out of his body into the small sweat lodge. A magic was filling him and he felt no fear as it continued to sweep through the room. His mind kept going back to the feelings of conflict, anger and then the fear he had felt at seeing the barge. He suddenly realized that these emotions he felt were not just his, but were from the other men inside this small lodge as well. Then he realized that they were the fears of an entire people, a collective fear that all who called Salmon Creek home now had to live with.

His thoughts were suddenly distracted when the chief slowly reached to his right and grabbed a small branch and placed it on the stones. Instantly a bitter odor filled the sweat lodge and a stinging sensation came to his eyes. The brush burst into a small flame before quickly burning out, leaving a smoky residue to linger. Mondo became aware that every breath he took brought this smoky air deep into his lungs.

The silence continued to grow until it overcame him. Time disappeared, lost its meaning in the magic of the moment. Mondo's mind continued to lose control, his thoughts drifted free. A lifetime of experiences that made him who he was grew to become meaningless as he sat in this holy place.

Slowly one of the men started to hum, a soft guttural sound that came from deep inside. The humming resonated through the sweat lodge, filling his mind and heart and carrying his soul along on each sound. His mind laughed at him as he tried to hang on to some sense of reality, but it was now impossible. Finally he cast himself free from all that he was, all that made him who he was, he cast himself into a spirit world that bordered on madness.

The guttural hum soon gave way to a soft chant, each tone so complete, so perfect. It sounded as if the pure language of the universe was being sung. The other men started to sing along, softly filling the sweat lodge with their voices. The words had a musical quality about them, like a stanza repeated over and over, and Mondo realized it was a holy mantra they were singing. Ever more so he felt his soul being carried along by the magic of the night.

All of his thoughts became shadows as he tried to look deep into his mind as it raced before him. His spirit was opened up, and he was helpless to control it. He was entering a place that he had never been before, a place where the conscious mind gave way to the soul.

An amazing realization soon came over him as he suddenly understood that somehow, as impossible as it seemed, he knew this song that filled the small sweat lodge. Slowly he allowed himself to chant along. The words were as sure as his name, as sure as anything he had ever known in the past. Mondo joined in with the other men, matching their tempo, following along, repeating each magical word that they sang. Somewhere during the night he became aware that he was no longer following but joining, all four of their voices became as one. The four men's spirits joined and they went forward into an ancient world that no white man had ever experienced. On through the night the men sang softly. Sweat continued to pour from Mondo, his entire body covered with a glistening wetness that reflected in the dim glow of the stones. Somewhere in the night he once again became aware of the silence. The others had stopped singing. He opened his eyes to see the chief looking at him, he could see in the dim light tears streaming down the old man's face. The others face's were lost in the darkness but he could sense their eyes upon him. He continued to chant the song as he closed his eyes, allowing his spirit the freedom to dive deeper into this song that rose not from his mind, but from his soul.

Soon the song stopped and words started to come forth from his lips. It was his voice, his words, but they had no meaning to him. For five minutes Mondo spoke in a tongue that he had never heard before. Each words meaning was lost to him. Yet he spoke with power and authority, repeating over and over a phrase that at the moment seemed the most important thing he had ever spoken. A meaningless phrase to him, but to the chief and his two most trusted advisors, it was the sound of their spirit world talking to them. They knew and understood every word. The chief wept uncontrollably as he listened. The words from Mondo's lips were the fulfillment of the prophecy repeated over and over.

Chapter 11

The phone on his desk buzzed, indicating a call from his secretary. Michael Jensen reached over and hit one of two flashing lights on his phone console.

"Yea," he said his voice harsher than he meant it to be.

"Mr. Jensen, I have your party on the line, sir, the call you were expecting."

"Good I'll take it."

He heard the phone click over and saw his secretaries light go out.

"Mr. Donaldson, it's been a while."

The last time he had seen Mr. Donaldson it had cost him seventy-five thousand dollars.

"Michael, yes it has been a while. I assume there is something that I can help you with?"

Michael laughed to himself, what a line for a hit man.

"Yes there is, can you come to Vancouver?"

"Of course, when?"

"In a few days."

"Wednesday, late afternoon, would be the earliest."

"That will be perfect. I'll pick you up at the airport. Let me know your flight."

"Wonderful," he said then hung up.

Michael had no idea what it would cost him this time, but once again he needed to go outside of his people, and Mr. Robert Donaldson was his only choice.

Three days of babysitting this Indian was about all that Flick could take. The hell with the money, this was getting out of hand and he knew it. The phone call should have come by nine this morning at the very latest. He pictured the same, heavy voice saying it was time to give this guy a few more pills and send him to the ozone, or wherever these pills send somebody, then unchain him and leave. By the time this drunken Indian woke up Flick figured he'd be long gone. He would just stroll out of the Mayflower, get his money and never look back.

By early afternoon Flick was really starting to worry. There was no phone call, no message, not even his pager went off. This was all starting to go sideways and he knew it. By seven that evening he was fighting the temptation to grab his stuff and run.

Flick sat there with the television blaring, but his thoughts were somewhere else. He looked at the Indian who stared with vacant eyes. It was time for him to take another pill. He would have to wake him up, lead him to the bathroom, force a pill or two down his throat, handcuff him again, and then keep sitting on his ass until morning. Flick had this nagging feeling in the back of his mind and he couldn't shake it, and a long time ago he had learned to pay attention to those feelings.

Sure, he was trapped in a two bit hotel in the bad part of town with a drunken Indian that was worth a lot of money to somebody, somewhere, for some unknown reason. Hell, he thought, he'd been trapped in hotels with hookers, drug dealers, psycho's, and even killers and it never bothered him before. Still, he knew this was going bad fast. The whole arrangement hadn't made any sense in the beginning and it made less now. He knew he needed to run, but unknown enemies are impossible to stop.

Joseph was slumped on the bed, his head resting on the pillow.

Flick couldn't take it anymore, there had to be something he could do.

"Wake up asshole," he said, trying to hide the frustration in his voice.

Slowly the Indian opened his eyes.

"What are you doing here man?" Flick asked.

"You should know."

"I don't know shit, but I know this whole thing ain't right."

"Kidnapping never is."

Flick was surprised by his response. The guy's mind must be working better than he thought.

"What's your name?"

"Joseph."

"Well, Joseph tell me, who wants to make sure you're out of the way for a few days?"

"What makes you think this ends in a few days?"

The way he said it stopped the thought process in Flick's mind, his next question disappearing into a fog.

Didn't they say just for a few days, he asked himself? He looked back in his memory to the call and he was sure, just a few days and make some good money. He didn't even know who put this whole thing together. There was nobody he could call. Suddenly, a chilling thought ran through his mind. What if this was never going to be just a few days, what if this was going to come down really hard for this guy, like concrete shoes off the pier, or a one way ride down a dark, deserted logging road. A thousand different ways could be found to make this Indian disappear and when the cops came looking for him it would all end up in his lap, or worse, suppose he disappeared as well.

Flick slumped back in his chair, exhaled a deep sigh and suddenly realized that he had been a complete fool to ever take this job.

"You got no idea what this is about?" Flick asked, having a hard time keeping the tension out of his voice.

"I got an idea."

"Well, shit, give it to me."

"You figure it out, you're the man!"

Flick stood up, walked into the bathroom and closed the door. He stared into the cracked mirror over the sink and realized that he had been set up from the beginning and more than likely something was coming down that would leave Joseph and him both dead.

The cold water did little to ease his tension, his neck ached and his head still pounded. The three aspirins that he had taken earlier had done little. He knew it. Damn he thought as he stared into the mirror, he knew this was all going wrong.

In the next moment it all suddenly came together for him. He knew neither of them were going to walk away from this. He was going down with Joseph and both of them would be dead if he didn't do something fast. He sat on the toilet feeling his knees growing weak with the realization that both of them needed to run.

Finally he forced himself up and walked to the door, opened it and stared at Joseph trying to figure out what the hell to do now? Joseph sensed the fear that Flick could no longer hide.

"It'll all come down on you man," he said.

"Shut up, I'm going outside. If I hear you say one goddamn word I'll come back in here and cut your face off!"

With that threat Flick turned, opened the door and walked out slamming it behind him. He hurried down the hallway and outside into the night. He made his way two blocks to a payphone, dropped in some change and punched a number that he knew by heart.

"Pick it up Mahoney," he said to himself.

After ten rings somebody picked up the phone.

"Yeah," was all he heard, but Flick knew it was him.

"Manny, it's Flick. I got troubles and they could be big. I need to hide. You got a place for me?"

"Call me in ten," and the line clicked dead.

He hoped to God that Manny Mahoney could find a safe place for him.

Flick walked across the street and down a block to a small coffee shop and bought two large black coffees. He sipped his as he sat at an outside table, his mind racing with ideas as he stared at all the people who walked by. Didn't any normal people live in this city anymore, he wondered? Everyone he looked at seemed to have something crazy about them, body piercing, or tattoos, spiked hair or something. Hustlers and hookers strolled by wearing skin-tight skimpy clothes, laughing and strutting their stuff for another night of decadence. The street people were all starting to appear for another night of God knows what they do, all the creeps come out when the sun goes down, he thought.

As he drank his coffee he realized he couldn't leave Joseph behind. If he ran then whoever set this up was free to waltz in the door, make that drunken Indian disappear and put the blame on him. Jesus, he sat there thinking about how many people had seen him in the last few days. He thought of the old man behind the counter who looked up from his paper as he ran in from the rain that first night. That old man also had seen the girls' drag Joseph in. They wouldn't take a rap for him and he couldn't blame them. Hooking seemed pretty innocent compared to murder. Then there was the waitress in the diner that he had been in before running into the Mayflower, the woman at the corner grocery store. Man he thought, there were probably twenty people who could identify him as someone who had been hanging around. He knew there were enough fingerprints in that room to tie him and Joseph together.

He finished his coffee and walked to a different payphone and called Mahoney again.

"1675 Forest Way, number B, it's in the back. There's a key under a rock underneath the garden hose next to the front door. You have one hour to get there and disappear," Mahoney hung up.

Flick kept repeating the address in his mind as he made his way back to the Mayflower.

"Drink this," he said as he removed the handcuffs and handed Joseph a cup of lukewarm coffee.

"Take a shower, if you want to stay alive you'll do what the hell I tell you to do and not cause me any grief," Flick said with malice.

Joseph didn't say a word. He sat up, then rose to his feet, stretched and started drinking his coffee as fast as he could as he headed for the bathroom.

Flick gave him three minutes once he heard the shower running before he walked into the bathroom, pulled his knife out and flung the shower curtain back. Joseph seeing the knife froze with a look of terror on his face. Flick reached down to the temperature knob and switched it to cold. He kept his knife on him with a look in his eye that dared Joseph to move. For two minutes the freezing water spattered off of Joseph, who never reached for the faucet, he never said a word.

Finally Flick shut the water off and put his knife back in its sheath.

"Get dressed, we're leaving," he told him as he turned around and walked out of the bathroom.

Flick looked around the cheap hotel and tried to fight the panic that was setting in. Jesus he thought, it will be impossible to wipe this place down, but still he had to try. He grabbed a pillow and pulled the cover off and started wiping everything as fast as he could. A few minutes later Joseph walked out of the bathroom, saw what Flick was doing and without a word walked back into the bathroom, pulled the wet towel off of the towel bar and started wiping the bathroom down.

Flicked glanced through the opened door and saw Joseph wiping away as fast as he could. Crazy Indian he thought, this wasn't about saving his ass. Yet he had his first ray of hope in an otherwise very dismal three days. Joseph was as scared as he was and that was very good.

It was nine-fifteen when the two of them walked out of the hotel, Flick walking twenty feet ahead of Joseph. Only once did Flick glance back to make sure he was there. Finally three blocks from the Mayflower, Flick stopped and leaned up against a brick wall that was in between street lights. Joseph walked up and stopped beside him, he didn't have a clue what to do next.

"Listen man, this is how it's coming down. Somebody wants you dead and because I was stupid enough to get involved in this whole shitty deal they want me dead as well. You got that? We are both as good as dead if we don't run. We need to lay low and try to figure out what is going on."

Joseph didn't say a word. He just nodded his head in agreement.

Suddenly out of the corner of his eye Flick saw three young men walking toward them. Instinctively he reached behind him and put his right hand on his knife, but they walked by without a word.

"Thanks man," Joseph said.

"Yeah," Flick replied.

They walked two more blocks before they entered a convenience store. Flick bought a map of Vancouver then headed back outside. It didn't take him very long to find Forest Way. They started walking and hailed a cab a few blocks later. They rode in silence as the cab took them to the waterfront. Ten minutes after the cab dropped them off they were in another cab heading in the general direction of their safe house. Three blocks away from their destination Flick had the driver pull over. He paid him and they started walking through a quiet neighborhood looking completely out of place.

Once the cab disappeared Flick changed directions and they

walked until they found the address. Two small houses were sitting very close to each other at the end of a long driveway. Both were dark except for the glow of a small light in the front window of the house in the back. Flick sure as hell hoped Manny had his act together, but he always had in the past. Silently, they walked up the driveway until they could see the small letter B on the front porch of the back house. Flick nodded with his head as he looked at Joseph who walked up to the porch and knelt down trying to keep himself out of sight.

Flick walked over to the garden hose which was rolled up on a reel two feet off of the ground. He looked around then kicked over a small rock and there was a key. Without making a sound he made his way to the front porch and he inserted the key. The door opened and they quietly walked inside, the glow of a dim light shining from somewhere in the back of the house. Flick looked around, studied the room, looked into the hallway, then closed the front door behind them. Satisfied, he dropped down onto the couch and felt a load of nerves, tension and fear leave him in a deep sigh.

Joseph sat on the floor and neither said a word. They both knew that this little haven wouldn't last for long. They were running from the same invisible people and they were scared to death.

Chapter 12

t was close to noon when Mondo woke to find himself covered under a thick blanket in the back of the old car that he had driven out to the sweat lodge in. His legs ached as he sat up groggily, his body slowly reacting as he saw his clothes on the driver's seat. Looking around he realized that he was parked in front of Chief Yazzi's house. He climbed out of the car holding his clothes and quickly dressed, then walked up and knocked on the door. No one answered so he tried the handle and the door opened.

"Hello," he yelled but he heard nothing back.

He let himself in and checked the house but it was empty. Oh well, he thought and he started back to Smokin' Joe.

As he walked down the dock he saw the two men that had watched his boat the night before climb off and walk toward him, but they just smiled as they passed without a word. He climbed aboard and found everything in perfect order.

He dropped down onto the settee and just sat, trying to remember as much of the night as possible. He had no memory of leaving the sweat lodge or of driving back to Chief Yazzi's house. The night was lost in a fog. Grabbing a large pillow that he bought in Panama, he wrapped his arms around it and holding it close he fell over on his right side, feeling the warmth and comfort of being back on board. He closed his eyes, took a few deeps breaths and realized he had no idea what was going to happen next.

The old man was miles away from Mondo, deep in the forest standing before the most sacred place of his people. As a child and then a young man his father had brought him to this very spot, teaching him to remember this place, to etch this location forever in his memory. Only once had he entered into the most holy place. Yet he could still picture the small room, the treasures of gold and silver and strange statues from far away places. He remembered bright precious gems and many other things, but mostly it was the sheets of copper stacked to the ceiling, that he remembered the most. The entire chamber was a small cathedral carved from solid rock. Now he stood before the entrance, alone with just his thoughts, his fears, and his hope that the power of the Cross was true.

He was standing before a rocky ledge almost seventy feet high, with steep vertical rocks jutting out from the cliffs above him. It took a while before he could guess where the outline of the small entrance was. It was laying flat on the ground in front of a huge hanging rock. A surge of sadness flooded through him as he thought of the times he had brought his son to this very spot. How he had started to pass the teachings of this place from his generation to the next. Now his son was lost and maybe dead. Yet how could he live without hope? He could not surrender to the fear that his son was no longer alive. Now there was only one thing that he could do, and that thought terrified him.

The chief took three steps to his right, then lowered his shovel and carefully started digging and soon revealed a large flat stone. Using his shovel he scraped the stone clean as best as he could, then he knelt down on his hands and knees and brushed the remaining dirt away.

Pausing, he looked over his shoulder at the stillness of the forest around him and felt a connection that dated back millenniums. Standing up he wedged his shovel under the front corner of the stone and lifted it. As the stone rose he could see darkness underneath it, then the darkness became a small opening as he slid the cover stone back. Taking one last look around him he put his shovel down, stepped into the blackness and carefully lowered himself down. Once his feet hit the earth he crouched low, flipped his flashlight on and carefully bending over, he crept for twenty feet before he was able to stand again. Shinning his flashlight to his left he saw a bed of stone over seven feet long and waist high with a low overhanging ceiling. Lying there were the skeletons of ten gods, who in death looked just like men. Chief Yazzi walked over and stood before them. He ran his left hand down the leg bone of one, hoping and praying for the wisdom that its touch might still impart. Turning to his right he saw the stacks of copper. These thin individual sheets of copper were made with handles cast at each corner and they were stacked to the ceiling in four tall columns. In the past, copper was the most precious material there was to his ancestors. No one ever talked about where this magical metal came from, only that its wealth was beyond measure. At famous Potlatch's and weddings these copper sheets were exchanged as the highest of honors. Now, Chief Yazzi stood before hundreds of sheets of copper, representing unimaginable wealth to his people in days past. Slowly, moving to his right he ducked down under another low ceiling and walked to the altar that held the sacred Cross. Reaching the altar he grabbed a golden lamp, its wick protruding out from a small, slender tube. He reached into his pocket and pulled out a lighter and lit the lamp then set it back down, before he turned his flashlight off. In the dim glow of the lamp he picked the ancient Cross up. It took two hands and its weight amazed him. It was gold with four rings of alternating black and white stones inlaid in a circle around the center. The bottom of the Cross extended out from the stone circle a foot ending in a base of gold. The relic made him think of something he'd seen in church when he had been forced to go as a boy. A holy relic that would sit high for all to see, yet he knew that this mosaic pattern, this golden Cross was like nothing he would ever have found in a modern church. The stones were cut perfectly, each piece carved with a slight curve, making the circle possible. It looked as if each stone was poured into place, the craftsmanship so perfect, each inlay separated by a thin sliver of gold. The circle radiated out over five inches before ending in a band of gold. Just staring at it took his breath away. He turned it over and gently ran his fingertips over the written inscriptions on the back. Symbols that no longer had any meaning for the living, yet held truths beyond human comprehension from an ancient past.

Holding the relic before him he feared what he was doing, for he understood that he was about to violate a trust that dated back over five thousand years. A shiver ran through his entire body, sending spasms of fear through his heart and mind and he almost fainted. What if he was wrong? He knew this moment would haunt him his short remaining lifetime.

Walking to his right he sat on another small bench of smooth rock and put the Cross down next to him. He started to think of the story he had been told as a child, how so long ago a great cloud floated upon the water and came to his people's summer camp overlooking the great sea. His people had gathered and watched this cloud from the cliffs. They built a huge fire trying to force this evil away, yet it continued to come closer. It took three days from when the cloud was first seen until it stopped just outside the waves that crashed upon the beach. His people were all terrified, for none of their holy men had prophesied such an event. The cloud sat for days before one of the bravest of the men dared to paddle out to it. This young man climbed upon the cloud and found strange looking men who were too sick to move, men too weak to defend themselves. He rushed back to tell the village elders. A council was held to decide what to do with these strange men. After much debate the wisdom of the ages prevailed and the men were not killed but were brought ashore and nurtured back to health. All but three of them lived to become one with his ancestors. The great cloud sat upon the waters for over two moons allowing many gifts to be brought to the village. Then one night a great storm lashed the land and the cloud disappeared and was never seen again. The gods, whose skin was white like the dead, and had hair colored the fury of the sun became one with his people and started to teach. As the gods grew in strength they continued to share wonders. They taught about the night sky and about the world so far away. They told of many different people living far across the waters. They brought wisdom to the people. It was through this wisdom that the neighboring tribes came together, putting their weapons of warfare down and becoming as brothers and sisters, living in peace. They realized that so much more could be gained from cooperation than could ever be gained by war. The gods of the cloud brought wisdom, compassion, knowledge, and they shared it with all.

His thoughts drifted back to the present as he looked around him and then looked at the Cross. His mind started racing with the fear that he was making such a mistake, but there was nothing else he could do. His people would need a chief to lead them in this fight and he knew his time was short. Cancer ran through his body. He only hoped that he could live long enough to see his son return, if he was still alive. Only his lost son could lead the people, could rally them together once he was gone. As he prayed in that most holy of places he had to hope that the power of the Cross could break the white man's hold upon his son.

Instinctively, he had understood last night that only one man could be trusted to carry this holy relic into the darkness of Vancouver. Only one man could have any hope of finding his son. For last night in the sweat lodge Captain Mondo had sung the ancient song of his ancestors.

Chapter 13

As far back as he could remember adversity was a game to be played with only one goal, to overcome and win. Fear of failure rarely entered his mind and when it did he forced it out so quickly that it never had time to settle. Yet, tonight was different. Ever since he received the call that woke him, his mind had fought against this creeping fear.

"Thunderbird has run, along with the watcher. They have forty minutes on us. I have people on it," the voice on the line had said, then paused as if waiting for some sort of instruction that could make everything right.

"Find them goddamn it!" he shouted before he slammed the phone down.

Michael lay in the darkness, his mind running with different possibilities for over ten minutes before he got up, walked downstairs, poured himself a Scotch and dropped onto his leather couch.

So the Indian has run, along with that bastard Flick, well . . . he thought, that changes everything.

Joseph Yazzi was a huge bargaining tool and Michael understood the potential risk if he ever returned to his people. Even though he was just a drunken, homeless Indian living on the streets of Vancouver he was still the Chief's only son. Michael knew that if the native population of Salmon Creek decided to fight against Mountain Resources and Joseph stood next to his father they could be very powerful and cause a lot of problems. The more disorganized and splintered the First Nation people were the better. Removing the possibility of Joseph ever being able to return to his people was critical to his planning. The people of Salmon Creek must be leaderless and lost. The easiest way to sever any ties that they could possibly have with the strength of their past, with their spirit world, was to remove the old man. Chief Yazzi had guided his people for a very long time and that was about to end, one way or another, he knew that for certain.

As he absentmindedly rolled the ice cubes in his empty glass he knew he needed to call some of his people in government and tell them to start the process of removing the entire disputed land issue from the courts. The time had come to force the First Nation people to open up their lands to logging. Millions of hectares of prime forest were just too tempting to be left alone, locked in an antiquated court system that could resolve nothing. By forcing the government to change its stance on the disputed land issue, the Native People would finally see the inevitability of the outcome. Logging was coming their way. They could benefit from it, take the money and use it however they wished, or they could lose any hope of ever regaining their lands.

This battle might have to be fought in the media as well, he knew, but right now it was too early to tell. If necessary he could convince people all across British Columbia that First Nation people needed to take more control of their financial situation and rely less on government handouts and that a comprise must be reached. When it was shown the financial windfall the Native People could received in exchange for logging contracts it would be easy to get the media buzz working in his favor. His influence with the press was even more powerful than in Parliament.

He would make it all look good, a grand splattering of hyperbole across the headlines, but as in any business deal, further negotiations would have to be spelled out. That was where he would make his fortune, in the fine print. Mountain Resources would promise much and in the beginning they would abide by their agreement, but only in the beginning.

Michael knew it was dangerous to force politicians into corners, but he also knew that at times it was the only way to get things done, and he wanted things done now! He smiled as he thought of the photos he had of the two politicians with hookers in the Marriot

Hotel. Those photos were some of the best money he had ever spent. It had taken a few years but each man had succumbed to the threat of exposure and the greed of cash and now there was no way out for them. After they each had accepted his first fifty thousand dollars he knew he had his political partners.

The phone call could wait until the morning. But he was determined that by noon tomorrow the Government of British Columbia would start to look at the disputed land issue in a new light. He was sure of it.

He poured his glass half full of scotch and wandered over to the window, then look down on the city streets below. He could see people scurrying around. As he stared he knew that he had the power of life and death, he could make or break people, destroy lives or bring the lowly up to new heights, but tonight his thoughts returned to that bastard Flick Shagwell. He thought he had picked the right scum bag to watch Joseph Yazzi. His people had assured him that Flick would do as he was told, take the money and not say a word to anybody. Well, maybe Flick was smarter than his people had thought.

He walked back over to the couch, drained his Scotch and pulled the comforter over his shoulders as he lay down. He knew some of the best answers came in that twilight place between consciousness and sleep. His mind was running, Flick Shagwell sure had screwed everything up.

Stephen Cartere received the call in his office at Parliament shortly after eleven in the morning. It was a short conversation. He said little, just listened. When the call was over he stood at his desk, and with sweaty palms called his secretary and informed her that he needed to speak to Mr. Thomas Egan, British Columbia's Minister of Forestry. He and Thomas had been talking for months about ways to create an environment where the Native People would be forced to open up their lands for logging, all under the pretense of helping them raise much needed revenues. The First Nation disputed land issue was something that had been simmering just out of sight for a very long time. It had been tied up in the courts for years and could easily continue to be there decades longer. This whole issue was a no win politically, yet he had no choice, people wanted things changed and had come to him with their request, and to these people it was political suicide to say no.

"Thomas, it's Stephen, I think we need to talk again. Did you see last week's editorial demanding that the government improve the health care possibilities of First Nation people?" there was a short pause as he listened to Thomas's reply.

"Good, we're in agreement. I think we should meet. I really want to make an announcement soon, within the next week if possible of our intent to take serious our commitment to Native people. As you know I already have contracts with Mountain Resources drawn up and just waiting for the correct political climate, if you will."

Another short pause as he listened.

"Yes, it could be seen that way, yet I prefer to see it as government in action, decisive, effective, taking the hard shots and doing what is right. You and I know it could take decades under normal channels. There is growing pressure from the public and we need to act now."

After his short conversation he hung up and sat back down in his chair. He realized that his palms were sweatier now than before he made his call. Little did Stephen Cartere know that Thomas Eagan had spent a fateful night in the Marriot as well.

The next day the headlines had yet another story about the plight of the First Nation People, and how through neglect and government abuse they were falling through the cracks of the very system that was designed to protect them. The front page article ran on and ended on the bottom of page three with the idea that it was time for Native people to take more control of their financial destiny by allowing logging on their tribal lands. The article went on to say that now was the perfect opportunity for both sides to come together and sort out the many disputed land issues that they faced. Native people owned millions of dollars of timber just waiting to be harvested. Why should it be up to the tax payers of British Columbia to help pay all of their bills, the newspaper had asked?

The uproar that followed filled the call in talk shows, filled the editorial response pages in all the local newspapers. Suddenly a concept that had been cultivated in the back room of Mountain

Resource had grown to front page news. The pot was being stirred and that was just what Michael Jensen wanted.

As Mondo lay on his bunk feeling drained from his experience in the sweat lodge he started thinking about this strange little town, with its beat up streets, and forlorn buildings. He couldn't shake a feeling of despair that overcame him as he thought about this place, and he wondered where this feeling came from. Was it from the physical world of his five senses, the world that he could see, feel, taste, and grab hold of, or was it something else? Was he picking up the feelings of a people who knew they had no hope, who were forced to live in a world that they couldn't control, a people whose values and beliefs were so different from the white man who now occupy their ancient lands.

The word occupy startled him. In that moment he understood that these people were living in occupation. They were a conquered people, ravished by bullets and disease until all they could do, all they could hope for was to surrender and accept whatever the white man promised. Their ancient wisdoms and traditions no longer held any hope for them, could no longer guide them in a world that was not theirs. No wonder Mondo thought, as he started to fall asleep, no wonder he felt such despair here.

It was late afternoon when he heard a soft knock on the side of the hull. He climbed up the companionway steps and looked out to see Chief Yazzi standing there. There was something about the old man that seemed very strange but he couldn't quite put his finger on it.

"May I come aboard?" he asked, his voice soft, seeming to have lost any authority and pride. Something was amiss and Mondo couldn't figure it out. The old man carried a large, stained, canvas bag with thick heavy straps over his right shoulder.

"Of course, please," Mondo climbed out of the companionway hatch and reached his hand down and helped pull him aboard and then they climbed down inside.

"I have wanted to see the inside of your boat. It's very . . . um . . . its very small," the chief said.

Mondo laughed, but he could sense how uncomfortable the old man was.

"Yep, but it's all I need."

"That sounds strange coming from a white man. I thought all white men wanted more and more, bigger and better?"

"I don't, want a cup of coffee?"

"Thanks."

Chief Yazzi sat down and watched Mondo as he worked in the galley. It was only when Mondo turned to hand him his cup that he realized the chief still clutched the canvas bag tight to his chest.

"What's in the bag?"

The old man didn't respond at first. He just sat there looking at Mondo. Whatever was going on with Chief Yazzi, Mondo knew to be quiet. He sipped his coffee for a few minutes just watching, realizing the anguish and turmoil that seemed to fill the old man.

Finally Chief Yazzi put the cup down on the small table and he started to speak.

"I know, and I think you know that you are here for my people. I now understand what you must do for us. In this bag is a treasure that is more important to my people, to my ancestors, than anything you could ever imagine. This goes back to Neskiwaii, this is a part of the mystery that you came here for.

"I am loaning you what is in this bag and I have only two requests. The first request I . . ." he stopped talking, reached over and grabbed his coffee cup. He took a long sip, as if savoring it, but Mondo could tell that he was trying to find the right words.

"I need you to find my son. He is lost in the white man's world of Vancouver. I need you to show him what is inside this bag. He knows of this relic, he will recognize it and I pray its power will break the white man's poisonous grasp on his soul. I ask you to find my son, Joseph Yazzi, show him what is inside this bag, and then bring him back to us."

Mondo just sat there not saying a word, and it was a long two minutes before Chief Yazzi started to speak again.

"I can see your heart my friend and even now in my weakness and fear your spirit reaches out to mine. Please take this, it is the best picture I have of him," he said as he reached into his shirt pocket and handed a small faded black and white photo of a young man to Mondo.

"That is my son."

Then slowly Chief Yazzi stood, leaving the bag on the settee, he turned and started walking for the companionway steps.

"Chief, how can I possibly find your son?"

The old man stopped and turned.

"That is beyond me. Let the gods of my people lead you."

Then without another word he climbed up the steps and a moment later Mondo felt Smokin' Joe gently roll as he climbed off of her.

Mondo sat stunned by what he had just heard. A few minutes later he casually reached over to pick the bag up. It was so heavy he was completely taken by surprise. Standing up so he could get his body directly over the bag it took both of his hands to lift it off of the settee. Thinking back he was amazed at how easy the old man had carried it. It had to be gold, he thought, nothing else could weigh that much and fit in the canvas bag. He looked inside to see something wrapped tight in an old woolen blanket, held in place by a few pieces of thin cord. Sitting back down he started to feel a panic set in. How could he possibly find Joseph, and what could possibly be inside this bag?

Chapter 14

An hour after Chief Yazzi left Smokin' Joe Mondo was standing by the side of the road at the outskirts of Salmon Creek waiting to catch the Island bus that would take him to Victoria. He had called Jonathan and left a message telling him that he was coming, that it was important, and that he needed to see him tonight. Somehow Mondo couldn't imagine unwrapping whatever the old man had given him without Jonathan.

It would be a long, boring bus ride with little to do besides think of how impossible it was going to be to ever find the chief's son. At least he had something to read, he had the old book about Neskiwaii and a book he had just started that held the promise of keeping his interest, titled Sunset Run. There was nothing else he could do but settle in for a long bus ride, and try to keep his fears in check.

It was after ten when he finally climbed off the bus in Victoria. Looking around he realized that this was a bad part of town. He grabbed the canvas bag Chief Yazzi had given him and flung it over his right shoulder keeping a good grip on it. With his left hand he carried his duffle bag, which had some spare clothes, a shaving kit, an extra pair of shoes, and whatever else he thought he might need for a few days and he hurried inside. He instantly picked out three tough looking guys standing in a corner casting quick glances his way, like vultures waiting for a kill. He knew he wasn't going to hang around here. Walking outside he hailed a cab and headed for Jonathan's apartment.

"Just a minute," he heard after he rang the doorbell.

Jonathan opened the door wearing a broad grin.

"Come in. I got your message."

Mondo walked in and dropped his duffle on the floor, then carefully set the canvas bag down on the sofa. Even though he had been sitting for a very long time he dropped down next to the bag feeling drained.

"You look beat Mondo, what's up? You want something?"

"No I'm fine but I have something to show you."

"Really, what . . . is it about Neskiwaii?"

"I think so, sit down and look in the bag."

Jonathan sat down looking at the canvas bag like a child on Christmas morning.

Mondo reached over, picked the bag up and handed it to him.

"Its heavy," he said before he released his grip.

The bag almost fell from Jonathan's hands.

"Jesus it is heavy," he said as he let it sit on his lap.

Jonathan looked at Mondo, then at the bag, then back at Mondo as a bewildered look grew on his face.

"I haven't looked at it yet."

"It's gold, isn't it?" Jonathan said, his eyes widening as he spoke.

"Just open it up and tell me what it is."

Jonathan sat back on the couch, exhaled a deep breath and pulled whatever was wrapped in the old blanket out of the bag and let the bag drop to the floor. He looked at Mondo with a strange look as he slowly unwrapped the blanket.

"My God . . ." he said as he lifted up a golden Cross with alternating circles of narrow black and white stones that created a halo out from its center. The small stones alternated within the rings as well, black offsetting white, creating four narrow bands, a mosaic of perfectly cut stones, edged in gold.

He looked at Mondo, letting the Cross sit back on his lap. Mondo read his face. Whatever this was Jonathan recognized it.

"Do you know what this is?" Jonathan finally asked.

"Not a clue."

"Where did you get this?" his voice so soft that Mondo could hardly hear him.

"It's a long story. Jonathan what is it?"

Jonathan held up the ancient Cross with both hands. He turned it over studying its golden backside and then turned it back looking at the strange inlaid rings of black and white stones.

"Mondo, this . . . doesn't exist. It is part of a myth . . . a story that for some reason won't go away. This Cross is the seal of a great city, of a great people."

He turned and looked at Mondo allowing the relic to once again sit in his lap.

"This Mondo, is the Cross of Atlantis."

Mondo laughed, but then checked himself. There was nothing funny about the look on Jonathan's face.

"Atlantis, Jonathan, really?"

"Really . . . Mondo."

Mondo felt his entire body slip backward into the old sofa. He closed his eyes, picturing the old man's face when he handed it to him.

"I don't believe it Jonathan."

"What don't you believe? You don't think there is any truth to the story of Atlantis? Well . . . I'll tell you one thing for sure. There is no doubt in my mind what is sitting on my lap."

Jonathan stood and gently laid the relic on the sofa. He walked out of sight, down a short hallway and was back in less than a minute, holding a large book in his hand.

Sitting down without saying a word, he started flipping pages as if he knew exactly what he was looking for.

"Look at this, you tell me," he said as he handed the book to Mondo, the page opened to a drawing of the exact Cross that sat on his sofa. There was no doubt in Mondo's mind that he was looking at a drawing of the relic that Chief Yazzi had given him. Under the picture was a small caption; The Cross of Atlantis.

"You see Mondo, the description of this Cross was first found in some of Plato's early writings. The first actual drawings of this relic were discovered in ancient Phoenician text found in Alexandria. Most scholars didn't give the writings or the drawings much attention, I mean really, who believed in a Cross of Atlantis?

"The Phoenicians claim that this Cross dates back to the beginning of time, to the great sea people that once sailed the world. Believe me when I tell you this Mondo, what you have brought here tonight, what sits on the couch next to me, I am certain is the Cross of Atlantis."

Mondo looked at Jonathan, studied his face, finding it impossible to believe.

Jonathan picked up the relic and held it, studying it, turning it over and over, as if it was now weightless. He brought it up close as he gently rubbed his fingers over the fine inlay work, then turned it over and studied the back.

"These symbols Mondo, they may be the earliest known written language ever."

After studying the relic for a few more minutes, he put it down on his lap and looked at Mondo.

"How in heavens name did you get this?"

"The chief of what is left of the people of Neskiwaii gave it to me. Jonathan what does this mean? How could this relic, this Cross, how the hell could an old Indian on Vancouver Island have this to give to me, how could he have it?"

"He can't Mondo. It can't be real." Jonathan said in a soft whisper as the reality of the moment struck him. "It is absolutely impossible. We have to be analytical," he said with a small laugh as he closed his eyes and took a deep breath then slowly exhaled. Opening his eyes a few seconds later he looked at Mondo and it was easy to see that the magic of the Cross had somehow disappeared.

"First, we both know that this can't be real. It must be a forgery, but how in god's name, even a forgery . . . even that would be impossible. Second, even if it is a forgery it is impossible for it to be found on Vancouver Island. It's beyond the realm of comprehension."

"That's fine Jonathan, it's beyond comprehension, but just the same it's sitting on your sofa."

Jonathan was speechless. His mind was running with the implications and he felt like his head was going to explode any second. Mondo found it impossible to believe him.

"Scotch Mondo, I believe I could use one," Jonathan said as he stood up.

"Bring the bottle."

For the next hour they studied the relic and looked at numerous books that Jonathan brought out. The more Jonathan talked and the more he showed Mondo books that either had drawings or written descriptions of the Cross of Atlantis, the more he had to admit that this indeed was what they had before them. The Scotch seemed to lighten the mood and both of them started to believe.

"Don't you have any photographs of this Cross?"

Jonathan looked up at him, and laughed.

"Photographs, you still don't get it Mondo. There has never been anything to photograph. All that history has is drawings and written descriptions. There has never been an actual Cross found!"

"Do you believe in Atlantis?" Mondo asked.

"I don't know if I believe in Atlantis per say, but I absolutely believe that around 3000 to 4000 B.C. something phenomenal happened. Like I told you before, what we call the beginning of civilization, from the pyramids to the Mayan calendar, to Mesopotamia, Stonehenge, even to the beginning of the Chinese culture half way around the world, it all started at the same time. How is that possible? It's not without some sort of contact. It is impossible for science to explain how this awakening, if you will for lack of a better word, ever happened."

Jonathan was beside himself, it was just too much to consider. The magic of the relic, the Scotch, the scientific potential of what lay on the couch, it was beyond belief. He took another drink of Scotch and seemed to lose his train of thought.

Finally, with a laugh he continued. "Look in the bible Mondo, I'm sure you've read some of it. You've heard about Noah's Ark. Do you have any idea how big that boat was? It was huge. Where in God's name," Jonathan started laughing again, "that's a joke, I think, maybe . . . anyway, where in God's name did Noah learn to build an Ark? Think of the cargo a boat that big could carry, or people. Suppose a fleet of ships, some the size of Noah's sailed from a calamity that destroyed a civilization. Suppose these people were cast out onto the ocean to survive however they could. Think of the culture and wisdom they would bring with them. You know Mondo I have thought for years that there is only one way to explain what happened around 4000 B.C. Somebody showed the entire world. From one beginning we all flourished.

"What about the tower of Babel?" Jonathan continued, his

excitement almost uncontrollable, "you know the story. It sure sounds like a pyramid to me. Don't you see that even our religion bears truth to what we are talking about. If Noah could build a ship to survive an ancient flood, or some sort of natural calamity, then so could others. What if Noah was from Atlantis, or whatever ancient civilization you want to call it, the name doesn't really matter, does it? What if the whole flood story is based on truth, maybe not a worldwide flood but a flood big enough to destroy a civilization? Melting ice sheets, glacial dams exploding, volcanic eruptions, hell I don't know, but do you see what I am talking about? Once we look at these stories not as some fairy tale from old, but fact, we open up a world of possibilities."

"Jesus, Jonathan, if this Cross is real, then this is one of the greatest treasures ever discovered. I mean what you're saying about this relic, it would be like finding the Ark of the Covenant, or the Holy Grail, whatever that is. This would be like . . ." Mondo couldn't think of the right word, he couldn't think of much at all, his mind was spinning out of control.

"Mondo if this is real, then this is one of the most important scientific discoveries ever. If this is the Cross of Atlantis, and if as you say an Indian chief from Neskiwaii gave you this, you have made one of the greatest discoveries in history. This is like finding proof of alien life. God Mondo, nobody will believe this, even if we hold a press conference tomorrow and show the world. Nobody will believe it."

"We can't do that Jonathan."

"Do what Mondo?"

"We can't tell the world."

"What, my god we have to!"

"We can't. I'm taking this to Vancouver and I'm showing it to Joseph Yazzi. That is after I find him."

"Who the hell is he and what does he have to do with the Cross of Atlantis?"

"As far as I know he's a drunken, homeless Indian living on the streets of Vancouver somewhere. What he has to do with this relic, god only knows."

Chapter 15

Mondo was awakened by the sound of a door closing softly. Fear filled him as he bolted upright, confused, momentarily not remembering where he was, until he realized that he was on Jonathan's couch. He slumped back down as he watched Jonathan slowly tiptoeing in front of him having just closed the front door. Carefully he reached down with his foot and kicked the canvas bag that he had wrapped tight under his feet last night.

"Sorry I woke you. I had to go out and get a paper and a battery for my digital camera. I want to photograph the Cross lying next to the front page, that way we can prove the date."

Mondo sat up, shook his head trying to clear cob webs.

"I don't think I ever fell asleep last night," Jonathan said, "I kept thinking about coming back out and waking you up. I'm sure it was after three the last time I looked at the clock."

Jonathan walked over to the coffee pot, poured a cup for Mondo, put it in the microwave for a minute, and handed it to him.

"Thanks," Mondo said as he brought the lukewarm coffee to his lips.

He hadn't slept very well either. There was that same recurring dream that he often had. He was working in a factory someplace with thousands of other people, all mindless drones, and for some reason he never remembered to punch the time clock so he never got paid. He had no idea what the dream meant.

"Jonathan I have to go to Vancouver today, you know that."

"Mondo, I won't try to change your mind, but you need to realize that what you have is more important than one man's life. It is more important than any man's life, yours or mine."

"I know that, but I can't fail Chief Yazzi. You should have seen him when he gave me the Cross. It almost killed him. I think he would sacrifice his son, even himself to keep it safe. It's just that he thinks the fate of his people rests with me finding his son Joseph. So, you see . . . I need to do this."

Jonathan walked over to the sofa and sat down next to him.

"What happens if you lose the Cross? What happens if somebody finds out what you are carrying with you? How many people would betray you, kill you for its value? Just its weight in gold must make it worth millions, but as you know its true value is beyond description. I bet collectors would pay, god Mondo, I don't have a clue, it's priceless! How can you carry it around with you? How can you leave it out of your sight for one second? You are planning on going to Vancouver carrying one of the most precious relics, one of the greatest discoveries in human history in your duffle bag! Then you have to find one man, a homeless drunk in a city. You don't even know where to look. Suppose somebody else is looking for this guy, what if this Chief Yazzi, hasn't told you everything?"

"I know."

Jonathan was completely right.

"I need to make a call," Mondo said.

"Sure no problem."

Mondo got up, put his pants on and walked over to the phone. He kept looking at Jonathan and then the canvas bag, feeling for the first time that maybe he couldn't trust him as much as he had thought.

"Don't worry Mondo, I don't have the balls, or maybe I'm a man of to much integrity. I don't know, but I thought about it."

"I know Jonathan, I know."

Mondo looked at the clock as he punched in the phone number. It was seven-thirty, she might still be home.

"Hello," it was Naomi.

"Good morning Naomi, its Mondo."

"Mondo, what a treat, are you okay?"

"I'm good. I'm at Jonathan's. I need to ask a favor of you."

"I thought you were calling me up for a date, I'm disappointed," she laughed.

"Naomi, please grab a pen and a piece of paper. I need your journalist skills."

"That's almost as good as a date, hang on."

"Okay what?" she said a few seconds later.

"I went to Neskawaii and I found a huge surprise. I found a giant barge called BELWOLF IV. It definitely looks like it's part of a huge commercial logging operation. Find out who owns it for me. Find anything that you can about it."

"Okay, is that it? I thought this was going to be full of mystery and intrigue. I'm somewhat disappointed in you Captain Mondo," she said with that cute little smile in her voice that caused him to instantly picture her diving into the pool at Bora Bora. He shook his head and forced it out of his mind.

"Listen Naomi, there may be more intrigue and mystery than either of us wants. Also I'm going to email you a picture. See if you can find out what it is. I'm not sure, so don't show the picture to anybody don't even describe it to anybody. Okay?"

"Oh the intrigue does start," she laughed again.

"Something like that, I'm heading to Vancouver today. I have to find somebody. I'll call you in a day or so. If you need to get hold of me before that leave a message with Jonathan. I'll keep in touch with him."

"Okay Mondo, but well . . . I don't work cheap."

"I'm afraid of that. I'll call you in a few days. Thanks Naomi. Tell your brother hi."

"Bye Captain."

He hung up and looked over at Jonathan who seemed to be listening to every word he had just said.

"Get your camera ready, we might as well take some pictures," Mondo said.

They took over twenty pictures of the Cross. A few of the photos Jonathan took with the self-timer, allowing both of them to be in it. They held the relic like it was a trophy size salmon, big grins on each of their faces, the successful hunters with the prize. Jonathan also insisted that a few of the pictures be taken with just the Cross and the newspaper held next to it. It seemed disrespectful somehow

Jonathan had said, to present to the world the Cross of Atlantis with him and Mondo in the picture looking like a couple of idiots.

"I need to email one of these pictures to Naomi, can I do it here"? Mondo asked later.

"Sure, in my office."

Mondo followed him down the hall and into his office and watched as he plugged a line from the camera into a port on the back of a laptop.

"It's on its way," he said.

"Thanks Jonathan."

"For what?"

"For being a man of integrity."

Jonathan gave him a funny look, and started to say something before he just turned away.

They walked back into the small living room and Mondo grabbed the Cross, wrapped it in the old woolen blanket, put it back in the canvas bag, and buried it in the bottom of his duffle.

"I'm going to take the ferry to Vancouver. I'll call you tonight. I'll call you daily if I can and let you know what I'm doing. I hope to god I can find Joseph Yazzi and get him back to Salmon Creek."

"What if you succeed and the chief wants to forget that he ever gave you this relic, what if he doesn't want the world to know about it?"

"I can't answer that. It seems we have an obligation to science to make this discovery known. I just don't know, besides last night you said this had to be a fake. Have you changed your mind?"

"I don't know what to think."

"Me neither. I'll grab breakfast somewhere."

"I'll drive you to the ferry if you want."

"No, I'll take a bus. I might as well start acting like a homeless person. Joseph Yazzi is living on the street and that's were I will have to go to find him."

"Mondo this is insane."

"You're absolutely right."

It took Naomi less than an hour to positively identify the picture she had been emailed, and she was shocked. She didn't believe for one minute that this was anything but a hoax. Yet it didn't seem like something Mondo would do. He had sounded so serious on the phone.

She went through her purse and found Jonathan's business card. She called him at home, no answer. Next she tried his office but nobody answered the phone there either. She desperately needed to talk to him and there was nothing that she could do. After a very frustrating ten minutes trying to get hold of Jonathan she decided to start looking into BELWOLF 1V, at least it would give her something different to think about.

Jonathan didn't go to work that morning, he couldn't. After years of frustration and ridicule, last night had proven to him that he was right. There was no way of telling how this would all turn out, but he now had proof that early man had sailed the oceans of the world, and even more important, the story of Atlantis was based on fact. As much as he had tried to convince himself and Mondo last night he knew that the Cross that he had held was no forgery. It had to be real. It was priceless and whoever announced its discovery to the world would be immortalized. This was one of the greatest discoveries of all time. This discovery was bigger than Mondo, or an Indian chief and his lost son. It was bigger than a dying Indian people.

He walked the streets of Victoria for the entire day struggling with what to do next.

Naomi had a very hard time finding anything about BELWOLF 1V. She spent an hour on the internet before she stumbled on an article that mentioned the barge and a large logging operation in a very remote area of northern British Columbia. The article went on to describe the barge as a mother ship, self sufficient for crew and equipment, built solely for the purpose of logging remote forests that would be otherwise inaccessible. From helicopter pads, to supply depots, to crew quarters, the barge was a floating city.

Tracking down its owners took another hour and what she found wasn't good. It was owned by a Canadian corporation that seemed to have no records, no other business in Canada, except ownership of the barge. As she dug deeper she found that same corporation had an office in the Cayman Islands. The Cayman's are one of the largest off shore banking centers in the world. Bogus corporations hide millions of dollars of profit in these banks. Most corporations there are nothing more than a mailing address and maybe a law firm to handle any problems that might arise. Naomi knew this wasn't right. Her instincts told her that this was a huge story. She knew that something big was going on and that Mondo was right in the middle of it.

awn Peters was exhausted and she hadn't slept well in over a week. Already her schedule at school was starting to run away from her. It had last year and she promised herself and her school counselors that this year would be different. It was just so hard to not get involved. She often wondered why people always asked her for help, asked her to share some responsibilities, handle some task when there were plenty of other people more qualified to do the job. She knew the answer even though it bothered her to admit it. She just had the hardest time in the world telling people no. Her desire to help others and to do the Lord's work was once again interfering with her education. What she really needed was someone to teach her an assertive training course.

The call came at seven-thirty waking her from a troubled sleep.

"Hello," she whispered her voice hoarse from a late night of street evangelism.

"Dawn darling," she knew instantly that it was Todd De Bijous, the gay manager at the mission.

"Dawn honey, I don't have anybody for tonight. Can you please, possibly come and help?"

That was about the last thing that she felt like doing. She lay in bed with the phone six inches from her head feeling that once again she was being taken advantage of. She sure wished the Lord would help her say no once in a while.

"Okay Todd, what time? You know I'm really busy at school."

"Oh Dawn, such a sweetheart, thank you, I knew I could count on you. Listen I'll try to keep your time short. If you show up at two we can have the kitchen going by then. I need you at the front door maybe until six tonight?" he said with a hint of question in the back of his voice.

Dawn knew she would be lucky to get out of St. Josephs Mission before eight.

"Okay, see you tonight."

She hung up the phone, rolled over and pulled the covers over her head. It was useless. She knew the late night street ministries were starting to take their toll.

Dawn had started her second year of college with high hopes. After struggling last year because of so many outside distractions she had promised herself that she would not over commit this year. Now she had been back to school for a little over a month and she had already become a regular at the food mission.

Yet she often thought wasn't that what her life was about, ministering to others in Christ's name?

She climbed out of bed, trying not to wake her roommate and walked into their tiny bathroom and turned the shower on. It would take a minute or two for the water to get even lukewarm. She glanced at herself in the mirror and then turned away. She had always been bothered by her looks. As far back as she could remember people had been telling her how cute she was. When she was little it was fine, it really didn't mean anything, and she just grew up with it, not even thinking twice about what it meant. Once she began junior high school and she started to blossom into a beautiful young woman her looks became a curse. Suddenly she had more attention than she ever wanted. Men of all ages started to drive her out of her mind. During high school it just got worse. An afternoon at the mall with her girlfriends would usually turn into an ordeal of male harassment. The thing that really bothered her was that everybody thought she should enjoy the attention. For some reason because she was put off by it all, she was stuck up, conceited, rude and just mean. That was about the last way she would describe herself, yet that is what she often heard.

Many of her girlfriends seemed to enjoy her company, not so much for herself but for the attention that she always seemed to bring around her. The smiles, the smirks, the second glances, the rude comments all started to drive her inside of herself, forcing her inward away from the out going friendly person she was. She often wondered why guys didn't get it. If they really wanted to get to know her, it was easy, just be nice. Slowly she continued to close herself off because it was just easier that way.

In her senior year of high school, at a Campus Crusade for Christ rally she walked forward and gave her life to Christ. She never realized when she was walking down those bleachers and up onto the stage that she was stepping out of her old life and into a new one. She was leaving behind what had been so superficial, so worldly and stepping into a life that held the promise of true insight, of meaning and of a relationship with God.

Her life changed overnight. Her friends started to change as well. She went from Friday night parties to Friday night bible studies, from sleeping in on Sunday morning to going to church services full of young people with guitars, singing, handclapping and shouting hallelujahs to the Lord. As graduation grew closer she knew she wanted to go to a Christian University.

"Study the bible?"

"Can't you do that at home?"

"Why go to college for that?"

"What kind of job will that get you"?

She had listened patiently to so many people who tried to change her mind, and it didn't take her long to realize that she had to get away from everybody, from her friends, her parents, even her past. She needed to start living her own life and it was impossible to do that in Grand Island, Nebraska, a town that she had spent her entire life in.

After high school graduation she cut her hair short, threw away her make up, climbed into her car and headed for Vancouver, British Columbia for a summer of street ministry before she started classes in the fall.

In some ways it seemed such a long time ago. Maybe it felt that way because she was finally settling into her own life. She was making it and at least she hadn't flunked out of school, not yet anyway. Time was now the big issue in her life, the lack of it, but at least she wasn't in Nebraska and she was serving the Lord.

Dawn pulled her car into the parking area behind the mission a few minutes before two. Already she could see the line that was starting to form around the entrance. How often she had looked into their faces and wondered about each person's story. How did they all end up homeless, living on the streets, trying to survive day by day? She wondered about the people that they must have left behind. Many must have children, loved ones, maybe even a spouse. A sense of sadness overcame her as she tried to put herself in their place. What hope did these people have? Was their life reduced to just a safe place to sleep and a belly full of food? What hopes and dreams could they have when it seemed that they had lost everything such a long time ago? No wonder so many turned to drugs and alcohol, what else was there?

St. Joseph's was non-denominational, which basically meant that no church could put its name on the building. It was all done in Christ's name and that was what drew her. Yet she was amazed at the bickering, the petty human drama that she witnessed so often from the staff. She thought that it should be so different. By putting others first and doing the Lord's work people should be able to get along much better than they did. It was a hard realization for her to accept that people were just people, with all of their human frailties regardless of their spiritual beliefs.

She walked in the back door and saw Todd scurrying around as usual. He was one of her favorite people at the mission. He was here because he really cared for the homeless. His gay lifestyle had shocked her at first probably because he was so open about it, not for one moment trying to stay in the closet. This had really bothered her when she met him and yet now she often laughed to herself as she remembered thinking she was going to have to convince him of his wrong doings. It didn't take her long to realize that Todd was one of the most non-pretentious people she had ever met. As a matter of fact she had grown to really like him.

"Oh Dawn, thanks so much. Please take the front door, you're so good up there," he said with a smile as he rushed by, then stopped in his tracks and looked at her again.

"I'll try to have you out by eight at the very latest," he said before he rushed off again. She remembered him telling her she could leave by six. Oh well, she knew she would be lucky to get out of here by ten.

Mondo walked off the ferry in Horseshoe Bay and looked around him. People were rushing everywhere. Cars were pulling on and off of ferries, traffic and confusion seemed to dominate the entire area. In the distance a car alarm went off and across the street somewhere a car started blasting its horn at someone or something. He thought back to Smokin' Joe tied up so peacefully in Salmon Creek and he knew he was absolutely crazy for being here.

On the ferry ride from Victoria he had started to realize how impossible it was going to be to carry this Cross around with him. The thought of losing it haunted him. He had been so tempted to leave it with Jonathan for safe keeping but he knew he couldn't. He kept thinking back to the look on Jonathan's face last night when they talked about what this discovery meant. How it would force the rewriting of ancient history if it was revealed to the world. He had read the conflict in Jonathan's eyes as he had held the relic. The stare that Jonathan had given him when he tucked the Cross back in the bag and wrapped it under his feet as he crawled into the sleeping bag last night, still bothered him. Mondo was smart enough to know that Jonathan Beckwith was struggling with what to do about the relic and that thought scared him, could he trust Jonathan enough to keep the Cross a secret?

Mondo wondered what he would do in Jonathan's situation. He knew that he was looked at by most in his field as being "out there," his ideas so speculative and unscientific. Even the man at the museum had rolled his eyes when he suggested that they go talk to him. It wasn't hard for Mondo to imagine that Jonathan had been shunned most of his academic career. Yet last night Mondo had proven to him that he was right. Jonathan's speculation on early human sea voyaging was correct. It was the only answer that made sense. The very concept of early civilization would have to be completely rewritten once the Cross was made public. Jonathan could now prove to the world of skeptics that the only thing positively known about ancient history was that science had it all wrong. The very concept that had been consuming him for years, something that he had been ridiculed for so long, he was now able to prove. What scholar wouldn't want to be the person that opened the debate on one of the greatest mystery's of the ancient world. Mondo understood how incredibly important this was to Jonathan, and that's what scared the hell out of him.

Chapter 17

t was three short blocks from where Mondo walked off of the ferry to the first city bus stop he saw. He sat down on a small bench and tucked his duffle bag under his feet. Already he noticed how differently people looked at him, his shabby, homeless appearance putting almost everybody off. Most people ignored him, while a few cast nervous, quick glances his way as they rushed past. He even had two logger types on the ferry boat give him a hard time about getting a job and being a bum. It was amazing, people's perception of him. His new role as a homeless person was starting. Two days of not shaving and wearing some grubby clothes, blue jeans with a torn knee and an over sized jacket, had transformed him into an outcast street person. It was amazing how little it took, he thought.

The bus was scheduled to arrive in twenty minutes. He studied the route, and decided to head for Stanley Park. On a nice day like today a lot of street people should be hanging out.

The entire homeless issue was so foreign to him. It had never even crossed his mind and now suddenly he was being thrust into a lifestyle that was so different from anything he had ever experienced. In the last five years there had never been a time when he had to think about being homeless, not with Smokin' Joe. His home was wherever he sailed her.

Ten minutes later an older man walked up and sat down beside him. The man looked like a homeless person, at least Mondo thought so. His dirty clothes, scraggly beard mostly dark with streaks of white and gray, his long hair, all seemed to highlight him as a street person. They exchanged glances but neither said a word. After a few minutes the man looked at Mondo again, and then nudged him with his elbow.

"Hey, got a smoke?" he asked.

"Nope."

"Why not?"

"Why not, because they'll kill you, that's why."

The old man laughed, his nicotine tinted teeth showing through his silver smoke stained beard.

"Yep, I guess your right, where are you going?"

"Stanley Park, thought I'd hang out for a while, what about you?"

"Don't know . . . that sounds good, I think I'll go to Stanley as well," he said with a laugh.

"Tell me, where do you sleep around here?"

"The best place is the Front Street Mission. It's in a bad part of town, man, like you don't want to be wandering around after dark if you can help it."

"Thanks, what's your name?"

"I used to have a Christian name you know. But since I ain't a Christian anymore, I thought that name didn't make sense anymore, and seeing as how I always wanted to go to Albuquerque . . . well friend that's my name, Albuquerque."

Mondo laughed.

"Well, Albuquerque, I'm Mondo, not much of a Christian name either, how you doing?"

"Good bro, I'm doing alright, at least right now."

The old man looked at Mondo as if sizing him up.

"How long you been on the street?"

"Not long, you know the story, lost my job, old lady kicked me out. I got people in Seattle, might head that way, what about you?"

"Three years, give or take, been all over the damn country but I tell you Vancouver's the best. Less chance of freezing to death here, man . . . in Calgary I almost didn't make it. Yep, came within an hour or so of becoming a popsicle. I was rescued by some sweet old ladies working for the mission. Pulled my frozen ass into a shelter, threw me in a warm bed and brought me back to life. Bless those sweet ladies."

Mondo wished he had a smoke. He would have given Albuquerque the whole pack.

"Hey Mondo," he said a few minutes later, "I don't have money for the bus, want to help me out?"

"No problem."

"Thanks Man."

Five minutes later they climbed on the bus. Albuquerque followed Mondo and sat down next to him. Mondo felt awkward sitting there, watching the city go by feeling like he was a fake. How do homeless people act, he asked himself? Are they all drug addicts? Do they suffer from mental problems? What makes a person so incapable of being able to deal with society that they just fall through the cracks? As he sat on the bus heading for Stanley Park he realized he didn't have a clue.

It seemed that Albuquerque was happy to ride in silence, so Mondo continued to let his mind wander, his thoughts drifting, thinking about what it must be like to be so down and out that the street is the only place you can call home.

"Tell me Albuquerque," he said a few minutes later, without really thinking it through, "what would you want for Christmas?"

"Christmas, a . . . Jesus Christ, you Santa or something?"

"Sorry man, dumb question, I know, but I'm curious, what would you want?"

"Man, I ain't thought about that one in a whole lot of years, but you know somethin' . . . I don't wish for money, no I'm fine without it. I'd just give it away if I had it. I tell you though . . . man," he stopped and gave Mondo a strange sad look, and then he sat in silence for a minute before he continued.

"Why'd you ask that damn question man? . . . I guess if you really need to know, well . . . I guess I wished that my daughter still loved and respected me."

Mondo didn't know what to say, Albuquerque's answer to his stupid question tore his heart out. Right then he realized two very important things, one was no personal questions and the other was that each person on the street had a story. It shocked him to think that Albuquerque had a daughter, maybe even more kids than that, he probably had a wife once upon a time, maybe a house in the suburbs. More than likely he had a real job and even paid taxes. How could he end up like this, homeless, living on the streets with nowhere to call home?

"Sorry Albuquerque."

"Well just don't ask any more damn questions about me. I ain't much but I'm all I got," he laughed as he said it, adding a little musical bounce to the end of his sentence. He sat for a few seconds with a deep smile on his face before he looked at Mondo and repeated, "I ain't much but I'm all that I got, oh . . . yah." All the way to Stanley Park Albuquerque kept singing this little tune over and over, driving Mondo and most of the other people sitting around them crazy.

"This is it man, our stop," he finally said as he nudged Mondo with his elbow.

They walked off the bus into a beautiful day. The sun was shining, and hundreds of people were just milling around. The park was packed.

"Let's grab a bench. I know a good one, follow me," Albuquerque said leading the way.

Mondo threw his duffle bag over his right shoulder and started off after him at a fast clip. The sidewalks and streets were full of people. Old couples walked slowly hand in hand as groups of young kids rushed here and there laughing, joking, hugging and acting cool. So many people were out enjoying the day. Mondo saw lots of street type kids hanging out also. The whole park had a feeling about it that he couldn't quite figure out, until he realized that it was just a carnival. That was it, he laughed to himself, a damn carnival.

They walked past a huge lawn and down a narrow trail surrounded by tall trees and lush green bushes and shrubs. It was cool in the shade, and they continued for another five minutes before coming around a turn and seeing a large group of young people, twenty or more hanging out.

"Hey Albuquerque," he heard a few people yell out.

"Where the hell you been, man?" somebody shouted, his voice lost in the crowd.

A young man walked up and slapped Albuquerque on the back, then gave him a big hug.

"Man, I thought you'd split or something."

"Hell, Brandon I split and already returned. Man I'm faster than a speeding bullet you know me, why I'm into the cosmos and back again and you don't even know I left."

They started laughing.

"Brandon this is Mondo, new to the streets, he's a good guy."

Brandon reached his right hand out and grabbed Mondo's.

"Welcome to the streets man, it's a jungle," he said, then he climbed up on the bench and hollered.

"Hey Albuquerque's got a friend. He's new, his name is Mondo."

"Hey Mondo welcome to our world," he heard somebody say.

Mondo walked over and sat down on one of the benches with a few people sitting around. He felt completely awkward. It was all he could do to try and maintain some sense of composure. He figured that anybody who lived on the street would be pretty good at reading body language and he feared what his was saying. For the next few hours he just sat trying to take it all in. It was amazing how easily he had been accepted.

Later in the afternoon a lady with bright red hair who had been hanging around most of the day walked up and sat down next to him. She was probably mid-forties, dressed very colorfully with a bright scarf tied around her head and flowing down over her shoulders. She smiled and then gave him a hard look before she asked, "you a cop?"

"A cop, Jesus lady, a cop . . . really," he said with a laugh.

"Well, you must be new to the streets."

"I'm really new, it shows?"

"It shows. Want some advice?"

"Yea, please."

"Okay rule number one, besides always look over your shoulder is never ask anybody about their lives, got it? We all left something and probably someone behind and most of us don't want to think about it. That's rule number one."

"Thanks. What's rule number two?"

"There ain't no rule number two dummy, just watch your butt and don't ask any questions," she laughed.

"Sounds easy, so tell me just because I hate rules, what's your story?"

She started laughing again, then grabbed him by the shoulders with both of her hands and pulled his face to hers and gave him a friendly kiss on his cheek.

"Damn that's good, your funny, you'll do just fine around here. I'm Patty, that's all you need to know. Let's just say I'm a little down on my luck right now, but I have good friends and it's a great day, and besides what else do I really need?"

"Not much, I guess Patty, I'm Mondo."

"That's right, not much, hey, what kind of name is Mondo, anyway?"

"It's my nickname and it's way too long of a story. My good friends used to call me "Too Good" but that started to sound a little to braggadocios for me, then suddenly Mondo came along and well it just stuck."

"I like it Mondo, it's got a ring to it."

Soon Patty was off talking with other people. He watched her as she flowed so easily from one group to another, her body language one of self confidence and jive all mixed together.

Mondo sat there the rest of the afternoon, listening, talking, and trying to take it all in. But in the back of his mind he never could stop thinking about Joseph Yazzi.

Around four or so people started drifting away. Mondo was talking to somebody and when he looked up Albuquerque was nowhere to be seen. Shit, he thought, now what? Somehow by hooking up with Albuquerque he had hoped to follow him around and get some idea of what to do on the streets. Where was he supposed to go now? He didn't know one person in this entire city, and he knew for sure that he couldn't spend the night in Stanley Park. When it was dark and he needed to sleep what was he supposed to do, roll up in a little ball and sleep under a tree? He didn't even know where to get something to eat.

Patty was talking to two young girls that he thought couldn't be over fifteen. Runways, he thought. He walked up to them and they stopped talking and he knew he was intruding on something important.

"Sorry, Patty but I got no place to go and I need somewhere to get something to eat and a place to crash, any ideas?"

"Oh honey, in my younger days I would have just taken you home, but seeing as I don't have a home," she said with a laugh, then looked at the two runaways, who started laughing with her.

"Well I think it's off to the mission for us. They don't run out of food but beds are a little harder to find at times. We ought to go," she looked back at the two girls.

"You two gonna be alright?"

"Yea, sure we're fine, we're staying at Jakes. You know him, he's crazy but he doesn't let anybody bother us."

"Well that's good, be safe, real safe. You two . . . I don't know, you two can't wander around the streets for very long before you get hurt, know what I mean?"

The look on their faces told Mondo they'd already been hurt, hurt bad.

"Yea, love you Patty, and thanks."

The girls gave her a kiss on the cheek then they started walking down the path that Mondo and Albuquerque had used earlier.

"You ready to go cowboy?" Patty asked him with a smile.

"What about Albuquerque?"

"Albuquerque, what about him, do you see him around here?"

"Nope."

"Well, then don't worry about him."

ondo sat on a bus next to Patty and watched it all roll by. The city looked so proper and normal at first, nice cars, fine shops, lots of flashing neon. Luxury and wealth seemed to jump out at him everywhere he looked. He saw nicely dressed men and women, many carrying shopping bags making their way through the streets and traffic. Taxis lined the roadways, people rushing here and there, couples arm in arm, business men in three piece suits, some laughing with others, some looking so serious. The entire feeling of Vancouver was one of well being and wealth. In less than three blocks it completely changed. The well dressed gave way to street people, ragged clothes, wildly colored hair, tattoo's and body piercing. In one short block he noticed four people slumped in doorways, either dead or more than likely just passed out.

The store fronts changed as well. Now it was pawn shops, porno stores, cheap hotels and cheap looking restaurants. The streets were littered with trash and he just couldn't get over all the people hanging out. He felt like he entered a different city, a different world. Only three short city blocks separated the wealthy of Vancouver from this.

"Mondo, welcome to Downtown Eastside, stick with me I'll show you around, you got a lot to learn," Patty said with a smile.

"You got that right," he replied meaning every word of it.

They climbed off the bus at Hastings and Main Street.

After walking only a few blocks Mondo was amazed at how many people knew Patty. It seemed like almost everybody said something to her as they walked by. The funny thing was nobody stopped to talk to her and she never slowed down to talk to them. It was a lot of "hey how you doing?" or "what's up?" or "what's new?" A string of one liners followed them, and Mondo wondered if living on the street made people like that. Could the unknown of daily life make it necessary to know so many, to consider everyone a friend, but at the same time demand that you keep everyone at a safe distance, was it a survival skill?

They walked up Hastings for three blocks before turning on Jones Street. Mondo saw a line of people, mostly men standing in front of an old gray three story building. They walked to the end of the line and waited their turn to get into the Carnegie Community Center. It was a shelter for the hungry and homeless, a safe haven to meet the most basic of human needs.

A few minutes later Mondo noticed a young, skinny kid in his early twenty's, crossing the street, walking toward them. There was a strange bounce to his hurried steps and a few moments later Mondo realized that he was heading right for Patti. She turned, looked at the kid when he was a few feet away from her and Mondo could see a visible change in her expression. Suddenly the skinny kid got right in Patti's face and started yelling. There was so much anger in his tone that it shocked Mondo. Soon Patty was yelling back at him and both were using a mouthful of profanities. The people around them all took a few steps back and turned their attention to the two of them. The young man was getting angrier and angrier and finally Mondo had enough. He walked up, put his arm around Patty and looked at the kid.

"Time to leave man," he said, his voice harsh with no hint of compromise.

"Who the fuck are you?" the kid yelled back.

Mondo brought his glance from the kid's face, down to his hands and saw that both were clenched tight in a fist.

"I'm a friend of Patty's, that's who."

It was at that moment that Mondo noticed the craziness in the kid's eyes, and it suddenly dawned on him that this guy was high as a kite, drugged out on something and that could make this situation real bad, real fast.

"Just turn around man and walk away, that's what I'm telling you."

"Nobody tells me shit, you got that."

"Well I am."

117

Mondo was trying to bluff his way through this. The last thing he wanted was a confrontation with some guy his first day on the street. The silence between them lingered, and a few of the onlookers started to tell the kid to leave as well. Finally he turned around and stormed off, still spewing a mouth full of profanities.

Patty watched him walk away then turned and looked at Mondo, "Don't be my fucking hero man, I don't need it!" her anger seeping out in every word she said.

Mondo didn't say a thing. He was about as lost and out of his comfort zone as any time he could ever remember. He took a step back, looked around him for a few seconds before he shrugged his shoulders, and started feeling like a complete idiot. Soon the line started moving and they followed it into a large open cafeteria something like he remembered from high school. There were rows and rows of tables with long benches and they were full of people. A staff of over ten stood behind a long glass counter dishing up food to those in line.

He followed Patty and let them put whatever they wanted on his plate and he was pleasantly surprised to receive a large helping of fried chicken, mashed potatoes, a small green salad and a little plastic cup of fruit. God, he thought he didn't eat this good at sea. They walked to the end of the line, grabbed a drink from a large tray and headed to a table that had a few empty seats.

Mondo was trying to forget about the hassle with the skinny kid. He didn't know what to say to Patti and he figured he'd just try to skip the whole issue. They sat down and started eating in an awkward silence, and he could tell the altercation had rattled her.

It soon dawned on him that the room was amazingly quiet. Looking around, he wondered what was going through these people's minds. What were they all feeling at this moment? Did they find a sense of peace, a comfort in the simple fact of being able to get a good meal in a safe environment? It made him think of the feelings he often experienced on Smokin' Joe after struggling through a storm. There was that strange sense of peace once things started to settle down, that feeling that everything was going to be alright, that the future was to far away to worry about and the present too beautiful, and satisfying to ignore.

"Sorry I was a bitch to you. It was sweet of you . . . telling Joey to split," Patty said interrupting his thoughts.

Mondo glanced at her, but didn't say anything.

She kept her eyes on him and he could sense her inner struggle. "What's wrong?" he asked.

"Oh Mondo, you just don't get it, I know. That's okay you're so new to all of this."

"Get what?"

"Well it's just that . . . on the street it's all about being able to take care of yourself. It's a respect thing and you can't ever show anybody you're afraid, you can't let anyone think you're weak. It's really like the damn animals in the jungle, its all about not needing anyone but yourself."

"Haven't you ever wanted to need someone?"

The look on her face told him much, told him that under her tough street shell was a woman that had loved, been hurt and wanted to love and be loved again.

She didn't say anything at first, just locked her brown eyes on him staring with a sense of sadness that even he could see. Tears started to form and she brushed them away.

"Fuck you Mondo," she suddenly said as she stood up, left her plate on the table and walked out the door.

He almost jumped up and ran after her but somehow he couldn't and she disappeared without a backward glance. He felt more alone at that moment than he could ever remember in his entire life. The longer he sat there, the more he knew that his new life on the streets was like nothing he had ever experienced.

An hour after Patti left, Mondo finally forced himself to get up and walk outside. Slowly he started walking up Jones Street, his duffle bag on his right shoulder. An overwhelming feeling of panic was trying to set in and he felt it with every step he took. He was so alone and out of his element. People kept walking by, all looking like they knew what they were doing, knew where they were going. Patti's words about not showing weakness kept coming back to him. How many people, he wondered had been just as scared their first few nights on the street as he felt right now? Facing fifty knot winds at sea seemed like a cake walk compared to this. He casually looked in a doorway as he walked past a run-down hotel and was shocked to see a woman sitting with a needle in her arm. She glanced at him and he could see a wave of pleasure on her face as she squeezed the syringe.

What the hell am I doing here, he thought, and he suddenly pictured Jonathan telling him he was insane to go to Vancouver and he knew once again he was right, this was crazy.

He realized that there was no way he could sleep on the street. He walked a few more blocks before he found a cheap hotel. He paid seven dollars, climbed three sets of stairs, then let himself into a room that was the worse place he had ever seen. There was one ugly picture on the wall, and the bed had an old gray military blanket on it, with one stained pillow crammed up against a cheap headboard. He flopped onto the mattress and dropped his duffle bag at his side. He reached over and pulled out his backpack, unzipped the small pocket in the front and brought out the picture that Chief Yazzi had given him. He studied Joseph Yazzi, memorized his dark brown eyes and jet black hair, the small dimple that showed on his left cheek. Staring at Joseph Yazzi he wondered how the hell he could ever find him.

That night he walked the streets until almost midnight. He looked like any other homeless person wandering around. He kept his eyes to himself and always stayed focused on who was around him. Keeping himself in the light of a building or under the glow of a street light just seemed smart. As he walked he was shocked at the amount of drug use he saw everywhere. The stench of marijuana seemed to permeate entire blocks. He saw more people shooting up, watched the hookers parading themselves up and down the streets. God he wondered, what came first for these poor people, was it drugs that led them to a life on the street, or was it their inability to cope in society that led to drugs, and for the first time his heart started to go out to these street people. He saw so many deals going down that after an hour he didn't even look twice. There were offers from hookers and dealers, from johns in fancy cars and gay guys on the street. This was a world that he wanted no part of, yet he was here and he couldn't leave until he found one man, a drunken Indian that he hoped to god was still alive.

Chapter 19

The Salty Elephant is an upscale restaurant three blocks from Parliament in downtown Victoria. It's known for its great lunches and even better for its private rooms where many a confidential government business meeting has been held. It was the perfect location for Stephen Cartere to get together with Thomas Egan, the British Columbia Minister of Forestry, and discuss the disputed land issue once again. Stephen knew he had to be very delicate today, but he also knew he had to get the sense of urgency that he felt across to Thomas. This issue had to be resolved. The small town of Salmon Creek would remain untouched but the lands surrounding it, lands that had been locked in the courts for the last twelve and a half years, needed to be dealt with immediately.

Ever since First Nation people started going to court claiming ownership rights of disputed landholdings, it had thrown the logging industry into chaos. How could this industry survive if it had no more trees to cut? The entire First Nation land issue had to be resolved once and for all and now was the time, Stephen knew. The decision making process had to be removed from the courts and placed back into the hands of the Minister of Forestry. Let the answer be a political decision that would set into motion the possibility of another ten to twenty years of logging in British Columbia. The eighteen thousand hectares of the Killiatt Wilderness was an incredibly large landholding and that was one of the main reasons that Mountain Resources had chosen it. The other reason it was chosen was that it was about as far away from anywhere as possible.

Its remoteness would hopefully make it easier to keep the entire operation far from the eyes of the general public.

Stephen sat in his office, leaning back in his chair wondering if he would need to go the extra mile. How far would he have to go to pressure Thomas? Would he be forced to break the law? Extortion and bribery could send him to prison but they were very effective. With the money already set aside in case it was needed and the dirty secrets that he held he should be able to accomplish his goal. A shiver ran through him when he realized that if Thomas refused to agree with him, he would be forced to use whatever tools were necessary. That however was not the way he was going to handle the matter today. He was certain that Thomas thought this lunch meeting would be just another round of their ongoing discussions about the disputed land issue. Little did the Minister of Forestry realize that the time for talk was over. Today Stephen would propose action. Thomas would be surprised, maybe even shocked but he would have to listen. In the end Stephen hoped to god that he would agree with him. Thomas could become richer, or he would be destroyed politically, socially and humiliated to the point that he would probably end up in divorce court, those were his only options.

Stephen understood that from a politician's point of view it was much easier to let the whole issue stay in the courts. No one wanted to take a stand, everybody was afraid to. This had become a no win situation, yet as he sat in his office he knew that if it was handled correctly he could use the disputed land issue to enhance his political career. Let him show the people of British Colombia that he wasn't afraid to tackle the hard issues, that he was a man who looked at both sides, and then made the tough call and did what was right. The public wanted this settled and he needed to get it done. In the long run it didn't matter to him who really ended up owning the land just as long as Mountain Resources could log it all.

He reached over, grabbed his phone and dialed Mrs. Whatcom, his secretary.

"I will be leaving momentarily for lunch with Mr. Egan. I should be back in an hour or so."

"Very good sir," she replied.

He stood up, walked over to the coat rack, grabbed his sport coat, and walked out the door.

Thomas Egan was already on his way to the Salty Elephant, and he knew this meeting was going to be a lot different then their past meetings. Stephen was going to come down hard on him about the First Nation disputed land issue, and he knew it. It helped that he had people who he could trust in Parliament, people who told him what was going on behind the scenes. That's how it worked in this city he thought as he walked, it's all about power, who had it, who wanted more of it, and what they wanted. A few of his colleagues' in Parliament had come to him and privately suggested that he take a good look at what Mr. Cartere was proposing, and that he take back from the courts the entire disputed land issue. He knew that he could. It was within his power to legally transfer the entire issue back to his office and back to him. With his signature he could open up enough disputed lands to re-energize an industry.

As he entered the restaurant he wondered what approach Mr. Cartere would take. Would he come off as he had in the past, the caring, decisive politician that wanted to resolve this issue? He hoped so, although he feared otherwise.

He walked through the lobby and into a small hallway that led to the bathrooms. Half way down the hall on the right was a door. There was no sign on it but he knew it well. He opened the door, entered, then gently closed the door behind him, feeling his apprehension growing with each step he took. It was a large room with enough seating for over fifty people, but today it would just be him and Stephen. He hung his jacket up on a fancy metal coat hanger, walked over to the table and pulled out a chair. He sat down facing the doorway that he just entered, somehow he felt better not having his back exposed.

"Thomas, it is so good to see you again. I hope you're hungry, how is the wife?" Stephen said as he walked in a few minutes later, he was all smiles.

"Everything is great Stephen, its good to see you."

Thomas did everything he could to keep his voice clear and full of confidence, but he felt neither. He was about to betray almost everything he had ever held dear to him since he started politics.

That hooker had turned out to be the biggest mistake of his entire life. Now, he knew there was no turning back. There was nothing he could do but reluctantly agree with whatever proposal Stephen was going to make. God he was starting to hate himself more and more. The disputed land issue was going to become his issue, and with just his signature he was going to open the flood gates of logging on the last virgin rainforest left in North America.

Michael Jensen was at the airport waiting for the flight from San Francisco that Mr. Donaldson was on. He was leaning against a huge concrete pillar near the luggage area watching the neon sign above the carousel flashing Brad's flight number. A few minutes later the conveyor began spitting luggage out.

He always felt very uncomfortable around Brad Donaldson. Ever since he had first used his services, the man had made him feel that way and very few people ever made him uncomfortable. The man was as charming and elegant on the outside as he was merciless, cruel and extremely intelligent on the inside.

Using Brad had become too easy for him and he knew it. It was becoming more and more of a risk and soon he would have to minimize as many risks as possible. Just one more job he whispered to himself, just one more.

He watched as Brad walked to the conveyor, waited for a few minutes then grabbed a small suitcase and started walking for the exit. Michael followed after him and as they crossed over the skyway into the parking area he walked up along side of him.

"Hello Brad, it's good to see you."

"Michael, a pleasure as always."

"I have the Mercedes, this way."

He motioned with his right hand and they walked in silence for the next few minutes. Once in traffic Michael seemed to relax a little.

"I have you staying in the Sheraton," he said as he reached under his seat and pulled out a large manila envelope and handed it to him.

"There is a cell phone in here and it is how we will communicate, as usual no calls except through the cell."

"Fine."

Brad pulled out the two black and white photos and looked at them. Studied them, committed both of these gentleman to memory.

"Where are we at Michael?"

"We've had a bit of a delay, a minor setback since I talked to you a few days ago. Nothing to serious and I believe we will have it all taken care of within twenty-four hours. I have people on it and I assume that this new timetable works for you?"

Brad laughed softly, "My time is your time, so to speak."

"Yes, I know," he replied, trying to keep any hint of his increasing paranoia out of his voice.

Fifteen minutes later the Mercedes pulled into the underground parking garage of the Sheraton Hotel. Brad Donaldson climbed out, retrieved his suitcase from the trunk, and then walked up to the rolled down driver's window.

"I'm going out tonight, I need some entertainment. I will be available after ten tomorrow. Good luck in fixing your minor setback," Brad said with a sarcastic laugh, then he turned and started for the elevator.

Brad Donaldson loved coming to Vancouver. He had his people here just like he had people in many different parts of the world, but he wouldn't need any of them tonight. All of the arrangements had already been made, the same house he had used in the past was available and he was sure there would be no problems. No, he thought as he made his way into the lobby, tonight was just for him.

He had no trouble checking into the hotel, his forged passport had fooled every person he had ever shown it to. He made his way up to the seventh floor and entered his suite. It was to his liking. It was plush, large, expensive and overlooking the city below. He kicked his shoes off, walked over to the bar and made himself a gin and tonic then walked back to the window and gazed out over the city skyline. A surge of excitement overcame him as he stood there. It had been a long time since he had been in Vancouver and he smiled as he thought that they never did find her body. She became just one more missing person, one more unsolved disappearance in a city that had a lot of unsolved disappearances.

He finished his drink and laughed, he was a bastard he knew, but he didn't care, and he certainly didn't give a shit about any of them. It was all about the terror on their young faces that he loved so much. It was all about that moment when they realized there was no escape, when they fell to their knees begging him for their lives, screaming out in a room that no sound could escape from, that moment was what drove him.

He set the empty glass down on a small end table near the sofa, never taking his eyes from the city that glared in the darkness below him. Soon he would shower, take himself out to a fine dinner, and start the hunt. The streets of Vancouver would have a killer loose on them tonight.

Chapter 20

The noise of the street made its way into his sleeping brain, cars and sirens jolting him awake. He rolled over and looked at his watch that was laying on the cheap plastic bed stand. It was almost ten. That was the latest Mondo had slept in a very long time.

His thoughts went back to last night and all of the people, crazy people he had watched as they paraded through the streets of lower Eastside. Just thinking about another day on the streets made him want to stay in bed all day. As lousy as this room was, at least it was his.

Finally he climbed out of bed, and throwing some clothes on he thought about what to do with the Cross. It wouldn't be safe if he carried it with him but leaving it in this cheap hotel room didn't seem much better. After thinking for a minute he took the pillow out of its stained case and put it under the bed, then he jammed the canvas bag and the Cross into the pillow case and propped it up against the headboard. It looked like a lumpy pillow. Looking around his room he shook his head in disbelief and headed out the door.

Walking down the three flights of steps gave him time to clear his mind a bit and he started to come up with a plan for the day. He made his way to the front-desk and paid for another night, then went out onto the street heading for the Carnegie Community Center. There was a short line out front and he didn't have to wait very long to get inside. The center that had been completely full last night was now almost empty. An older, overweight lady gave him a large plate of scrambled eggs and he grabbed a cup of coffee, walked over and sat down at a table. Drinking his coffee continued to kick start his mind, but as he sat there he realized how frustrated and emotionally drained he was. Just one night on the street made him grasp how difficult, if not impossible it was going to be to ever find Joseph Yazzi.

After eating and finishing his second cup of coffee he headed out the door. He had another decision to make this morning as well, his appearance. Who did he want to be today? Was he going to be another down and out homeless person, or was he going to become somebody who wouldn't draw attention to himself once he left the Lower Eastside? He laughed when he thought how easy it was to go either way, just by the clothes he wore and the amount of stubble on his face.

Back in his hotel he grabbed his razor and walked down the hallway to the only bathroom on the entire floor. He took a quick shower, shaved, combed his hair and put on some decent clothes. Ten minutes later he was standing at a bus stop waiting to catch a bus, the Cross hidden inside the canvas bag covered by his jacket. There was no destination in his mind, he was going to get on the bus, keep his eyes open and hope to god that a safe place to hide the Cross jumped out at him.

It was one-fifteen when the city bus pulled up and he climbed on. Within a matter of minutes he left the Lower Eastside behind. Again he was amazed at the contrast, without even thinking he took a deep breath and exhaled as if trying to rid his body of the tensions from yesterday and last night. He pulled out a city map and started following the progress of the bus. The streets flew by, people and cars, traffic and chaos all seemed beyond affecting him as he stared out the window.

One of his first thoughts for a place to hide the Cross was a bank safety deposit box, but he knew right away it wouldn't work, the Cross was too large. A minute later he thought about a locker at the airport. He looked at the map and found Vancouver International airport, it was a few miles away. Settling back into his seat he thought that maybe he had finally found a safe home for the Cross. A few minutes later as he looked out the window watching the city flashing by he saw a sign for Ballard's Gym and Spa. A health club would have lockers he thought. He jumped up and climbed off the bus at the next stop.

Looking at the map he figured that he was about three miles from Lower Eastside. The health club was across the street and down two blocks. Walking back toward the club he came to a signal at 48th street. Once the light turned green he started to cross, looking for traffic as he went. On his right down a block he saw a large parking area and a sign for Oakridge Mall. That would be his landmark, his reference point for the gym. He kept walking and on the next block he found a small mom and pop type neighborhood store and went in. He spent a few minutes looking around before he found the hardware section and walked up to where the padlocks were hanging on the wall. His first thought was to buy the biggest, most indestructible lock they carried but then as he thought about it he knew a lock that big would look very out of place in a gym locker room. He bought a small brass lock and walked out the door.

Just as he was walking up to the entrance of the gym the front door swung open and three middle-aged women strolled out laughing and carrying gym bags. He stepped back from the door to let them pass and they gave him a fleeting glance and a smile, and one of them held the door open for him.

"Thank you," he said as he walked inside. Such a simple gesture in the Lower Eastside would never have happened.

A row of workout machines was to his left facing a large glass window that peered out onto the sidewalk and street. A few people were working out but for the most part the gym was empty. To his right was another large window that looked out over an Olympic sized swimming pool, the glass roof over the pool letting filtered streams of sunlight through. In front of him was a long counter with fitness magazines on the left and a large assortment of nutrition bars and bottled drinks for sale on the right. A tall, thin man wearing a name tag that said his name was Fred watched him enter from behind the counter.

"Good afternoon, can I help you?" Fred asked with a warm smile.

"Yes, I'm thinking about joining, I wonder if you have any introductory specials?"

"Sure do, first month for half price. It's regularly fifty-nine dollars a person per month, so our special brings it down to thirty. If you want your own locker by the month it's another ten bucks."

"That sounds good, sign me up?"

"You don't want to look around first?"

"No I don't think so, it looks nice, why, do I need to look around?"

Fred laughed, "No, but I'll tell you we have a hot tub, a steam room, as well as a sauna. There are classes and work out programs throughout the day and in the evening also. After we do the paper work I'll give you a schedule."

"Great, let's do it."

Mondo had felt a wave of relief overcome him when Fred had mentioned the lockers.

"I need an address, telephone number and payment for the first month in advance." Fred said looking up at Mondo from the paper work he had just spread out on the counter.

Mondo looked at him then said, "I'm anchored out on my sailboat. I just arrived, I don't have a phone, is that okay?"

"You live on a sailboat?"

"Yep."

"Man, I'm jealous. I always wanted to live on a sailboat. Travel the world, see exotic ports. You ever sailed offshore?"

"A little," Mondo replied with a laugh.

"Well, it must be something to be out there. The captain of your own ship, in charge of your own destiny living out your own dreams not having to take bullshit from anybody."

Mondo laughed again. Poor Fred had read too many glossy sailing magazines for his own good. Fred looked back to the paper work sitting on the counter.

"You don't have a phone number I can use, or an address? Man I don't know, I don't think we can do this."

Mondo looked at him and shrugged his shoulder.

"Sorry Fred, I don't."

"I'm not supposed to accept any members without all of the info filled out. Tell you what, just for the hell of it, I'll put my phone number down for you. What marina are you going to stay at?"

Mondo had no idea what to tell Fred. He didn't even know the name of a marina in Vancouver.

"I don't know, I'm not sure, does it matter?"

"Well like I said I can't take this application without filling in all the blanks. It's my boss, you know, damn rules. Hey, let's look in the phone book, all we need to find is a marina that lists its street address, then I can use that. I don't care if you live there or not, just need an address."

"Great, and thanks Fred."

A few minutes later all the paper work was finished and Mondo walked down a flight of stairs holding a gym schedule, and a towel along with his large canvas bag. The thought of a sauna and steam bath sounded really good to him. The locker room was huge, two long double rows of lockers were on his left and another row of double lockers were straight ahead of him running off to his right and disappearing behind a wall. A sign with an arrow pointing to his right said showers. Most of the lockers were locked and he remembered Fred telling him to just pick an empty one and use it. Mondo walked half way down the row of lockers on his left and opened an upper door. He stared looking inside this small locker while all of the fears and emotions of the last few days came crashing into his brain at once. He had found a place for the Cross, now all he had to do was find Joseph Yazzi.

Chapter 21

t's always dangerous to increase the circle and Michael Jensen knew that better than most. All through his business career that motto had served him well. The larger the circle, the more people that became involved, the harder it was to keep it all manageable. So far there was only one person who could connect him to Joseph Yazzi and Flick, and that person was Harvey Langdon.

Michael sat in his car driving back from the Sheraton thinking about Harvey and the years they had worked together. Their business relationship started during his second year at Pascal & Pascal and back then it was a rather simple matter of blackmail. It had taken Harvey less than a month to find enough information to silence two board members who opposed Michael's nomination as vice president. It seemed that almost everybody had skeletons somewhere and most of those skeletons were usually kept well hidden in a bedroom closet. That is the first place to look, he remembered Harvey telling him. That little bit of wisdom had paid off very well. He now had two politicians in Parliament listening to his requests because they also had skeletons.

By bringing Brad Donaldson into this he had expanded his circle by one hundred percent, but there had been no other choice. Never had he asked Harvey to kill for him and he knew better than to ever mention it. Harvey was extremely good at what he did, but he was no killer.

Michael pulled his Mercedes into the parking garage of his condominium, drove fifty feet to the guard office and stopped in front of a yellow metal barricade that blocked his way. He glanced up and recognized Stanley, a young black attendant who often worked there.

"Good afternoon Mr. Jensen," Stanley said as the barrier slowly rose out of the way.

"Yea," he replied as he hit the gas a little harder and squealed his tires.

Riding the elevator up to his penthouse suite he wondered how long it would take to find Joseph and Flick. Having Brad in Vancouver was just to close for his comfort.

Three hours after filling all of the paperwork out at the health club Mondo was back in Lower Eastside. He felt so relieved to have found a safe place for the Cross, and much of the tension he felt had drained away as he had sat in the hot tub.

On the bus back to the Lower Eastside he also had thought of a way to look for Joseph Yazzi. He climbed off the bus as close to the Carnegie Community Center as he could. This time he walked to the back of the building and knocked on a door that was wide open.

"Just a minute, if your hungry go to the front," he heard somebody yell.

He knocked again and a moment later a young man, mid thirties with a cell phone to his ear walked around the corner and looked at him.

Mondo's clean cut appearance must have startled him because he gave him a funny look then brought his right index finger up in the air like a signal.

"Just a minute," he mouthed as he continued to listen to his call.

A few moments later he closed the phone and put it in his pocket.

"Hi, how can I help you?"

"I was wondering if you need any volunteers?"

"You're asking to volunteer? You just can't knock on my back door and ask to volunteer. Thanks, but it doesn't work that way, at least not here. You need to go downtown, fill out some forms, wait a week for a police background check and then come back and fill out an application."

"Jesus, all that to volunteer for free?"

"Yep it's crazy, but I always seem to have enough help and I don't write the rules."

"Oh well, thanks anyway."

Mondo turned and started to walk away, but stopped when the young man called out.

"Why don't you go down to St. Joseph's Mission, they're always looking for help. Ask for Todd De Bijous, tell him John from Carnegie sent you over."

"Where's St. Josephs?"

"It's less than a mile away, walk up Main to 21st, turn left on Malcolm, go three or four blocks, you can't miss it."

Mondo repeated the directions over in his head as he turned and started walking away when John called to him one more time.

"Hey, thanks for caring, I wish more people did."

Walking the street, seeing all of the people hanging out still amazed him. The wild hair, the body piercing, the dreadlocks and shabby clothes made him feel so out of place. As he continued walking he started thinking that a lot of these young street kids were probably here because they wanted to be. Maybe it was cool to hang out in the Lower Eastside, get high, maybe get laid then go home to the folks and complain to them about their greedy, capitalistic life style.

What bothered Mondo as he walked towards the mission was thinking about the people who weren't here because they wanted to be. What about the people who just kept falling through the cracks until they hit the streets of Lower Eastside and couldn't fall any further? How many people he asked himself, that wandered these streets, could ever in their wildest dreams have pictured themselves as homeless? His thoughts drifted back to Albuquerque and his daughter. It's hard for successful people to have sympathy for the homeless, he knew. Even he had to fight the thought that most of these people were here because they were lazy, or addicted to drugs, that somehow it was their fault. In just two days on the streets he had seen the hopelessness that most of these people lived with. He could read it in their eyes and see it on their faces. Mondo understood that it didn't matter what you were in life, what you had achieved in the past, if life beat you down hard enough there was no getting up, and he thought that most of these people had been beaten their entire life. Everybody has a story, he kept thinking over and over as he continued walking until he found the mission.

There were about twenty people waiting to get in and as he made his way to the end of the line he saw a young woman come out from the front door, take a quick glance over the crowd, and rush back inside. She must work here, he thought.

The line went fast and once inside he was greeted by the smell of food and a warm smile from the young lady that he had seen a few minutes earlier.

"Welcome to St. Josephs. There is plenty of food and remember Jesus loves you and so do we."

Mondo was surprised, almost taken back.

"Well thank you, I'm looking for Todd De Bijous, is he here?"

Dawn Peters looked at him and knew she was right, this guy wasn't your regular street person, and it wasn't just his clean appearance that made her think that. There was something in the way he carried himself that made her notice him when she had walked outside to do a head count a few minutes earlier.

"Yes, he's here, I can get him now or if you like you can have something to eat then talk to him? We have ham and mashed potatoes today."

There was such a gentleness about her and Mondo sensed it immediately.

"I can't pass that offer up. But I would like to talk to him after I eat, okay?"

"I'll ask him to come over, but for now follow the line, grab a plate and enjoy."

He followed the person in front of him, wondering what it was about that young woman that made him instantly like her.

All through dinner he watched her at the door greeting people as they entered. Each person that walked in, regardless of their appearance she seemed to reach out to in a way that made them feel welcome. It was the first time he had witnessed such care and concern since he reached Vancouver.

Soon his thoughts were distracted when out of the corner of his eye a man walked up to him wearing a kitchen apron and wiping his hands on a small towel that he had tucked into his pocket. He pulled a chair out and sat down with a smile. Mondo thought that maybe everybody who worked here took happy pills before they started, but his crazy thoughts were interrupted.

"I'm Todd," he paused looking at Mondo, waiting for him to reply and then continued, "De Bijous, Dawn said you wanted to talk to me."

"Oh . . . yes sorry," he said shaking his head snapping back to the moment.

"I would like to volunteer here. I'm . . . well I'm new to Vancouver, and I'd like to help out if I can?"

"Believe me, there is always room for a helping hand, and I assume a warm heart. Is that why you're here, because you care?"

The question made Mondo think fast, something about Todd made him want to be as honest as he could.

"I'm new to Vancouver and I'm also new to living on the streets. Right now I have a cheap room a few blocks away, but I'd feel better if I could help out, you know give something back."

Mondo didn't tell him that his other reason for volunteering was to see as many homeless faces in one day as he could. Maybe, just maybe, Joseph Yazzi might walk in the door.

"When do you want to start?"

"Right now."

"Follow me," Todd said as he stood up," I'll introduce you to our staff. You've already met Dawn Peters, and as you know I'm Todd, we have Stephanie and Sammy working tonight. What's your name?"

"My friends call me Mondo."

"Well Mondo, I will assume that we can call you that as well around here. You're hired."

Mondo followed him into a large kitchen, and Todd handed him an apron just like the one he was wearing then steered him towards a sink full of dirty dishes.

"You have to start out at the bottom around here Mondo," he said laughing again. His laugh was almost as warm as Dawn's smile.

"I'm afraid there is little room for promotion . . . but we will try to get you out of dish detail just as soon as you finish them all."

Chapter 22

Flick had big worries and he was scared to death because somebody who was willing to spend a lot of money was looking for him and Joseph Yazzi. Nobody seemed to know who it was but his friends told him to get out of town and not look back. He wished he could, but that was the wrong approach and he knew it. There was no way he could run from someone that he didn't know, some invisible enemy; it could never end that way. No, he would have to stay and find out who was behind this whole insane Joseph Yazzi deal. Joseph was the only lead he had and trying to get an answer from that drunken Indian hadn't been easy. He had said about three words since they made it to the safe house.

Still, Flick thought as he walked up to the television, took one long look at Joseph and then turned it off, there wasn't much more to go on.

"I'm leaving for a few hours. You stay here and don't do anything stupid. Don't answer the phone, the door, nothing and don't even think of going outside. You screw up and I'm out of here and you can do whatever the hell you want. You got that?"

He could see the fear on Joseph's face.

"Yeah."

"Good, so I'm taking a walk. Keep the television low and keep the blinds closed, I'm coming back so don't worry."

He gave Joseph one more hard look before he grabbed his jacket and walked out the door glancing at his watch, it was ten-forty. Walking through this quiet residential neighborhood he felt that at least for the moment he was safe.

He walked for half an hour at a brisk pace before leaving the serenity of the suburbs behind and hitting traffic and neon, commerce and confusion on Van Isle Blvd. After another ten minutes he hailed a passing cab and climbed in. He had put enough distance between himself and the safe house. Now it was time to refocus and start thinking about the rest of the evening. He had to find Gloria and fast, that was his number one priority. She was running scared, and he had no idea if they had found her yet. It was almost impossible to believe but the two hookers that brought Joseph into the hotel were now running for their lives. Both had somehow been identified, and Lori was still in intensive care after the beating she had received. He felt terrible, he didn't know her as well as he knew Gloria, but god, you just don't beat a woman like that, besides he thought, what the hell could she tell them.

Flick had the cab drive past Charlie's, a late night bar and dance club, but he didn't have the driver slow down. All that he did was casually glance out the window as they drove past. It was almost eleven-thirty and lots of people were hanging out waiting to get inside. There was a line of fancy cars parked in front waiting for valet parking and all the beautiful people mingled. God, he hoped he was dressed good enough to get in the door. Charlie's was for the high class, a party place for those that wanted a good time without any notoriety. The club was known for its tight security, and highly effective bouncers. The paparazzos didn't even bother with this place. They would last about two seconds before they were physically removed.

The cab pulled over three blocks after passing Charlie's in front of a movie theater. Flick paid the driver and headed toward the movies until the cab was out of sight then he turned and started for Charlie's. He knew that Gloria had friends there, knew she used to work out of there, but if he knew that then who else did? Still, there was nothing else he could do, he had to find her, and that would be impossible on the street.

Flick kept his composure as he walked up to the door. All the finely dressed people hanging out made him feel like a dirt bag, but screw them he told himself. If it wasn't for Gloria he would never bother coming to a stuck up place like this. He watched the bouncer eyeing each person, and if he didn't like you then Flick knew you didn't get in, such bullshit. The doorman was about two hundred pounds and a little over six feet tall. Not very big but it didn't matter how big you were if you were very good, and everybody that worked at Charlie's was very good at whatever they did. The bouncer gave him a nod as he walked past him following the crowd that clambered through the door and he was ushered in.

The carnival was in full swing. The music was loud but seemed dimmed over the chatter of voices and drunken laughter. The setting was dark and shadows danced on the walls from the row of lights that dimly glowed from the ceiling. Colored lights flashed throughout the dance floor as a sea of people gyrated back and forth to the music coming from a five piece blues band. The bar was busy as gorgeous young waitresses in sexy revealing outfits hustled up to the drink counter shouting orders. Customers waited in long lines trying to grab the attention of one of the three bartenders that were running behind the mahogany bar. Flick drifted near the bar, stood for about ten minutes before he ordered a drink. The wait didn't bother him, he was in no hurry, he had all night and he hadn't a clue what to do next. One thing for certain though there was no way he could ask about her, that would be a sure recipe for trouble. He slowly sipped his gin and tonic as he walked to a corner near the bathrooms and leaned against the wall. His only hope was that somebody would walk by and jiggle his memory, something, a face, a second glance, anything.

After ten minutes he started milling again, walking out near the dance floor making his way around empty chairs vacated at the moment by the many dancers who rubbed and bumped each other in erotic passion. He was just skirting around an empty table when out of the corner of his eye a young woman, mid twenties with a short tight low-cut dress and wearing long earrings grabbed his arm spilling what was left of his drink. With a laugh she smiled at him and said, "Let's dance honey," and pulled him out on the dance floor before he could do anything besides set his empty glass down on a passing table. In another time and another mind-set he might have enjoyed this, but he couldn't stop thinking about Gloria. How the hell could he find her?

Slowly the music started to make its way into him. His body started swaying to the rhythm, his feet moving to the tempo of the band, his thoughts relaxing as he looked at this stunning young lady that he was dancing with. He brought his eyes to her and smiled as she smiled back, hell he thought.

The song ended on a sizzling guitar lick and Flick held out his hands to her. She grabbed them and he pulled her to him, pulled her face to his. He smelled her perfume, felt her tight against him. He reached down brought her face up to his looking for that first kiss.

"Easy, I'm a friend of Gloria's."

He stopped, looked at her and smiled. He had never seen her before. The band started another song, a slow one this time. Flick didn't say a word, he pulled her tight against him and they started swaying to the music.

"That's why I'm here, I need to find her," he whispered in her ear.

"She was hoping you might show up. I'm Linda. I'm a good friend of hers. She gave me your picture. She's scared, really scared, what they did to Lori, you know . . ." she let her words drift off.

"I want to help her."

"She told me a lot about you Flick, that's your name right?"

"Right," he said as he had a sudden impulse and pulled her tighter.

"Tell me Linda, what is a beautiful thing like you doing after the show?"

"Flick," she said with a smile that turned into a grin, "are you hitting on me?"

"I do believe I am, but first things first, do you know where Gloria is?"

"Maybe?" she said with a flirty look on her face.

"Okay, so what do I do with that?" he said as he brought his lips down to hers, giving her a hard kiss, cutting her words off.

"What do you want to do with it Flick?" she answered back with a smile after the kiss, and he could feel the sexual tension growing.

He laughed, "I need to find Gloria, I can't think of much else besides that right now, sorry. But if I knew I could find her . . . well . . . I could relax and let myself go, know what I mean?"

Linda gave him a smile and wrapped her arms tighter around him as she stood on her toes and brought her lips up to his right ear.

"So if you knew where Gloria was you could . . . um . . . unwind a little?"

"Oh I do believe I could," he whispered, "do you know where she is?"

"Maybe, maybe I do Flick, if you're a real good boy, that is," she said as she pulled him close, ran her hands down over his ass and brought her lips back to his.

Chapter 23

The chance encounter with Linda gave Flick hope about find-ing Gloria. Even after she had taken him home and the passion that started on the dance floor continued through most of the night, he still couldn't stop thinking about Gloria. He had been so surprised how much it upset him when Joseph had hit her that night in the hotel. He felt like killing the bastard then, and that was strange because there were so many young women out on the streets that it was impossible to care after a while, but when it came to Gloria he cared a lot. It was a deep felt care and he understood where it came from and that made it all the more real.

Flick let himself out of Linda's apartment around five in the morning. He called a cab on his cell phone and was back at the safe house by six.

When he let himself in Joseph bolted up from the couch the look on his face one of fear and then relief, and Flick knew he was damn glad he had returned. Flick glanced at him then sat down. He ran his fingers through his hair, shook his head trying to get Linda out of his mind.

"We need to be out of here by noon. I talked to a friend and I think I can find one of the girls that brought you to the Mayflower," he gave Joseph a hard stare. It was time for a few answers.

"The other girl is in Intensive Care at City Hospital, somebody beat the hell out of her and I'm sure it has to do with you. I want you to tell me what is going on, and no bullshit man, no bullshit at all."

Joseph stared at him for a few seconds, collecting his thoughts, wondering if this could really have anything to do with the offer he had received a few weeks ago.

"Okay," he said softly, "a few weeks ago some dude came up to me on the street, gave me fifty bucks if I would get into his car with him. I told him to go to hell, I don't go for that shit, but he laughed, told me he didn't either. Well, fifty bucks is fifty bucks so I followed him into his car. It was parked right on Aurora Avenue, with plenty of people and traffic around so I wasn't scared, but I don't go for that, alright."

"Alright man, just tell me," Flick said as he studied him. If this guy was lying he would know it, and if he was he would take him out on the streets and leave him.

"So this guy gives me fifty and tells me there's another two thousand. All I have to do is to call my father and tell him that I'm okay but he needs to back off and let some logging happen around Salmon Creek. I told the guy he was crazy. I haven't spoken to my father in years. Then it dawned on me, I was supposed to make my father think that this was a ransom for my life, like they'd kill me if he fought the logging. Well, that really pissed me off. It's blackmail or something like that and I told him so. But he just laughed and told me how much money two grand was and all I had to do was read what he had written down," he stopped talking and looked up at Flick, tears were starting to form, when he continued his voice was even softer.

"Man, I haven't talked to my father in over two years. I sure as hell wasn't going to call him and tell him a crock of shit even for that much money."

"So what happened?"

"I told the guy to fuck off, kept his fifty and climbed out of the car. I forgot all about it until you walked in the hotel that night, then I thought oh, here's trouble."

Flick leaned back in the chair and didn't say a word. He learned a long time ago that if somebody was lying the best way to discover it was to stare em down in silence. The liars always felt the need to keep talking. Joseph just put his face in his hands and let out a deep sigh.

After a minute Flick asked him, "Why would somebody do that?"

"Do what"?

"Why would somebody want you to call your father and tell him a bunch of shit for two grand? Who is your father, the chief or something?"

"Actually he is. He is the chief of my people. We live out on the west coast in the middle of nowhere."

"Still, two grand, it don't make no fricking sense, not to me."

"It does if you're trying to force my father into something. That's all that I can think of. Somebody is playing really heavy handed with my father, with my people and somehow they thought using me could help."

"Can it help?"

"Man, I don't know. I mean I'm my fathers son, his only child, I'm sure I've . . . well . . . I'm sure I've broken his heart."

"Why?"

"Why, Jesus, I'm a drunk, a drunk Indian is about as low as you can get, at least for my people."

Flick looked hard at him and let him know he was judging his story, trying to see if it was true.

"I ain't lying to you man, I don't know what is going on but it has something to do with my father, and with my people. God, I feel like shit," he said as the tears started rolling down his face.

The silence between them lasted almost five minutes. Joseph was trying to stop the tears, but it seemed to Flick that years of pent up emotions were finally being unleashed. Let the guy cry them out, he thought.

Flick stood up, walked into the kitchen, found a coffee pot and some coffee in a cupboard along with some different breakfast cereals and a few boxes of rice milk. Damn, he thought, Mahoney thinks of everything. A few minutes later he brought a cup of coffee out to Joseph, who by now had stopped the flow of tears, but sat there looking like a very beaten and defeated human being.

He grabbed the coffee from Flick and started drinking it but he never looked up at him. Flick was turning back into the kitchen when Joseph said, "Thanks man, thanks for not leaving me."

Flick didn't say a word. He sure wasn't going to tell him that he would have left him a long time ago if he thought he could get away with it.

By twelve-thirty they were out of the safe house and heading for the city in a cab. Joseph never asked where they were going, just kept his head down and didn't say a word. Once they climbed out of the taxi Joseph realized he was in Lower Eastside. They walked a few blocks, then while waiting for a light to turn green Joseph asked him, "What's your name, if you don't mind me asking."

"You don't need to know my name. You don't even want to remember my face. When this is over you'd better hope to god we never meet again."

"I got to call you something."

"Jesus man, call me Dexter, how's that?"

"Okay Dexter," he laughed, knowing that was a fake name and a dumb one also.

Flick felt at home in the Lower Eastside. It was his turf and also Gloria was hiding close by, staying with a girlfriend.

On the north side of Lower Eastside, near where 21st met Harrison Flick knew a cheap hotel that he had used before. The old guy that owned it was an asshole but he was a straight shooter as far as keeping his mouth shut and not getting involved in anybody's business. If somebody came around asking about him, he knew the old man wouldn't say a word, not for an extra hundred that he would slide his way.

"We're checking into a hotel, I doubt you got any money?" Flick asked him.

"I got some money, keep it in my shoe, in my sock really. I got a hundred or so."

"Good, cause I don't plan on spending my money to keep your sorry ass alive."

Joseph looked at him and realized he was starting to like this guy. Dexter wasn't nearly as tough as he wanted him to believe.

They walked until they reached 21st street, turned right, then continued a few more blocks before he followed Flick into a hotel. They entered a clean, little lobby with a few chairs to the left surrounding a small coffee table with some magazines on it. Nobody was behind the desk but there was the sound of a hockey game coming from somewhere. Flick walked up to the counter, hit the little bell once and waited.

"Just a minute, right in the middle of the damn game, Jesus Christ," they both heard from around an open door.

An old man walked out and looked at both of them. If he recognized Flick he didn't show it.

"What?" he said.

"I'm from the health department. We want to look around," Flick said. It was the same line that he used every time he stayed here. He hoped it made some connection with the old guy, because connections on the street were about the best thing a person had going for him.

"Don't rent by the hour."

Flick laughed, that was what the old guy had told him the last time he was here. Flick didn't say a word as he pulled his wallet out and slipped two, one hundred dollar bills on the counter.

"I don't want it for an hour I want it for the night."

The old man turned around to a desk drawer that was behind him and opened it then handed Flick a room key.

"Check out is eleven, or it's another hundred."

Then he turned and hurried out of sight back to his hockey game.

"No questions," Joseph said as they started up the stairs.

"Not in this place," Flick smiled back.

It was the first time Joseph had ever seen him smile.

Chapter 24

E ven though he was in the back corner of the kitchen looking at a sink full of dishes Mondo tried to keep an eye on the men that walked through St Joseph's front door. It was awkward at times studying their faces, trying to be discrete as he glanced at any man that had the slightest resemblance to Joseph Yazzi. To have Joseph walk in the door was an incredible long shot. The odds were so against it that he knew it was crazy, but it was all he could think of doing. If the so-called power of the totem didn't in some way bring him and Joseph together he doubted he would ever find him.

From his corner he was also watching Dawn. Her warmth and caring nature seemed to just go on and on throughout the evening. Mondo found her fascinating and he wasn't sure why. Something about her radiated such a sense of peace and caring. He had felt it the moment she had first spoken to him. How could she greet all those people and not be burned out by the end of the evening, he wondered?

Washing the ever growing pile of dishes was more than he had bargained for, and he had been at it for hours. He was going as fast as he could, trying to keep an eye out for Joseph and finding himself staring at Dawn a little more than he should. He soon realized that she hadn't taken a break all evening and the line still stretched out the door. Finally he rinsed his hands off, wiped them on his wet apron and walked up to Todd.

"Todd, I've been watching Dawn, she hasn't slowed down a bit. Let me bring her something to eat. I can handle the door for a few minutes."

"Not as good as she can."

"Well, you got that right, but she is going to burn out if you don't give her a break."

Todd nodded his head in agreement.

"Your right Mondo, she loves the mashed potatoes, give her a good helping. I reckon the dishes will still be there."

"Thanks."

Mondo walked over behind Sammy who was dishing plates of food up as fast as she could and made a plate for Dawn, then he walked behind the counter and started her way. For some unknown reason she turned and looked at him, saw the plate of food and gave him a cute little smile, then silently mouthed an exaggerated thank you.

"I think the greeter needs to eat. I know I can't do your job as good as you but, I'll try," he said as he handed her the plate.

"Thank you. I'm Dawn Peters, and you are?"

"I'm Mondo."

"Well Mondo, to tell you the truth, I haven't eaten since breakfast. Thanks this is very kind of you. I won't be long."

She walked over to a nearby table, pulled the chair out, then almost as if in slow motion she turned and gave Mondo another glance followed by a warm smile before she sat down and started eating. He turned his attention to the line of people coming through the door.

It sure was easier to keep an eye out for Joseph this way, he thought.

As the hungry started passing by him he did everything he could to make each person feel welcomed. He had a growing empathy toward the homeless, and it made him think about his life. All of the adventures and travels, the blessings that he had received so far, it all could have turned out so differently. What was it, he wondered, that enabled him to live his life so close to the edge and never fall off. There certainly was no financial security in the way he lived, yet he knew he would never end up like these homeless people. He was starting to realize that it isn't so much about the troubles that life brings to your front door it's all about your ability to bounce back. It's more about the belief that you can get up, dust yourself off, look

adversity in the eye, tell it to go to hell and keep going. Somewhere in their past each one of these people he watched this evening had been crushed by something that just took it out of them.

Twenty or thirty people must have gone by him before Dawn stood up. She walked back toward him, smiled, as she gently touched his left hand and said,

"Mondo, that was so sweet of you to think of me."

He took the empty plate from her, smiled back and said "no trouble," then he headed back to his ever growing pile of dishes.

Todd was right about the dishes still being there. In the short ten minutes or so that he was at the front door the pile had doubled. God, he thought was this the best idea he could come up with?

As the evening continued, he noticed the line at the door was finally slowing down. The rush was starting to end. He was still washing as fast as he could but now he was getting ahead of the piles. Soon the front door was closed and locked for the night. Sammy was putting some of the food in plastic containers and putting them in the large double door stainless refrigerator. Stephanie had left a few minutes earlier after giving Todd a kiss on his cheek. Mondo looked at the clock near the back door and was surprised to see it was after ten. He was just finishing when Dawn walked around the corner.

"Need a ride anywhere?" she asked.

"Well, as a matter of fact I do. I'm staying a mile or so away. You don't mind?"

He left the question hanging out there.

"Mind, after you brought me dinner, kept me from fainting right there on the floor. No Mondo I don't mind."

Mondo laughed, his dimples showing.

"Sweet dimples," she said, then seemed embarrassed by her quick remark.

"Let me talk to Todd real fast if you don't mind, I'd like to come back again," he said trying to ignore her comment.

"Sure, I'll wait."

Mondo walked into the small office that was in the back of the building and knocked on the open door.

"Todd, got a minute?"

Todd swung around in a small swivel chair and looked at Mondo.

149

"Yep, what's up, and hey thanks for your help."

"I'd like to volunteer again."

"Any time, you don't even have to make an appointment, just show up, there will always be something for you to do."

"Thanks, see you soon."

He walked back to where Dawn was standing. "I'm ready if you are?"

"Great let's go."

He followed her out the back door and climbed into her car.

"You could be taking a chance giving me a ride, you know, I could be some psycho or something," he said with a smile in his voice as she pulled out into traffic.

"Believe me, Mondo. I don't think I have to worry about you. I have a sense about people, I really do. So I'm curious."

"Curious about what?"

"About you, and by the way, where do you live?"

"Right now I'm down near Jones street in a hotel called the Ambassador," he found himself somewhat embarrassed to admit that he was staying there. At least he didn't have to tell her he was sleeping under a bench.

"Just tell me which way to go."

"I will if I can remember, so why are you curious about me?"

"Because you don't fit."

"Is it that obvious?"

"To me it is. I've been volunteering on the streets for the last year and believe me you don't fit."

"Well I guess that's good. I'm not really a homeless person. I live on my sailboat, which right now is on the west coast of Vancouver Island," he paused not sure how much she really wanted to hear.

"Okay. You have a sailboat that you live on and it's on the outer coast somewhere, so what are you doing here?"

"You really want to know?"

"Yes, I do."

"Tell you what, why don't we go get a drink somewhere? This story is a lot longer than you think."

"I don't drink."

"Okay, what about a Starbucks or something?"

"That would keep me up all night."

"Well Dawn," he laughed, "I guess I can give you the condensed Readers Digest version. You see I'm on a quest, I know that sounds stupid, but I am. I'm trying to find somebody. A homeless, drunken Indian who lives on the streets of Vancouver and I don't have a clue where to look for him."

She didn't say anything for a few seconds, just focused on her driving.

"You want me to tell you more?" he asked.

"Yes, please."

"Okay, so without getting into to much detail, the man I'm looking for is the son of the chief of this little town called Salmon Creek. For some reason his father thinks I can rescue his son from the evil clutches of the white man's world."

"Do you think you can?" she asked as she looked at him then turned her attention back to the road.

"I don't know. It seems pretty impossible to me but this old man said there are powers that I have no idea of that can make it happen. What do I know? The reason he needs to find his son is so he will return to his people and fight against a logging company that is ready to cut down their forest. The chief believes if they start logging, it will be the end of his people."

"How did you ever get involved in something like this?"

"You wouldn't believe it if I told you, and I don't think you have the time to hear the story. I have a picture of this guy and I would like to show it to you, maybe you've seen him."

"Sure where is his picture?"

"It's in my hotel room."

As soon as he said it he felt awkward, like he was giving her a line.

She glanced over at him and in the soft glow of the passing street lights he could see her smile.

"Really Mondo, in your cheap hotel room, I don't think I want to venture there, thank you just the same."

He laughed, "Dawn I'm not that kind of guy, really, but that's where his picture is. His name is Joseph Yazzi."

A few seconds later she asked "isn't the Ambassador around here, I remember it being somewhere close?"

He glanced out the window trying to find a landmark.

She suddenly pulled her car over into an empty parking place.

"Can't pass up a good place to park, Mondo go get your picture. I think your hotel is in the next block. I'll sit here and wait for you, if you don't mind."

"Thanks Dawn, I'll be right back."

He climbed out of the car, looked around and saw the neon sign for the Ambassador ahead on the next block. He closed her door and took off walking at a fast pace. He raced up the stairs, found the picture and was back in her car within a few minutes. She turned the dome light on as he handed her the picture and studied it for a minute, then she flicked the light off.

"I've seen him around. It's been a while but I do recognize his face."

"Any idea how I can find him?"

She was silent for a few moments then she turned and looked at him.

"Sorry Mondo, not a clue."

Chapter 25

The man sat in the car, cell phone to his ear shouting and moving his hands wildly about. A passerby would have thought he was having a fight with his wife, but he wasn't. Harvey Langdon had just pulled his car over a few minutes earlier and he was extremely frustrated, pissed off and scared to death. This was coming undone fast and he sure didn't want Michael to think it was his fault.

He thought it was strange when over a month ago Michael had called him and told him he needed to find a homeless Indian who was living on the streets somewhere in Vancouver. The name Joseph Yazzi meant nothing to him. He had no idea what Michael was thinking, but he had learned a long time ago that it didn't make any difference, just find him Michael told him. It had taken five days and six of his best people working the streets before he found the guy. Then it was three hundred dollars a day to have one of his people follow him around so they wouldn't loose him. It hadn't made any sense.

After two days of following this Indian around Michael told Harvey to go have a talk with him. His instructions were simple. Offer him some money and tell him all he had to do was to make a phone call. It sounded pretty easy and Michael had even scripted what he was supposed to say. All Harvey had to do was drag his ass to a phone, put the script under his nose, dial a number for him if necessary, and pay him off. Shove enough money at him and it should be fine, Michael had told him.

Well, he and Michael both missed that call. After Joseph Yazzi stormed out of his car with his fifty dollars he knew that it was going to take a lot more effort to make him play along. Harvey had been the one to suggest grabbing the guy, stuff him in a hotel somewhere for a few days, and soften him up. Shit, he thought, he had even recommended that they use Flick. Now Flick and Joseph Yazzi were both running and he had to find them within twenty-four hours. That was damn near impossible. Finding Joseph had been hard enough and he wasn't even hiding. That damn Flick had been around long enough to have a few tricks up his sleeve, and that worried the hell out of Harvey.

Now he had twelve people on the street looking for them. Twelve, god he thought, he never had to use that many at one time. There was something way to urgent about this and he didn't like it one bit. In the back of his mind he was starting to fear that maybe these two were going to disappear forever and if so what then?

He hollered into the cell phone cutting the person off, "listen, you've got less than eighteen hours to find them. Somebody on the street knows where they are and I need to find that somebody, you need to find that somebody. It's time to start turning all the rocks over," he listened as the person he was talking to started to make excuses again.

"Listen to me, I don't give a shit about any of that, find them, you have eighteen hours, just find em!"

He closed his phone and took a deep breath.

"Goddamn it," he shouted.

Flick sat in the oversized chair and felt a surge of relief. They were once again safe, at least for the moment. The two of them could probably stay here a few days before having to leave, and a few days sounded really good right now. He looked over at Joseph and wondered about him. He had little reason to doubt his story, the guy had told him the truth as far as he could tell.

A little strategy was forming in Flick's mind, a step by step plan that would hopefully give him a clue as to who was after them and why. Once he figured out who they were he would have to come up with a plan to get them to back off.

"Man, what's your last name and where did you say you came from?" Flick asked Joseph.

"Why?"

"Why, damn it because I need to know that's why. You want to be on the street by yourself? I doubt it, so tell me what's your last name and where the hell do you come from?"

"Yazzi, I'm from Salmon Creek."

"Where's that?"

"It's on the west coast of Vancouver Island, its all tribal lands."

"Y-A-Z-Z-I," Flick spelled it out.

"Yes like that."

"Listen Joseph Yazzi, I'm heading out, I got a few people to find. You don't go anywhere, got it? I'll be back in an hour or so, I'll bring you something to eat. You stay right here man," he said as he stood up and looked down at him.

"Okay."

The B.C. Tel van didn't look out of place as it pulled off of the main road two miles east of Salmon Creek and into a circular driveway. The driver, a B.C. Tel employee with over fifteen years working for the phone company climbed out and unlocked a chain then pulled his van up to a small building and parked. He climbed out and walked up to the metal door, unlocked it and let himself inside the central switching station for all telephone calls coming in and out of Salmon Creek.

It took him less than five minutes to isolate Chief Yazzi's phone line. Once he accomplished that, he attached a small relay that would transmit all phone activity on that line to his van parked ten feet away. From the inside of his van all calls were recorded as well as the number that the call originated from. This information was available to anyone who knew the right phone number to call. The driver was a little concerned that he would have to leave the van here, but he had covered himself by not signing his name when he checked the van out. Finishing his work, he walked outside locking the switching station door behind him. He locked the heavy chain that was strung across the driveway into the station, making sure the three red flags were still attached as he had found them, then waited for his ride back to Victoria.

Whoever wanted this tap paid him good and that was all he cared about.

Flick made his way down into the heart of Lower Eastside before he stopped at a pay phone. These phones were getting harder to find since everybody started using cell phones. Still a pay phone was the safest way there was to make a call. He put the coins in and dialed Mahoney.

"Manny it's me," he said relieved to get his friend on the first call.

"I'm alright and thanks for the house. We're gone now. What's going on? What have you heard?"

"I don't know what you did Flick, but you must have pissed somebody off, there are a lot of people looking for the two of you. Word on the street is there is a lot of cash for whoever finds you, a lot of cash," Manny said, his English accent difficult to understand.

"No word about who wants us?"

"No but it's big. That's all I know. Call me in a few hours. I'll see if I can dig deeper."

"Thanks Manny," he said and hung up.

He walked three more blocks before he found another pay phone. He put his coins in and dialed operator information.

"Yes, good morning, I'd like the phone number of a Yazzi, that's Y-A-Z-Z-I (he spelled it out to the operator); the town is Salmon Creek."

He waited less than a minute before the operator came back with a Charles Yazzi and his phone number. Flick wrote it down, thanked the operator and started walking towards the address that he had for Gloria.

As he walked he wondered what he should tell Joseph's father. How straight should he play it? There was little doubt in his mind that old man Yazzi must know who was behind this. It basically was extortion as far as he could tell. Somebody powerful and rich wanted to keep this old man out of their plans and was willing to play real hard ball to achieve it.

He walked until he found the apartment that Linda told him

Gloria was living in. Casually, he continued to look around him as he walked. One of the nice things about the Lower Eastside was if you weren't a street person you really couldn't hide very well. The people that were searching for him would look pretty conspicuous just hanging out. At the end of the street he waited for the light to turn green then he crossed, turned to his left, and circled around the block before he walked up to the apartment building. He opened the rusty front door and quickly let himself in. He was standing in an entryway with an ornate metal door that blocked his access to the stairs about fifteen feet in front of him. To his left was a row of small mail boxes and under each box was a buzzer that would ring the owner and let them know somebody was downstairs for them. A small round speaker covered with a chrome grill was for the intercom. He ran his eyes across the names until he saw C. Johnston, the C stood for Christy. He reached over and pushed the buzzer, holding it for thirty seconds. After waiting over a minute with no reply he hit the buzzer again, holding it even longer. Another minute passed before the cheap speaker crackled, "who is it?" he heard a woman ask.

"It's Flick, I need to see Gloria."

There was a long moment of silence before he heard. "I'll be right down."

Chapter 26

I t was good to see Gloria again he thought as they sat in Christy's small living room. The similarities between her and Sandra were amazing. From the first time he had ever seen her on the street he couldn't get over how she reminded him of her. God if there was one thing he would do over in his life it would be Sandra. Thinking about her while trying to explain his plans to Gloria was to damn distracting. It was time to put Sandra out of his thoughts, yet he had been trying to do that very thing for the last year and a half with little success.

Sandra Boichet was the only woman he had ever loved. She was the only woman he had ever felt enough of a connection with to make him know that love was worth the risk. The three years that they were together were not all bliss and romance. No, he knew a lot of the issues that they faced were his. But in the end he couldn't compete with heroin. She died sitting right there in his favorite chair in their small house in Burnaby. He knew that it would be with him for the rest of his life, finding her like that, the needle still in her arm, her face a pale sickening white, her eyes hauntingly dull and empty. There was no way he could forget or ever forgive himself for not trying harder to save her from that damn drug. Of all the drugs on the street, only heroin scared the hell out of him.

"Okay, so you're good with this?" he asked Gloria.

"You think its best don't you?"

"I do. You need to get out of town and my buddy is a good man, there won't be any hassles, I promise you. He's driving to Montreal in a few days and I think you need to go with him. Let things cool off around here, then if you want to come back okay, but for now you really need to leave. You know Gloria this might be a great time for you to get off the streets for good, go to college or something. I don't want to see anything happen to you."

Gloria pulled the shawl tight around her shoulders and tried to figure out what was going on with Flick. It was like he had become her big brother or something.

"Flick I have to know, why are you doing this for me?"

"Why not?"

"Because there are a thousand girls out on the street and for some reason . . . well for some reason you've . . ." she paused trying to find the right word. He didn't give her the time to figure it out.

"Listen Gloria, I could tell you all sorts of shit, but I won't. You remind me of someone that I will miss everyday for the rest of my life. I couldn't help her and now she's dead. I can help you and in some sick way that makes me feel better. This is about me and my demons as much as it is about you. That's it Gloria, that's really it."

They both sat in silence for a few minutes.

"What was her name, Flick?"

"Shit . . . if I tell you will you go to Montreal?"

"Flick, I'll go to Montreal even if you don't tell me. I just would like to know."

"Sandra, Sandra Biochet. We were together for over three years. I really loved her."

"What happened?" she asked with such care and concern.

"Overdosed. Never, I mean never do heroin Gloria. You see what it does."

Flick was about in tears and he couldn't believe it. Gloria couldn't believe it either. She stood up and walked across the small living room to the chair he was sitting in and knelt down in front of him. She put her head on his lap and wrapped her arms around his waist. She couldn't remember the last time she had felt such concern from anybody for her. Not from her mom, not her moms boyfriends, not even the ones who raped her. She couldn't ever remember feeling what she had just felt from Flick. God, she wondered is this what it is like to have somebody really care about you.

Neither of them said anything for a few minutes. Gloria just rested her head on his lap, feeling a security and comfort that was like a breath of fresh air all the while he gently stroked her long brown hair with his fingers.

"I got to go," Flick finally said, embarrassed yet some how relieved at the same time.

"Okay," her voice so soft he almost didn't hear her.

She brought her head off of his lap and stood up. He looked at her and then stood and wrapped his arms around her and held her close.

A minute later he lightly pushed her back and looked into her eyes.

"Gloria get off the street, make a new life for yourself, do it for me, do it for a Sandra Biochet that you never knew."

He let her go and started for the front door as she just stood there wanting to say so much but not finding the right words. At the door he turned and looked at her. He didn't say anything either. It was as if in some strange way both of them had just made a connection with another soul that they both so desperately needed. Flick reached into his wallet and pulled out five American one hundred dollar bills and put them on the small oval wood table next to the front door. Then he brought his eyes from the money back to her. Gloria just looked at him wishing he would stay.

"Do it for Sandra Biochet," he said softly as he turned away from her and let himself out the door.

Flick couldn't wait to get out of that apartment and back out to the street. The emotions that he had just experienced seemed to have sucked the air from his lungs as they sent his mind careening down a very painful ride on memory lane. Touching that deeply on Sandra's memories might be good in the long run he thought as he quickened his pace, but right now it hurt like hell.

He walked five blocks before going into a small coffee shop and buying a large coffee with a five dollar bill and receiving a lot of change back. On his way out the door he grabbed a napkin to write notes on. Then he walked another few blocks before he found a pay phone. He pulled a handful of change out and put it on the little metal lip that the phone book hung from.

Okay, he thought to himself, now it's Joseph's dad's turn. What the hell was he going to say to him? Shit he thought, he didn't have a damn clue. He pulled the napkin and a pen out and put them next to the change.

He dialed the number and was surprised that it cost over a dollar for the first minute, he would have to talk fast before he ran out of money. The phone rang and rang and he was starting to think that nobody was home when it was suddenly picked up but nobody said a word.

Jesus he thought and after a long wait he figured it was up to him. "Is this Charles Yazzi?"

After another long pause he finally heard a voice, "Yes this is."

"Listen, I'm a friend of your son Joseph, right now we're both in Vancouver and somebody doesn't like us, any ideas who they are?"

"You're with Joseph?"

Flick could picture some gray haired old geezer of an Indian talking about as slow as possible. Well, he had better start talking fast. He only had a few more dollars in change.

"Did Captain Mondo find you?" the old man asked.

"What? Cut the crap, somebody is trying to kill us and I want to know who and why. Who is after us and what does this have to do with you and logging around Salmon Creek, wherever the hell that is?"

"Will you tell Joseph that I love him, that his people need him, we need . . ."

"Listen, just shut up, or there won't be a Joseph or me to talk to! Somebody tried to bribe your son into calling you and telling you not to resist the logging that they are planning, or your son wouldn't see the light of morning. Know what I mean? Well, those people are after us and I need to know who the hell they are. You got about one more minute before I run out of change for this damn phone so start making sense."

"Fine, yes . . . Mountain Resources that is the company. They want to log our native lands. They won't stop until they have cut down our forest. Michael Jensen is his name. He is the one who is behind this. He is a dangerous man, able I believe to kill if necessary."

Flick was writing as fast as he could.

"Why don't you just let them cut a few damn trees down and not fight this?"

"Because that is what we have done for the last one hundred years. There is very little left and they will not stop until it is all logged."

"Listen Chief, I got to go. I'm about out of change. Your son is fine. I'll tell him that I talked to you."

"Please, please for an old man with not much time left find Mondo."

"Who?"

"Captain Mondo, I sent him to Vancouver to find my son. He is our only hope."

"Captain Mondo, Jesus. Okay, sure I'll tell him."

"Sir," Flick was shocked at the humility in the voice, shocked in the way the old man seemed to reach out to him through the phone with nothing but a desperate plea.

"Please sir, find him."

"Yeah, sure, okay."

Flick hung up and started down the street.

Fifteen minutes later he opened the door to their room and found Joseph sitting on a chair watching TV.

"I told you I'd be back, here's lunch, or breakfast, hell I don't know and I don't care," he said as he flung a bag of fast food at him.

Flick walked into the bathroom and ran the water on cold for a few seconds before splashing it on his face. It momentarily seemed to ease his anxiety, seemed to snap his mind back to the present. As he looked in the mirror he thought that the day had gone pretty good so far. Gloria was going to be alright and he had two names, Mountain Resources and Michael Jensen. That was a hell of a lot more than he had this morning.

He walked back into the room, sat down on the side of the bed and kicked his feet up on the bed. His head was still killing him and he kept thinking that there was something else he was supposed to tell Joseph, something else besides his father loved him, and that his people needed him. Right now he wasn't even going to tell Joseph that he had talked to his father.

As he lay there thinking about Gloria, and Sandra, Mountain Resources and a Michael Jensen his mind kept trying to look back into the one thing that he knew he was missing. He looked at Joseph who wasn't paying any attention to the television but was staring at him with his right hand in the fast food bag.

"Oh yeah, I almost forgot, we need to find some guy named Mondo, Captain Mondo, you ever heard of him?"

"Never."

"Well, I got a feeling that we are going to have to start looking for him real soon."

"How soon is that?"

"In the next twenty minutes."

Chapter 27

Five minutes after Flick hung up from Charles Yazzi, Harvey Langdon's cell phone rang. He was just pulling off of the Second Narrows Bridge. Fumbling for the phone sitting on the passenger's seat he almost ran a bicyclist off of the road.

"Yeah"

"They're in Lower Eastside, Flick just called the guy's dad."

"Awesome," he said trailing the word with a sigh of relief.

"Okay here is what I want. Have Grady's teams pull off we don't need that many people now. Take Eddie and Jake and whoever they want and get them into Lower Eastside. What else did you hear?"

"The old man told Flick about Mountain Resources and about Michael as well."

"Shit," he interrupted, "okay what else?"

"The name Mondo came up, a Captain Mondo. The old man asked Flick if he had found him."

"Found him . . . what?"

"Yeah the old man said he sent this Mondo guy to Vancouver to find his son and that he was their only hope. He told Flick to find him."

"Mondo, any idea who this guy is?"

"Not a clue, that's about it, although the old man told Flick he thought Michael was capable of murder," he let the last word hang.

Harvey had wondered that very question on more than a few occasions.

"Yeah, don't worry, it's all right, thanks. That wire tap was a great idea. I see why I pay you what I do."

He hung up without waiting for a reply. They were in Lower

Eastside, damn that made sense, he thought. Well, it was his turn to smile now. He would have his best people there in less than twenty minutes. The circle just got a hell of a lot smaller around those two.

"Here's the problem as I see it Joseph. If you stay here you're going to go crazy just sitting around. If we both go out on the street together we're just too damn conspicuous. So, I guess its either you hang out here or we walk the streets separately and start looking for this Captain Mondo."

"Who's this Mondo guy, some super hero or something?"

Flick laughed, "Well I doubt that, but let's just say that we need to find him. Now believe it or not he is actually looking for you and that's good. For once we got somebody on our side, and we need to find him."

"How?"

"I've been thinking about that. This guy is trying to find you so he must know you're on the streets and he must know you're a drunk, sorry but you said it yourself. So, I asked myself where I would look if I was trying to find you. Well, first I'd go where most of the homeless hang out, which is right here in Lower Eastside. Then I asked myself what next? What could I do to see as many homeless people as possible? Well you know what I would do? I'd hang out in a mission. I'd volunteer and look at every face that came in the door. That's about all I could think of."

"Makes sense I guess."

"I'm going to look in the phone book, write down all of the missions in Lower Eastside, then in an hour or so we can head out and I'll give you a list to check out. I guess you'll just have to ask if Mondo is around, you know play it real casual, like he's a friend or something, just be cool man, can you do that?"

"Yeah sure, no problem," but there was a problem for Joseph Yazzi and he knew it, he hadn't had a drink in four days.

After a great workout in the weight room and then a steam bath followed by a long shower Mondo didn't want to go back to his life on the streets. He felt like going sailing. The sun was out and a little breeze blew as he walked out of the health club and toward the bus that would take him back to Lower Eastside. The Cross was safe. The health club was a perfect place to hide it.

He glanced at his watch as he climbed on the bus, it was almost noon. This ride would once again transport him from the wealth and prosperity of Vancouver into the despair and poverty of Lower Eastside.

Climbing off the bus he looked around and felt that same sadness, so many people down and out, all just struggling to get by one day at a time. He made his way to his hotel, paid for another night then headed up the three flights of stairs.

Five minutes later he was walking towards St. Joseph's Mission. He had a pair of sunglass on which made it easy for him to study the men who walked by. None of them could follow his eyes as he looked at every face that had the slightest resemblance to Joseph Yazzi.

He wondered about Dawn and if she would be at the mission, but did it matter he asked himself? He was going there to try and find Joseph yet last night after the short time that they spent together, he knew he wanted to see her again. It was her spirit he realized, she just had this glow, and she didn't have to say a word for it to shine.

A block before the mission he saw a pay phone and had a sudden thought to stop and make a few calls. He grabbed his wallet and took out a business card then dropped some change in the phone and punched the number. After three rings Jonathan answered.

"Hello."

"Jonathan it's me, Mondo, thought I'd say hi."

"Boy am I glad you called," Mondo could hear the tension in his voice, "I was worried sick, is everything okay, is everything safe?" he said.

"Fine, I have everything safe, don't worry."

"Worry, how can I not worry? Listen I've thought a lot about what you showed me. I have come to the conclusion that it can not be a fake."

"Jonathan, you told me it can't be real."

"I know it can't be, but it is even less likely that it is a fake. Nobody would create such a forgery and give it to an Indian chief on Vancouver Island. Do you understand what I'm saying? Do you know what this means?"

"It means a complete rewrite of ancient history."

"That's it Mondo, a complete rewrite."

"Well it's safe, don't go crazy over it. I still haven't found Joseph Yazzi. I'm starting to think its going to be impossible."

"This whole thing is beyond impossible, beyond stupid if you ask me. Just keep it safe, understand me, by the way where are you staying?"

Mondo started to tell him, but in the next second he changed his mind.

"I'm moving everyday. I sleep wherever I can."

"You can't be carrying the Cross with you!"

"No it's stashed and it's safe. Don't worry, Jonathan it's safe, nobody will find it."

There was a pause from Jonathan and once again Mondo remembered the look on his face that night at the condo.

"It's safe Jonathan. I got to go, I'll call you soon."

"Wait, Naomi has been driving me crazy, call her."

"Okay, I'll keep you posted, thanks Jonathan."

"For what?"

"For being a man of integrity."

Then he hung up before Jonathan could say anything.

He pulled more change out of his pocket and punched in another number.

"Naomi hi," he said when she answered.

"Mondo, where are you?"

"I'm in Vancouver. Did you get the picture I emailed you?"

"I did, Mondo I've been talking to Jonathan, he won't tell me much but do you know what that is a picture of?" she said her voice full of excitement.

"Yes, Naomi I do. I know it's impossible and it can't be real but Jonathan thinks it is. I can't tell you much more. I hope in the next few days to get this all figured out and I'll let you know what's going on."

"Mondo what are you going to do with it?"

"Well, right now I have to find somebody, and show it to him. Then I guess I have to get us back to Salmon Creek, that's all I know for sure."

"Get us?"

"Yeah, the guy I'm looking for, which is why I have the Cross in the first place. Listen Naomi it's crazy and I hope that soon I can get this all sorted out, okay, until then I just don't have any answers."

"Okay Mondo, by the way I found out something about that barge. It's owned by a corporation that is headquartered in Grand Cayman Island, so I'm sure that it's just a front, a dummy corporation. I dug a lot more and found that the barge is used as a base of operation for logging projects when the logging site is not accessible by road. Is somebody going to log near Neskiwaii?"

"That's what this is all about, and I have a bad feeling that it could turn real ugly, fast."

"Don't get hurt Mondo."

"I won't. I'll keep you posted."

"Alright call me. I have to know what's going on."

"Naomi, I never could keep a secret from you, I'll call you."

"Bye, Mondo, be safe,"

He hung up and continued toward the mission, walking until he reached the back door of St. Josephs, then knocked once and walked in.

"Todd," he yelled.

Todd was sitting in the far corner with a phone to his ear. At hearing Mondo he spun around with a startled look on his face, spilling a cup of coffee he was holding.

"Jesus Mondo, sorry," he said as he stood up and brushed the coffee off of his pants with his hand.

"You come by to work?" he asked as he cupped the phone to his waist.

"Yeah, thought I'd help out."

"Great," he said as he brought the phone back to his ear but kept his left hand over the mouth piece.

"You might as well go say hello to Helen, she's serving today. I think I'll have you help her."

Mondo found Helen, introduced himself and was soon serving meals to all who were waiting. He kept thinking about the expression on Todd's face. Something had set him off and Mondo was starting to feel like he couldn't trust anybody.

Chapter 28

At one o'clock Flick and Joseph walked outside and stood in the sunshine. Flick reached into his pocket and pulled out a list of the five missions that Joseph was going to have to check out.

"Remember man, be cool. You have to really keep your eyes open. If we're looking for this Mondo guy, then maybe somebody else is, just be back here by eight-thirty at the latest." Flick said as he struggled with a sense of apprehension about letting Joseph loose on the street. Hell he thought, it wasn't his job to babysit this guy anymore.

"Remember eight-thirty, don't be late," he said as Joseph headed off toward his first mission.

Flick pulled a piece of paper out of his pocket and looked at the seven missions he had written down. Maybe he could get to them all, maybe not, but at least he was starting. He figured the best way to ask about Mondo would be to stand in line with everybody else and when he got to the door just casually ask for him. Anything else would make him stand out to much.

Joseph couldn't get over how nice it felt to be outside. It seemed like he had been trapped in cheap hotels for way too long. Walking past his first bar, hearing the laughter and tasting the smell of cheap beer he knew he wouldn't make it through the day without giving in. He almost stopped and went in the door right then, but he kept walking. He would try to check out at least two of the missions. That was the least he could do, he thought.

✳

It was close to five-thirty when Dawn walked in the back door of St. Josephs. Mondo heard her, turned around and smiled at her. She caught his smile and returned it before she hung her coat and purse up and walked over to him.

"Hey, Mondo, nice to see you here, you're going to become a regular, just like me," she laughed then made her way to the front door and started making everyone feel welcome.

Mondo kept dishing food up, wondering about Joseph Yazzi and if this little plan of his was going to work, and if it didn't what then?. There was no way that he could see himself returning to Salmon Creek without Joseph. He remembered the look on the old man's face when he had given him the Cross and made it so plain that having his son return was the most important thing in his life.

The time went by slowly as he kept piling food on people's plates, kept looking for Joseph and also watching Dawn as she greeted yet another person. Over the noise of the crowd he couldn't hear her but he could imagine her telling each person who entered that Jesus loved them and so did she.

It was close to six when Mondo glanced up and saw a tall skinny guy who for some strange reason instantly caught his attention walk in the front door. He stood in line nervously, his eyes darting around the room as if he was looking for someone or was guilty of something. Maybe he was hiding from somebody Mondo couldn't tell but something about him was wrong. He watched as the guy reached Dawn, then leaned over and whispered something in her ear. She looked at him for a second before she stepped back and brought her face away from his. Whatever he said must have bothered her because she took another two steps back as the guy got a mean expression on his face. In the next instant he grabbed her arm, pulled her close, and said something else. Dawn tried to get free but he held her tight. He just stared at her and Mondo was about to run around the counter when he let go of her arm, turned around and stormed out the door, almost knocking over three people. As soon as he disappeared Dawn looked over at Mondo and he could see fear on her face. She glanced back at the door ignoring two homeless men who walked by without her saying a word to them.

A moment later she turned around and walked to Mondo.

"Did you see that guy?" she asked her voice full of tension.

"Yeah, I did what happened?"

"He asked for you."

"What?"

"He asked if Mondo was here, like he was a friend of yours or something. I almost sent him over to you but I . . . I don't know, there was just something about him that I didn't like."

"He asked for me by my name?"

"Yes, he said is Mondo around."

"Wow, well I think you did the right thing, I don't know who he was or why he wanted to talk to me but I didn't like him either."

"I have to get back, what time do you work till?"

"Until you leave," he said with a smile.

She rolled her eyes at him, smiled and went back to the door.

Who ever that guy was, it was bad news and Mondo knew it.

It was a very long two hours before it finally started to slow down around eight. Dawn had taken a break and gobbled some dinner but she was back at it in a few minutes. Mondo had made his way to the back and had a short dinner break as well. He saw the pile of dishes but at least that wasn't his department tonight.

He was still filling plates, watching Helen putting things away, and he never gave a second glance to the young man that walked up to the counter, held out his plate and as soon as he put some food on it said, "Thanks Mondo."

Before he even thought he replied, "Sure no problem, you're welcome."

Then he stopped in his tracks, adrenalin instantly rushing through his body. The guy gave him a smile and stood there looking at him.

"Chuck Yazzi sent me to find you. My name is Flick, we need to talk."

At the old man's name even more adrenaline rushed through him. He didn't know what to think. If that first creep hadn't scared the hell out of him he probably wouldn't have thought twice. Now this guy was standing here obviously not interested in food looking right at him. Mondo knew it was too late to lie his way out of this one. He glanced up and saw Dawn staring at them both.

"Listen man, give me a few minutes, I'll come talk to you."

"Okay," he said and walked with his plate to an empty table, sat down and started picking at his food.

Mondo felt like a complete idiot. All he would have had to do was say something, anything besides what he did and the guy would have just kept walking. He wondered if he had just made his first big mistake on the street. Well, he might as well go talk to him, at least he knew Chuck Yazzi, but then he thought, what did that matter?

"Helen, please cover for me for a minute will you?" he asked her trying to keep a sense of composure in his voice. She gave him a funny look because they both knew she was finished with serving, but she started dishing up food for the next in line. Mondo looked over at Dawn as he started for Flick's table. She watched his every step. He gave her a half hearted smile as he pulled out a chair and sat down. Mondo looked at Flick, tried reading him, tried to get some sense of what was going on. He couldn't tell a thing as Flick looked at him and gave him a strange little smile.

"Listen Mondo, my name is Flick. I've been with Joseph Yazzi for the last four days. I called his dad and he told me to find you. It was amazingly easy you know, really it was."

Mondo didn't know what to think, his thoughts racing back to the Cross, praying that he had covered his tracks well enough.

"Okay so," Mondo replied trying to keep all of the tension he felt out of his voice.

"It must seem strange to you, me walking in here and knowing your name."

"I want to know what you want."

"I think you have to tell me that. Charles Yazzi practically begged me to find you. He kept saying find Captain Mondo. He said you were his only hope. Why are you so important to him, Mondo?"

"Why the hell did you call him?"

"Because I've been taking care of his son for the last four days and somebody bad is after us. I didn't have any other option but to call him. You want to tell me what's going on?"

"I don't know what's going on."

Flick laughed, "That's right man, you don't know me from shit, but listen to what I tell you. Somebody is after Joseph Yazzi. About a month ago they tried to pay him to call his father and tell him not to fight the logging that is going to start around Salmon Creek. Well he told the guy to go to hell. A few weeks later they basically kidnapped him for lack of a nicer word, stuffed him in a cheap hotel and paid me a grand a day to watch him. The whole deal stunk from the beginning but a grand a day well I went for it. A few days later I started to get really bad feelings about it all, and I listen to those feelings. I suddenly understood that we're both going down and it was time to start running and we've been running since."

"You know where Joseph Yazzi is?"

"Yep, we're staying in the same hotel room. He's supposed to be back there by now."

"I need to see him, can you do that?"

"I can but you need to do something for me."

Mondo figured as much.

"What?"

"These people aren't going to go away. Whoever they are they scare the shit out of me. I got to get this figured out and find some way to get them to back off."

"You think I can help?"

"I don't know man, can you?"

"I don't know Flick. I don't know about you and I don't know about the guy earlier today."

Flick picked up on it immediately.

"What guy earlier today?"

"Some guy came in here a few hours before you. He didn't look right if you know what I mean. He walked up to the lady at the door and asked for me, by name. She didn't like him, so she told him she never heard of me. Then he just turned around and stormed out the door."

"You're telling me that in the last two hours somebody else walked in this place and asked for you by name?"

"That's right."

"Oh shit!"

Chapter 29

The headlines of the Vancouver Sun were hard to see in the dim glow of the street light. Joseph Yazzi stumbled past the newsstand, then caught himself and walked back ten feet and read the headlines again. The alcoholic stupor that he had spent the last three hours creating seemed to disappear in a flash. He read the bold headlines again and then stumbled over the finer print.

"Hey buddy they're for sale, it ain't a library," a fat old man hollered at him from behind the counter.

Joseph ignored him and kept reading.

A minute later the fat man got up, walked over and pulled the paper from his hand.

"Listen asshole buy it or screw off, you bum."

Joseph looked up at him and the man was taken back by his tears, and they both stood there for a fleeting second, Joseph too drunk to do much of anything and the newsstand owner shaking his head as he looked from the headlines and back at him.

"What's the problem?" the fat man said, and then he turned his attention to the paper and read the bold headline: LOGGING SOON ON DISPUTED LANDS?

The fat man looked at Joseph and knew that somehow this drunken Indian was shocked by the headlines.

"Here, take it," he said as he handed the paper to Joseph and walked back to his small chair and sat down.

The world was spinning too fast for Joseph to make much sense of it. The paper seemed to have equilibrium of its own as the print danced in front of his eyes. Tears continued to flow making reading even more difficult. Finally he opened the paper, took the front page, folded it up as best as his drunken mind could and crammed it in his back pocket. He left the rest of the paper sitting on the counter and staggered off.

An overwhelming sense of failure hit him as he stumbled down the street. His people needed him, his father needed him, yet his guilt and shame were too strong to overcome. He was a drunken Indian, a disgrace and he knew it. He was as lost to his people and their ways as he was lost in the white man's world. Walking into the first bar he came across he pulled the remaining money he had from his right pants pocket and ordered two beers.

"Shit," Flick said again as he slumped back in the chair and pushed the plate of food away from him. Mondo didn't know what to think. How could anybody in this city know him? Something was going on and it suddenly seemed a lot bigger than simply finding Joseph Yazzi.

"He talked to her?" Flick said as he glanced over at Dawn.

Mondo just nodded.

"Can you get her over here?"

"Yeah."

Mondo looked at Dawn who had been nervously glancing at the two of them. Ever so slightly he waved her over with his index finger. A scared look came over her as she walked up to the table and stood there. Flick looked up and smiled.

"Please sit down. I'm one of the good guys, my name's Flick."

Dawn sat down, not knowing what to expect.

"I've been looking for your friend Mondo, unfortunately it seems somebody else is also. What did the guy say to you?"

Dawn looked at Mondo then back at Flick, were there good guys and bad guys now, she thought? She looked again at Mondo not knowing what to do.

"It's okay Dawn just tell us both what happened."

"Okay, well the guy gave me the creeps the second he walked in the door and I can tell about people you know," she glanced at Flick when she said it then continued. "He seemed really pushy. In a hurry, he didn't even smile when I said hello. He just leaned over and whispered in my ear, he said, I want to talk to Mondo. My first thought was, okay no problem he's right there. But something just made me take a second look at him. The moment we made eye contact he got really mad, grabbed my arm and told me to get him. It was like an order or something. Right then I knew this wasn't good. I told him I didn't know anybody by that name. He looked at me with these really mean eyes, I mean really mean eyes, then turned around and left without a word. I'm not sure he believed me."

She looked at them both and then closed her eyes and sighed gently as she thought about the guy.

"That guy was evil," she said a few moments later.

"Okay so who is this guy and why was he looking for you?" Flick said as he looked at them both.

"I don't have a clue," Mondo said with a sense of apprehension.

"How many people know you're in Vancouver?"

He had already been thinking about that. There was Chief Yazzi, Jonathan, and Naomi. Somehow he couldn't see Albuquerque or Patty having anything to do with this.

"Only three people."

"Only three people, you're kidding. Do you trust them?" Flick asked.

"Yes I do. I trust each of them completely," even though he did have a few doubts about Jonathan, he didn't mention it.

"That doesn't make sense. Who else could be interested in you and why?" he looked at Dawn and Mondo and then shook his head, as if waiting for an explanation.

Dawn looked over at the door and saw that Todd had taken her place.

"I should get back."

She got up and started greeting the last of the stragglers still coming in the door.

Flick and Mondo looked at each other.

"Did you see the guy she's talking about?"

"Yeah, I did."

"What was your take on him?"

"He didn't seem like somebody I'd care to meet. I agree with Dawn there was something wrong with him."

"Here's what I think. I think that somehow they know Chief Yazzi told me to find you. How could anybody know that?"

"There's only one way that I can think of, they listened to your phone call."

A slight smile appeared on Flicks lips for just a second, before it disappeared.

"Mondo that's what I'm thinking. They must have a tap on his line."

"Jesus, who are these people Flick?"

"Well the old man told me two names, Mountain Resources and Michael Jensen. He also told me he thought Michael Jensen was a killer."

"Is that who set you up to watch Joseph?"

"Probably, although I'll never know for sure, but it adds up."

Mondo glanced over at Dawn as she was locking the front door. At least that creep wasn't going to come back tonight.

"You know Flick, why can't we set up some sort of trap for these guys."

"How?"

"Well suppose you call Chief Yazzi again. Tell him you've found us and were all staying in a hotel somewhere, then we stand in the shadows and see if anybody comes rushing in. At least that way we would know for sure if they have his line tapped."

"Not a bad idea. Listen Mondo, I don't know how to get this across to you but we are all running from the same people and they want the same thing, Joseph Yazzi. I've got myself in the way and now they have their sights on me. I have a feeling they have you in their sights too. I hope they don't have Dawn on their radar screen."

"What does she have to do with any of this?"

"Nothing but they don't know that. We sure don't want her involved."

Mondo picked up the way he said we and it set him at ease, he was starting to believe Flick.

"Here's what I think we should do. Joseph and I are staying at this hotel on Harrison, it's called The Rivera. I'm heading back there now. Joseph will be wondering what happened to me. Why don't you come by as soon as you can? You can meet Joseph and we can figure out what the hell we're going to do. By the way, why does the old man want you to find his son? What are you suppose to do once you find him?"

"Bring him back to Salmon Creek."

"Good luck," Flick laughed, "I don't think that will ever happen. He feels like a disgrace to his family and people. I don't think he has enough nerve to ever show his face there again."

"Well, I hope you're wrong."

Flick, stood up and looked down at Mondo.

"The address for the Rivera is 1438 Harrison, room 211. You need to come by tonight man. These people are not going to stop."

Mondo knew Flick was right. At least he was going to find Joseph Yazzi and that seemed like an incredible stroke of luck.

"I'll be there in an hour or so," Mondo said as he stood up.

Flick smiled, walked to the front door. Dawn fumbled with a set of keys and finally let him out then she walked back over to Mondo.

"What's going on, are you in trouble?"

"I don't think so, but you know I trust Flick. Somehow I think he's a straight shooter."

"Be careful."

"You bet."

Mondo felt a sudden need to explain it all to her.

"Listen Dawn, I don't think I can come back here anymore, not for a while anyway. I just can't risk you getting dragged into this," he paused looking at her then he reached out and gently grabbed her right hand and wrapped it in his.

"I don't know if our friendship can go anywhere and I guess it's stupid for me to even think about it, but I want you to know something. I really like you, I have from the moment I first met you."

He didn't have any idea what her reaction was going to be, but he felt a lot better clearing the air.

"Mondo, thanks for being honest, and thanks for trying to keep me out of whatever is going on around here. I really want to be your friend. You seem like such a nice guy, and I have a real hard time meeting nice guys, but you need to know that I'm in love with Jesus and I only have room in my heart for him. So maybe we both worried about something that we didn't have to."

Mondo smiled and she smiled back.

"Can you give me your phone number?"

"Sure let me get my purse."

He followed her over to where she had hung her purse and coat, and watched as she pulled out a pen and a small piece of paper and wrote her phone number down then handed it to him.

"Do you want a ride home?"

He was about to say yes but he changed his mind, he didn't want to get her any more involved than she already was.

"No thanks, but I'm ready to go are you?"

"Yes."

"Well I'll walk you to your car."

"Such a gentleman."

"Todd we're out of here, see you soon," he hollered towards his little office, then they turned and walked out the back door. The moment he closed the door behind him and looked out at the parking area he knew something was wrong. It was much darker than it should be. He looked at where the two flood lights normally shined over the parking lot and both were dark. Something wasn't right, he thought. He put his arm around Dawn and hurried into the darkness.

"Mondo. What's wrong?" she said softly but he didn't reply.

Ten feet from her car he caught a quick movement out of the corner of his eye. He spun to his left and watched as two men walked out from the shadows. One of them was the guy from this afternoon. Mondo grabbed Dawn and pushed her behind him. Both men walked to within five feet of them and stopped. In the dim light of a far away street light Mondo glanced down and saw the pistol pointing right at them.

"You shouldn't tell lies sweetheart," the skinny guy with the gun said as he walked two steps closer and shoved his pistol into Mondo's stomach.

"You're much too sweet to be a good liar."

Chapter 30

The barrel of the pistol was jammed so hard into Mondo's stomach he couldn't take a breath. There was nothing that he could do. He looked at the guy and saw that there was no mercy in his eyes.

"I say we take a little walk, Captain Mondo, you too sweetheart," he said.

"She's got nothing to do with this, just let her drive away," Mondo replied.

"Sorry, I think it's a little late for that now," he said as he pulled the pistol back and motioned with it towards the street.

Mondo took a step, but Dawn didn't move.

"I said you too darling."

"I'm not going anywhere. Don't you know that Jesus loves you? Why are you doing this?"

The man with the gun and his partner both looked at her, then each other and started laughing.

"Well, I'll be Pete, we got a holy roller here," the gunman said still laughing.

"Maybe we should pray for forgiveness, what do you think, Eddie?" his partner said.

Pete was two feet to Mondo's left standing relaxed with his arms at his side. Mondo kept watching the gun, watching every move that it made.

"I'm not leaving," Dawn said defiantly.

"Oh yes you are bitch," Eddie snarled as he took a step closer to her raising the barrel skyward, his right hand cocked to hit her with the side of the pistol. That was the moment Mondo was waiting for. He lunged, grabbed the gunman's downward arcing hand as he threw his body into Dawn knocking her out of the way. Mondo forced the barrel up at the same time bringing his right knee hard into Eddie's groin. The pain was so intense that Eddie's knees started to buckle, his grip on the pistol weakening as he started to fall. Mondo ripped the gun from his hand and was frantically trying to swing the barrel around and grab the handle when Pete came flying out of the darkness and tackled him, sending them both crashing to the ground. The gun flew from his hand and disappeared as it slid under a parked car. Pete landed on top of Mondo and brought his right fist down hard toward Mondo's face. Without even thinking Mondo deflected the punch by slamming his left hand into Pete's right elbow causing his fist to fly past his face and slam into the pavement. Mondo swung his left hand back across his body and hit Pete in the face with the back of his knuckles. The powerful blow staggered him and before he could recover Mondo leaned forward and hit him with a right, sending him flying backwards. Mondo jumped to his feet, spun to his right and kicked the still hunched over Eddie in the face, snapping his head back and sending him crashing to the ground. His head made a sickening noise as it hit the pavement. Pete was trying to get to his feet as Mondo turned and charged him. Just as he stood Mondo landed a powerful blow to his midsection. Pete gasped and started to double over the wind knocked out of him, his lungs making a hollow sucking sound as he tried to catch his breath. Pete was going down and he couldn't stop himself. Mondo brought his right knee up as he grabbed Pete's long hair and pulled his head down smashing it into his knee. Pete's nose shattered into a bloody pulp as he was thrown backwards. He was unconscious before he hit the pavement. Neither man moved. Dawn was trying to get up as Mondo rushed over to her.

"You all right?" he asked.

"God, Mondo," she cried, her voice quaking with fear.

He helped Dawn stand, then he rushed over and knelt down by the parked car trying to find the gun. He couldn't see anything in the darkness. He jumped up, ran around the other side of the car but still couldn't find it anywhere.

"Damn," he shouted then looked over at Dawn as she slowly staggered toward her car. He forgot about the pistol and ran up to her.

"Let's go," he shouted as he reached down and grabbed the driver's door, pulled it open and pushed her into the driver's seat. Running to the other side of the car he saw Eddie lying dangerously close to the left back tire.

"Wait," he hollered as she started the car.

He ran over to Eddie and dragged him out of the way.

"Let's get out of here," he said as he jumped in the car.

Dawn's car burned rubber as she threw it in reverse and backed out of the parking spot. She slammed the car in gear, and hardly slowed down when she raced into traffic causing tires to squeal and horns to blast.

Neither said a word for the first block. Dawn kept glancing in her rear view mirror trying to see if any cars were speeding after them.

"My Sweet Jesus, that was scary," she said, her voice cracking.

"Are you all right?"

"I don't know. I've never had a gun pulled on me. Did you see his face when he was about to hit me, he was crazy."

"Dawn I'm so sorry."

They drove another block in silence, neither being able to understand what the implications of this attack might be.

"These are some pretty bad people aren't they?"

"I think so, and so does Flick. You know Dawn I hate to say this, but I think you're in deep with us now."

"I know Mondo," she said softly.

"Dawn, I am really sorry."

"Now what?"

"We need to find Flick. Tell him what happened and hope to god that he's on our side."

"What if he's not?"

"I don't know, but I think he is. I think he was telling us the truth. He told me he had Joseph Yazzi, and that's who I came to find."

"Do you know where Flick is?"

"Yes I do, he's staying at the Rivera hotel on Harrison street."

She glanced over at him as he sat there watching her drive. There was such sadness in her face and it was the first time he had ever seen it.

"What's wrong, besides, what we just went through," Mondo asked then thought it was a stupid question.

"It's just that he was going to hit me with that gun and drag me away and there was nothing that I could do to stop him. Not even the Lord could have stopped him."

Mondo laughed, "Well you know Dawn, I hate to say it but maybe, just maybe, the Lord," he drug the word Lord out a little, " maybe the Lord used me to stop him, how's that for divine intervention."

She smiled at him then stared back at the road. She didn't say anything for a minute before she glanced over at him. "You know maybe you're right, Captain," she drug Captain out in a cute mocking tone, "you know the lord does work in mysterious ways," she laughed.

They drove until they found Harrison then turned right and started looking for the Rivera.

"I hope we're going the right way," she said.

"Me too, let's drive five or six blocks before we start to worry."

In the next block they both saw the Rivera on the right and Dawn slowed down a little.

"Just keep going, let me check it out," he said. She drove three more blocks then turned to the left, drove half a block and pulled into a parking area for a twenty-four hour grocery store. She pulled to the far back corner and turned her car off.

"This seems as good as any place," he said.

As she started to open her door, he gently put his arm on her shoulder. She turned around and looked into his caring, blue eyes. In that instant her heart went out to him, she wanted to hug him, to kiss him, to tell him that she was falling in love with him, but she knew she never would and it all passed in a fleeting moment.

"Let's do this," he said "you walk twenty or thirty feet in front of me. Don't look back at me, not even once. When you get to the Rivera walk in like you are staying there, don't hesitate, okay."

"All right."

They climbed out of the car and he let her walk ahead before he started following behind her. His mind was spinning with the realization that he had just dragged her into this nightmare.

As he continued walking he found himself thinking more and more about her. What was it that attracted her to him so much? He knew it was her sweet smile and caring heart but there was more and for the life of him he couldn't put his finger on it.

They walked out onto Harrison and turned towards the Rivera. There were a lot of people on the street. More than a few times somebody bumped into her, gave her a scowl and kept walking. He hoped she didn't turn around and he hoped to god that nobody was waiting for them. At the entrance to the hotel Dawn didn't slow down. She pulled her purse to her as she walked up the stairs and looked in it as if she was getting out a key. Perfect he thought.

He followed her in and continued until they were both hidden from the glass doors at the entrance.

"Room 211," he told her.

They found 211 and Mondo knocked. He heard somebody get up and walk over to the door.

"Stand behind me," he told her softly, "and be ready to run if anything happens, all right?"

"All right."

They both heard a chain unlock and then a dead bolt slide back before the door opened and Flick was standing there.

"Come on in," he said as he stuck his head out the door and glanced up and down the hallway.

"Any problems?" Flick asked, as he locked the door behind them.

Mondo and Dawn looked at each other but said nothing. Mondo quickly glanced around the room, then walked into the bathroom and looked around. He reached for the closed shower curtain and pulled it back. There laying in the bathtub covered with puke and passed out to the world was a middle aged Indian.

Mondo walked back out of the bathroom and looked at Flick.

"Joseph Yazzi?" he said as he nodded his head towards the bathroom.

"Yep, Mondo, meet Joseph Yazzi."

Chapter 31

Flicked studied them as they told him their story about the attack in the parking lot. He was watching their eyes as they talked, looking for any sign that might give them away if this was all bogus. What could they possibly gain from such a fabrication, he wondered? Once they finished he didn't say a word, just stared at them trying to make them uncomfortable, using his old trick of trying to trap a liar. Neither of them seemed to have much more to offer. This was going bad so fast Flick couldn't believe it.

"So what do you think we do next?" Flick asked.

Dawn looked at Mondo but didn't say a word. This was so foreign to her that she was absolutely clueless.

"I'm not sure. It was pretty simple when all I had to do was find Joseph and try to get him to go back to Salmon Creek. Now I don't know. Somebody sure turned the dogs loose on us, what do you think Flick?" Mondo said looking at him, returning his stare.

Flick shook his head slightly and let out a deep sigh.

"Well we have to assume that there are a lot of people in Lower Eastside looking for us. One thing in our favor is they probably can't identify you and Dawn, but they sure as hell have pictures of Joseph and me. So that means if anybody has to go out on the street it's the two of you."

"What can we do on the street?" Mondo asked.

"I make all of my calls from pay phones, can't be traced that way and even if they do you are long gone in thirty seconds, so I need you to make a call for me. We're going to need food and we also have to be out of here tomorrow bright and early. So that means a driver, and a place to go."

"My cars just a few blocks from here," Dawn said.

Flick looked at her and thought she wouldn't last five minutes on the street with these people after her.

"Honey, I'm going to assume that they have found your car and somebody is sitting within a hundred feet of it with a cell phone on their lap just waiting for you to show up. No, I think for the moment your car just sits."

"Okay," she said her voice so soft that they barely heard her.

"What about Joseph?" Mondo asked.

"I say he won't cause us any problems until morning when he will have one hell of a hangover and he will be begging us for another drink."

"I need to get him back to Salmon Creek."

"That's your thing Mondo, I just need to keep us alive," Flick replied.

Nobody said a word for the next few minutes, each lost in their private thoughts.

"I just can't stay here forever. I mean I think that maybe I should just walk out, get my car and hope that they don't bother me. I don't know anything about what's going on," Dawn said breaking the silence, her voice echoing her fears.

"That might be okay tomorrow once we're gone from here. But how about for now you hang tight." Flick said not looking at her.

"I have classes, I have a roommate. I can't just disappear! She will call the police. Maybe that's what we should do. Call the police right now," she said as she glanced from Mondo to Flick and back to Mondo.

Flick smiled as he looked at her, she sure was naive he thought.

"That might not be in our best interests. I have a dislike of the police and they really don't think very much of me either."

She looked at Mondo trying to get some support from him.

"Dawn, I think Flick is right, we need to lay low at least until tomorrow. I'm going to go make Flick's call and get some fast food somewhere," he said as he stood up. That was about all that he could think of doing at the moment. This was starting to come down to street survival 101, and he was out of his league.

"Flick, give me the number and tell me what you want me to say."

Flick stood up and walked over to the small table near the television and ripped off the cover of a magazine. He wrote Manny's phone number down and handed the torn cover to Mondo.

"Here's what I want you to tell him. First you say Manny, my watch says it's twelve-thirty-four. Don't forget that Mondo, that's one of our little secret numbers. Then tell him you're with me and we have to run, there's four of us, and we need a driver and a house. Tell him you'll call him back by nine tomorrow morning."

"All right I can do that."

Mondo glanced at Dawn who was still sitting on the bed wearing such a confused look.

"Dawn," Mondo said, "Why don't you come with me, call your roommate. By tomorrow I'm sure your life will be back to normal, but if you're not up for it I can call her for you."

Dawn laughed, "I can just image if you called and told her I'm spending the night somewhere else. She wouldn't believe it. No I think I'll tag along and call myself."

She glanced over at Flick as if asking his permission.

"Just be careful."

"All right, we'll get some fast food somewhere and we'll be back in half an hour," Mondo said.

She stood up and followed him to the door.

"Just be real careful. Make sure nobody follows you back here, all right," Flick said, his nervousness impossible to hide.

Harvey Langdon was furious, and it took all of his self control to keep his mind focused. It should have been so damn easy, and it could have been all over by now. All that Eddie would have had to do was to call him and tell him of his hunch. But that goddamn idiot had to try and be a hero. Well, he got what he deserved. He had a skull fracture and would be in the hospital for a while, hell he might never be the same. At least Pete could get around, but his face was never going to look right.

Harvey wasn't quite sure what to do next. He hated to bring more of his people back into Lower Eastside, but he needed to get this wrapped up now. The fact that Mondo had slipped through his hands was going to come down hard on him even though it wasn't his screw up. Shit he thought, what damn idiots he had working for him. He grabbed his cell phone, punched in the number and waited.

"You might as well bring Grady and his crew back. Have them meet me at Logan's in twenty minutes."

He hung up the phone. At least he had one good break. It hadn't taken his people ten minutes to find out that the woman Mondo left the mission with was a regular volunteer named Dawn Peters. It had taken them even less time to pull up a photo of her from the internet. Now the entire team could identify three of the four people they were after. Only Mondo didn't have a face and he was really starting to intrigue Harvey. Pete told him he must be a black belt or something. Well Harvey laughed, as he put his phone in his pocket, he sure took care of Eddie.

Fifteen minutes later he was seated around a table with four people.

"We are still assuming that Flick and Joseph are in Lower Eastside," he said as he slid a picture of Dawn, along with a description of Mondo to each of them.

"We now have one more face to look for. I also know that she is driving a white 1997 Toyota Camry license plate WCH 732. It's an American plate from Nebraska. We can't assume that Mondo and Dawn have met Flick, but we can't rule it out, so this is how I want it played. You will call me if you have any information, any at all. You let me decide what is important. Also this Mondo guy is a black belt, so be careful. Use a few of your favorite contacts on the street, but we want this kept close to home, I don't want this getting away from us."

He stared at each one of them trying to let the seriousness of this seep into their minds.

"Eddie and Pete screwed this up big time and I don't want any more screw ups people," he said then he stood up and left without another word.

The four remaining people slowly made their way from the restaurant in the next five minutes.

Harvey had another trick up his sleeve that he didn't mention at the meeting. He reported Dawn's Camry stolen. He would let the police do some of the hard work. If they found her car it would be on the radio and he had one of his people monitoring the police frequencies. Yeah, he thought as he drove away let the police do something for once.

It was going to be an awkward phone call and Michael knew it. Having to call Brad Donaldson with bad news wasn't going to be easy anyway he tried to phrase it. He was driving his Mercedes through traffic feeling pissed off that they hadn't found Flick and Joseph, and also thinking about Brad and the problem that he had become. How does one take out a hit man he thought as he pulled up to a red light and waited impatiently? He laughed when the answer came to him.

"Just hire another hit man," he said under his breath.

Probably not, he reconsidered as the light turned green.

No, he reasoned the best way to take him out was to do it himself, nobody else to worry about. He'd done it before and he could do it again, he thought.

With the self assurance that he could handle Brad Donaldson, he flipped open his phone and punched the number to Brad's cell and waited through three rings before it was picked up.

"We are still working on our little problem, sorry, it shouldn't be much longer," he said aware of his breath, keeping his voice calm.

There was a short pause on the line.

"As you know, my time is your time . . . so to speak."

"I understand. I will let you know as soon as I have more information."

"Very well."

He closed his phone and threw it on the seat. This was turning into a disaster and he knew it. It was bad enough when it was just Joseph and Flick that needed Brad's special attention, but now there was this Mondo guy and the woman from the mission. It's too bad for them he thought, but he couldn't leave any loose ends.

Harvey hadn't told him the whole story of who screwed up and let those two get away, but he would find out and they would get the beating of their life. It may be hard to find a killer, but he had plenty of brutes that loved to beat somebody up for a few bucks.

Chapter 32

Out on the street the night was starting to get cold. Mondo pulled his jacket tight and continued walking twenty feet behind Dawn. Their plan was simple. She would lead the way and stop at the second pay phone she saw. It should only take a minute or two for her to call her roommate and let her know that all was well and she wouldn't be coming home tonight. Then Dawn would keep walking until the next pay phone. She would walk past it and stop a short distance away while Mondo made the call for Flick. Then it was onto a burger joint and back to the hotel.

Mondo once again started to let his mind wonder as he walked behind her, wishing he had more of an insight into what made her the way she was. She certainly seemed happy at the mission greeting people, trying to help the homeless, but there had to be more to her. Was her love for Jesus so large that she had no room in her heart for anybody else, he wondered? By focusing on Jesus was she really keeping other people away, a religious barricade to protect her from something, maybe something in her past? She seemed so honest and committed at the mission, the way she reached out to everyone who walked through the door, but that wasn't the real world. At the mission she was reaching out to those who would never try to reach back. What would her reaction be if someone reached out to her, what would she do if somebody fell in love with her?

She stopped at a group of pay phones before he realized it and it brought his thoughts crashing back to the street. He walked thirty feet past her and sat down on a bus stop bench. Mondo watched as she dialed a number and had a short conversation. He laughed to himself as he thought of what her roommate must be thinking. This had to be pretty out of character for her to not come home at night. She hung up and continued walking. On the next block she entered into a convenience store passing a group of phones.

Mondo stopped and dialed the number Flick had given him and repeated his message. After he hung up he kept the phone to his ear while he waited for her to buy whatever she was standing in line for. Watching her through the window as he pretended to talk made him feel funny, like he was a stalker or something. There was a long check-out line and as she finally reached the cashier Mondo was surprised by the young man's reaction. It seemed that for a split moment when he looked up at her he was taken back by surprise. His mouth dropped and he took a step backward, his body language telling Mondo that something had just happened. It was even more chilling when the next moment he turned his back on her and reached for the phone. She stood there nervously grinding her two thumbs behind her back, waiting while the clerk talked on the phone.

He was on the phone for less than thirty seconds, before he turned around and slowly started to help her. Mondo studied the guy and he was definitely taking his time. Suddenly it all came clear to him. This guy recognized her, called somebody and was now stalling as long as he could. Mondo let the phone drop, walked into the store and cut in front of the person standing behind her.

He leaned forward and whispered in her ear, "Time to go," then he grabbed her elbow and steered her toward the door. Once outside they started walking as fast as possible without drawing any attention to themselves.

"What was that about?" she asked.

"I'm just really paranoid. I think that guy recognized you and he called somebody and was stalling for time."

"I think you're right, we need to get out of here," she said with a sense of urgency in her voice.

They rushed down the street and then had to stop and wait for a long light to turn green. As soon as the light changed they were off and almost running down the next block only to be stopped by another red light. A minute or two ticked off while they waited for the light and they were both still very nervous. Suddenly a white van raced around the corner right in front of them going the other way. They both looked at the van and for one second Mondo's eyes met with the drivers, then in the next instant the driver slammed the brakes on and the van slid sideways, cutting across three lanes of traffic and heading right at them.

"Run," Mondo shouted as he grabbed her hand and they started running for their lives. They both heard horns blaring and then the van screech to a halt. Mondo turned to see one man jump out the passenger door and start after them. In the next second the van burned rubber as it turned the corner and started chasing them. Mondo grabbed Dawn's hand tighter and pulled her toward the shadows of a house. They ran down a driveway, past a parked motor home and through a back yard. At a tall fence he stopped, grabbed Dawn and threw her over as she struggled to climb it. He glanced behind him and saw somebody still racing after them. Mondo jumped the fence with ease, his adrenaline pumping, fear driving him on. Dawn was already ten feet in front of him going as fast as she could heading for the front of the house. He caught up with her just as they reached a six foot gate and some garbage cans to his left. Flinging the gate open he turned and grabbed the metal lid from one of the garbage cans.

"Keep running," he whispered to her as he followed her out the gate then jumped to his left and squatted down behind the fence. Dawn was half way across the street when Mondo heard the guy that was chasing after them. Just as their pursuer was about to run out through the open gate Mondo leaped to his feet and hit him in the face with the open side of the garbage can lid. The impact swept the man right off his feet and the gun went flying in the air. Before he hit the ground Mondo lashed out with a kick that slammed him into the fence. Before the man could react, Mondo hit him in the stomach with a punch that was so powerful the man crumpled and didn't move, then Mondo turned and charged after Dawn. She was across the street waiting for him hiding in the darkness between two houses. He reached her and they took off running through another backyard. Again they jumped a fence and kept going.

For twenty minutes they didn't slow down, they just kept running through more backyards and down quiet dark streets. Finally Dawn couldn't go any more.

"I have to stop," she said as she gasped for air.

"This way," he said as he saw a long dark driveway across the street from them. There were no lights on in the house. Slowly they made their way fifteen feet up the driveway and stopped, the glow from the closest street light over ten feet away. Both Mondo and Dawn leaned against a short fence trying to catch their breath, fearing what would happen if a dog started barking or a house light went on.

"Mondo, I think you were right about that clerk, it's the only way they could have found us. How can we go anywhere? We can't!"

He reached out and pulled her close to him, wrapping his arms around her and for a few minutes he didn't say a word. There really was nothing he could say. He had dragged her into this nightmare and he wasn't sure if they would survive the night.

Finally they knew it was time to move. They walked out to the sidewalk and looked around. It was quiet and no cars could be seen as they continued walking, but Mondo was worried, and it just wasn't about a white van anymore. By now there could be ten cars roaming the area searching for them. Any car could be a threat, any parked car they walked past could have a person sitting in it, holding a cell phone, just hoping to see them walk by.

There was another problem Mondo thought of as they walked, and it was that they were completely lost. In their mad dash to escape he hadn't given any thought to where they were heading, and now it was impossible to even guess which direction would bring them back to something they could recognize and use as a landmark. After walking a few more blocks a car suddenly turned down the street they were on three blocks behind them. Before its headlights could flash on them they ran into the nearest yard and dove behind some shrubbery. They lay flat on their stomachs and watched as the car slowly made its way down the street. Nobody would be driving that slow, not even a ninety year old grandmother, Mondo thought. The car was going fifteen miles an hour at best, its headlights casting flashes of brilliance through the dark shadows on the street. The car pulled along side of where they were hiding and kept going. They both rolled over and watched its red lights disappear down the street.

Neither moved, both of them just lay there realizing how dangerous this night had become.

A few minutes later, Mondo was just about to stand and Dawn was already on her knees getting up, when something coming down the street caught his eye. He grabbed Dawn's right wrist and pulled her hard back down to the ground as a minute later another car drove slowly by with its headlights off.

"Smart," he said softly.

The first car was a decoy, and it almost worked. Another minute and they would have been out on the sidewalk totally exposed. The car continued past them until it disappeared out of sight.

"We have to be really careful. We need to keep in the shadows as much as possible," he whispered as he looked at her in the darkness. He promised himself right then that he would see her through this and that nobody would ever hurt her, no matter what it took.

They started walking again, Mondo constantly looking behind him while Dawn kept her eyes glued to the road in front of them.

"Dawn," he whispered," I am completely lost. I have no idea which way to go. Do you?"

"Let's keep walking. I think I'll recognize a street soon."

They walked for three hours, constantly dodging cars until they reached a main street in Lower Eastside. It was close to two o'clock when they finally reached the Rivera. Both of them were exhausted and Dawn was close to tears. They made their way up the stairs and as softly as possible knocked on Flick's door. They stood there for a few minutes, waiting, with no answer. Finally Mondo knocked again and a minute later a door across the hall opened. They both turned at hearing the door to see Flick with a little smirk on his face.

"I thought there might be some trouble, so I switched rooms. Come on in, I guess I was right about the trouble," he said taking one look at them.

Chapter 33

I t was after midnight when Michael climbed into his Mercedes and started out of town. His nervousness was mixed with excitement. This was now another test, one that would force him to overcome his fears, clear his mind of any outside distractions, and focus on what needed to be done.

The act of killing had never been easy for him and he was glad of that. He liked to let others do it for him. Yet, tonight there was no one else he could turn to. Brad Donaldson had become a liability. He knew too many secrets and that was no longer a risk Michael was willing to take. There was no loyalty in this business, every secret had the potential to turn into blackmail or worse.

There was little doubt in his mind that Brad would sell him down the river in a heart beat if he was forced to. No, Michael thought it was time to end their business relationship and there was only one way that this type of business could end. With only one of them walking away. After killing Brad, he figured that taking care of the rest of his problems wouldn't be too hard either.

Michael checked his watch, it was twelve-thirty, he had a few more miles to drive and a few more minutes to focus and get himself under control. Rubbing his right leg against the console he felt the .38 caliber that was tucked tight in its boot holster. It was a very big gamble to bring this gun with him, and it had gone against his instincts, but in the end his mind had overruled his fears. This pistol was incapable of firing, it had been reworked by a trusted gunsmith and it all looked right, but it wouldn't fire. He knew Brad would find this pistol, he was too much of a professional not to.

The gun that he would have to trust tonight was the small .22 caliber Colt that sat on the passenger seat. It was very uncomfortable to wear so he waited as long as possible before he would have to tuck it into the special holster that he made. The holster was nothing more than a jock strap, with a thin strip of foam padding and a piece of Velcro. Michael was amazed at the times he had been patted down by professionals, yet none of them ever checked his balls. Men had a complete phobia about patting down another man's groin. It was the perfect place to stash this little gun.

He turned into the long driveway that led to a nice rambling house sitting peacefully alone surrounded by acres of farm land. Pulling up to the house, he turned the car off and before opening the door, he slid the Colt down his pants. Then he opened the door, the dome light showing anybody that may be looking, that he was alone. He walked up and rang the bell.

Brad opened the door, greeted him with a smile that Michael didn't trust for one second.

"Welcome Michael," he said in that same non-emotional voice of his that had always driven Michael crazy. He wondered if anything ever rattled Brad's cage.

"Care for a drink?" Brad asked.

"Sure, gin and tonic."

"Good, follow me, the bar is this way."

Michael followed Brad down a long hallway that led to open French doors on his left. Just as he walked through the doors into the living room he caught a movement out of his right eye. A big man dressed in black pants and a black turtleneck who must have weighed over two hundred and fifty pounds seemed to come out of nowhere.

"Oh, Michael please excuse John, but he is rather paranoid," Brad said with that same smile.

John walked up to Michael and started patting him down. He ran his hands down his legs and felt the .38 in his boot. Without a word he yanked Michael's boot off and pulled the pistol from its holster. Brad was standing near the bar watching. John brought the gun over and handed it to him before he turned and disappeared down the hallway.

"Michael, I am surprised at you," Brad said.

"I don't like to go anywhere without it, so don't take it personally," Michael said keeping himself completely calm as he walked up to the bar and took the drink out of Brad's hand.

"Now Michael," Brad said as he sat down and motioned for him to sit as well, still playing with the .38, "I do believe you about this gun, I can understand, a man in your business, and all, but really, bringing a weapon to our meeting, that's a little unnerving."

Michael laughed out loud.

"Brad, just forget it. I need to talk to you about my problem. It seems to have grown somewhat out of hand and I hate that fact. So for the moment I would like for you to plan on spending another twenty-four hours here."

"Why did you have to come here to ask me that, why wouldn't a phone call do," Brad asked, his voice now having an edge that Michael hadn't heard earlier.

Michael had asked himself that very question and he had a hard time coming up with a believable answer. This could have easily been taken care of over the phone.

"Well Brad, I wanted to talk you in person. I need to get a sense of what you're thinking and a phone call is just too impersonal for that."

Brad smiled a half smile as he leaned back into the couch and Michael doubted he believed a word of it.

"Michael, I am sorry but I will be leaving tomorrow. I don't like slop and this is about as sloppy as I have ever seen from you. I think it best if we sever our relationship," he said, all the time playing with the .38.

Michael didn't say anything for a few seconds his mind racing with the implications of what Brad had just told him. He suddenly feared that Brad was feeling the same way about him.

"That creates more of a problem for me," he said keeping his voice steady.

"Yes, I think it would, but you see Michael, your problems are not my problems. So what do I care?" he said as he casually twisted the pistol so it was pointing at Michael.

"That's true Brad, and you're right this is getting very sloppy. Still, I would throw in another fifty thousand for you to stay twenty-four hours."

Brad looked at him and it seemed as if each man knew this little game was about to end, a game that only one of them would survive.

"That is very generous of you," he said as he cocked back the pistol and looked to see that a shell was in the chamber.

"Very generous Michael, and I am tempted, but I think not," he said as he suddenly whipped the pistol up, pointed it at Michael and pulled the trigger. In the next two seconds Brad pulled the trigger three times before Michael was able to reach down into his pants pull out the .22 and fire one round that went cleanly through the front of Brad Donaldson's forehead and exited in a bloody mess before striking a large mirror on the far wall and shattering the glass.

Brad was dead before he hit the floor. Michael jumped up ran to the wall next to the French doors and started flipping off the lights. In five seconds he had turned the entire downstairs into darkness, except for the lights that shined from the top of the stairs to his left. Charging back through the French doors he dove down landing hard on the floor, then spun around so his body was in the living room and just his head, arms and the gun lay in the hallway. In what seemed like the next second the upstairs door flew open and John came charging out and down the stairs carrying a small Uzi pistol. Before he could react to the darkness and stop himself he was already half way down the stairs. Michael fired two shots that staggered the big man. John started to bring his Uzi up, but another round sent him down to his knees where he seemed to pause for a moment before tumbling down the remaining few steps. He lay there moaning as a bloody froth bubbled out between his lips. Michael stood up and walked over to him, looked down, then shot him once in the forehead. He turned, walked back into the living room, looked at Brad, and picked up the .38 putting it in his pocket. He grabbed his empty gin and tonic glass and took it to the bar where were he wiped it clean then holding the very bottom of the glass with a towel he set it back on an open shelf with similar glasses.

Michael looked around and felt an incredible eerie silence. It permeated his entire being. His adrenaline was running, filling him with a sense of his invulnerability. He had risen to the occasion, he had taken care of a problem and it filled him with a high that was as close to addiction as he had ever known.

He walked back to John, picked up the Uzi, and started up the stairs. Carefully he checked the entire upstairs, peering into each room, searching any place that somebody could be hiding. There could be no witness.

Satisfied that the upstairs was empty he started walking through the downstairs making his way through the kitchen and another long hallway. At the end were two doors, one on his right and the other on his left. He opened the door on his right to an empty bedroom. When he opened the door on his left a feeling of shock overcame him and he almost gagged. Sitting there huddled on the floor was a naked young woman, probably early twenties he thought. She had been beaten so badly that even her best friends wouldn't recognize her. She had numerous cuts on her arms and legs and her entire body seemed covered with black and blue bruises. The room reeked of vomit and feces. Jesus Christ, he thought that sick bastard. Her hair was a mess, full of caked, dried blood mixed deep into her strawberry blonde curls.

Her eyes were nothing but deep sockets of black and blue, the swelling so large that it almost completely covered her deep blue eyes that stared out at him with a blank emptiness.

She sat on the floor wedged up against the bed, slightly rocking back and forth, as she held her arms tight to her chest and looked up at Michael. He tried for a second to picture her as a beautiful young woman but it was beyond his abilities to see past all of the damage that she had suffered. A tight choke collar with deep metal studs cut into her throat and was connected by a short leash to a metal bed post. Her eyes were fixed on him, her breathing coming in shallow, soft gasps.

Michael walked over and knelt down beside her, reached out and gently pulled her face up towards his.

"I am so sorry," he whispered.

"So sorry," he said again as he gently let her face fall from his hand. Then he stood up and walked back to the doorway. He turned and looked at her one more time, feeling a sense of sadness that surprised him.

"I am so very sorry," he said as he raised the .22 and fired once.

Chapter 34

B y ten-fifteen in the morning they were all laying on the floor of an old ford econoline van feeling every jar and bump that it took with its worn-out suspension. The van was the type that had side windows, so anyone who cared to look would just see an empty, old beater going down the road with a young black driver. Where they were being taken Flick had no idea but he didn't worry. Mahoney had come through again and they would have a safe place to hide.

Mondo kept thinking about last night and how everything had changed the moment they walked out to the parking area and had been confronted by Pete and Eddie. What had been a mission to find one man had now turned into a fight for survival and he had Dawn to worry about as well. Somehow he had to think of a way out, someway to end this so she could get on with her life. There was no way he was going to allow her to become a victim in all of this, no way at all.

He was also hoping for a chance to talk to Joseph, who right now looked like he had a hangover from hell. He was curled in the fetal position at the back of the van and he hadn't said a word to anybody since they woke him up this morning in the bathtub. Mondo wondered what his reaction was going to be when he saw the Cross. Would it somehow snap him out of this drunken stupor that he lived in?

Dawn sat completely lost in her thoughts. Her entire life had just vanished and she couldn't imagine how to get it back. This morning she had seriously thought of telling Mondo and Flick that she was heading to her car and back to her old life. Yet, the helplessness she remembered feeling when Eddie was about to hit her with the gun haunted her. That moment had even shaken the very foundation of her spiritual beliefs. It had stolen something sacred from her and she feared that it might be gone forever. How could she live if she didn't have enough faith to believe in the protecting hand of the Lord? So it was with a heavy heart and a fear of not knowing what else to do that she had finally climbed into the van. She had the rest of the day to think this through and she really did feel better with Mondo close.

They drove for about twenty minutes before coming to a stop. The driver reached down on the seat, hit a garage door opener, and the van pulled into a small one car garage with an overhead light on.

The young driver turned the engine off and said with a laugh, "End of the road, hope you folks enjoyed the trip, tips are greatly appreciated," as the garage door closed behind them.

Joseph was the last to leave the van. Mondo actually had to reach over and push him hard to get him to stir. Finally they all walked into a small utility room with a washer and dryer on their left before walking up two steps into a kitchen.

"Make yourselves at home. I'm leaving the van if you need it. Manny said it's clean so there will be no problems if you are pulled over in it. You're good here for three days. There's a Vancouver city map on the dining table with this house and its address highlighted so you can find your way back," the young black man said as he walked to the front door and left without a backward glance.

"You must owe this Manny guy big time," Mondo said as he looked at Flick.

Flick laughed, walked to the refrigerator and opened it. There was plenty of food for three days.

"Manny and I go way back, and in a way he owes me, will always owe me, but that's a different story. I haven't had to use him in a long time."

"So this isn't a general run of the mill, average day in Flick's life?"

"Hardly."

Dawn was sitting on the sofa looking at the two of them and she hadn't said a word since they walked in the house. Both Mondo and Flick could imagine the turmoil and conflict that was running through her mind. Joseph stood by the utility room doorway, his left hand on the door jam looking completely lost.

Flick closed the refrigerator door holding a quart of milk.

"Joseph, this is Mondo, he's a friend of yours, a friend of your fathers."

Mondo watched him flinch as Flick mentioned his father. The word seemed to cut right through him, and in that instant Mondo realized just how difficult it was going to be to get him to return to Salmon Creek. Joseph just kept standing there like he was waiting for someone to tell him what to do next. Flick walked to a cabinet, opened it and pulled out four bowls then reached into a higher cabinet and brought out a box of cereal.

"Breakfast for all," he said.

They gathered around the kitchen table eating cereal and fruit. It was Dawn that finally broke the silence.

"What now?" she asked casting her glance directly at Flick.

"Dawn, that's a great question," he replied.

Everybody sat there looking at each other, nobody having a clue as what to do next.

Harvey was sitting across from Michael in a small sandwich shop off of Ballard Way. It was dark and they sat in the furthest booth from the door. Michael was in better spirits than Harvey had anticipated. He wasn't sure why and that unknown factor had him nervous, really nervous. It wasn't like Michael to be so casual about something this important, especially when it all went to shit as it did last night.

"Listen Harvey, their probably long gone by now. We need to rethink finding them. Maybe instead of running all over the city we should put your people at the ferries and airports. What I really need is to keep Joseph from getting back to Salmon Creek."

"What about Flick, Mondo and the girl, are we letting them all go?"

Michael leaned back in the booth, ran his fingers through his jet black hair and looked at Harvey.

"No we're not. I'm not letting Joseph go either. I just think it's time to look at our objective again."

Harvey sat waiting for a lecture, but it didn't come. Michael really was acting very strange this morning.

"Listen Harvey, we've been through it with Flick and Joseph and this entire screw-up. We can't keep chasing them. I mean he's just a drunken Indian, right?"

Harvey sat in stunned silence trying to gain a sense of composure as he listened to Michael. Harvey knew that giving up were two words not in Michael's vocabulary, so what was going on?

"What do you think Harvey?" Michael said after a few moments of awkward silence.

"I agree we can't keep chasing them, we had our opportunity," Harvey paused, afraid to ask the thought that had been running through his mind for the last few days.

"You know Michael you never told me what you plan on doing once we find them."

A smile formed on Michael's face, for just a second but Harvey saw it and he didn't like it one bit.

Mondo walked over to where Joseph was on the couch and sat down next to him.

"Your father sent me to find you. He needs you back in Salmon Creek," he said staring into Joseph's face trying to read any emotions that might escape.

Joseph slumped back into the couch, closed his eyes and he let out a deep sigh. His words were slow as if each thought had to be separately processed before being spoken.

"I am dead to my people. There is nothing that I can do."

"Your father doesn't think so."

"My father. My father lives with hopes that are just shadows, it is too late for shadows, and it is too late for hope."

He closed his eyes and rested his head back into the couch.

Mondo stood up and walked into the kitchen where Flick was just finishing drying the dishes. He walked past him, waved his index finger and they both walked out into the garage. Flick closed the door behind them.

"Flick I need to go into town, I have to get something. It's really important. Can you make sure Joseph stays here until I get back?"

"Yeah, no problem," Flick said, wanting to ask more but deciding not to.

"Good, just keep him here. If he decides not to go with me back to Salmon Creek then I've done all I came to do."

Flick looked at him again, and Mondo knew that something was bothering him.

"How does this end for Dawn?" Flick asked.

"I don't know, but we have to make sure it does. I'll be back in an hour. Keep Joseph here and keep him sober."

Flick laughed.

"I can do that."

Fifteen minutes later Mondo was pulling the van into a parking space at the health club.

"Good morning Mondo, come to work out?" Fred the want to be sailor asked.

"No Fred, just grabbing something."

Mondo walked down the stairs to the locker room and to his locker. Nobody was around. He pulled out his key, opened the door and grabbed the dirty canvas bag. He sat down on a bench holding the bag on his lap and thought about all that had transpired since he first heard of Neskiwaii. His thoughts went back to Albuquerque and Patti, to the hundreds of homeless men and women he had seen in the last few days. He realized that he could never look at them the same again. Never would he cast a judgmental glance their way. He felt sad as he thought about the thousands of street people who just couldn't make it in the real world. People who for whatever reason had turned to drugs and alcohol to ease the pain of life. He ended up sitting there for ten minutes just thinking about the homeless, thinking about a hundred different Albuquerque's and Patties. What a sick society he thought that couldn't find some way to reach these people.

t was with extreme apprehension that Mondo climbed out of the van and walked into the house carrying the canvas bag over his right shoulder. Dawn was sitting on the sofa reading a bible she had found while Flick couldn't be seen anywhere. Joseph was staring at the television, lost in a game show that somehow Mondo knew he wasn't the least bit interested in.

"Hi Dawn," he said as he walked into the living room.

She glanced up and gave him a weak smile, then she went back to reading. That smile made Mondo more determined than ever to make sure that when this was all over she would never have to look over her shoulder in fear again.

"Joseph, come here," he said with a hint of authority in his voice.

Joseph glanced at him then over to Dawn. He hesitated for a few seconds before he finally got up from the chair and followed Mondo down the hallway to a bedroom.

"Close the door behind you," he said as Joseph stood at the door with a confused look on his face, "I have something for you from your father."

A panicked look came over Joseph and he stood there for almost a minute before he slowly walked into the room and closed the door behind him.

"Sit down," Mondo motioned to a small chair in front of a desk in the corner.

Mondo was starting to think that Joseph couldn't make a decision by himself if his life depended on it.

"Listen Joseph, listen really, really carefully. Your father sent me to find you, to give you something. Well, after one day on the streets I thought it would be impossible. Maybe your father's magic is more powerful than I thought . . . I don't know. I just want you to understand. I never met your father until a week ago, and yet he believes beyond a doubt that his gods brought me to Salmon Creek, so I could bring this to you. What I want you to know is that your people need you. Your father needs you. They are going to start logging and your father and your people are going to fight them. Joseph, do you understand? They need you there."

Mondo stood up and walked over to him and dropped the bag on his lap.

"He told me to give you this, so here it is."

Mondo walked back to the bed and sat down, never talking his eyes from Joseph, who reached up with trembling hands and grabbed the canvas bag. He brought his eyes up and stared at Mondo.

"Just open it."

Joseph opened the bag and he brought out the Cross still covered in cheap burlap. His hands were shaking so much he almost couldn't control them as he carefully started to unwrap the relic. Slowly the burlap fell to his lap, and in the next second his body shook a violent spasm as if it was going into an epileptic fit, his breath escaping from him in a deep gasp. Tears started to form before bursting into a cascade of uncontrollable sobs. Joseph bent over at the waist clutching the Cross to his chest, sobbing, his body shaking to the point of almost convulsions.

Mondo stood up and walked out of the room. Whatever demons Joseph had to face, he had to face them by himself.

Dawn looked up and watched Mondo as he walked into the living room. She smiled slightly and put the bible down on her lap, staring at him with a questioning gaze. He sat down next to her, gently grabbed her right hand and wrapped it in his. So many thoughts ran through his mind as he sat there.

"Is everything alright with Joseph?" she asked as they both could hear his sobbing.

"I doubt it. But I think . . . I hope anyway that it is a new beginning for him."

His heart went out to her as he looked into her face. This woman who just wanted to serve people in the name of the lord, and who was now hiding from evil men who would track her down and never let her be. He knew he could never let that happen.

"You know Dawn I am so sorry that you are swept up in all of this. I promise you that before I leave, before we say goodbye, I will make sure that you never have to worry about these people. I promise you."

Then he reached over, brushed her hair back from her face and gave her a gentle kiss behind her ear. She looked at him surprised as if this token kiss was so unexpected, then she reached out and gently brought Mondo's lips to hers and kissed him with passion that she could no longer hide from him.

She drew away from the kiss and brought her eyes down to the bible sitting on her lap. Mondo was so surprised that he didn't know what to say. They both sat there for a minute, neither speaking, each lost in the magic of what had just happened, lost in the beauty of a simple kiss.

"Dawn, you really are such a wonderful person."

"Shut up Mondo, or I'll start believing you," she said with a laugh.

She looked at him and there was so much she wanted to tell him, but instead the awkward silence continued.

"Tell me about your religion will you?" he asked a few moments later, trying to break the silence.

He saw the fear and confusion she felt, then with a sigh she settled back into the couch, turned her eyes away from him and sat for a few moments as if gathering her thoughts.

"I don't know what to tell you, where to start. I certainly don't want to get into my whole life story. I guess you just need to know that when I asked Jesus into my heart and he accepted I felt a new purpose, a new peace, and a new direction in my life. I . . . honestly . . . at times, I have been so afraid of losing that. I have had to force myself to believe when it didn't seem as real as it should. There are times when emotions rule my life and then there are times of clarity where it all seems so real and understandable. I don't know Mondo, but I somehow think that if I didn't have faith I wouldn't have a thing worth living for."

He sat on the couch still holding her hand, feeling closer to her at this moment than he ever dreamt he would. She was really not much different than him, he realized. Maybe not much different than many of the street people he had seen the last week. Religion had become her way of dealing with a world that was out of control and seemed to be going in a direction that had little meaning for her. He saw a little tear and he let go of her hand and wiped it from her face.

"Why the tears Dawn?" he asked in a soft voice.

She shook her head as if she didn't really know herself, then another tear and before she could stop tears began streaming down her face. Mondo reached over and pulled her to him holding her tight, wrapping her in the comfort of his embrace. Dawn spent the next five minutes just letting it all out. The frustration, the pain, the years of self doubt, all flooded from her as she sat in his arms. He didn't say a word the entire time.

Finally she pulled away and sat up, wiped her eyes and laughed.

"Boy, you must think I'm a basket case," she said.

Mondo smiled, looked into her bright blue eyes.

"In all honesty, I think you are about the most wonderful woman I have ever met."

She reached out and brought his lips to hers once again. She kissed him with such passion, passion that she never knew she was capable of. Her kiss was filled with a deep longing for a love that she had never allowed herself to feel, never allowed herself to believe in. Mondo gave himself completely to her, losing himself again in the beauty of her kiss.

When she finally brought her lips from his he saw such honesty, such vulnerability. Then she stood up without a word and walked to the bathroom, leaving a stunned Mondo without a clue as to what really just happened.

A few minutes later Joseph walked out of the bedroom holding the canvas bag with the top of the Cross sticking out. He walked over and stood in front of Mondo for a minute, not saying a word before he sat down on the floor.

"I am going to return to my father, I would like your help," he said.

"Joseph that would be my pleasure."

"I am ready, when you think the time is right."

"Soon."

Slowly Joseph pulled the relic out from the bag and held it up.

He cast his glance from Mondo, to the Cross and then to Mondo again. Slowly, as if each word could not be rushed, as if the meaning was too important he said, "I pledge to you, to my father and to this most sacred gift that I will never taste a drink of alcohol again. Never will I allow myself to be poisoned by what I despise, by what I now forsake. I do this for my people, for my father and for myself."

Mondo couldn't help it, the sincerity of what Joseph had just said, a statement that would change his life forever was just too powerful. Mondo burst into tears, the emotions of this morning just too much for him.

Chapter 36

Mondo was still sitting on the sofa and Joseph was staring out the window, his heart already back in Salmon Creek, when Dawn walked back into the living room.

She glanced at Joseph but didn't say anything as she sat down next to Mondo.

"Feel better?" Mondo asked her.

She smiled, shrugged her shoulders, and gave him a half-hearted smile.

"I guess," she said then looked at Joseph and softly called his name.

"Yes."

"Are you alright?"

Joseph smiled and looked at her with a long penetrating gaze, "I am fine. I am going home soon."

"That means you're both heading back to Vancouver Island?" she asked, her voice betraying her apprehension about Mondo leaving, as she looked at him.

"I'm not sure if it's today, but we are heading back there soon. Does anybody know where Flick went?" Mondo asked.

"Oh, sorry, he told me to tell you he was heading somewhere, somebody came and picked him up. He wrote a number down. It's by the phone if you want to call him."

Mondo stood up, walked to the phone and dialed it.

"Flick, it's Mondo."

"How is everything there?"

"Pretty good, we need to talk. I'm ready to take Joseph and head for Salmon Creek."

"Well that's good . . . but what about Dawn?"

"That's why we need to talk. I've got to put an end to this before I leave. Remember when we talked about setting a little surprise for some of our friends, I think we need to do that."

"Actually Mondo that's why I'm not there, I've been putting the pieces together. I'm getting a ride back to the house. I'll be there in an hour and I'll tell you what I have been thinking about."

"Great see you then."

An hour later Mondo and Flick were standing in the garage next to the old beater van.

"It's the only way that we can ever put an end to this," Flick said as he and Mondo stood close to each other and talked in whispers.

"You might be right, but it's pretty risky."

"Yeah it is, but we need to flush this Michael Jensen and his people out into the open. We need to get across to them that it's over as far as we are concerned."

"Well, I can't think of a better plan."

"Good, then it's time we move."

Mondo walked back into the house, while Flick opened the garage door and then climbed into the van and started the engine. A minute later Dawn and Joseph followed Mondo out of the house and they all climbed in, Joseph still holding the canvas bag close to his chest. Once they were all inside Flick turned around and gave them a smile. "One more new place, after tonight I think we'll be able to do whatever we want without worrying whose after us," then he backed out of the garage, hit the automatic door button and drove away.

At six-fifteen that evening Harvey Logan's cell phone rang.

"Yeah," he said in a curt voice. He had been bothered all day by his meeting with Michael and he just couldn't shake the feeling that something wasn't right, that somehow the game had changed and he was the last to know about it.

"We've just recorded another call to the old man. We know where they are hiding."

Harvey listened for another minute and then hung up. He pulled his car over into a Denny's parking lot, closed his eyes and took a deep breath. Now what, he asked himself, although it seemed obvious. There was nothing he could do but call Michael. However, he did have one other choice, and right now it seemed the smartest thing that he could ever do. Get on the freeway, head east and never look back.

He punched in Michael's number and waited for him to answer. Instead of hearing Michael the phone rang through to his voice message. After listening to the short recording Harvey said, "We've located them and they are all together. They will be there tonight . . . it's your call."

Hanging up, he threw the phone on the passenger seat feeling completely drained by this entire ordeal. What should have been so easy had turned into a nightmare and it was still far from being contained.

He pulled out of Denny's and started driving home, all the time thinking that whatever Michael wanted from him he was going to have to do, he had no choice. Michael scared the hell out of him too much to do anything else.

Harvey was trying to unlock his front door when his cell phone started ringing. He cursed to himself, opened the door and threw his jacket on the dining table before glancing at the phone and seeing it was Michael calling him. He damn near let the call go to voice mail but he knew he couldn't.

"Michael," he said with a confidence in his voice that he didn't feel.

"Where are they?"

"They are down by the waterfront. They're staying in one of the old Matson liner warehouses, near Front Street. I think there are some old living quarters upstairs and that's where they are."

"You think, Harvey or you know?"

"Michael, we just listened in on Mondo's call to the old man. He said he found Joseph and that for right now they were all safe and staying in the Matson warehouses, so that's about all I do know."

Michael thought it through as he took a sip of Scotch and sat back on the leather sofa in his office.

"Okay let's do this. Get one of your people down there and have him locate exactly where they are staying. Once that is established, let me know and we will get a small team and we'll go pay them a visit. I want your most trusted people on this one, understand?"

"Why?" Harvey was surprised that he had the nerve to ask the question.

Michael was silent for a moment and that made Harvey even more uncomfortable.

"Listen Harvey don't ask me any damn questions, just get me three of your best people, have one of them check it out and call me when you have established contact."

Harvey's phone went dead and he threw it across the room where it bounced off the wall and landed on the carpet. He damn well knew why Michael wanted his most trusted people. He was going to kill them all and he didn't want to have to worry about who else knew about it. Harvey walked to the front window and looked at his silver Audi parked in the driveway. He knew he should climb in the car, and head east, damn he was screwed either way, and he knew it.

The old Matson buildings were huge. Once these warehouses had been part of a very busy waterfront complex. Freighters that traveled the world had been loaded and unloaded out of the three warehouses that made up the Matson waterfront complex. Now it was an empty ghost of itself, abandoned when the Port of Vancouver established its new facilities three miles away. All ocean goods were now transported in containers and the Matson property was left to rust. Every once in a while there would be talk of tearing it all down and rebuilding it with offices and condo's, turning the eyesore of old warehouses into a trendy new waterfront community, but for the present the three warehouses and all the land around it stood forlorn and deserted, a grim reminder of progress and the casualties that it leaves behind. A six foot chain link fence surrounded the complex and a small building at the far north corner housed the caretaker who just happened to be good friends with Matthew Mahoney.

The front gate was unlocked when the van pulled up to it and they drove through, then parked in front of warehouse number three. This warehouse had a large crew dormitory on the second level. There was also a small third story apartment that was for the captains and officers, and it was still comfortably furnished.

Flick walked back, locked the gate and then they all went inside. Mahoney already had four of his best people hidden in the miles of scaffolding and over head walkways that made up the ceiling of the warehouse. Huge rusted cranes and rails with large pulleys and long chains still hung in mute testimony to the heavy loads that once moved so easily in and out of this warehouse. Mahoney's people had spread themselves out, taking up positions that gave them a clear line of sight of anybody who walked through the front door. The ground level of the warehouse was empty and anyone who walked inside would have nothing to hide behind, nowhere to run. Each of Mahoney's people had a high powered hunting rifle and now they waited patiently.

Mondo, Flick, Dawn and Joseph settled in for one more night on the run. They kept the lights on and made no effort to keep away from the windows. They had set the trap, now it was time to wait and let the hunters come to them.

Chapter 37

Harvey gave Michael a little smile a moment after Flick walked by the second story window.

"Okay, Michael, they're all there. Flick was the last we needed to I.D. It's your call," he said, feeling worse by the minute. Being an accomplice to murder was something he didn't take lightly.

Two other people that Michael had never met before were standing next to Harvey. One was a very attractive woman in her early thirties. The other was a large black man who looked like he should have played professional football. Michael wondered why Harvey had picked these two from all of the people he used. Well, that didn't really matter he thought a moment later, as he looked at the woman again. Depending on how this all came down he might get to know her a little better. He was thinking of finding a replacement for Harvey and it might as well be someone he could screw.

Michael glanced at his watch and hit the illumination button; it was nine-thirty-five. He looked at his people and saw that only Harvey wasn't carrying a gun. Michael had his favorite 9 millimeter in his shoulder holster. The woman was carrying a small Uzi, and the black man had a sawed-off shotgun in his right hand and a large bolt cutter in his left. They had more than enough firepower for what he intended.

"Let's go," Michael said, and they started across the street. They kept themselves in the shadows and had no trouble getting to the gate. It was locked as expected. The black man handed his shotgun to the woman, then brought the bolt cutters up to the large padlock and cut through it with ease. He reached around, unhooked the chain, and swung the gate open. Once they were inside he wrapped the chain around the gate and inserted the lock back through the chain. Unless somebody looked very closely, it all looked right.

They continued to walk, keeping themselves hidden until they were next to the door of warehouse number three.

"Listen, people, I want this clean, you just follow my lead," Michael said as he looked at each of them. When his eyes met Harvey's he noticed the fear in them, and Harvey didn't hold his gaze for more than a second before he looked away. Poor Harvey, Michael thought, you have been so useful.

Michael twisted the door handle. It was locked. Reaching into his jacket pocket he pulled out a small metal can three inches high and an inch wide. After removing the lid, he unhooked a small tube that was taped on the side and carefully screwed it into the short nozzle that extended from the top of the can. Glancing around at the three of them he shook his head back and they each took a few steps away. He inserted the tube into the keyway and pulled the trigger and a steady stream of foamy liquid ran into the lock before overflowing and running down the door. Michael reached into his pants pocket and pulled out a lighter. Taking a step back, he flicked the lighter open and held the small flame to the bottom of the foam which by now had dried to a thick paste. The foam instantly ignited and burned its way up the door and into the lock. A thin stream of gray smoke appeared before it turned into a flame, in the next second it suddenly shot out from the lock as if it was connected to a blow torch. In twenty seconds the flame died out and the handle glowed a dull red. Michael kicked the lock, and the door swung open.

"Leave the bolt cutter, we'll pick it up when we're done," Michael whispered, not looking at the black man. Carefully they walked into the dark warehouse closing the door behind them.

In the far corner to their left they could see a set of stairs in the dim glow of a light coming from above. Michael, holding his .9 millimeter led the way as they started across the empty floor. They were seventy-five feet into the warehouse, about half-way across, when all the over-head lights came on in one blinding flash.

"Move and you're all dead," they heard a voice from somewhere.

Their eyes had become so adjusted to the darkness that it was impossible to keep them open.

"Drop the guns now!" somebody shouted.

Michael and the woman dropped their weapons but there was a moment's hesitation from the black man. The sound of rifles cocking echoed through the empty warehouse.

"I said drop it, asshole!" the voice bouncing off the empty walls.

The shotgun fell to the floor. All four stood there knowing they had been set up and had walked into a trap.

Matthew Mahoney walked down the stairs, wearing a fake beard, his hair dyed black. It would be impossible for them to ever identify him. Carrying a shotgun he slowly walked toward them.

"I think you're looking for some dear friends of mine. I don't like that, and they don't like it either. They're sick of running from you so I'm just going to kill you four right now. What do you think about that?" he said.

Nobody said a word as he stopped ten feet in front of them. Not even Michael had a thing to say, but Harvey definitely was as good as dead if they ever got out of here alive.

Slowly Flick and Mondo walked down the stairs then over to Mahoney. Mondo carrying a roll of duct tape and Flick a small digital camera.

"I've got enough rifles pointing at your heads to blow each of you away in about one second," Mahoney said, an evil smile on his face.

"Now, I don't really give a shit who kills you. I don't give a shit which way it comes down. I just have to make sure that you don't bother my friends ever again, you understand?" he said as he walked a few feet closer and stared into each of their faces. Three of them were scared to death, but the man who was leading them across the room when the lights went on looked back at Mahoney with eyes that held no fear, only rage at being so stupid. This one, Mahoney knew, was a killer, and he also knew he would never back off. Mahoney took another step forward then smashed the butt of the shotgun into Michael's stomach. It happened so fast that Michael couldn't do a thing. He doubled over and fell to his knees as a huge gasp flew from his lips. Mahoney kicked him in the chest, sending him crashing to the concrete floor. He took his eyes from Michael and stared at the others.

"I'm not like you people. I don't enjoy killing, but you see they're my friends you're after," he said, then he looked down at Michael who moaned on the floor.

"So tell me, if I don't kill you, how do I know that you will leave my friends alone?" He left the sentence hang out there as if maybe there were another way for this evening to end.

"How about we just turn around and never look back?" Harvey managed to say, even though he was scared to death.

Mahoney looked at him and laughed. "Just like that, you give me your word and all is well. What the fuck do you think, man? How do I know you don't come after all of us, this shit will!" he said as he looked back at Michael, then kicked him again.

None of them said a word, as a smile started to grow on Mahoney's face, then he chuckled softly.

"I have an idea," he said as he pointed the shotgun at the black man.

"Take your clothes off, asshole."

The black man was so afraid he didn't hesitate and a few seconds later he stood there naked, his clothes in a pile at his feet.

Mahoney glanced at Harvey, then at the woman.

"Both of you, off with your clothes, now!"

Mahoney looked at Michael and put the barrel of the shotgun an inch from his head. "I still don't know what to do with this asshole, tell me what's his name?" he said as he looked at Harvey.

"Michael Jensen."

"So this is Michael Jensen. I should have known," Mahoney said.

He pointed the shotgun back at the black man, then looked over at Mondo and gave him a nod.

Mondo walked up to the black man and quickly started wrapping him in duct tape, locking his arms and legs tight to his body. After ten wraps Mondo shoved him over and he hit the ground with a groan. He wrapped Harvey in duct tape as well before pushing him over. He felt like a shit when he started wrapping the woman in duct tape but he knew she could kill them all just as easy. Soon all three were lying naked on the cold concrete floor with so much duct tape wrapped around them they could hardly move.

Michael was lying on his back with his legs pulled tight to his chest, trying to get his breath back.

"Take your clothes off, asshole," Mahoney said putting the barrel back to Michael's face.

There was nothing that Michael could do and slowly he took his clothes off.

Mondo walked over and wrapped Michael in tape like the others.

"Come on down people," Mahoney shouted.

Four men appeared in the overhead darkness and started climbing down.

"Thanks, I'll catch up with you guys later," Mahoney said as they reached the main floor. The four walked out the door without a backward glance.

Flick walked over to the four naked people on the floor. He pulled his digital camera out and started taking pictures of them, getting close-ups, capturing the fear on their faces. Even Michael was now scared to death.

"The way I see it is this. If I let you live, and if you ever come close to my friends, these pictures are going to be on the internet so fast you won't believe it. I'll put these pictures on places that you don't even know exist. The whole world will see you like this. Then I will personally hunt you down and kill each one of you, got it? If you live tonight, you walk away and never, I mean never, look for my friends again, or so help me God . . ." Mahoney said, not finishing his sentence.

Mondo glanced behind him and saw Joseph and Dawn standing at the bottom of the stairs watching. His heart went out to them. They shouldn't have to witness this brutality, but there was no other way. He waved them over and soon all four of them were standing next to Mahoney, staring down at the duct-taped killers. Mahoney reached into his pants pocket and pulled out a small pocket knife. He held it for everybody to see, then threw it across the floor were it landed about forty feet away.

"Start crawling," Mahoney said.

Then they all walked out of warehouse number three.

Chapter 38

The beat-up old van carrying the four of them drove into the twenty-four hour grocery store parking lot a little after midnight. Mondo was driving and he pulled up to where Dawn had left her car, but it wasn't there. Sitting in the space was a big truck.

"Your car's gone," he said.

"What!" she exclaimed as she sat up on her knees and looked out the front window.

"Shit! Sorry. My car can't be gone!"

"Well, it is," Mondo said as he pulled the van into a vacant spot a few parking spaces away.

They all climbed out and stood there wondering what had happened to her car.

"It must have got towed," Joseph said.

"Towed? Why, I wasn't parked that long, was I?" she asked, looking at Mondo as if he had any clue how long was too long.

"You probably did get towed, Dawn. Sorry," Flick said as he walked about ten feet to his right and stopped before a small sign attached to a fence near the dumpster. The sign read Andy's Towing Service and a phone number was written in bold letters.

"I'll call him," Flick said as he pulled out his cell phone.

A few minutes later he walked back to where they were standing.

"Yep, it's at the police station. Your car was reported stolen and when the cops found it they towed it."

"Stolen, how could that have happened?" Dawn asked.

"Probably our friends that were looking for us, I bet they reported it stolen trying to track you down," Mondo said.

"Now what?" she said as she slumped against the side of the van.

"No problem," Flick said as he punched some more numbers on his cell phone.

He looked at them as he was waiting for his call to go through, and said, "The guy from the towing company gave me impounds number, hang on . . . yes, my girlfriend's car was reported stolen and you guys towed it. Well, it never was stolen in the first place, so how do we get it back?"

He listened for a few minutes, then hung up and looked at Dawn.

"It's at 6th and Broward at the police station. You can get it in the morning. Bring your I.D. and a check for two hundred dollars."

"Two hundred dollars!" she exclaimed. "I don't have that much."

Mondo put his arms around her. "There is nothing we can do tonight. I'll loan you the money. We can drop you off at your apartment now or if you come back to the house I can give you a ride in the morning."

"Two hundred dollars, God, I'll be broke." She seemed to have not heard Mondo's offer of the loan.

"Let's get in the van and head back to the house. We can deal with this stuff tomorrow," Flick said as he climbed in the driver's seat.

"Dawn, what do you want to do?" Mondo asked her.

She stood there, uncertain, trying not to listen to her feelings. One part of her wanted to say goodbye to everyone, head home and get on with her life, but she hesitated because, in her heart, she wasn't quite ready to say goodbye to Mondo.

"I'll go with you guys. You can give me a ride tomorrow, Mondo?"

"It would be my pleasure," he replied with a smile.

It took the black man over thirty minutes to roll to the knife. He finally freed his hands and feet, then stood up and started ripping duct tape from his body feeling the sting of each piece. Once he was finished he walked over to the others.

"Cut me out of here," Michael screamed, he had been humiliated and made such a fool, and Harvey would pay for it.

"Shut up," the black man threatened. "Your fucking crazy idea. I ought to kick the shit out of you," he said as he stared down at Michael, who suddenly became very quiet.

The black man walked over and knelt down next to the woman, smiled at her and ran his fingers over her exposed skin.

"Tell me, sweetheart, you ever had a black man before?"

She didn't say a word just looked at him, feeling very helpless.

"I asked you a question, bitch," he said, his voice suddenly very threatening.

"Jesus, Jackson, leave her alone," Harvey shouted.

"Go to hell, Harvey. It seems none of you are in a position to say much, are you?"

Jackson took the knife and started cutting the duct tape around her legs. He stopped cutting at her waist, then slowly ripped the tape from her skin, hoping to see some grimace of pain on her face. She didn't show any.

"Listen, Jackson, I said leave her alone, she's special, got it? You mess with her and you'll be looking over your shoulder for me for one hell of a long time," Harvey said with enough anger in his voice that it pulled Jackson back to reality.

The big black man stood up, walked over to Harvey and looked down at him.

"You threatening me, Harvey?"

"You're goddamn right I am. You touch her and you might as well kill me because I'll be coming after you. Is she really worth it?"

Jackson stood there for a minute glancing back at the woman then looking at Harvey.

"No, Harvey she ain't worth it," he said as he threw the knife down, got dressed, and walked out the door.

Harvey rolled over, grabbed the knife, and slowly worked the blade around until he was able to start cutting through his bonds. After a few minutes he walked over to the woman and cut her free.

"Thanks, Harvey," she said softly.

"No worries."

Once Harvey and the woman were dressed, they both stopped at the same time and glance down at Michael.

"Goddamn it, cut me out of here," Michael shouted at them.

Harvey still held the knife as he looked down at Michael, and he knew he didn't want a damn thing more to do with him.

"Go to hell," he said as he threw the knife across the floor, then he turned and putting his arm around the woman they both walked out of the warehouse.

The runaround at the police station the next morning took over an hour, and both Dawn and Mondo were very frustrated by the time a policeman pulled her car around to the front parking area and told them they could leave. Mondo followed her and walked up to the driver's door as she started to open it. She hesitated once she got the door opened and in that moment she realized this really was goodbye.

"Mondo, I guess our paths are going separate directions today. I . . . I'll miss you," she said as she quickly glanced up into his big blue eyes and saw the sadness on his face.

"Dawn, you really are special to me. I don't want to lose track of you. We can keep in touch, we can email, something, I don't know . . . I just don't want it to end today."

She stood there in a silence that very quickly became uncomfortable for both of them.

"Mondo, listen to me," she said as she reached out and wrapped her hands around his.

"I can't see you any more. I'm not going to email you. I don't want to keep thinking about you, I can't," her voice very soft, as she brushed a tear away with her right hand.

"Dawn, why?"

"Why, Mondo? Because I have never met a man like you before that's why. I've never felt what I feel for you," she said as she turned away, letting go of his hand.

"Because, Mondo, I love you. Don't ask me why, or how, because I don't understand it. I don't know . . . it's stupid. I don't even know when . . . but I love you, and I can't do that. I don't know how to do that. Do you understand me? I don't know how to love you. You need to walk back to the van, drive away and never look for me . . . you need to forget me . . . please," her words cutting him to the core.

"I don't think I can forget you."

"Please, Mondo." She was crying hard now, tears streaming down her face.

Looking at her brought a flood of emotions over him and his tears just started. He suddenly realized how much he cared for her, how much she meant to him, how these last few days of worrying about her safety had caused him to fall in love with her. He didn't want to lose her, not now, not today, not ever. He closed his eyes and tried to catch his breath as he slowly stepped back from her car.

"You're sure about this?"

"No," she managed to say in-between sobs, and then she climbed in her car, slammed the door shut and pulled away into traffic.

The drive back to the safe house was one of the saddest times that he could ever remember. He kept reliving that moment when she drove away and he lost sight of her car. Just like that, she was gone and he would never see her again. His heart ached and he wished to God he had chased after her or done something, anything.

He pulled up to the house but didn't bother opening the garage door. Jumping out of the van he knew that he would have to force the heartache away, deal with Joseph and get them both back to Salmon Creek. Mondo walked up to the front door and knocked twice, then waited. It took only a few seconds before Flick opened the door.

Joseph was standing in the living room holding the canvas bag and Mondo thought that he probably hadn't let it out of his sight since they got back to the house late last night.

"You ready, Joseph?"

"Yes, I am ready."

Mondo looked at Flick and gave him a weak smile.

"What are you going to do now that this is over?"

"I think I'm headin' to Montreal, got a friend to look up," he said with a smile.

"Take care, Flick, you're a good man," Mondo said as he extended his hand.

"Same goes for you, and I just want to say if it was me, I'd keep in touch with Dawn. There's more to her than you might realize."

"Thanks," Mondo replied. Flick's comment cut his heart wide open.

"You want a ride to the ferry?" Flick asked.

"Yeah."

Mondo walked past Flick, down to the bedroom and grabbed his duffle bag. He turned and walked into the hallway, then glanced into the other bedroom that Dawn had slept in. It turned a knife in his heart and his thoughts went back to the kiss and the shared tears on the couch yesterday, and with a sickening feeling he understood that it was over. She was gone and he would never see her again.

Chapter 39

The dirt bike slowly made its way up the steep, rutty remains of the six mile long service road. The driver had to swerve around fallen logs and make his way through washed-out ravines and other obstacles as he carefully picked his way along what was now barely a trail. He hadn't been up here in years, and Billy would never take his bike up here for fun, it was too rough. At times the bike barely had enough speed to keep himself and his passenger from falling over as it continued to make its way through mud, limbs and other debris. But Billy wouldn't fail, not with Chief Yazzi on the back. The old service road was the only way to get to the top of the mountain range that separated Salmon Creek from Swartz Bay and the barge.

Fear had swept through Chief Yazzi when he learned that the Provincial Government had decided to take back the disputed land issue from the courts. In one day, years of effort had been erased, and he and his people knew that logging was now certain. With the barge already in place there was very little time to find a strategy to fight back with.

Now it was up to Billy to bring the old man up to Bald Mountain so he could look out over his ancestral lands, lands that the government now called the Killiatt Wilderness area. He knew that others would be following him soon. Twelve more dirt bikes would soon be scrambling over this road, each carrying a respected elder.

It promised to be a nice day and the sun was already warming the air when the bike reached the top. Billy pulled over and kicked his feet out to support the bike as his passenger slowly climbed off.

"You are a good driver, Billy. Go back, I'll be fine." Chief Yazzi said as he waved goodbye and started walking the short distance to the vista point that would let him see clearly for miles to the south.

He was looking forward to this time alone, a time of solitude that he so desperately needed. There had been so much confusion from the moment the attorneys in Victoria had called with a warning of the government mandate that would soon open up disputed lands to logging.

As he sat watching the world around him, the peace of the forest called out to his weary soul. He needed to be here, needed to taste the air, to hear the silence of the forest, to see the majestic glory of what he would soon fight for. This would be his last battle he knew, and maybe his most important. If logging was allowed to start here, it would not stop. He thought about the giant redwood trees of Northern California and felt a growing sadness. Over ninety-five percent of one of the most majestic trees ever to grow on earth had been cut down and forgotten.

As he gazed out over the Killiatt, a land owned by his people since the beginning of time, he knew he would fight and if it took his life, then so be it. It would make a great newspaper headline he thought with a laugh: CHIEF RUN OVER BY LOGGER'S BULLDOZER. There was no doubt in his mind that he was ready to die if necessary, but could he force his son to pay that price as well? He knew that if he fought Mountain Resources they would kill Joseph. They had told him as much and he didn't doubt them at all. This was the unbearable pain that he suffered with. His son had been found, he was still alive, but for how long? Yet he knew there was nothing he could do for Joseph. It wasn't even a decision that he could make. If only it was that easy. As much as he loved his son, this logging must be fought. If Joseph could not be saved, then maybe his blood would be the first to fall in this battle.

He sat down on a large rock outcropping and brought the binoculars to his eyes. The barge was pulled up to the beach. This ugly monstrosity of human achievement was anchored close enough to allow a large landing ramp to extend out from its deck to the sand. On the sandy beach, from the end of the ramp up to the solid ground some twenty feet away, was stretched some type of

227

temporary roadway that had already enabled one big bulldozer to be off-loaded. There was a flurry of activity as he looked through the binoculars. Small aluminum workboats hurried between the barge and the small dock that was already built on shore. This was the beginning of a war. The enemy was establishing a beachhead and the fighting would start soon, he knew.

He closed his eyes and lost track of time, the silence of the forest filling him as if it were the sweetest music he had ever heard. When he finally opened his eyes, he let his thoughts wonder trying to understand why the souls of the white men were so blinded to the greatness and beauty of what surrounded them. Certainly they couldn't see it, for if they could they would never act the way they do. Often he had talked with his trusted friends about what would happen if the Mother Goddess, who gave birth to the earth and all that live upon it, no longer desired to nurture mankind. What would happen if she finally tired of the pollution and filth that the white man so carelessly littered her world with? Would she still continue to bless humanity, in spite of how she was treated, or would she strike out and remove the single species that threatened the very existence of all life on this planet? Chief Yazzi had little doubt that she was capable of such a feat. She was the Mother of all life, life was her gift, and it was hers to take back.

The silence and peace continued to engulf him, strengthen him, and give his soul the courage that he knew he no longer had. This was his land and each tree belonged to him and his people, to all the people of this beautiful planet. It was not for the few to kill, to steal so they could get rich. The forest was the gift of life to all. Don't all things that live breathe the air that the forest gives us? Mother of all, he thought as he stood up, protect us from this insanity.

Soon he could hear the sound of more motorcycles coming his way. He started walking back to the small clearing where they would soon be arriving. The quietness had done its job, it had cleared his mind and enabled him to think, to find a way forward. He would fight, and he hoped his people would fight as well, for their very existence was entwined with this forest. He knew this logging operation was the beginning of the end for the last remaining virgin forest in British Columbia. Yes, he would fight. Fight as his ancestors had with all that they could, until they were overwhelmed with disease and superior weapons and forced to submit to the slavery that they still lived with to this very day. He suddenly understood that victory was certain regardless of the outcome. His people would defeat the logging company or die trying, either way there was victory, compared to doing nothing.

In the next twenty minutes the rest of the elders arrived. Each man walked to the bluffs and sat down near him, watching the enemy far below. Even the two who had been paid by Mountain Resources now wished they had never allowed themselves to be bought. The fact that soon this forest would be nothing but a burning scar upon the land deeply affected all of them.

"My friends look and see our enemy, study them. We stand alone against the white man and his destruction, and nobody will come to our aid. Our government who we put our hopes in, has betrayed us. For greed and profit they will kill what is not theirs to kill. They will kill what is ours. I cannot allow that. I make this decision for myself, for we must all look into our hearts to find our own ways. Will you fight with me and maybe die with me, or will you stand by and watch as they kill what we hold so dear?"

He looked at each of the men sitting around him, men he had known his entire life. He loved each and every one of them. After a few minutes of silence he started talking again.

"We will need to develop our strategy. How best to fight this white man and his machines? I feel that only through public outrage can we be victorious. Our enemies are so powerful they have even twisted our government. I don't know if they will allow much about this in the news. I fear if this becomes violent our white government will send in its soldiers as in the past and we will suffer from their strength. They will be able to portray us as killers and we will lose the support of whites throughout British Columbia. Yet I fear only through bloodshed will we be able to stop them."

In his heart he was now finished speaking. He had said all that he needed to. After a few minutes of silence another spoke.

"I have thought much about this day. I have a plan," he said.

"Good, share it with us."

For the next three hours they sat, each man free to speak his mind, to judge the words of others. Nothing is held back in a council of war and all are given the opportunity to speak.

It was close to noon when they heard the first of the returning motorcycles. Their timing was good; nothing more could be accomplished by staying here. A strategy of warfare had been established, a course of action set, and soon there would be blood upon the land as it had been in the past.

Chapter 40

A belch of thick black smoke rose from the rusted exhaust pipe of the huge bulldozer, its steel mesh tracks tearing fresh earth and casting it aside in its wake. This was the second large piece of equipment to be off-loaded from Beowulf 1V this morning. Tommy Landford had to take advantage of the high tide and get as much ashore as he could in the next few hours.

For the last eight years Tommy had run Beowulf 1V and its crew like his own private army. He liked that analogy, because each time they started a logging operation it was war, and he always won.

Bud Hansen, one of the men that Mondo had fought in the bar, walked up and stood next to Tommy. They watched the bulldozer as it started to pull a large flat-bottom skiff out of the water and winch it up to the top of the beach. The skiff was full of choker cables and heavy come-alongs, chain saws, and fuel cans.

"Still think we'll have trouble with the Indians"? Bud asked.

"No doubt in my mind, and I really hope we do. I'm tired of these damn tree huggers thinking all of this is theirs," Tommy said as he swung his arms out wide, as if trying to draw the entire forest to him.

"I want to kick some ass, and I don't see how we can lose. We have the law on our side, so what the hell can they do to stop us? No press is ever going to come out here. Hell even if some damn reporter did find us, the papers would never print it. Our people have that all taken care of, they don't want the public to know shit."

Gracefully Tommy swung his two hundred and ninety-pound frame away from the rail and looked down at Bud, who was a big man in his own right.

"You ready for a little war, Bud?"

"Damn right, Tommy, and I hope that shit from the bar is still around, I've got some unfinished business with that boy."

Tommy laughed and almost said something smart-ass about Bud and George both getting their butts kicked, but he decided to hold back. Let Bud stay pissed off, he thought, it couldn't hurt.

"When do we start cutting?" Bud asked a few minutes later.

"Not sure, I'm still waiting for word from the mainland. Right now it's just get everything set up and ready to roll. Man, it's going to be something to see all of this," once again he stretched his arms out wide, like Moses before the Red Sea, " all cut down and hauled away. We are going to be rich after this one, Bud."

Tommy stood there for a few more seconds, his mind running before he started talking again.

"I know I always say this, but I still have that place in the Bahamas and I'm thinking after this job, it might be time to get out of this business and just drink rum and go bone fishin' every day."

Bud laughed and looked at the huge man.

"Tommy, I've heard that for the last year and a half."

"I know, it's always just one more damn job, isn't it? You know something Bud? I must really love what I do."

Mondo carried his duffle bag over his right shoulder with the canvas bag and the relic buried in the bottom. He and Joseph walked up the boarding ramp for the eleven-fifteen sailing to Vancouver Island. Once on board they settled into a small booth as the ferry started to back out and head west.

Watching the water sliding past brought Mondo's thoughts back to Smokin' Joe, back to the peace and harmony, the serenity that he so often felt when he was sailing. He shook his head and let out a deep sigh as he thought of the difference between his short homeless experience and living on his boat. Seeing the homeless as he had, living in their shoes, had been such a shock to him.

A short hour after leaving Vancouver they were standing at a bus stop in Sidney, waiting for the city bus that would take them downtown. Joseph had been very quiet the entire ferry ride over, and Mondo could only guess what was going through his mind.

"You nervous?" he finally asked Joseph.

Joseph turned and looked at him, and a small smile grew on his face as he slowly shook his head.

"No, I am not nervous. I am ready, my father knows that I am coming, and he is ready as well."

"How does your father know you're coming?"

"He knows," Joseph said with another smile.

The bus pulled up and soon they were downtown, waiting for another bus that would run them up-island and to Salmon Creek. It seemed like months ago to Mondo when he had arrived late that night on his way to Jonathan's trying to get some answers. Why does time play tricks like that, he asked himself, still trying to figure out how Joseph's father could possibly know they were coming.

The fury and humiliation that Michael felt hadn't gone away. After freeing himself from the warehouse, making his way home and sleeping through the night, he was still filled with rage. The phone call he had just hung up from didn't help either. Harvey was gone. Three of his people had driven over to Harvey's with the instructions to bring him back to Michael's. They found Harvey, some of his clothes and his car gone. There was no doubt in anybody's mind that Harvey was not coming back. He was running and there was nothing that Michael could do about it. He would have to forget Harvey and vent his anger in another direction. Trying to find Flick would be impossible, so that left Chief Yazzi and his people, and if they wanted a fight then, goddamn it, he was going to give them a beating they would never recover from. The more he thought about it, as he absent-mindedly wandered around the inside of his mansion, the more he knew that he wanted to hurt as many people as he could. This was no longer just about money, this was about revenge and pride, and he wouldn't lose.

It was with deep fear that Dawn returned to the mission and started greeting the homeless again. She had become so confused in the last few days that she didn't even know what she believed anymore. After saying goodbye to Mondo she was an emotional wreck. When Todd called and told her it was an emergency, and asked if she could please return just for a few hours tonight she didn't know what to tell him. She left him hanging on the phone for almost a minute before she just gave in and told him she would be there.

It had been easier than she hoped once she showed up and started helping. She seemed to fall back into a routine that was so easy for her, reaching out to others. Her problem was the one person she wanted to reach out to more than anyone she had ever met, she knew she would never see again.

"Dawn, thank you so much," Todd said after locking the front door and closing the mission for the night.

"You're welcome," she replied.

Todd knew something was really bothering her and he didn't know what to do about it. It wasn't any of his business. Yet, he really liked her, really cared about her, and he knew that something was going on.

"Dawn, come sit down," he said as he reached for her hand and led her over to a table.

"What's wrong, darling?" he said with such sincerity that it made her sit back, close her eyes and take a deep breath.

"Todd, you have no idea what I have been through the last few days."

"I know that you disappeared. I tried calling you. Even your roommate was really scared. I don't know what happened, but I just want to see if there is anything that I can do. I want to help."

"I just need some time, that's all."

"Listen Dawn, I have eyes and I know about people. Whatever this is, it has to do with Mondo."

He paused, hoping she would continue the conversation but she didn't say a word. After a few minutes he stood up and smiled at her again.

"Dawn, if you love Mondo, then you can't ignore it, you can't throw it away."

It was close to ten when she finished her work and walked out the back door. She was so busy thinking about what Todd had said that she didn't even notice the two men who walked up behind her as she started to unlock her car. Only when she suddenly felt their presence and turned did she fear again. Before she could scream, one of the men grabbed her and cupped his large hand over her mouth. She tried to bite him, tried to pull his hand away, but she wasn't strong enough. In the next second the other man picked up her legs and they carried her toward a waiting van. She continued trying to scream but she could hardly breathe. Suddenly the side door of a white van opened and she was thrown into it, landing with a hard crash. The door slammed closed and she felt the van accelerate so fast that she was thrown against the back door, hitting it so hard that she went flying to the floor. When she spun around, the first thing she saw was the back of a young man driving, then she stared at the passenger seat and almost fainted. The man sitting there was smiling at her with such a sinister smile. She remembered his face, remembered his name as he lay moaning on the floor, and she knew she was staring into the eyes of a killer. Michael Jensen was looking at her and she knew she would never see Mondo again.

Chapter 41

D arkness began to settle over Salmon Creek, and from a distance it looked so tranquil, almost fairy-tale like as the last of the orange and reddish hues of a dying sunset fell into the Pacific Ocean. Seven men including Chief Yazzi stood in a moment of silence as they cast their gaze north toward their homes and their loved ones. Their camp was nestled in a small half-acre level area near the top of Bald Mountain that sheltered them from strong southerly winds as well as from the searching eyes of their enemies.

Tonight each man knew that he had a very important task to fill once they arrived at the logging camp. It would take almost two hours to hike down the mountain and over three to get back. Except for Chief Yazzi they were all dressed in black sweat pants, comfortable tennis shoes and a long-sleeved black sweat shirt. Each of them carried a small VHF radio tuned to a pre-assigned channel on their belt. Five of them also carried backpacks with eight sticks of dynamite, one hundred and fifty feet of primer cord, and matches. The sixth man carried a smaller pack that held a roll of duct tape, a small hand-held GPS unit, two pairs of night vision goggles, and one taser stun gun.

After watching the last of the sunset, they sat down around the soft glow of the small fire and said little. Each man understood that tonight was another step forward in a battle that would soon likely turn into bloodshed.

At ten o'clock Chief Yazzi stood, followed by the others a moment later. They reached their hands over the dying embers, bringing their grasps into one firm handshake.

"I am too old to go with you tonight. I will wait. I will be here for your return. Go with the gods of our people," the old chief said, then watched as they turned and disappeared into the darkness.

The old topographical maps they had studied made it easier as they struggled down the steep incline of the old service road. None spoke as they walked. All were deep in thought, feeling a bond of unity that raced back generations. This bond gave them strength. It united them with their ancestors, who also had been forced to fight for what was theirs.

One man was chosen as the group leader and occasionally he would stop and check his GPS, holding a small flashlight between his teeth while reading the map. There was no rush, no sense of urgency, each man knew they had all night.

Once they reached the valley floor they carefully continued toward the logging camp and the barge. The group stopped half a mile from the beach and, after a short rest, two of them started scouting the way ahead. The young men doing the scouting were the best trackers the village had. Carefully they kept themselves in the darkness, following the glow of a star high above the horizon. Every fifty feet they stopped and scanned the area ahead of them, staring through their night vision binoculars, looking for the telltale glow of any person who might be trying to hide. Once they were sure it was safe, one ran back and brought the rest up to the waiting tracker. Then they repeated the process. It took another hour for them to get a hundred feet from the beach.

As the men lay hiding behind a small rocky ridge, one of the scouts pointed to his left and handed the night vision glasses to another. It took him only a moment to make out the form of a guard hiding in the darkness about seventy-five feet up the beach from them, a rifle propped in his hand. The man brought the glasses down from his eyes and studied the direction he would go. Then, holding the taser in his right hand, and wearing a small backpack, Leonard Dancing Hawk slowly crawled off into the darkness.

It took ten minutes for the scouts to find two other armed guards. One of them was thirty feet to their right, sitting next to an over-turned skiff that rested just in the tree line. The third guard had fallen asleep his rifle on the ground, his head slumped over resting against his jacket that was bundled up against a huge tree. It was decided to let the third man continue sleeping.

It took Leonard twenty minutes to get to the first guard. Slowly, he brought the taser up and lined the sights on his target. Bringing his left hand up to support his right, he took a deep breath and pulled the trigger. Two metal darts flew from the gun and hit the unsuspecting man in the back, and the electrical shock sent a vicious spasm through the guard. Leonard Dancing Hawk crawled over to him, reached into his backpack, pulled out the duct tape and started binding the man's hands and feet. Once he was wrapped tight, Leonard made two wraps around the man's head, sealing his lips, making it impossible for him to utter a sound, then slowly Leonard turned and started back.

Once with the group, Leonard rested for a few minutes before he looked through the night vision glasses and started off after the second guard. It took him thirty minutes to stun this man, wrap him tight and return to the group. It was now time for the second part of the plan. Each man had already picked his target and slowly they started crawling in different directions, none making a sound.

Leonard crawled to the large bulldozer, while another man headed off in the direction of the huge log skidder, and another crept down to the dock. A fourth crawled to seven skiffs that were pulled up on the beach and filled with logging equipment, as the last man made his way toward more machinery piled at the top of the beach. The leader stayed right where he was and constantly scanned the area. If he needed to warn any of them he would simply hit the microphone button on his radio, which would send out one very short, soft tone.

Once they arrived at their targets, each man started to place the dynamite. The bulldozer had three sticks in both tracks as well as two that Leonard wedged in the engine compartment. With incredible stealth and silence, they went about their task. Once finished, each man hit the microphone button on his radio, sending a short beep back to the leader. It took ten minutes before they all had clicked once. Everybody was ready. Time seemed to stop as they lay there in the stillness of the cold night, not a sound could be heard. Then a minute after hearing the last click, the leader hit his radio microphone button. Almost instantly, snakes of light started to fizzle at a fast pace. The men were up and running, all of them racing for the trail that would lead them back to Bald Mountain.

The explosions rocked the night. The concussions sent shock waves that slammed into each of them, almost knocking them over. They all stopped and turned, looking behind them as huge balls of flames rocketed skyward. More explosions sounded as equipment and diesel fuel, gasoline and different oils started to burn and explode. The night sky was suddenly a blaze of burning embers. The men didn't linger, they turned and started the long run up the mountain.

Chief Yazzi had been patiently sitting in a small folding chair, watching the few dim embers of the dying fire. Once again he had found what he needed in the peace and quiet, in the beauty of this place that surrounded him. The stars seemed so close he knew he could touch them if he really tried. His thoughts drifted back to his people, to his ancestors, to a thousand generations who had stared at this same heavenly display, and he knew he was connected to each and every one of them. By walking the same land, breathing the same air, drinking the same waters that his people had cherished since the beginning of time, it brought his soul and theirs together. Tonight was a gift for all of them.

He had been sitting for so long that soon his eyes grew heavy. He had almost fallen asleep when the first explosion startled him so much he fell out of his chair. In the next second the beach burst into flames. The entire barge and beach lit up in the glowing explosions that sent machinery and equipment hundreds of feet skyward. He got to his feet and his heart reached out to all who had known battle with the whites. It made little difference to him that most had tasted defeat. Tonight his ancestors rejoiced in this first victory. The war had started, the invaders had been dealt a setback, but he knew they would not be defeated this easily.

Chapter 42

As morning began to break Tommy Landford was beside himself with anger. He couldn't believe that they had been able to sneak in here and do the amount of damage that he saw as he looked out from the barge.

All of the heavy equipment was destroyed, so was most of the dock and many of their crew boats. The skiffs on the beach were destroyed as well as most of their chain saws. The small equipment didn't worry him. That stuff could be flown out by helicopter and they could be back to work by this afternoon, but losing the bulldozer and skidder, that was big.

He hadn't slept since the explosions woke him up from his deep sleep and sent him flying out of his cabin. He had stood there for an hour, watching as the fires burned, until they slowly started to go out and the darkness returned.

Now the scene looked right out of a war zone. None of the crew came by to talk to him. They all knew enough to leave him alone and stay out of his way. The two guards that had been stunned had already been freed and were downstairs trying to get warm. The third guard swore to everybody that he was wide awake all night and that he didn't see a thing, but nobody believed him.

Tommy walked down to the kitchen, poured himself a cup of coffee and headed back out on the deck. Somehow, in spite of this mass destruction and chaos, his mind was calm and focused. The war had started. Finishing his coffee, he threw the cup overboard, walked back to the supply room and grabbed a chainsaw. He checked that it had gas and oil, then he walked down to the ramp and climbed into one of the small crew boats that had been tied to the barge last night. Starting the engine he roared away and headed for the beach. He ran the skiff right up on the sand lifting the outboard a moment before the prop would have struck shore. Looking behind him he saw all of the crew leaning against the railing watching him. He stepped out of the skiff and headed up the beach and back into the forest. Glancing around him he saw a huge old-growth cedar, and started the chain saw. In fifteen minutes the giant cedar came crashing down, smashing onto the beach for all to see. Then, turning the saw off, he let it drop to the forest floor and walked back to the beach, and looked at the barge. The silence was broken by joyous screams as his men hollered his name, jumping up and down as if they had all just won the lottery.

"Let's start cutting this goddamn forest down," he shouted.

Even as he climbed into the skiff and started back to the barge he knew there wasn't a lot they could accomplish until they replaced the heavy equipment. They could spend a day logging, but after that the crew would start tripping over fallen logs, and that was just too dangerous. Tying the boat up and climbing back on board, he knew the Indians had won the first round, but he didn't care. He knew they would lose in the end.

Once back in his office he picked up the satellite telephone and called Mountain Resources. He was told that Michael wasn't in, so he left the secretary a good description of what had happened last night and also a list of what he needed. He also told her that he thought Michael should bring the police in, but it was up to him to make that decision.

As the bus pulled into Salmon Creek, Mondo looked over and studied Joseph, trying to get a sense of what he was feeling. What thoughts and emotions were running through his head? Joseph had been very quiet the entire trip from Vancouver, and now as the bus pulled over, he turned and looked at Mondo.

"Thank you for believing in my father's ways. I am home because of you," he said.

They were the only two passengers to climb off the bus. The air held the scent of forest mixed with a hint of salt. It was a sweet perfume to Mondo and it overwhelmed him as he grabbed his bag and started following Joseph to his father's house. By the time Joseph and Mondo reached the street that Chief Yazzi lived on, the entire town was learning of their return. Chief Yazzi stood at his open door and as soon as he saw his son he rushed to greet him. Father and son met and embraced, holding tightly to what each had thought was lost forever. Tears streamed down their faces. Mondo stood silently watching this reunion. Even before they reached Chief Yazzi's house, cars started pulling up and screeching to a halt. People began piling out, people on bicycles started showing up and kids running completely out of breath suddenly appeared. It seemed that people were emerging from everywhere. From side streets and doorways, cars, and on foot, the entire town was suddenly surrounding Joseph and his father welcoming the lost son home.

Joseph stopped at his father's doorway, turned and looked out at his people.

"I have returned to you. I was lost to the poisons of the white man. Now, because of our friend here," he pointed directly at Mondo, "because of this white man I am here. We must always know that not all whites are our enemies. I have missed you all so much," then he followed his father into his house.

What amazed Mondo was that the entire group followed Chief Yazzi and Joseph right inside. The little house was becoming so packed Mondo thought somebody might go right through the floor. He stood there, watching the joyful confusion, feeling out of place, and he decided not to follow the crowd. Smokin' Joe was calling him and he needed to get back to his home. A short time later he was back on board, nestled in his sanctuary and after living on the streets he knew this was all he would ever need. He set his bag on the floor, then dropped down onto the settee and closed his eyes, feeling such a deep tiredness. It was as if all the tensions, fears, and frustrations of the last week flooded through him at once. Thinking back, he tried to pinpoint exactly what was causing these deep emotions and he knew instantly, it was Dawn. He shouldn't have let her go like that, not without trying to stop her. Now because he didn't try, she was lost forever. He knew he acted like an idiot at the police station. Why didn't he just tell her how he felt? As he sat there it became harder and harder for him to believe that he would never see her again. He remembered her tears, the sorrow on her face as she told him to leave and to forget her. He slumped over on the settee and stretched out, feeling a flood of mixed emotions overwhelm him. He was home, he had found Joseph and returned him to his people, but he had lost something of his own, something that he didn't realize how desperately he wanted, until she walked out of his life.

It was just starting to get dark when Chief Yazzi knocked on the side of Smokin' Joe and Mondo invited him onboard. Carefully the old man made his way down the companionway steps and sat down. He looked at Mondo and gave him a huge smile.

"Thank you, Captain Mondo."

Mondo reached into his duffle bag, and pulled out the bag holding the Cross. He walked over to Chief Yazzi and sat next to him. Then he held the Cross, still wrapped in burlap, up for both of them to look at before he gently put it on the old man's lap.

"I showed this to a friend of mine in Victoria. He works at the museum, he was very excited."

"What did he say it was?" the chief asked slowly, and Mondo knew he was having a conversation with a very wise and extremely crafty old man.

"He told me what it is. He also knows that it is impossible for you to have this."

"Is that right? Impossible, that is a very big word . . . how do you explain it being here, if it is impossible?"

"I can't and he couldn't. There is no way that the seal of an ancient city, a city destroyed over six thousand years ago, could be here. It is impossible."

"Yes, you're right, just as finding my lost son in Vancouver seemed impossible."

Mondo looked deep into Chief Yazzi's eyes, trying to read them, read anything that might help him understand better where this conversation was going.

"He is right, it is beyond understanding that my people have this treasure from the past, yet here it is. It has been with my people since our very beginning. The story of this Cross and the people who brought it to us is as old as my people. Only a few of us even know about the treasures that we have been given."

"Treasures?"

"Yes, Mondo, treasures."

"You're telling me that there is more?"

"Much more."

Michael Jensen walked around his living room, the cell phone inches from his ear, listening to Tommy Landford's loud voice as he told him what had happened last night. Adrenaline pumped through Michael and he was feeling that rush of excitement that came with danger and death. The war had started, and he couldn't have been happier.

He was pacing his large living room, trying to keep his mind focused on the call, but it was getting harder with each passing minute. All that he could think about was Dawn, as she sat on the couch, her hands folded gently on her lap, looking completely lost and terrified.

He almost started laughing at her as he kept trying to focus on what Tommy was saying. She looked so saintly sitting there and he couldn't get the picture of feeding her to the lions out of his mind.

"Listen Tommy, I'm not calling in the police, not yet. I don't want the press. I'll arrange for another barge from Gold City, and I'll have all of the equipment on it you want. It will be there within forty-eight hours. Also, I'll be flying out there tomorrow and I'm bringing a guest, so I want the honeymoon suite," he said as he watched Dawn's expression.

"Yeah, the honeymoon suite," he said again. He didn't care what Tommy was thinking, he wasn't even listening to him anymore, his attention was captivated by the look on her face.

"Lastly, I want to make those bastards bleed, so you think about it, the war has started. I want them hurting so bad that they will wish they never had been born."

Clicking the phone shut, he stopped walking and looked at her. Slowly she brought her eyes up to his, and he saw the fear, the hopelessness that she felt. A deep smile appeared on his face as he walked over and stood looking down at her, feeling a rush of excitement that was almost uncontrollable. He sat down and grabbed her right hand, squeezing it hard, inflicting pain, causing a small gasp to seep from her mouth. Then slowly he brought her hand up to his lips and started kissing it, never taking his eyes from hers. The moment she started to turn away he grabbed her head and twisted her face back toward his, locking his eyes on hers.

Dawn watched in horror as that same evil smile grew on his face. At that moment she understood what he was going to do and that there was nothing she could do to stop him. She was shaking so hard she could hardly breathe, fear flooding her mind.

"Please, no," she managed to say with words so soft that Michael sitting right next to her almost couldn't hear.

"Please, no," he mimicked back, "but Dawn, my love, I've already reserved the honeymoon suite."

Chapter 43

hree skiffs pulled into the head of the bay at dawn. Each had four heavily armed men inside and they stopped one hundred yards from the end of the pier. Lloyd Reineck looked around in the growing light. He was sixty-five years old and hard as nails after forty years in the logging business, and he knew exactly what was expected of him.

"Drop the anchor," he whispered and a moment later he heard a splash as the man in the bow let the anchor and chain drop overboard. The other two boats came alongside and tied up.

"We'll rotate one skiff back to the barge every three hours, but for now let's just kick back, drink some coffee and enjoy the morning," he said with a smile as he sat down and looked around.

Nobody was coming in or out of Salmon Creek by boat unless he let them, and he knew the fun was just beginning.

Forty minutes later three logging trucks, two carrying full trailers, pulled off the highway and started making their way to Salmon Creek. The empty logging truck in the lead was painted bright red and it had orange flames shooting out from under its engine cover. The red logging truck started to slow down a hundred and fifty feet before the turnout to the telephone switching station. The driver down-shifted and hit his engine exhaust brake, causing his motor to scream as the truck slowed even more. At twenty miles an hour he swung his truck off the road, broke through the chain barrier, and aimed his truck at the side of the building. The heavily reinforced bumper took the jolt without even jarring him. The logging truck crashed right through the side of the building, smashing equipment, sending lumber, plywood, roofing and over a hundred thousand dollars worth of high-tech equipment careening into a jumbled pile of debris. After crashing through the wall he slowed his truck to a stop, then, smiling, he watched his rear view mirrors as he started backing out, smashing more telephone equipment with every turn his tires made. Once on the road he waited for his friends who had stopped and watched his demolition to pull their rigs behind him. Then all three drivers, keeping their right hands on their air horns, headed into Salmon Creek, creating a reverberating shock wave that echoed off the mountains. As they reached town the driver of the red truck hit his brakes, sending a signal to the two truckers behind him. He slowed down, then stopped in the middle of the road and watched his mirrors as the other trucks came to a stop, then started working their trailers until they ended up across the road.

Nobody was driving in or out of Salmon Creek, all telephone communication with the outside world had just been destroyed, and the bay was blockaded. Salmon Creek was now under siege.

The driver of the red logging truck sat anxiously as his two friends climbed down from their trucks, walked the short distance to his and climbed inside.

"Let's go kick ass," the driver said as he handed his friend riding near the window a shotgun.

"Yep, let's kick some ass," he repeated as he roared off into town with his air horn still blasting away.

Mondo was surprised at the sound of footsteps on the dock so early in the morning. He lay there for a few seconds before he felt a sharp blow to the side of Smokin' Joe. Instantly he was up, racing to the companionway steps. He slid the hatch back and was shocked to see over a dozen men, each carrying rifles or shotguns, standing next to his boat. He recognized two of the men from the bar fight. George looked up at him, and gave Smokin' Joe another kick with a heavy pair of logging boots.

"We ain't done with you, boy," he said, then George turned and followed his friends toward town.

Mondo rushed back inside, got dressed and was running down the dock in just a matter of minutes. He could see the group of men ahead of him walking down the middle of the street, and he sure recognized trouble when he saw it.

He turned to his right and ran as fast as he could, charging down another street that he hoped would lead him to Chief Yazzi's house. He had to scramble over a few fences and almost got bit by a dog, but soon he reached the old man's house. The front door was wide open and as he ran inside he was surprised to see at least ten men standing in the living room. Joseph was talking. He looked up and saw Mondo charging in.

"Welcome, my friend."

"You've got some people coming that aren't too friendly, do you know about them?" Mondo asked.

"Yes, we know about them. We know that they have blockaded the road into our town, and we know that they have destroyed all telephone communication with the outside. They also have armed guards at the entrance to our bay."

Mondo slumped down in the chair and looked at the men around him.

"Jesus Christ," was all he could say.

"It seems the war has come to us," Joseph said as he looked at Mondo, then at the others around him.

"I want no confrontation," Joseph continued. "I will go talk with them. My father will stay here. I will find out what they want, though I can guess," he said and then gave Mondo a strange look.

"What do they want, Joseph?" Mondo asked.

"It seems some of our people destroyed much of their equipment on the beach the night before last. I think they want revenge, probably blood, if I know the white man."

"You just can't walk out there by yourself!" Mondo said as he stood up.

"What you can not see will protect me. I will be fine."

Each man standing there gave Mondo a little smile then looked at Chief Yazzi, who with a slight wave of his right hand sent them all rushing out the front door. Suddenly the room took on an ominous quiet as the three of them stood there.

"Joseph, those men were armed to the teeth. I don't think they are playing around."

Joseph walked over to Mondo and put his arm around him.

"By the time we meet I will have over twenty-five rifles pointing at them. I don't think there will be bloodshed, not this morning anyway. Please stay here with my father," he said, then strolled out the door as if heading for a picnic.

Mondo turned and looked at Chief Yazzi.

"You're going to let him walk out there by himself and meet those men?"

"It is his way. He has returned and he now speaks for my people."

Mondo glanced out the open front door and watched Joseph walking down the street. He looked back at Chief Yazzi, who didn't seem concerned at all. In the next moment he ran out the door. Mondo caught up with Joseph just as he reached the corner of the main street.

"What are you doing?" Joseph asked, with a very surprised look on his face.

"Hell if I know."

The group of men was a block away and coming fast. Joseph and Mondo continued another twenty feet before stopping. Tommy and his men didn't stop until they were ten feet away, all their guns pointing right at them. Mondo glanced at Joseph and was surprised by the expression on his face; there was no fear.

"What do you want?" Joseph asked, his voice firm, in absolute control with no hint of any emotion.

Tommy Landford took a step forward and leveled his shotgun right at Joseph.

"Listen, you son of a bitch. You people blew up a lot of my equipment. I came to arrest your chief and make sure you damn Indians never try that again."

"Maybe you should leave our land, go take your evil somewhere else," Joseph replied with malice in his voice.

"You bastard, I'll send you to hell if I want," Tommy said as he cocked the shotgun.

"Listen, shit!" Mondo shouted. "You can't start shooting people, this isn't the Wild West!"

"Shut up, boy," Bud said as he stepped forward and pointed his rifle at Mondo.

The two groups stood there for over a minute, nobody saying a word.

"Like I said, I came here to arrest your chief, and I ain't leaving until I do, so where is he?" Tommy said, still holding the shotgun directly on the two of them.

"I am the chief," Joseph replied.

"Don't bullshit me, boy. You're the drunkard that lived like scum in Vancouver. I came to get your father."

"Nobody will touch my father. I am the chief. If you wish to talk, then do so."

"I ain't talking boy, I'm taking," Tommy said.

Suddenly from down the street they could hear the blast of a truck's air horn. Mondo and Joseph turned to see a large red logging truck racing down the road, its horn blasting, aiming right at them. The truck kicked up a trail of dust that made it impossible to see behind it as it raced closer. Suddenly, when the truck was less than fifty feet away the driver slammed on the brakes and turned the wheel, causing the truck to start sliding sideways. Expertly the driver steered the truck so that the rig slid another twenty feet before coming to a stop, blocking the road. In the next instant the passenger door opened and a man jumped out and pointed a shotgun at Mondo and Joseph.

"Like I said," Tommy repeated, "I came to take. I'm taking your father and maybe you back to the barge and I don't expect any more shit from you damn Indians, you got that?"

"I think you are sadly mistaken," Joseph said.

Tommy stared at Joseph and Mondo and he realized that this wasn't going as he had thought. He figured by now this damn Indian would be quaking in his boots. In the back of his mind he knew he was missing something. Slowly he started looking around him. He was shocked to see armed men standing up from roof tops, weapons pointing at him and his men. He looked and saw rifles pointing from doorways and opened windows, behind trees and parked cars . . . well he thought, goddamn it!

"You damn Indians better keep away from my beach and my stuff or next time I'll come shooting first."

"When you do, you will die," Joseph said with no hint of fear.

"Let's get the hell out of here," Tommy said as he turned and started leading his men back to their boats.

The red logging truck slowly started turning itself around and in a minute was driving back down the way it had come.

Mondo stood there looking at Joseph, watching his face, trying to guess what he was thinking.

Finally Joseph looked over at him.

"What, my friend?"

"You seemed pretty sure of yourself."

"Sure of myself?" Joseph laughed. "Sure of myself? Mondo I was scared to death."

Chapter 44

B y noon Tommy Landford had had two satellite telephone conversations with Michael. The first call was filled with rage as he told him of the confrontation they had earlier this morning. Those damn Indians had outsmarted him again and he knew it. Thinking back to seeing those rifles pointed at him and his men made him realize that this was going to be a tougher fight than he had first thought. Still, he had the law on his side, and if it came down to it he knew Michael would play that card, if he had to. Michael was going to win this and there was no doubt in his mind.

The second call was from Michael an hour later with much better news. The barge with new equipment would leave Gold City today and should arrive tomorrow. One skidder and a cat were loaded as well as a few skiffs, chain saws, fuel, and two cases of twelve-year-old Scotch. Tommy liked the Scotch idea. He knew that his men were as mad as he was. Let them fuel their rage with alcohol and then we'll see who wins this damn war, he thought.

Tommy knew there was no way to live down today's humiliation, but soon he'd make up for it. They'd kick ass and start cutting their goddamn forest down, and when they were all finished there wouldn't be a damn thing left standing.

Tommy slumped back in his small cabin and ran his fingers through his jet black hair. A surprising thought suddenly raced through his mind. Maybe, just maybe he thought, after this job he really should retire to the Bahamas.

*

Chief Yazzi, Joseph, and Mondo sat in the living room drinking coffee. It was surprisingly quiet and Mondo figured it wasn't up to him to keep the conversation going. There was no discussion of a strategy to fight the loggers. No mention of the blockade that surrounded Salmon Creek. When Joseph and his father did speak it was about the old times that they shared. About the hunting trips and good years in the past when fishing was plentiful and their people had all that they needed. They talked of life in a happier time when the influences of the white man seemed so far away.

After the years they had been separated, Mondo thought they would have so much to talk about. As he sat there he started to think that maybe they wanted to talk privately and were waiting for him to leave, but he soon realized that wasn't it either. In some strange way he finally understood that whatever had happened in the past, the years of Joseph living on the street were now meaningless, no longer a part of the present and therefore not worth discussing.

Finally Chief Yazzi put his coffee cup down and looked at Mondo, smiling with that mixture of wisdom and mischief.

"It seems that you have far exceeded your own beliefs by bringing my son home. I can never thank you enough. I will truly be indebted to you forever. What can I do to possibly repay your bravery?"

The expression on his face made Mondo laugh, because they both knew the answer.

"Tell me about Neskiwaii, tell me about the Cross of Atlantis, and tell me about your treasure."

"Oh yes, Neskiwaii, I almost forgot," he laughed. "Your friend in Victoria would like to know more as well, wouldn't he?"

"Absolutely."

Chief Yazzi sat back in his chair and looked at Mondo. The mischief left his face and he grew serious.

"Neskiwaii is a sad chapter for my people. In one day their world ended, and only a few survived the massacre. The village was never rebuilt and it is still a place of great sorrow. Yet buried near Neskiwaii, as you know, is a gift from the gods. That is the real reason for the massacre so long ago. Those that attacked came because they had heard of the great riches that we were trusted with. My people were betrayed, yet they never revealed the location of the treasure and therefore were destroyed.

"You see, Mondo, we are the keepers of this ancient treasure, but it is not ours, and we understand that the time will come when we must return it."

"Return it, to who?" Mondo said, surprised.

"It belongs to the world. We have kept it safe since the beginning of time, but I fear what the future now holds. Look and see what the world has become. Nuclear weapons are still being created, for what, I ask you? Why does the white man continue down this insane road? We will never understand, but we know that we will be part of whatever the outcome is. I fear that our mother, who gives us the earth and sky, the air and the water that we all breathe and drink, I fear she will grow tired of us. If she does, then time will end, and it may be ending soon."

"Why do you say that?" Joseph asked his attention focused completely on his father.

"Look at the Mayan Calendar."

"I have never heard of this calendar," Joseph said.

"The Mayan calendar ends on December 21, 2012. I cannot tell you what happens on that date, no one can, but I have eyes to see the direction the world turns, and it turns towards destruction because of evil men who control this world. Men who lie, cheat, and feel no compassion, men who steal all that they can and give back nothing in return."

"Does that effect what you do with the treasure?" Mondo asked.

"Maybe . . . I don't know, but there is power in the treasure. You have seen it change my son, maybe it can change the world."

"Change the world? Do you mean change the way people think?" Joseph asked.

"Yes, maybe . . . hopefully."

"Is it possible Father?"

"I don't know, son, I really don't know."

Silence filled the room as each man became lost in his private thoughts. Mondo wondered about the date that the Mayans picked so long ago; could it really be the end of the world? How could they possibly know that? It is beyond reason to think they could see into the future. Yet Mondo now knew that anything was possible.

"How do you know when to reveal the treasure to the world?" Mondo asked a few minutes later.

"I don't know."

"You don't know? Maybe now is the time."

Chief Yazzi sat there for a few minutes and didn't say a word. He glanced between Mondo and Joseph and each of them could see the turmoil that he felt. The silence grew until Mondo found it uncomfortable. He stood and looked at them both.

"I'm going back to Smokin' Joe."

Just as he turned toward the door there was a soft knock and in came two men. They seemed surprised to find Mondo there. They looked at Chief Yazzi and then back at Mondo and he could sense their unease.

"Hello, my friends. Please, Mondo is a part of our people. You can say anything in front of him."

They pulled out two chairs and sat down around the table. Mondo sat back down as well.

"A barge has left Gold City. It has enough equipment on board that they will be able to start full-scale logging once it arrives. I think what we accomplished on the beach will be short lived if the barge reaches Swartz Bay," one of them said.

"Can we stop the barge?" Joseph asked.

"Maybe, I'm not sure how," the same man replied.

The room became silent as each man thought about what the arrival of the barge meant.

"There must be a way to stop it," Joseph said.

More silence and Mondo was thinking fast, "I have an idea," he said.

All eyes turned his way, and he suddenly felt uncomfortable. Had this become his war, he asked himself? But he already knew the answer.

"Yes," Chief Yazzi asked.

"Well, it seems to me we can't sink the barge, it's probably built of steel and you would need a cannon to blast it out of the water. The best hope we have is to delay it from arriving. Even if we can stop it for just a few days it will help." He looked at them and knew they were waiting for him to continue.

"Okay, so this barge will be towed by a tug boat of some kind. I say we try to foul the tug's propeller by having it run over some type of rope, something that could get wrapped tight in its propeller and might lock the engine up."

"How would we do that?" Joseph asked.

"We need to find a narrow pass that we are sure the barge will have to go through. Then we run a rope just under the water. If we leave enough slack in it there is a chance the propeller will pick it up. If it does, it will wrap the line around the propeller shaft so fast it will lock that engine before they know what happened. It might even break something. It could even pull the shaft out of the transmission if we're lucky."

He looked around at them and felt each man weighing his words.

"It happened to me in Mexico. Smokin' Joe pulled into an anchorage late at night and ran over a fishing net. The damn thing pulled the shaft right out of the transmission, took me a week to fix it."

"That might work, and I know just the right place. If we ran a rope across Jackson Narrows, just before the fork to Shellcha Rapids, and the tug boat propeller was fouled, there is a chance the currents would carry the barge and tug down the rapids. If that happened, they would crash into the rocks off of Long Point, maybe even sink," one of the men said.

A smile grew on Chief Yazzi's face as he looked from Mondo to the other men sitting around the table.

"That is a good idea. I think we should try it."

"What about the barricade of our harbor? Plus I know they have spies that will be watching what we do." Joseph asked.

"Yes, you are right, just as we have our spies. Still, I think a small skiff under the cover of darkness could sneak out of the harbor. Maybe some of our old fish nets might work to trap the barge?" Chief Yazzi said as he looked at Mondo.

"I don't know if nets would be strong enough. That tug boat is going to have a lot of power and that propeller is going to try to rip right through whatever we use."

"What do you suggest?" Joseph asked.

"I have some one inch line on board. It's three hundred feet long, hopefully that is long enough."

"That is a good plan. I know Jackson Narrows. Three hundred feet of rope will be more than enough," Joseph said.

"Good, Mondo, I like your idea, tonight we will lay our trap," Chief Yazzi said and that little mischievous smile of his crept back across his face. "Tonight we will fight again."

Five miles away from Salmon Creek as the crow flies and two hundred feet from the barge, Leonard Dancing Hawk slowly shifted his weight trying to ease the cramping that was starting in both legs. He had been sitting for over three hours watching the barge. The long telephoto lens of his digital camera rested on a small mound of dirt covered with an old shirt spread out to keep his camera clean. Chief Yazzi had suggested that he have his camera ready as he watched the barge and the loggers. He stretched his right leg, feeling the stiffness, and he was about to stretch his left leg when he heard the unmistakable sound of a helicopter. Forgetting about his cramps he grabbed his camera and focused on the barge as a helicopter suddenly appeared and landed. A minute later he snapped five pictures of a man and a young woman climbing out of the helicopter being greeted by a huge man with jet black hair. The two men exchanged handshakes and started talking in a very friendly manner. Switching his view from the men to the woman he was instantly struck by the fear on her face. He took two close-up pictures of her before one of the men forcefully grabbed her by the arm and they all walked out of view.

Leonard made it back to Salmon Creek by seven that evening. He was tired, and the two-hour hike to the top of Bald Mountain, and then the jarring ride on the back of a small motorcycle had taken its toll on his body. He ached and his mind was foggy as he walked into his small house, gave his two children a hug and a kiss then dropped down on an old faded sofa. He could smell dinner cooking and he caught a glimpse of his wife as she moved about the kitchen. His daughter suddenly jumped on his lap unexpectedly and almost knocked the wind out of him. He wrapped his huge arms around her and gave her a tickle that brought a bundle of laughs, as she twisted and turned in her father's grasp. Looking deep into her beautiful, fragile eyes he was suddenly very afraid of what her future held.

It was only as he looked at his daughter that he thought of the woman on the barge and of the photos that he had taken of her. As tired as he was, he knew he should get up, walk over to Chief Yazzi's house and show him the pictures. Something about the look on her face really bothered him.

He continued to tickle his daughter for another minute before he forced himself off the couch and into the kitchen. His wife smiled at him as he gave her a kiss before telling her he was going over to Chief Yazzi's for a few minutes. She gave him a sweet smile and patted his rear as he turned and headed for the door.

Chapter 45

M ondo pushed his inflatable dinghy away from the dock and inserted two oars in the oar locks. Silently he rowed as he looked at the young man sitting in the stern. He had been told his name was Billy and he would guide him to where they would set their trap. It was close to two-thirty in the morning and the night was bitter cold. The darkness made seeing the outline of the two skiffs that blocked the entrance to Salmon Creek almost impossible. Mondo rowed until he reached the shore, then, keeping his dinghy in a few feet of water, he skirted by the loggers, who seemed to be asleep. Bracing his feet against three hundred feet of one-inch line that lay piled on the floor, he pulled at the oars. It would take an hour of hard rowing before they could be sure they were far enough away not to be heard when he started the engine. Mondo knew it would be a long night.

Chief Yazzi had told him the barge was anchored three miles east of the narrows. Checking his tide book, Mondo found that slack water was at six-thirty this morning and he knew the tug would be going through the narrows at slack. Once the tide started rising and the currents started to flow it would be impossible to control the barge.

His plan was simple. Tie one end of the line on the east side of Jackson Narrows then string the rope across the channel and tie it on the other side. The trick was going to be trying to judge how much line to use and how deep it should be. If it was too deep the propeller would miss it, too high and it might be seen.

Mondo continued rowing, checking his watch every ten minutes or so until an hour had finally passed. Putting the oars down, he fumbled in the darkness and with two pulls started the engine. The noise of the outboard was kept to a minimum as he motored along at only five knots. A few minutes later Billy reached over, grabbed the tiller from Mondo's hand and turned the throttle to full speed. The inflatable jumped up on a plane and quickly gained speed as they started racing through the darkness.

Billy drove the dinghy like a crazy man, skimming past the close shoreline, the only light coming from a slim moon that had just risen over the high mountains. There was nothing Mondo could do, he just resolved himself to trust Billy's crazy driving and hang on.

They must have driven for almost an hour before the boat slowed and headed toward shore. Billy lifted the engine up and locked it in place as the dinghy glided softly to a stop on a small pebble beach.

"Climb out and we'll drag the boat up the beach," Billy whispered.

They both stepped out and pulled the boat up on the shore. Mondo looked around trying to guess in what direction the other end of Jackson Narrows lay, but he couldn't see a thing in the darkness. Together they started to drag one end of the rope out of the dinghy as Mondo made his way to a low-hanging tree. Billy continued to feed the rope until Mondo had enough. He tied a knot around a thick low-hanging branch, then he walked back to the dinghy and they pushed it into the water. Billy started the outboard as Mondo fed rope out over the stern.

It took about ten minutes before Mondo felt the bow of the dinghy gently reach shore again. Billy jumped over the bow, followed by Mondo, and they both pulled the dinghy up the beach and tied it off to a large driftwood log.

As Mondo stood on the beach he knew that his strategy could easily fail. It all came down to getting the line tight enough to rest just below the surface and keeping it there. The rope would want to sag in the middle and depending on where the barge went through the narrows it might be impossible to take enough of the slack out.

As he sat on the beach waiting for dawn Mondo thought about this whole crazy situation that he found himself in. It was amazing to think that this all started not that long ago with a rainy afternoon at the museum. Now here he sat, bundled up against the cold, on some deserted beach halfway up Vancouver Island, trying to sabotage a barge full of logging equipment and help save a people, that, a few weeks ago he never even knew existed.

His thoughts continued to run and soon another day started to twinkle in the morning dawn. Billy was sitting a few feet from the dinghy, resting against more driftwood. Mondo checked his watch. It was five-thirty, about half an hour before he expected the barge. He stood up and started walking around the small beach they had landed on. There were large trees running down to the shore and lots of scattered driftwood.

Walking over to the dinghy, he grabbed the end of the rope and started making his way up the steep hillside, looking for a good tree to wrap the line around. The higher he could get, the more control he would have over the line. Thirty feet up from the beach he found a large madrona tree and took two wraps around it. The paper-thin red bark peeled away, leaving the smooth outside edge of the tree. Glancing out over the narrows, he could only guess where they had tied the other end. Even now the water boiled through the narrow pass, kicking up eddies and back currents, creating torrents of flowing water.

To his right, less than half a mile away, was the channel that led to Shellcha Rapids. This small finger of water branched off from the main waterway and was forced between the narrow rocky shores, creating an incredibly powerful set of rapids. White water exploded against huge rocks that stood in the mouth of the channel, forcing water upward as well as down deep into the darkness. If that barge drifted into those rapids, even at slack water, it could very easily capsize.

It was impossible to see his rope in the water. Even now, in the light of morning, he lost it only twenty feet from shore.

"Billy, I need you to grab some brush and cover the dinghy, then come here. It might take both of us to pull this line tight," he said softly.

Billy seemed to come back from where his thoughts were, stood, grabbed some branches and cut them off with a pocket knife. He laid the branches over the dinghy and then walked up to Mondo.

The two of them stood in silence, and Mondo felt like a hunter, and he knew the prey was getting close. The light continued to increase and the sky soon became crystal blue without a cloud in sight.

They heard the tug before they saw it and soon it slowly made its way around a large point of land and into view. They both stood and watched as a steady stream of black exhaust poured from its red smokestack. The tug was heading for the middle of the channel, its tow pulled up tight only a hundred feet behind it. The water had smoothed out considerably and Mondo was amazed at the difference slack water could make. He looked at Billy, who kept glancing from the tug and barge back to him as the tug continued its slow crawl.

"We have to pull it tighter," Mondo said as he wrapped the line once more around the tree, pulling with all his strength. Billy grabbed the line and pulled as hard as he could.

The tug and barge were now in the middle of the narrows and the barge was starting to be pushed sideways by the current. The black smoke continued to belch from the red smokestack. Mondo could only pray now, there was nothing else they could do. The rope was pulled as tight as they could pull it and it stretched out above the water a good thirty feet from the shore, before disappearing into the dark waters. They strained, knowing that if it wasn't wrapped around the smooth madrona tree it would be impossible for them to hold it. Waiting made time stand still. Suddenly both men felt the rope jerk tight, then the line started whipping out of their hands. The bark peeled as the rope was pulled even tighter, the line stretching even higher over the water before it suddenly came to an abrupt stop and then slowly dropped to the ground at their feet.

They studied the tug, trying to gauge its forward momentum. The tug didn't seem to slow down and Mondo feared its sharp propeller had cut right through the rope. A few minutes later they could see the barge slowly start to drift closer to the tug. Two men had rushed out of the wheelhouse, ran to the stern and looked over into the water. The barge continued to come closer to the slowing tug and there was nothing that anybody on the tug could do. Mondo and Billy watched as the crew of the tug frantically ran to the bow as the barge slowly started to turn sideways and crash into the back of the tug. The barge, carried by its momentum continued forward, forcing the tug's stern down as the bottom of the barge started to climb over it. Mondo's heart almost stopped as the front of the tug began reaching skyward, its stern being swallowed by the barge. For a second it looked like the barge was going to continue right over the tug, forcing it down into the depths, but suddenly the tug skidded out from underneath the barge and shot forward twenty feet before coming to a stop.

The barge continued to drift and soon it passed the tug, which was now slowly being towed backwards through the narrows by the barge. Mondo watched as the crew, still at the bow, dropped the anchor. Slowly the tug started to straighten out as its anchor grabbed and the barge started to swing around behind it. The towline soon became stretched tight and Mondo could only guess at the incredible force of the barge as it pulled on the stern of the tug. The tug started following the barge in a slow jerky motion and Mondo knew that the anchor wasn't holding.

The barge continued to pull and slowly the stern of the tug started to sink. Mondo could see the decks getting lower as the tow cable grew straighter and started to pull itself out of the water. For a moment the anchor seemed to hold, and Mondo thought that maybe the barge and tug would stop moving. In the next moment the stern of the tug was pulled down even further, and Mondo knew it would sink if nothing was done. He watched as one of the panicked crewmen raced to the stern and released the drum that held the steel tow cable. The tugs stern started to rise, just inches from being swamped, as the barge slowly began to float away. The tug suddenly looked almost peaceful sitting there, as the barge drifted closer to the rapids. Billy and Mondo watched the barge hit the first of the huge rocks at the entrance to Shellcha Rapids, then continue to smash against the rocks, bouncing back and forth as if trying to cast itself free from the current's grip. Slowly it continued down the rapids until it hit another group of large boulders, grounding its heavy flat steel bottom into the rocky pinnacles. Quickly the water rose over the deck and started to flood it. The barge tilted to starboard and, in the next moment, the side that was lodged against the rocks rose high and the equipment on board started to slide. The weight of the skidder and bulldozer forced the left side under and that was all it took. As the equipment continued to slide the barge capsized, turning its ugly streaked bottom skyward as it threw all that it carried into the raging waters of Shellcha Rapids.

Chapter 46

Mondo and Billy stood in silent disbelief as they watched the capsized barge continue to smash its way down the rapids. The equipment that had fallen overboard was completely out of sight, lost in the depths. Sadness overcame Mondo as he realized that the war once again had escalated and it was going to get a lot uglier real soon. When the first blood would be spilled he had no idea, but he knew it was coming.

The tug was still anchored in the narrows, water swirling around it as the current continued to boil.

"Time to go, Billy."

They walked down to the dinghy, uncovered it and slid it into the water. Mondo jumped in and Billy pushed off from shore. Lowering the outboard Mondo started it, spun the boat around and off they went, crashing over waves, sending plumes of saltwater flying. They started across Jackson Narrows, both watching the tug which was anchored closer to them than they liked. Mondo watched as one of the crew men ran back into the pilothouse and returned moments later holding a rifle. A shot rang out and they both instinctively ducked down into the dingy, knowing it wouldn't protect them at all. A series of shots rang out and all they could do was hang on and keep going as fast as possible. Mondo was keeping his head down, at the same time trying to see ahead of him, the throttle full speed when suddenly Billy jerked upright and flew right out of the boat. Mondo instantly backed off the throttle and spun the dinghy around so fast that it almost flipped over. Billy was floating face down, making no effort to swim as Mondo pulled up to him, Billy's blood already staining the water a crimson red. Another shot rang out as Mondo reached over and pulled Billy into the boat. He was already dead, the bullet leaving a bloody wound where it exited his body. Two more shots rang out before the dinghy was racing at full speed away from the tug. Keeping his head down, staring at Billy's lifeless body, Mondo burst into tears, grieving for a brave young man he hardly knew.

The water smoothed out as he left the narrows, then he turned to his right following the channel, and the barge disappeared out of view.

It would be a long trip to Salmon Creek. He was glad he had his handheld GPS and that he had looked at the charts before he left last night. All the way back he couldn't stop thinking that Billy's death was just the beginning.

As he raced around the last corner before entering the bay of Salmon Creek, he suddenly saw the loggers two boats still anchored out. He had completely forgotten about them, and he was beyond fear. His anger at Billy's death had put him over the edge. He hit the throttle, giving his outboard every ounce of power, as he raced toward the surprised loggers. The dinghy was now only fifty feet away, racing on a collision course with the nearest skiff. At twenty feet one of the loggers tried to grab his rifle, but it was too late. At ten feet Mondo slammed the outboard motor to starboard, causing the inflatable to dig deep into the water, creating a huge rooster tail wave that slammed into the logger's skiff. The wave hit two men squarely in the chest and they were flipped over board before they had any time to react. Mondo never looked behind him as he raced into the harbor past Smokin' Joe, backing off on the throttle at the last moment before he pulled up to the dock. Turning the outboard off, he broke down in tears again looking at Billy whose blood mixed with salt water still splashed back and forth in the bottom of his boat.

As he walked to Chief Yazzi's house carrying Billy's body, his clothes became soaked in the young man's blood. By the time he reached the old man's house at least fifty people walked with him. Chief Yazzi and Joseph moved aside as he carried Billy and laid him down on the old sofa.

Joseph knelt down next to Billy and began to weep, his sobs soon echoed with the tears of many. Finally Joseph stood and looked at those standing around him, his face reflecting the terrible sadness that they all felt. He walked a few steps to Mondo, put his arms around him and pulled him close.

"I had no idea it would come to this. I had no idea how much my people needed me. Thank you," he whispered.

He glanced at his father and for a moment he was silent. Slowly Chief Yazzi nodded his head and all that watched knew beyond a doubt that Joseph now led the people.

"It is now war!" he shouted as he turned and looked at those standing around him, "as it has been so often in the past, innocent blood has been spilled, a brave young man that we all loved is now gone. I call the elders. Go gather them, bring them, today we fight!"

Then he sat down next to Billy's lifeless body, and gently reached his right hand over and closed his staring eyes. The house was soon empty of people and Joseph stood in the doorway, his thoughts a thousand miles away. Mondo and Chief Yazzi knew his mind raced with the thought of warfare, and of the death and destruction that they all knew would soon fall upon their little town. There was no way they could successfully fight against the loggers because they would be fighting the government of British Columbia as well. They understood that once they started fighting, the white man's army would come and crush them as they had in the past.

A council of war was held in Chief Yazzi's small house. Twelve men sat around the dining room table and discussed the best strategy. Even Leonard Dancing Hawk, who had been so anxious to start the war, was now somber. The men never argued, all listened to each others words of wisdom. There was no hint of defeat in any of them. No man expressed his thoughts about the futility of their efforts, yet each man knew they couldn't win.

It was almost one o'clock when Chief Yazzi stood and walked over to Mondo who had said little through most of the meeting.

"Let us take a walk," he said and even in the gloom of this desperate hour Mondo saw that strange smile on his face.

Mondo grabbed his backpack as Chief Yazzi grabbed the canvas bag that held the Cross from a closet and then they walked outside. They reached the main street and stood for a few minutes before a battered green car pulled over as it was driving by. The driver smiled, reached over and rolled down the passenger window.

"Chief Yazzi, Mondo, can I give you a ride?"

"Yes, thank you," the old man said as he opened the front door and they climbed in.

"I would like to stop by Billy's, then would you please gather two dirt bikes and a driver for each. Make sure they have plenty of gas. Can you do that for me?" he asked.

Mondo was amazed at his humility.

"Yes."

They spent about ten minutes at Billy's, Chief Yazzi softly talking to his mother. Mondo was standing off at a distance, wondering about the Cross and what the old man intended to do with it, and still grieving for Billy. Then two loud dirt bikes pulled into the yard and a few minutes later they were both hanging on as they roared away from town.

Soon they were slowly making their way up Bald Mountain. Mondo was hanging on, trying his best to anticipate each jar and bump as they continued up a road that he was surprised the dirt bikes could travel. They continued for over an hour before the bikes pulled into an open clearing and they slowly climbed off.

"Please wait for us. We will be back before nightfall," Chief Yazzi asked his driver.

"Now I am afraid we must walk, Mondo," he said, then he turned and they started down the back side of Bald Mountain. The hike was hard and Mondo kept thinking about having to climb back up this mountain in a few hours. Little was spoken as they made their way down the narrow steep trail, Chief Yazzi trying to conserve his energy, the canvas bag and the Cross over his right shoulder.

After a very tiring hike they reached level ground and the coolness of the deep forest. The size of the trees amazed Mondo. They seemed to reach to the heavens and he couldn't believe that the loggers could just come in here and cut them all down without a second thought.

There was no trail now, but the old man seemed to know his way as they walked around huge trees and through low-lying brush. Occasionally Chief Yazzi would glance over his shoulder at Mondo with that little smile of his, then he would turn his attention back to finding the way.

For twenty minutes they walked in the silence of this majestic old growth forest. Finally Chief Yazzi stopped near a small running creek and waited for Mondo to walk to his side.

"We are here. This is the most holy of places," Chief Yazzi said.

As he looked around Mondo couldn't see anything that made this spot any different from the forest they had just walked through. Trees and brush, moss and huge ferns covered the area. There was a long rock outcropping off to his left. It was at least seventy feet high, and ran for a couple hundred yards before disappearing in the trees.

Mondo pulled his pack off, turned on his GPS, and in less than a minute he had locked in their exact position.

Finally, in a hushed whisper, the old man spoke.

"Do you see it?"

Mondo just shook his head.

"I am not surprised. It has been here for over five thousand years. It has been undisturbed for most of that time."

Mondo glanced around him, then walked a few feet and leaned against a huge cedar tree, its long branches gracefully swept down, almost touching the earth.

Slowly Chief Yazzi walked away from Mondo and over to the huge outcropping of rock. He stopped a few feet in front of it, then knelt down and brushed the earth away. A moment later he dug out a short handled shovel. He gently put the canvas bag on the ground, stood and walked a few feet to his right before he started digging. The earth came up easy and soon he was on his knees brushing away the last remaining loose earth from a large flat stone.

Standing, he wedged his shovel under the front right corner of the stone and forced it up. Mondo rushed over and together they lifted it up a few more inches and slid it back and out of the way. Mondo stared down into the darkness of a tunnel then looked over at Chief Yazzi.

"A treasure awaits you," Chief Yazzi said.

Chapter 47

The smell of fresh coffee radiated out of the small kitchen on BELWOLF IV. Breakfast was being cooked, and the crew gathered around eating and drinking coffee as a loud chatter filled the small room. Another day was starting and they were all anxious for the barge to show up. They had been sitting around long enough and they were ready to log.

Dawn was sitting by herself and she was scared to death. She couldn't believe that Michael didn't care that the crew knew she was here. From the moment she had climbed off the helicopter, there had been no effort to hide her presence.

Last night Michael and Tommy had gotten so drunk that when Michael climbed into their small cabin he immediately passed out. She doubted she would escape his lecherous plans that easily tonight. Somehow she had to get off this barge, but how, and even if she could, where would she run?

She sipped her coffee slowly, trying to think of something that she could do to escape, but her thoughts kept going back to Mondo and she couldn't force him out of her mind. She was still lost in her thoughts when a tall, thin man walked into the galley and up to the table where Michael and Tommy sat. He carried a large handheld telephone and he handed it to Tommy without saying a word, then turned and left. She watched Tommy as he listened to the call, a few seconds later his entire expression changed and a sudden seriousness came over him. His face turned pale and his hand holding the phone started to shake. Michael, who had been busy eating, suddenly looked up and started paying attention to the call. It seemed in the next moment the entire crew stopped whatever they were doing or saying, and the room became deathly quiet as everybody switched their focus to Tommy.

Unconsciously Tommy closed his eyes and let out a deep sigh, and a minute later he took the phone away from his ear and laid it on the table. The silence echoed in the small galley. He looked around the room and back to Michael.

"They sabotaged the tug, and they had to cut the barge loose. It went down Shellcha rapids, it flipped over and all of the equipment went overboard. The barge finally drifted up on the beach smashed to shit," he said, then slammed his huge fist down on the table.

"All of the equipment is gone, Jesus Christ!"

Michael had been so startled by him slamming his fist down that without even thinking about it he jumped backward and fell right out of his chair.

Every eye was riveted on Tommy as they all thought about the implications of what he had just said.

"There's more," he said as Michael pulled himself back to the table.

Everybody waited in silent anticipation for his next words.

"The crew on the barge shot one of them. Shot him right off of a small dinghy as two people raced away from shore. Those stupid bastards! Jesus Christ, what idiots! The last thing we need is people to start shooting around here."

Michael wasn't thinking about bloodshed. All he could think about was that another hundred thousand dollars worth of equipment had just disappeared in a heartbeat.

Joseph and the elders finished their meeting around two-thirty. They all understood there would be no holding back, it truly was now war. Even Leonard Dancing Hawk left Chief Yazzi's house with a very heavy heart. His thoughts kept going back to his two small children. How would this all end for them? What would his wife do if he were killed? As he walked to his house, he knew he was facing the same fears that had haunted his people ever since the white man had first arrived on their shores such a long time ago.

271

Mondo started through the tunnel, following Chief Yazzi and the glow of his flashlight. The darkness closed in on him and he had to fight his fear of claustrophobia as he struggled on. After crawling for about twenty feet he watched as the old man stood. When Mondo reached Chief Yazzi he stood up next to him and tried to see in the faint light. The old man took a few more steps and Mondo watched the beam of the flashlight as it came to rest on a carved rock shelf that looked like an altar. A match was struck and in the next moment a small lamp was lit. Chief Yazzi turned the flashlight off and set it down then took the canvas bag from his shoulder. He let the burlap fall to the ground as he reverently set the Cross next to the lamp.

The light from the lamp burned brighter and Mondo's eyes were starting to adjust to the darkness. Slowly he could start to make sense of what he was seeing. To his left was a large flat stone, and on it lay ten human skeletons. The sight sent a cold chill down his spine. He walked to the skeletons and then looked at Chief Yazzi.

"Yes, Mondo, those are the gods," the old man whispered.

Mondo turned to his right and walked about five feet until he was standing in front of three stacks of copper. Each sheet was an inch thick and they were stacked to the low ceiling. A few more steps brought him to a small shelf carved into the rock. Sitting on it were three small golden replicas of the stone carvings of Easter Island, and next to them a golden sphinx and a small golden pyramid. Mondo looked to his right and walked to another ledge. Sitting on it, carved from a black stone was a foot long replica of an ocean-going boat. Even in the dim light he could see the fine detail that showed the boat was built in the lap-strake design, with one board overlapping the other as it went up from the keel. Its up-turned bow was swept high, as was its stern, and it reminded him of the design the Vikings would one day make famous. In the silence of this place his thoughts drifted to Jonathan.

The lamp burned brighter and his focus became clearer as he studied the many treasures before him. Lying on the ground, piled against the wall, was a stack of swords and lances, all stained with a green patina of ancient bronze. He reached down and picked up one of the swords and ran his thumb down the edge. It was still amazingly sharp. Gently putting the sword back on the pile he continued exploring. Sitting on another shelf cut into the solid rock was a bowl of jewelry, precious stones, and a few gold coins. He gently ran his fingers through the bowl knowing its contents must be worth millions.

Mondo continued to walk inside the small chamber staring in disbelief at what he saw. He found another carving of a sailing ship, then he saw three bronze heads, each identical and about a foot high, sitting on another rock ledge. The faces were those of ancient Greek warriors, bearded men with proud features staring at him through empty eyes. For the next ten minutes he wandered inside the small room in silent disbelief. Chief Yazzi stood by watching, but never said a word as Mondo beheld treasures that would truly rewrite ancient history.

It was almost dark when they reached the top of Bald Mountain and the two waiting motorcycles. It had been a very difficult climb and Mondo wondered how Chief Yazzi managed it, yet the old man had set a fast pace and never wavered. Driving down the mountain in the fading light seemed almost impossible, and it was after nine when they finally reached Chief Yazzi's house.

They climbed off the dirt bikes and Chief Yazzi thanked both of the drivers before they drove off in a loud roar and he and Mondo walked inside. Joseph sat at the small table and Mondo walked up to him and looked over his shoulder. Joseph was looking at a topographical map of Salmon Creek, Swartz Bay and the surrounding area. There were thin red pencil lines drawn along the map and Mondo shivered as he thought of more bloodshed. Joseph gave him a smile, but it was half-hearted. Mondo pulled a chair out and sat down. He was bone tired and hungry, but his thoughts kept going back to the treasure and to Jonathan. Chief Yazzi was rummaging around in the kitchen when Joseph turned and looked at Mondo, but this time there was no smile on his face.

"What?" Mondo asked, knowing something was wrong just by the look.

Joseph didn't say a word. Slowly he reached under the map and pulled out a small stack of photographs and slid them across the table. It took Mondo a second to realize that he was looking at BELWOLF IV anchored in Swartz Bay. There was Michael Jensen, and off to one side in the corner of the picture stood Dawn Peters, and she was terrified.

Chapter 48

His knees grew weak, and he had a hard time catching his breath as he looked at Dawn and saw the fear that was etched on her face. Rage flooded through him as he looked at the photos. At that moment Mondo fully understood the type of man that Michael Jensen was. He would never back down and this could end only one way, somebody was going to have to kill him.

"God, I don't believe it, Joseph. Why would he do that?"

"Because he thinks he is invincible?"

"Is he?"

"I don't know."

Mondo ran his fingers through his hair and leaned back in the chair.

"Joseph, I have to get Dawn off of that barge."

Joseph nodded his head in agreement.

"Our plans are set Mondo. We will move into position tonight, but we can do nothing until morning."

"I can't wait until morning."

Mondo stood up, "Good luck, my friend," he said as he reached his hand out, then turned and started running for Smokin' Joe.

He was back on board in less than ten minutes. His mind had been racing all the way, trying to think of how he could possibly rescue her, and it seemed almost impossible. How could he get on board BELWOLF IV, find her, and get them both off without somebody seeing them? Standing at the chart table with his small day pack opened in front of him, he threw in a folded chart of the area, duct tape, flashlight, a hand-held GPS, and his razor-sharp fish-filleting knife. He was dressed in the darkest clothes he could find and he had a black stocking cap on his head.

At the foot of the companionway steps, he stopped and looked around his home. He loved Smokin' Joe and for one fleeting moment he thought of how wonderful it might be to take Dawn with him and show her some of the wonders of life aboard a sailboat. That thought lasted only a second, and he knew there was no time for wishful thinking, not now. Tomorrow there would be lots of time if things worked out, and he couldn't bring himself to ponder the alternative.

As he started to climb up the steps, he grabbed his fish-smacking billy club and threw it in his day pack, zipped it closed, and flung it over his shoulder.

In the still, quiet darkness of the night he climbed into his dinghy and pushed off from the dock. This time he rowed to his left, keeping himself in the shadows of the overhanging trees that reached down to the waters edge.

Making his way past the loggers took over twenty minutes as he slowly rowed, not allowing a sound to escape. The night had an eerie silence to it, and his neck and shoulders became sore as he constantly turned to see what was ahead of him. There was no way he could start his engine, and eight miles was one hell of a long way to row an inflatable dinghy.

Three times he stopped and checked his GPS against the chart to find out exactly where he was. Finally, just when he thought his arms couldn't pull the oars one more time, he came around a large group of rocks at the water's edge and saw the barge. Its outline was silhouetted against the shore by a bright spotlight that hung from the top of the crane.

Mondo stopped rowing and took a deep breath. He stayed there for a few minutes before he rowed the dingy into a small cove, dragged it up on a rocky beach, and tied it off to a tree. He opened his day pack, strapped his filleting knife on his belt, then threw his pack over his shoulder and headed for the barge. It was a lot further away than he had first thought. It felt like it took forever before he was finally hiding in the shadows near some lines that stretched from the barge to shore. He sat for fifteen minutes, just watching, calming his fears and trying to get some strength back into his arms and shoulders. He had seen three men walking the deck, all armed and all looking very aware as they patrolled. This was going to be almost impossible, he thought.

The helicopter was on a small landing pad and there was a cabin near it that had some light coming from a window. He would aim for that cabin and hope to God that's where Dawn was. Wrapping his hands and feet around one of the long lines that led from shore to the barge he started crawling, hanging upside down, holding on as best as he could, realizing just how vulnerable he was. Slowly, hand over hand he painfully pulled himself forward until he reached the barge. Grabbing the bulwark, he dragged himself up and over and landed on the steel deck. Without wasting a second he crawled over to some large wooden crates and hid. There wasn't a sound to be heard anywhere. Lying there trying to catch his breath, he opened his pack and grabbed his billy club.

A minute later he started crawling toward the small cabin near the helicopter. Pulling himself over the rough steel plating the deck was made from, was like crawling over sixty-grit sandpaper, but there was nothing else he could do. Twice he had to freeze and wait as a guard walked by.

He was a nervous wreck by the time he finally reached the cabin. Slowly, keeping hidden in the darkness, he rose to his feet and peered through the curtain, which was a thin blanket hung up from the inside. Looking at the lower left corner where the blanket left a small void he saw that he was looking into a bedroom and office. There was a small desk against the far wall covered with paperwork, books, radio equipment and, he recognized, a satellite telephone. He couldn't hear a sound and after a few minutes he knew she wasn't there.

He turned so his back was leaning against the wall, then slid down until he rested on his knees and looked around, and he didn't have a clue what to do next. It would be almost impossible to randomly find her and he had a much better chance of being discovered by one of the guards as he stumbled around searching. Crouching in the darkness he waited for something to happen, waited for anything to trigger a response that would lead him on. He didn't have long to wait.

The guard was smoking a cigarette, not paying much attention as he started to walk past Mondo. He never saw the billy club that came crashing down on his head, instantly causing his knees to buckle before he hit the steel deck with a thud. Mondo pulled his stocking cap off and crammed it in the man's mouth, then pulling his fillet knife out of the sheath held it against the guard's throat. The man's eyes were wide open with terror as he looked up.

"One sound and you're dead," Mondo whispered, "where's the girl?"

Slowly the man raised his right hand and pointed across the deck to the front of the barge, and a cabin that had a dim light glowing through a window.

"You lie to me and you're dead," Mondo said, trying to sound as tough as possible and not letting any of the fear that he felt echo through his voice.

Mondo reached over his shoulder, unzipped his backpack, and pulled out the duct tape with his left hand. He ran the tape three times around the man's head, forcing the cap into his mouth, making it impossible for him to utter a sound. He bound the man's hands and feet and then wrapped his body to a stanchion that held the bulwark in place.

Mondo brought his face down close to the man who still looked absolutely terrified.

"Make one sound and my friend, who is only five feet from you will cut your throat, you got it?"

The guard slowly nodded his head and Mondo turned and started crawling toward the front of the barge.

eonard Dancing Hawk met his men at the foot of the dock. As they gathered close around him in the silence of the night he looked deep into their eyes. All of these men he loved as family. All of them he had known his entire life, and he couldn't control the fear that by morning some of them might be dead.

He looked out into the darkness of the bay, knowing that his first task was to remove the blockade. Holding the two aluminum skiffs in the water he let four armed men climb into each boat before he silently pushed them off toward the unsuspecting loggers. As his friends rowed out into the bay he walked to the end of the dock, knelt down, strapped the night vision goggles on, and then sighted down his hunting rifle. The clarity of the goggles amazed him as he instantly saw the two boats with the loggers in them. The boats were tied together and he could see two armed men sitting, fighting sleep and boredom. He hoped they were wise enough not to fight, but if they did he would fire the first shot.

He watched as his men continued, praying that this wouldn't end in bloodshed. When the lead skiff was twenty feet from the anchored loggers one of them must have heard something, because suddenly they all jumped up and started pointing their rifles randomly into the darkness. When one of the loggers took aim directly at the first skiff, Leonard sighted on the man, let out a deep sigh and fired.

The shot exploded through the stillness of the night and the man was flipped overboard by the impact. In the next second the loggers started firing wildly and all hell broke loose. His men on the skiffs started shooting and the loggers continued firing blindly. It lasted less than ten seconds, but in that time five loggers were killed before the rest stopped shooting and dropped to the bottom of their aluminum skiffs trying to save themselves.

Dawn sat in the corner of the small cabin, shaking with so much terror that she could hardly breathe. She had just glanced up at Michael, and now she feared him as she had never feared another person in her entire life. He was standing two feet away from her, naked, his hard body reflecting the light from the candles that sat on a small counter.

"Do you like what you see?" he asked her, his tone so menacing.

She couldn't react. Fear had driven her over the edge. She kept her face in her hands, crying, trying in some way to deny what was inevitable. He was going to rape her and probably kill her and there was nothing she could do to prevent it.

"I said look at me," he ordered in a hushed but deadly tone.

Slowly she brought her eyes up to him, saw his naked glow, saw the evil on his face, and then watched as his wicked smile grew.

"That's better," he said as he grabbed her hair and pulled her face to his.

"That's much better," he said as he bent over and forced his lips on hers, tasting the saltiness of her tears still wet on her lips.

He pulled away from her, grabbed her right arm and forced her up against his naked body. She couldn't stand and as she started to fall he reached both hands behind her, pulled her close and forced his lips on hers again.

In the next moment he swept her up in his arms, carried her over to the small bed in the corner and dropped her. Michael ripped her blouse open and forcefully pulled it over her head. He knelt down on the bed and ran his fingers up her back and unsnapped her bra, flinging it away. Dawn couldn't breathe, she thought maybe her heart would give out and she would die right then. He pulled her close as he bent down and ran his lips over her breast, driving fear into her very soul.

Michael pulled his lips away a moment later and looked deep into her terror filled face. "I told you love, I really did reserve the honeymoon suite."

Mondo was carefully making his way forward, trying to keep in the shadows, but soon it became impossible as the light from the top of the crane was hanging directly over where he had to go. He knelt behind a low wall, staring at the fifty feet he would have to run before he could hide again. There was nothing he could do but try. Taking a deep breath he charged out into the light, waiting for a sudden cry from a guard or crew person. He ran as fast as he could and before he knew it he was back in the shadows. Slowly he continued toward the cabin, which stood off by itself near the bow on the port side of the boat. He had lost track of the guards and he had no idea when the next one would come around the corner. His club was ready and his fillet knife was back on his side. Finally he reached the cabin where a soft glow came through the window and its flimsy curtain. Slowly he straightened himself up and he dared to look. The soft light from a few candles allowed him to see into the room just as Michael brought his face up from Dawn's breast, the terror on her face tearing Mondo's heart apart. Instantly, without even thinking, his hand tightened on the billy club and he raced around the corner, searching for the cabin door. He prayed to god it wouldn't be locked as he reached down and twisted the knob in his hand. Mondo charged the fifteen feet across the cabin and by the time Michael could react there was nothing he could do. Mondo swung the club as hard as he could, catching Michael on the side of his head just as he turned, the impact making a sickening thud as it sent Michael flying off the bed into a crumpled heap in the corner.

Dawn took one look at Mondo, started to say something, tried to move before her face went completely white, and in the next second she let out a small gasp and fainted. Michael lay motionless in the corner, he didn't make a sound.

Mondo knelt beside Dawn and slapped her face. She stirred, muttered something that he couldn't understand, but her eyes never opened. He turned, looked around the cabin and saw a small washbasin. Running over to it he grabbed a cup, filled it with water and raced back to Dawn before throwing the water in her face. It was an involuntary gasp that came from deep inside, as she opened her eyes. Mondo knelt down and wrapped his arms around her. Dawn was somewhere between consciously being aware of his presence and some other far away place, and for the next few minutes he just held her.

"Dawn, it's me, it's Mondo, I'm here, I love you," he finally whispered, his face inches from hers.

"Oh Mondo God, I . . ." she tried to talk but her mind wouldn't work.

"Dawn, listen to me. We need to get out of here. Can you stand up?"

She nodded her head.

Mondo looked around and found her ripped blouse and handed it to her.

"Quickly, let's go," he whispered as she threw her blouse on and followed after him.

Mondo led the way out the cabin door, then knelt down and looked around. He couldn't see anyone but he knew they couldn't risk going back across the boat. Glancing to his left, he saw one of the long ropes that held the front of the barge to shore. Reaching behind him he grabbed Dawn's right hand and slowly led her over to the bulwark at the side of the boat.

"Can you climb down this rope?" he asked, but she was still shaking so badly he knew she couldn't make it.

He climbed over the rail and held his hand out for her.

"Trust me," he whispered.

She grabbed his right hand and swung her body over the bulwark and they stood on a small ledge about fifty feet above the water.

"Dawn, listen to me. Climb on my back and don't let go. If you do we're dead."

He turned his back to her and felt her jump up and wrap her arms and legs tight around him, then he grabbed hold of the rope and with a little kick, brought his feet up and started climbing toward shore.

His hands burned and his muscles screamed in protest as he dangled upside down with Dawn hanging on tight below him. Slowly, hand over hand he finally reached land. Dawn fell to the ground the instant Mondo stood up, her knees so weak it took a few minutes before she could get up and stand next to him.

They stood in the silence another thirty seconds before he grabbed her by the hand and off they went. It was very difficult for them to pick their way through the darkness above the steep cliffs that fell off into Swartz Bay. One false step could send them both tumbling down into the freezing water and the splash would wake everyone on the barge. Slowly he led her down to the waters edge and finally to the small bay where he had tied his inflatable. Dawn sat down on the side of his boat and took one long look at Mondo as he sat down beside her. Tears welled up from deep inside and all she could do was put her arms around him and hold him close as she tried to bury the sound of her sobs in his chest.

Chapter 50

n the quiet of the early morning dawn, seven boats carrying thirty-two armed men slowly rounded the corner into Swartz Bay. As soon as the barge was in sight Joseph raised his right hand and the boats circled around him, and in a hushed voice that held none of the fear that he felt he gently said, "Everyone knows what we must do. We are an honorable people. I love you all, be brave, be strong."

Two boats, one of them carrying the bodies of the five dead loggers started toward the stern of the barge as the rest turned to shore and the small bay they would use to beach their boats on. The first ashore were surprised to see Mondo's dinghy partially hidden in the far corner of the beach. They waited for Joseph then pointed out the inflatable. Panic filled him, and he had a sudden anguish that his friend was dead. Joseph walked over, looked inside and saw Mondo and Dawn sleeping in the bottom of the inflatable, their arms wrapped tight around each other. Silently, he stepped back and raised his index finger to his lips, then he turned and watched the other two skiffs as they paddled toward the barge.

The two boats stopped a hundred feet from the stern of BELWOLF IV. The man paddling the boat with the dead loggers in it dropped an anchor overboard then climbed into the other boat and they returned to the beach where the others were waiting. Once again Joseph gathered his men around him, but this time he said nothing. He placed his hand on the shoulder of the man next to him, bowed his head and in the silence and beauty of this place they all knew what they were fighting for. The silence filled each of them. Then Joseph and his men started hiking, and soon all of them were well hidden surrounding the barge. Now, it was a waiting game, and it wouldn't take long before somebody on the barge spotted the anchored skiff.

All of Joseph's men were wide awake, and all had their rifles aimed at the unsuspecting barge and her crew. Joseph hoped to avoid more bloodshed, yet what choice did he have? This was forced upon him and his people and he could see no other alternative but to fight for what was theirs.

A short time later Joseph watched a crew member as he made his way to the stern of the barge and started to light a cigarette before spotting the anchored skiff. The man turned and raced back inside, coming out a minute later with five or six other men. They all stared at the dinghy, and Joseph didn't give them any time to react as he raised his rifle into the air and fired the first shot. In the next instant all of Joseph's men opened fire. They aimed not at the men on board, but at the barge itself. Joseph's hope was not to kill but to intimidate.

Bullets ricocheted off the steel plating of the barge and its upper decks as everyone on board dove for cover. The overhead light hanging from the crane was shot out and it came crashing down to the deck in a thousand pieces. The fire-power of over thirty men all shooting as quickly as possible caused everybody on the barge to panic. Even Tommy Landford rolled out of bed and threw himself down next to his bunk as bullets smashed off the side of his cabin. One bullet found its way through his small window, sending shattered glass flying across the floor before the bullet passed through the wall. Joseph and his men fired over two hundred rounds before stopping after one minute as planned. The air reeked of gunpowder, and a smoky haze drifted across Swartz Bay, carried on a slight breeze.

The first person to move was Michael. He stumbled out of the cabin door naked, holding a wet towel to the side of his bloody head. He staggered to the rail, looking like a madman as he stared out through the haze of burnt powder. His movements were jerky and his hand holding the towel trembled.

"You bastards, you crazy bastards!" he screamed, his words having a slur to them that made it almost impossible to understand him.

Joseph aimed to the right of him and fired. The bullet struck metal creating a ringing explosion, but Michael didn't move, he didn't even flinch as another round was sent his way. Dropping the towel from his bloody head, he stood there screaming at them, raising his right fist in defiance and they all knew they were watching a man out of his mind.

Joseph climbed up on the rocks he was hiding behind until he was in plain view of all on the barge.

"Listen to me!" he shouted, "you will leave this place and never return. I give you until tomorrow morning. If you are still here we will return and kill you. That I promise," then he stepped back and disappeared into the forest.

"That's right," Tommy screamed into the satellite phone, "just ten minutes ago. Five of my men are dead and Michael's out of his mind. Those bastards shot up the barge, and my men are not sticking around! This has gone over the edge, my God, it's over the edge!"

He sat there trying to calm himself, knowing that he had to get his emotions under control, but it was impossible at the moment.

"You'd better do something, 'cause I'm out of here and this whole thing is going to blow up so fast you can't believe it. The press will find out, not even you can hide it now."

He listened for a few more minutes, nodding his head in agreement as a little smile started to grow on his face.

"Okay, you do that! You send in the army, the navy, I don't give a shit, I just want those bastards out of the way for good."

He switched the phone off and tried to gain control of his breathing. The government was sending in troops and those bastards were going to pay.

The first military helicopter landed on the only road into Salmon Creek just before nine a.m., creating a blockade only a hundred feet from where the logging trucks had temporarily stopped traffic a few days ago. Fourteen armed soldiers climbed out and immediately set up a checkpoint. They rolled two roadside barricade kits out of the chopper, as well as seventy-five feet of tire puncturing road mat. Ten minutes after landing no one was coming or going from Salmon Creek without government approval.

The one hundred and twenty-three foot military cutter, Mackenzie Spirit was one hour away from departing Esquimalt, and her orders were simple. Rush at full speed to Salmon Creek, and stop any and all boat traffic from entering or leaving the harbor.

Three troop trucks plus a mobile command center, including tents for cooking and housing, as well as another forty-three soldiers were already on the road having departed Nanaimo less than an hour after Tommy had hung up from his call. Tommy Landford had called the right person. The government was coming and they were as pissed off as he was.

There was no joy inside the small house of Chief Yazzi. They had been fortunate that none of their people had been injured, but they knew that they would soon feel the full power of the white man's rage. Mondo and Dawn sat in the living room. They had said little, as Joseph and his father talked about the response they both knew would come soon.

A knock on the door startled them all. A moment later the door opened and a young boy walked inside. He smiled at Mondo and Dawn as he walked to the kitchen table where Joseph and his father sat.

"Hello, Chief Yazzi, a helicopter with soldiers has landed and they have blocked the road. My mother and I were told to turn around and leave. There was nothing else we could do. They had rifles pointing at us. We pretended to drive away, but we know of the old river road. My mother is sitting in the car as close to town as the old road will let her drive. She told me to run and see you and ask if there is anything we can do?"

Joseph recognized him as a cousin of one of his people that lived a few miles off the reservation.

"Go back to your mother. Tell her to call as many of our people as she can. Tell her to call the newspapers. Tell your mother that we are trapped and the army has arrived," Chief Yazzi said.

Slowly, the old man turned and looked at Joseph, then Mondo and Dawn before reaching down and putting his right hand on the young boy's shoulder.

In a soft voice he said to the boy. "You are brave to have run all of this way, thank you. Tell your mother that we in Salmon Creek are at war and we will die soon without help."

Within an hour of the first phone call, over a hundred people had streamed into Salmon Creek to show their support for Chief Yazzi and his people. Cars full of native people pulled over and parked as close to the check-point as they were allowed. In the next hour the crowd grew to over three hundred. Soon a helicopter was flying overhead with the letters of television station KIRE written boldly on its side. The people waved their hands high and roared out in a loud voice as the press helicopter hovered low, a cameraman perched in the open doorway, secured by a tether, filming the ever-growing group.

Within ten minutes that live footage was being shown throughout British Columbia, then throughout the nation. All over Canada people dropped whatever they were doing and watched as a crisis was about to unfold on Vancouver Island.

Chapter 51

The telephone rang five times and had just started switching to the answering machine when Naomi rushed out of the bathroom with a towel wrapped around her.

"Hello," she said wondering why she hadn't let the machine get it.

"Naomi, it's Jonathan. Have you seen the news?"

The way he said it drove fear right through her.

"What! The news . . . what happened, is Mondo okay?"

"I don't know, but something big is happening in Salmon Creek. Turn on the television and see if anything is on. It's all over Canadian news."

Holding the phone to her ear with her shoulder, she ran over and flicked the television on.

"Jonathan, what's happening?" she said, her voice echoing the fears that were growing by the second.

Naomi clicked through the ten stations she received, but nothing was on except for regular viewing.

"Jonathan, I don't have all of the fancy news stations. Nothing is on down here. Tell me what is happening!"

"There has been some shooting in Salmon Creek."

Naomi dropped down on the couch. She felt her blood drain away and she couldn't catch her breath.

"Naomi, are you there?"

"Jonathan, my God, shooting! Who?"

"Right now it seems five loggers have been killed. The news is saying they were ambushed and murdered. They're making the native people sound like a bunch of bloodthirsty, crazy Indians. The press is totally one-sided on this."

"Jonathan, what about Mondo?"

"I don't know."

"What can we do?"

"Nothing, Naomi. I just wanted to let you know that something is coming down and I know Mondo is right smack in the middle of it all."

"There must be something we can do?"

"Naomi . . . I can't think of a thing."

"I'll stay by the phone. Please, Jonathan, you need to keep me posted. Will I be able to call you?"

"Yes, I'm at the museum. I'll be here all day following this. I'm going to make some more calls. If I find anything out, I'll call you."

"Jonathan, I'm scared to death for Mondo."

"Naomi . . . so am I."

She heard the click as he hung up, and she felt her world turn upside down. She didn't even try to get up from the couch for fifteen minutes. Her wet hair was dripping puddles, as her mind raced with the fear that Mondo could be in really big trouble.

Finally she forced herself up and over to the computer. She Googled Canadian news and what she saw shocked her. In bold flashing colors the on-line news page screamed out about the five loggers ambushed and murdered in Salmon Creek. The article said that at this time they didn't know who was responsible for the murders, but it was likely First Nation People. She scrolled down the page and was even more shocked when she clicked on the live video link and watched the continuing footage shot from a news helicopter. It looked like a thousand people were gathered in a huge field, and more cars and people were pulling in by the minute. Off to one side was a military camp with tents, jeeps, trucks and lots of heavily armed soldiers. Across the road was a huge barricade with a steel bar blocking any access, and armed guards were stopping all cars. Naomi thought it looked like Baghdad. God, she thought, this looks really bad.

*

"I cannot let you do this, Father. Please don't go," Joseph was pleading, but it didn't change Chief Yazzi's mind.

Standing next to the battered police car, he turned and looked at his son.

"Joseph, I will take the loggers that we held in jail to the soldiers. I will try to talk to them."

"You know what will happen. You will be arrested."

The old man slowly nodded his head in agreement and looked at his son.

"Yes, Joseph, I know that. There is nothing else that I can do. I am the chief of my people, though it is you who will guide us through this. I am sorry that you have returned to such sorrow."

Then without another word he climbed into the front seat and the driver pulled away, heading for the roadblock.

Chief Yazzi was amazed at how many soldiers there were as they slowed down to stop before the metal barricade a few minutes later. He knew that death was standing in the middle of the road and there was nothing he could do to stop it.

Slowly he opened his door and stepped out, looking at over ten soldiers with their rifles pointing right at him. Opening the back door, he let the loggers climb out. They walked to the barricade and were warmly greeted. Chief Yazzi followed a few feet behind them and stopped studying the young soldiers who pointed their rifles at him.

"I have returned your people to you. I am Chief Yazzi. Is there anything more that I can do for you?" he asked watching their confusion grow.

The soldiers looked at each other, wondering who the hell this stupid Indian was. Finally one of them turned to the tents and hollered somebody's name and a minute later a large man walked up to Chief Yazzi.

"I am in charge. My name is Major Jason Lafferty. Who the hell are you?"

"I am Chief Yazzi. I have released these loggers from our jail and I am turning them over to you. They have violated our lands and the treaties that we have upheld with your government."

"Listen, Chief," Jason said, his tone seething with anger, "I don't give a shit about your violations or treaties. Five loggers have been murdered and if you're the chief of this damn place, then you're under arrest."

"I have come in peace."

"Peace my ass! You and your people should have thought about keeping the peace before you started killing."

"I have come in peace and I will now leave in peace," he said then turned and started walking back to his car.

"I said stop, you crazy bastard!" Jason ordered, but Chief Yazzi didn't slow down.

Major Lafferty was almost speechless at the nerve of this old man.

"Stop, you idiot!" he screamed.

Then he turned to two soldiers who were standing next to him.

"Get that son of a bitch!"

They rushed after Chief Yazzi, and just before he reached the open car door, one of them hit him in the back with his rifle butt, crashing him into the front fender of the car, smashing his forehead on the windshield before he stumbled and fell to the ground.

In the next instant over five hundred people screamed in rage and started to rush forward to protect Chief Yazzi. Major Lafferty turned and looked at the angry mob. He knew this was about one second away from turning into a complete bloodbath, and that wasn't going to happen on his watch.

"Fire into the air!" he screamed, and twenty of his men raised their rifles and fired over the surging crowd. The flood of people stopped at the sound of the shots, but their rage continued. From somewhere in the crowd a stone flew through the air and hit one of the men standing next to the Major. In the next second a barrage of stones came flying from the crowd.

"Fire again," Lafferty ordered and his men fired over the crowd. The stones continued flying, the anger that drove the native people overcoming their fear of the white man's bullets.

One of the soldiers must have panicked, because in the next second suddenly two of the protesters crumpled to the ground. Both had been shot in the chest.

"My God, hold your fire!" Major Lafferty shouted, but to no avail.

The soldiers, many fearing for their lives, fired into the crowd. People fell, as others screamed, everybody running for their lives.

By now there were three news helicopters flying overhead and all of them captured the shooting live. In less than a minute the shocking news footage was being broadcast, not just in Canada but throughout the world. This was now a major worldwide event.

Chief Yazzi was pushed into the command center tent, told to sit down, shut up and not to move. Paramedics were treating the injured and already medical helicopters had been called in. Twelve people were shot, three were already dead, and it looked like more might not make it. Major Lafferty couldn't believe how quickly it all happened.

The sound of the gunfire had just faded away with the last echoes from the mountains surrounding Salmon Creek, and already Mondo, Joseph and Dawn were running down the street. They raced around the corner out to the rutted main street, looking for the next car to drive by and give them a ride to where the roadblock was. A minute later they climbed into the back of an old pickup truck and raced out of town.

The truck slowed to a stop a hundred feet from the barricade, as the three of them stood in the back and tried to see Chief Yazzi in the mass confusion of people. They couldn't find him.

"My father," Joseph said softly.

The faded green police car slowly started backing away from the barricade and the soldiers just ignored it.

When the old police car reached the truck, the driver rolled down the passenger window and looked at them. Tears streamed down his face.

"The soldiers have shot some of our people. I think some are dead. Your father has been arrested. At least he is not hurt," he lied, remembering the rifle butt hitting the old man from behind.

Mondo reached his arm out and put it on Joseph's shoulder. They stood there for a few minutes before three soldiers who had been standing at the gate suddenly started walking their way.

"We can do nothing by staying here Joseph," Mondo whispered.

Joseph nodded his head then he bent over to the driver of the truck.

"Please, we should go."

Dawn kept looking at Mondo as they rode back into town, and he understood what was going through her mind. Somehow, the two of them had to help the standoff come to a peaceful end. They were the only two white people that Joseph and his people trusted.

awn and Mondo sat on Joseph's front porch throwing ideas out as fast as they could think of them. Any idea that popped into their minds was discussed. The urgency that they both felt overshadowed everything else. Salmon Creek was about to explode, and they knew it.

"I just can't think of anything else that's not stupid," she said.

"Nothing is stupid at the moment, Dawn. There has to be some way we can get the government to back off long enough for this to calm down. We know that the logging is wrong, and it probably is illegal. So what's your stupid thought?"

"Well, maybe we should bus as many homeless people up here as possible. I think we could get thousands to show up."

"That's a thought, but we don't have the time. What else?"

"What else? I can't think of a thing, can you?"

"Actually I can."

"You can! What is it?"

Mondo stood up, reached his hand to Dawn's and gently pulled her up.

"Let's go talk to Joseph."

They walked into Joseph's house to find him sitting on the couch, his eyes closed, his head resting in the soft fabric. Hearing them enter, he glanced their way, smiled, but he looked very defeated at the moment.

"Joseph I want you to think about something. I have a plan to get the government to back off."

"How?"

"Listen, Joseph. Your father said the treasure wasn't yours to keep, that your people are only the caretakers of it. I think now is the time to reveal it to the world. Think about the impact it would have."

"We are cut off from the world, how can we do anything?"

"No, Joseph, we're not, not completely, anyway."

Joseph slowly opened his eyes and looked at Mondo.

"Even if it is the right thing to do, I see no way to accomplish it. I doubt I could find the treasure, and I am not sure who else knows where it is located," he said before casting his gaze back to the floor.

"I can find it."

"You can? Has my father taken you there?"

"Yes, he did Joseph. I can find the treasure."

Joseph thought for a few minutes, leaving Mondo and Dawn standing in an awkward silence.

"How can we tell the world? We are prisoners here," he finally said sounding totally defeated once again.

"Do you want to tell the world Joseph? It could save your people. I think I have a way to contact the outside."

Joseph let out a deep sigh, and gave them both another worried look.

"I would do anything to save my people."

"Joseph, I know you trust me. Let us show the world the Treasure of Salmon Creek."

Ten minutes later Mondo was standing at his chart table, his right hand holding the radio microphone, Dawn sat on the bottom rung of the companionway ladder, looking around the inside of Smokin' Joe.

Mondo's left hand was sweaty as he scrolled through the radio frequencies that were allowed for vessel traffic. Rolling through the numbers, he hoped against hope that whoever he contacted would take him seriously. Finally, he heard someone talking and he listened for a minute, waiting for just the right moment.

"Break, break, break, this is Whiskey Charlie X-Ray 3381, break."

Mondo knew it was very rude behavior to break in on the middle of somebody's conversation, yet this was his only hope of contacting the outside world, and it was too important to worry about petty protocol.

"Break, come back, this is the fishing vessel Hammerhead, over."

"Hammerhead, this is Smokin' Joe. I need a little help. I'm in Salmon Creek, is there any way you can do a phone patch for me?"

"Salmon Creek, man, what is going on up there? It's all over the news."

"It's not good, Hammerhead, that's for sure."

There was a pause on the radio before Hammerhead came back.

"I can run up to the house. I'm out on my dock. I could patch you through the ham-radio network."

"Hammerhead, you have no idea how important this is."

"Okay, Smokin' Joe. Stay on frequency and I'll run up to the house. I'll be back on the radio in a flash."

"Hammerhead, thank you, I'll be standing by on six-eight."

Mondo opened his chart table, grabbed his wallet and pulled out Jonathan's card. In a minute Hammerhead was back on the radio.

"Okay, Smokin' Joe, I'm here. What number do you want me to call?"

Mondo gave him Jonathan's home number. The phone rang and rang but nobody answered. Mondo couldn't believe that he finally had a way to contact the outside world and Jonathan wasn't home.

"Can we try another number, Hammerhead?"

"No problem, what is it?"

Mondo read off Jonathan's number at the museum. The phone in his office started ringing one minute after he stepped out and walked down the hall to the bathroom. In the three minutes it took him to return to his office he had missed Mondo's call.

"Hammerhead, I don't want to run this into the ground, but can you possibly try another number for me?"

"Mondo, I have friends in Salmon Creek, I'll do whatever I can to help."

"Thank you, here's the number."

A minute later Naomi grabbed her phone. "Jonathan, what's going . . ." she was cut off by Mondo.

"Naomi, it's me Mondo."

"Mondo . . . are you all right? What's going on?"

"I'm okay. Listen, Naomi, remember the picture I emailed you, do you still have it saved on your computer?"

"Sure, I do."

"Good, I need you to contact somebody, the Smithsonian, World Heritage Foundation, the United Nations, I don't know. Just call somebody and tell them that a treasure, one that will rewrite history is buried in Salmon Creek and I know where it is."

"A treasure . . . Mondo, this sounds insane."

"Just trust me, Naomi. It's real and it's here, I've seen it. You need to go through your connections and try to get somebody to believe you. Hold a press conference, something, anything, and maybe we can stop what is about to happen up here."

"What's going to happen, Mondo?"

"A lot of people are going to die, Naomi, that's the bottom line."

"Mondo I don't have any contacts like that . . . I can't think," he cut her off in mid-sentence.

"Naomi, just start, you have to get somebody to look at the photo I emailed you."

"All right, I'll try. How do I get in touch with you?"

"Hammerhead, you still there?"

"Roger that."

"I don't know your take on any of this, Hammerhead, but I need to keep in touch with the outside world. All of our phone lines are down and the army isn't letting anybody in or out. Can I use you as a contact?"

"I'll do whatever I can."

"Naomi, write down Hammerhead's phone number. I'll try calling you through him and you can leave me messages. That's the best we can do."

There was a long silence on the phone as Naomi tried to grasp what she had just heard.

"Naomi," Mondo continued, "this is one of the greatest discoveries in five thousand years. If you write it, if you and Jonathan can pull this off, history will remember your names."

"Mondo, right now all I want is for you to be safe."

"Just tell the world Naomi, you and Jonathan are our only hope."

"Mondo be careful."

"Bye, Naomi."

"Bye, Mondo," she said and hung up.

"Hammerhead."

"Yeah."

"Well, Hammerhead, you heard a lot, and I got no idea what you're going to do with it, but I need your help. This really is about to turn into a bloodbath up here."

"Mondo, I have more native blood in me than white. I'll help anyway I can."

A deep sense of relief flooded through Mondo at hearing that.

"Listen, Mondo, I'll come on frequency every hour on the hour and stay on for ten minutes, at least until I fall asleep at night."

"Thank you. Let's use channel thirteen for contact."

"That's for commercial traffic, Mondo."

"I know, but there will be less chance of somebody overhearing us and listening in."

"Thirteen it is."

"Hammerhead, I'll talk to you soon, and thanks," he hung his radio mike up, looked at Dawn, and gave her a big smile.

"Welcome to my home."

"It's cute, Mondo," she said with a grin.

It was too bad that Mondo hadn't made his initial contact with Hammerhead on a different frequency. Tommy Landford's radio man had been constantly monitoring the normal marine channels, having programmed his receiver to scroll through and stop at any voice transmissions that it found. He had been half-asleep playing a game of solitaire when he heard Mondo's first contact with Hammerhead. At the mention of Salmon Creek he almost fell out of his chair, then he hollered out the radio room door for somebody to get Tommy.

Together they listened to almost all of Mondo's conversation with Naomi. After the phone patch was over, logging didn't seem very important to Tommy any more, not compared to a treasure.

"UNESCO," the lady on the phone said in a pleasant voice.

"Yes, hi, my name is Naomi. I need to talk to somebody, it's really important and I just don't know who to ask for," she knew she sounded like an idiot already.

"I'm sorry, what did you want to talk about?"

"A treasure."

"Really . . . a treasure like a secret treasure, maybe Pirates of the Caribbean type treasure?"

Naomi could tell that in about two seconds she was going to be hung-up on.

"Please, don't hang up. There is a town called Salmon Creek, it's in British Columbia. It's about to turn into a war zone between the government and the native people. There is a treasure there that will rewrite history but we need to stop this bloodbath before it starts."

"I can tell you're upset, but we really don't have a treasure department, sorry, maybe you should try Disney World."

Naomi could tell the lady was laughing at her through the phone line.

"Listen, just one more minute, please," Naomi pleaded. "I want to email you a picture of just a small part of the treasure. Please, can I have an email address? I'll send you my contact information as well. Please, let me email you this photo."

The operator looked at her watch. It was just about break time and she didn't want to deal with this crackpot, but this lady sounded so convincing.

"Alright, I will give you the email address of Mr. Paul Deseno. He is one of our in house consultants. He might like to see your picture."

"Thank you, I know you think I'm crazy, but wait until you see the picture. People's lives are at stake here."

"Yes, I'm sure the Pirates of the Caribbean could be very dangerous." Naomi could still hear the laughter in her voice, but she did get Paul's email address.

"Thank you. I will send this immediately."

"Thank you for your call, Naomi," the lady said, but her voice had lost any of its friendliness.

Frantically, Naomi sent off the email with the photo of the Cross as an attachment, along with her name and phone number.

In the headquarters for UNESCO, or United Nations Educational, Scientific, Cultural Organization in New York City, Mr. Paul Deseno was just about to leave for the day when his phone rang.

"Paul, this is Margie at reception. I just got a call from a lady who told me about a treasure in a small town in British Columbia called Salmon Creek. It's about to go to war or something . . . anyway, she sounded so convincing, and she begged me to give her an email address of somebody that she could send a picture of the treasure to. So I gave her your email address, hope you don't mind?"

"Margie," he said in an exasperated tone, "is this a joke?"

"Please, Paul, just check your email. I have a feeling it's already there."

"Just a minute, Margie, you might as well stay on the line in case I have any questions."

"Okay."

Paul hit his keyboard, then scrolled down to his emails and clicked once.

There was an email that simply said "treasure" next to it. He shook his head as he clicked on it and watched as the picture slowly grew into the photo that Mondo had sent Naomi. Paul studied it for a few seconds, and his curiosity grew.

"Margie," he said, the phone still perched on his shoulder, "did this lady sound like a nut?"

"No, as a matter of fact I wouldn't even have bothered you, but she sounded so convincing. Why, is there a picture?"

"Yes, Margie there is a picture, but I don't believe what I am seeing."

"Do you recognize it? What is it Paul?"

"Margie, all I can say is thank you. I'll keep you posted."

Paul didn't even wait for her reply before hanging up and punching in the contact telephone number written on the email.

Chapter 53

The Citation jet touched down at John Wayne International airport in Southern California, refueled, and picked up one passenger before taxiing back out onto the runway and taking off for Victoria, British Columbia.

Paul Deseno was taking the biggest gamble of his academic career. After calling the contact number on the email, and talking to Naomi, his instincts told him she was far from crazy. They talked for fifteen minutes and in that conversation he learned of Mr. Jonathan Beckwith, who worked at the Provincial Museum in Victoria. He called Jonathan and their conversation lasted over twenty minutes, and at the end of it he still didn't know what to do, or for that matter what to even think. It was only after turning on the television in the coffee room, watching CNN news and seeing the story about Salmon Creek that he realized he had no choice but to go there. He forced himself to act before he really had time to think it through, before he could let his rational mind overcome his curiosity, and before anybody in corporate could stop him.

This was probably the biggest, wildest, goose chase he had ever heard of, and in the back of his mind he knew there was a good chance his career could be over because of it. Yet, did it really matter any more? He was sixty-two years old, and had been sitting behind that damn desk for the last twelve years, thinking all along that this wasn't what he had envisioned when he joined UNESCO.

The flight went fast, he and Naomi talked constantly. By the time they landed in Victoria, he couldn't wait to meet Captain Mondo.

His life sounded like a movie script. The seatbelt light flashed as the Citation made its final approach.

"Buckle up, Naomi," he said in a fatherly tone.

She smiled at him, noticing how dignified he looked in his trimmed grey beard and long wavy hair tucked back in a short ponytail. Paul Deseno definitely didn't look like a couch potato, desk riding, academic pencil pusher, she thought.

The Citation taxied to a small corner of the airport and was met by Canadian Custom and Immigration, who spent less than five minutes looking at passports. The officials had no clue as to the reason behind this surprise visit by UNESCO, but they were instructed to make the check-in as painless as possible.

After being cleared, they were escorted into a small waiting room, then through a set of wide doors and out into a lobby where Jonathan waited.

"Jonathan, so nice to see you again," Naomi said as she gave him a hug and kissed his cheek.

"Jonathan, meet Paul Deseno."

"Nice to meet you, always good to put a face behind a voice, welcome."

"It is my pleasure."

"I have a small plane chartered to take us to Gold City. From there I have a helicopter standing by. I see no reason not to leave now, unless you would like a break from air travel," Jonathan said, full of excitement.

"Not at all, I say we get to Salmon Creek as soon as possible," Paul replied.

"Splendid," Jonathan said, then escorted them out the door and toward his car.

Paul and Jonathan talked the entire flight. Naomi couldn't tell if Paul was just placating him and his crazy ideas or if he was genuinely interested, but neither of them stopped talking until the small plane touched down.

Fifteen minutes later they were airborne again, flying over some of the most beautiful forests, and mountains Paul had ever seen. The helicopter was so loud that conversation between the two of them stopped, but Naomi figured that if it was up to Jonathan he would have screamed over the roar of the engine the entire time.

Mondo and Dawn each hung on the back of a dirt bike as they carefully made their way up Bald Mountain. His backpack, carrying his hand-held GPS, VHF radio and flashlight, was uncomfortable, the strap digging into his left shoulder where the pad had slipped off. There was no way he could risk letting go of the driver, not even for one second to try and fix it. Mondo kept glancing back at Dawn about twenty feet behind him, watching her expressions go from exhilaration and excitement to fear as the dirt bike made its way up the almost nonexistent service road. Mondo had been hesitant to bring her along, but she insisted, saying that she was a part of whatever happened now, and after all they had been through there was no way she was going to sit in Joseph's house and wait. Mondo had resisted, but when she smiled at him and asked please, there was little he could do to hold her back.

He kept thinking how important this day could end up being. Not just to Joseph and his people but to the entire world. His hope was once Paul Deseno arrived and saw the treasure he would pull every resource that UNESCO had to stop the standoff. It was all he could think of, there was no plan B.

Still hanging on for dear life, he thought about the last few hours and hoped he hadn't overlooked anything. His last phone patch through Hammerhead he had kept as short as possible. He had given Jonathan the approximate coordinates for Bald Mountain and told him there was a place the helicopter could land.

After another twenty minutes or so of rough riding the dirt bikes finally made their way to the top of Bald Mountain and the two of them climbed off, stretched, feeling the pain and stiffness from the ride.

"We'll go back with the helicopter, thank you," Mondo said to the drivers before they turned and started back down the mountain.

Mondo and Dawn stood in the silence, looking at an incredible display of nature, the mountains rolling on one to the other in a silhouette of green that seemed to float out into the distant horizon. Mondo pulled his backpack off as he walked to a small rock shelf and sat down. He reached in his bag and grabbed his hand-held GPS and the VHF radio. Turning the GPS on, he waited until it found the satellites and when his exact location came up on the screen, he turned his radio on and scrolled down to channel thirteen.

"This is Smokin' Joe."

A few seconds later the helicopter replied, "Smokin' Joe, this is your party. Where are you located?"

Mondo read off the GPS coordinates.

"Roger that, we will be there soon, over," the entire conversation lasted less than thirty seconds.

Dawn walked over to where he sat and looked at him.

"Mondo, I'm so glad I'm here with you, to share this wonderful place."

"Me too."

He reached up and grabbed her hand, then lifted himself up and looked deep into her eyes. The glow that radiated from her smile melted him. Gently he reached out and brought her lips to his tasting the sweetness of her kiss. That moment blocked out the rest of the world, as they held each other tight in this pristine wilderness, so far removed from the trappings of the 21st century.

Holding hands, they walked over to a large flat stone, and sat down, looking far to the south, seeing Swartz Bay and the barge in the distance. They sat a while just enjoying the moment and the comfort they each felt.

"Look, Dawn, here comes the helicopter," he said as he pointed to the southeast, and then she saw its small outline reflected against the blue sky. Soon the copter landed and out climbed Jonathan, an older man that Mondo knew was from UNESCO, and Naomi. Mondo walked over and looked at the pilot, who gave him a thumbs up sign, as the blades finally stopped their rotation. Naomi was the last to climb out, and seeing Mondo, she rushed over into his arms.

"Mondo, I am so glad to see you're safe," she said, then suddenly felt awkward seeing Dawn standing twenty feet away watching.

"Naomi, Jonathan, and Mr. Deseno, this is Dawn Peters," Mondo said, twisting to his right and pointing at her. Dawn smiled, but she was surprised at the reaction she felt seeing Naomi.

"Captain Mondo," Paul said as he extended his right hand out, "it's wonderful to meet you. Naomi has told me much about your adventures and exploits."

"It's my pleasure to meet you sir," he replied, "we have a long hike in front of us. It will be hard and getting back up will be even harder. But I can guarantee you all that what you will see will leave you speechless."

"I am speechless already, the beauty of this place," Paul said as he looked south over Swartz Bay and the never-ending mountains.

"Are you aware that a logging company plans to clear-cut all that you can see?" Mondo asked him.

Paul turned and looked at Mondo.

"Surely you jest."

"Surely not. This is scheduled to be logged with government approval, and a lot of blood is going to be spilled before it's over. But for now, shall we start our hike?"

They all smiled and started following Mondo down the backside of Bald Mountain.

Tommy Landford, the radio man and Bud were sitting in the shade of the forest miles from the barge. They hadn't told anybody they were leaving, and even though most of the crew thought it was strange that the three of them took off, nobody dared ask why.

Tommy had his .357 magnum pistol strapped on his belt and Bud carried a shotgun. The radio man was just along because he already knew too much to be left behind. Tommy had been listening all morning to channel thirteen, and when he saw the helicopter coming in for a landing on Bald Mountain, he had a hard time keeping his excitement under control.

Bud didn't know about the treasure, but Tommy had told him that they were going to have a little meeting in the woods this afternoon, and the guy from the bar would be there. That was all Bud cared about. He had already made his mind up he was going to beat the hell out of that boy today.

Tommy had studied the topographical map of Bald Mountain and he saw the faint outline of the old service road. That was all he had to go on, but it was enough for him to make an educated guess. That had to be the way they were coming and the three of them were just waiting.

Chapter 54

Joseph stood in front of the barricade talking to Major Lafferty and over thirty of his soldiers. Fifty feet behind Joseph were twenty of his men standing next to five parked cars, and they were all armed. The last thing the Major wanted was any more bloodshed, but he had to gain control of this situation now.

"You must surrender yourself and all of the men who were involved in the shooting. That is not negotiable. I expect them here within the hour," Lafferty said, trying to keep his voice under control.

"I will give myself in exchange for my father. That is all you need. I am responsible for my people."

"I don't give a shit about that. I want those who pulled the trigger. That's my orders and that is what I intend to accomplish."

The two men stood five feet apart, each knowing that the other would not back down.

"I am sorry then," Joseph said turning away.

"Listen to me. I want them here in an hour or I'm coming in and I will take them, and I will not be responsible for whatever happens."

Joseph turned and studied him. He could see the fear in Lafferty's eyes, and he wondered if his fear was as easy to read.

"Release my father. Take me, that is all I offer. If you enter our town we will fight."

Major Lafferty laughed. "You will fight against the army? Are you crazy, do you want to die?"

"Die? No, I do not want to die, but I may have little choice in the matter."

The major thought about arresting him right then, but he knew he couldn't risk it.

"We have helicopters, soldiers, hell I can get tanks up here. There is no way you can fight against us."

"We can always fight," Joseph said, then turned and started walking back to his men.

Major Lafferty stood there feeling an overwhelming fear growing in the middle of his gut, and he knew this was going to get ugly very soon.

As they reached the valley floor all five of them were exhausted. The strain of climbing down Bald Mountain had taken its toll. Nobody complained, but Paul was definitely the worst of the group as he sat wheezing, trying to catch his breath.

"The good news is, it's pretty much level from here and we don't have far to go," Mondo said, glancing at Paul.

Paul smiled, then they all stood up and continued.

Mondo was holding his GPS, following the route back to the treasure. It would have been impossible to find his way through the dense forest without it. He was completely focused on the GPS, when all of a sudden he heard something that caused him to stop in his tracks. Twenty feet ahead of him, standing side by side were Bud, holding a shotgun, the radioman, and Tommy, holding his .357 in his right hand.

"My, my, what do we have here?" Tommy said in a sinister voice. No one replied.

"Nobody's talking, Bud, what do you think?"

"I don't know, Tommy, it's hard to say."

"Well, Bud, let me guess. I think they're a bunch of well . . . I don't know . . . maybe they're on a treasure hunt."

"A treasure hunt," Bud said, surprised, but playing along.

"I like a treasure hunt, especially when it can make us rich," Tommy said, looking at Mondo.

Paul stepped forward and said, "I am Paul Deseno, from UNESCO. I suggest that you let us pass and leave. If you cause any trouble I will bring down the wrath of the United Nations on you."

Tommy laughed, "That's about the best threat I've heard in a long time, funny as hell mister. The United Nations couldn't wipe its own ass! Now let me ask you a question. What makes you think I'm going to let any of you walk out of here?"

He paused and let his words sink in deep. Mondo and the others knew that these men would not hesitate to kill them.

"I suggest you show us a treasure, Mondo," he said, pointing the .357 right at him.

Mondo didn't move. His thoughts were running a million miles an hour. He stood there analyzing their situation, trying to find one thing that he could turn into an advantage, anything, but he couldn't think of a thing.

Bud lowered his shotgun and took a step.

"I told you boy, I ain't done with you. There ain't going to be any of your fancy ninja shit this time. Not with a stomach full of buckshot," he said as he slid the pump action on the shotgun that put a shell in the chamber.

"Now show us the treasure, or else," Tommy said, and Mondo knew he had no choice.

Two Apache attack helicopters slowly flew over Salmon Creek two hundred feet above the ground. Their orders were not to attack even if fired upon. Major Lafferty hoped to God that these crazy Indians would understand how hopeless their situation was and would surrender. This was getting to the point of no return and pressure was coming down hard on him to get this over with as quickly as possible. He had no idea why they didn't send in a negotiation team. Instead they sent him two attack helicopters. Damn, he thought, somebody wanted this to turn to shit, and if it does, his head will fall.

The helicopters circled the town for ten minutes. Nobody came outside to look at them, not a single person was seen anywhere. It seemed like the entire population of Salmon Creek had headed for the hills, but Lafferty and his people knew better. Each side understood that the time for negotiation was over.

Major Lafferty looked at his watch. It was ten-thirty-five. God, he thought to himself, he had less than four hours to find a peaceful outcome or his orders left him no alternative. By two this afternoon, his troops, along with the attack helicopters would enter Salmon Creek, and all he could think was, heaven help us all.

Mondo led the group, with Bud walking right behind him, the radioman and Tommy bringing up the rear. There was no thought of running. It would be impossible for all of them to get away, and he wasn't leaving anybody behind.

After twenty minutes Mondo stopped.

"Why'd you stop, boy?" Bud said.

Mondo turned, looked at him and had a sudden urge to cram that shotgun down his throat.

Mondo didn't say a word. He walked a few more feet, knelt down and dug up the shovel that Chief Yazzi had left. Glancing back over his shoulder as he stood up, he saw the fear in his friends' faces.

"Dig boy," Tommy said, as he walked up to him.

Mondo walked to his right and started shoveling the earth away, clearing the large rock with the shovel as best he could before kneeling down and brushing it clear with his hands.

"Here's your treasure," he said, standing up.

Tommy stood beside him, looking down at the large flat stone. "Open it."

Taking the shovel, he lifted the front corner and raised the stone up, then he slid it back and out of the way, revealing the dark entrance to the treasure chamber. A smile grew on Tommy's face as he looked at Mondo, then back at his two friends.

"Son of a bitch, I almost didn't believe it."

He turned to Mondo and slowly raised his .357 and pointed it at him.

"I'm following you down that hole. I'm just one step behind you, and I swear one false move and you're dead, and your friends will be next."

He motioned with his pistol, and Mondo had no choice but to drop down into the tunnel and start crawling with Tommy right behind him.

The light from Mondo's flashlight bounced off the narrow walls of the tunnel as he crawled until he could stand up. Tommy stood next to him, then reached over, grabbed the flashlight and started shining it around the room. Slowly Mondo started taking little steps to his right. Tommy ignored him as he followed the glow of the flashlight. A few more steps and Mondo was standing next to the pile of swords and knives on the floor that he had seen earlier. The beam of the flashlight continued to drift away from him and in a second Mondo reached down, grabbed a small dagger and stuffed it in his back pocket, pulling his shirttail out, hiding the small handle.

Tommy suddenly swung the light at him, "Don't move you son of a bitch."

Mondo stood motionless and didn't say a word.

Still holding the flashlight, Tommy continued walking around the room. He stopped in front of the bowl full of jewels, shaking his head in disbelief then took a few more steps before he was standing in front of the Cross. Switching the flashlight to his left hand he reached out and grabbed hold of it. In the dim glow of the flashlight Mondo could see the greed on his face, and he knew they wouldn't get out of here alive. Tommy put the Cross back down and looked at Mondo.

"Son of a bitch, this is a treasure."

Mondo didn't reply. He just stared at him wondering what the hell he could do.

The beam of the light continued to dance around the room. Tommy spent ten minutes looking around the small chamber before he walked back, grabbed the Cross and shined the light at Mondo.

"Time to crawl back out, boy," he said waving the light at the tunnel.

The moment the light left him Mondo grabbed the dagger and held it in his right hand with the blade pointing up his arm, concealing it as best he could.

Tommy held the flashlight and waited until Mondo was ahead of him, then they both started crawling.

As he reached the end of the tunnel Mondo stood, but stopped before he tried to climb out because the daylight was blinding him. He brought his left hand up to protect his eyes and squinted, then blinked twice before he could make out Bud and the other man standing twenty feet away, the barrel of the shotgun pointing down. Jonathan, Naomi, Dawn and Paul sat on the ground ten feet to their left. Mondo kept his right arm in close to his side knowing that either way he held the dagger, somebody was going to see it in the next few seconds. He placed his right foot high on the tunnel wall, then reaching out with both hands he started to pull himself up. Just as he raised his left foot off the ground the dirt gave way under his right foot and he fell back into the tunnel, landing on Tommy, who was just starting to stand. Tommy's right hand held the flashlight and the Cross and he couldn't do anything with it, but instinctively he reached out with his left, trying to grab hold of Mondo as he started to fall backwards. Suddenly, at Mondo's left side, appearing out of the darkness was a hand holding a .357 revolver. Mondo never hesitated, never thought twice as he brought his right hand down hard and in the last second twisted the dagger around and ran it right through Tommy's left hand. Before Tommy had time to scream, Mondo wrenched the pistol free and kicked backwards, sending Tommy rolling into the darkness of the tunnel. Mondo brought the pistol up and pointed it at Bud, who instantly started to raise the shotgun. Mondo couldn't force himself to pull the trigger, he had never shot anybody before. Suddenly, he felt Tommy grabbing his legs, trying to pull him down. Everything seemed to stop for a split-second as he looked at Dawn and saw the fear and terror on her face. Fighting against Tommy and knowing he was losing, he aimed at Bud and fired twice. The second shot hit the radioman, who staggered and fell into Bud, knocking them both to the ground.

Tommy jerked, trying to pull Mondo down into the tunnel. Mondo kicked back with his right leg but the big man was ready, and he grabbed it and pulled Mondo's feet right out from under him. As he started to fall he fired three times, hitting Bud twice in the chest just as he was getting to his feet. The shots sent Bud crashing backwards, the shotgun flying from his grasp and disappearing into the creek. Mondo was so off balance that, as he frantically reached out for something to grab hold of, his right hand smashed into the flat cover stone, knocking the gun out of his hand and sending it flying into the bushes. Desperately fighting back, he spread his arms out as wide as he could grabbing the sides of the tunnel as he pulled his left leg out of Tommy's grasp, and slammed it back into his face. He jerked his right leg free and jumped.

In the next second Mondo was outside the tunnel on his knees desperately searching for the .357, which was impossible to find in the brush and stickers. Tommy stood up, reached out, grabbed Mondo's right foot and pulled it out from underneath him, sending him crashing to the ground. Instinctively Mondo rolled to his right as Tommy jumped out of the tunnel and brought a huge boot down, missing Mondo's head by inches. Tommy was so off balance that he couldn't kick again, and that bought Mondo a few precious seconds as he scrambled back to his feet before Tommy lunged at him. Almost three hundred pounds of muscle powered by pain and fury flew through the air with incredible speed. Mondo dodged to his right, and Tommy's momentum carried him too far, leaving his side exposed. Mondo smashed his right fist into Tommy's kidney, a punch that sent the big man stumbling to his knees. With incredible speed Tommy picked himself up, turned and charged. Mondo struggled backward trying to fight him off, waiting for just the right moment. Then, as he had practiced a thousand times before, he reached out, grabbed Tommy's right hand, rotated the wrist, and twisted it to the right. Mondo's next move surprised Tommy as he suddenly changed direction and stepped forward, spinning underneath Tommy's right hand and snapping it downward in a twisting motion. Time seemed to stand still before the wrist lock forced Tommy to his knees. Mondo kicked out with his right foot, snapping Tommy's head back. Before Mondo could kick again Tommy wrenched his hand free and slammed it into Mondo's side, knocking the air from his lungs and driving him back until he fell on the ground. Tommy was still on his knees trying to stand when Mondo put all of his weight on his left arm, swung himself around, kicking with his right leg, he hit Tommy in the face, knocking him flat to the ground. Mondo jumped up trying to catch his breath as Tommy pulled himself back to his feet, blood running down his right cheek. The look on his face told Mondo that only one of them was going to walk away from this alive. Tommy charged, and Mondo somehow managed to jump out of the way. As Tommy tried to turn and grab him, Mondo found his breath, screamed a 'kiai' that echoed through the forest and kicked out with a powerful side-kick that caught Tommy completely exposed, smashing into his rib cage, stopping him in his tracks. Before Tommy could move Mondo screamed again, focusing all of his power, as he unleashed a high front-kick that slammed under Tommy's chin, sending him to his knees before he collapsed face first in the dirt. Tommy struggled to get up but he was too slow. Mondo jumped high into the air and brought his right foot down on the back of Tommy's head, snapping his neck as if he had dropped from the gallows. Mondo's momentum carried him forward as he stumbled, then fell, landing on his injured right side, creating a jolt of pain that almost caused him to black out.

In the next instant Dawn was at his side, tears streaming down her face.

Mondo knew some of his ribs must be broken and it was too painful for him to move. Before he could really understand what was happening, Jonathan, Naomi and Paul were all kneeling next to him.

Forcing the pain away for just one moment he sat up, and looked at them, still gasping for air trying to get the words out.

"Hurry . . . look at the treasure . . . we don't have much time," he managed to say.

Chapter 55

Major Lafferty looked at his watch as he sat in the corner of his tent, trying to keep his fear under control after hanging up from his superior officer. He had less than an hour before he was to enter Salmon Creek. He knew his superiors were taking their orders from the politicians in Parliament and they didn't understand the severity of this situation. They were hoping to intimidate these First Nation people into surrendering and he knew it would never work. For the first time in his military career he knew he should disobey an order. Whoever was calling the shots, some bastard hidden in the corridors of Parliament, was wrong to force this confrontation. Enough blood had already been spilled and if he took his troops into Salmon Creek he knew a lot more people were going to die. It was twelve-fifteen, and he didn't know what to do.

Mondo sat under a cedar tree, his side turning black and blue and the pain of Tommy's blow growing by the minute. He had hardly been able to stand and walk twenty feet before he had to sit down again. The thought of climbing Bald Mountain seemed impossible. Dawn and Naomi sat next to him while Jonathan and Paul were in the treasure chamber. Mondo looked at both of them and smiled, trying to ease their fears.

"Naomi, please tell Paul and Jonathan we need to leave."

She stood up and walked over to the tunnel entrance, knelt down and called to them, then she turned and looked at Mondo, his head resting on Dawn's lap, and she knew they truly loved each other.

Jonathan and Paul climbed out, slid the cover stone back into place, and threw some dirt on it before they walked over to Mondo as he carefully stood up.

"What do you think?" Mondo asked, looking at Paul and Jonathan.

Jonathan was speechless. All he could do was shake his head in amazement.

"It is beyond anything that I could have hoped for, anything I could ever have dreamed of," Paul said, Jonathan nodding enthusiastically next to him.

"We have to get back to Joseph and try to stop the army. Paul, now that you have seen this do you think you can get UNESCO to apply pressure to the Canadian Government to back off?"

"I don't know. We are non-political. Besides it could take months," he said, disappointment etched on his face.

Mondo looked at him.

"Months! You don't have an hour! Do you realize what is about to happen?" He shouted, his anger growing as he felt the hopelessness of the situation.

"First, a lot of Joseph's people are going to be killed and even more will be put in prison, then some goddamn loggers will come in here and cut this forest to the ground, do you understand that?"

He stared at Paul, then took three steps closer until he was standing right in front of him, his face just inches away.

"If that happens this treasure will be lost forever, because Joseph will be dead and I swear I will never reveal this location. If this turns into war and Joseph and his people are killed this treasure will never be found."

Then without another word, he turned and walked away, followed by Naomi and Dawn.

"What can we do?" Paul asked, looking at Jonathan.

"We can get in that goddamn helicopter, fly to Salmon Creek, park our asses in the middle of a war and pray that somebody has enough brains to listen to us," Jonathan said.

"Amen," Paul replied.

Mondo and the girls continued walking. Jonathan and Paul spent a few minutes looking around before they took off running after them. Even with the help of a good hiking stick Mondo knew it would be impossible for him to climb Bald Mountain. He walked in silence for a few more minutes thinking about what to do next, each step becoming more painful, until it was almost impossible to continue.

"Listen," he said as he stopped and looked at all of them, "you can't wait for me. You need to take the GPS and go as fast as you can and get to the helicopter. From there it's your call. But I hope you contact somebody and stop this insanity," he said handing his GPS to Jonathan.

"I don't know how to use one of these," Jonathan said.

"Shit, what about you, Paul?"

"Never had to use one, I can't even turn my computer on."

"Well, you'll never find the service road without it and you can't wait for me."

"I'll take them," Naomi said as she grabbed the GPS and looked at Mondo.

"How will you find the service road?" she asked him.

"I won't. I can't make it. I have another plan."

"What?" Dawn cried out.

"Listen Naomi," he said, ignoring Dawn's question, "take Jonathan, Paul and Dawn and get to the helicopter as fast as you can."

"Mondo, I'm staying with you," Dawn cried.

He looked at her, and this time he wasn't going to let her change his mind.

"Dawn, go with them. I want all of you to get to the copter now."

There was no doubt in any of their minds that he meant what he said.

"Mondo, I can't leave you, not again," Dawn whispered, tears already starting to form.

"Go, all of you, go as fast as you can, a lot of lives depend on you," he managed to say, his side throbbing in pain.

"What are you going to do?" Dawn asked.

"Just go," he said, before he turned and started walking.

They all stood there almost in shock, watching him walk away, before Naomi took off at a good run. They had no choice but to follow her. Soon Mondo was alone, leaning on his hiking stick, knowing that the only way he was going to get out of here alive was to head for the barge.

*

The charter helicopter took off, kicking a whirlwind of dust up into the air.

The pilot couldn't believe that they wanted him to fly to Salmon Creek. He had been listening to the news. There was no way he was going to fly there.

"You're crazy, I'm heading back to Gold City," he shouted at them over his right shoulder.

"I am a representative of the United Nations," Paul said as he flashed his ID card in front of him, "and this is an emergency. If you do not take us to Salmon Creek immediately I will see that you never fly a goddamn thing the rest of your life, do you understand me?"

"Listen Mister, there's a war about to start there and I ain't going, so forget it."

Slowly Paul reached into his front pocket and pulled out a small bronze knife he had taken from the treasure chamber. In the next second he reached up and held it to the pilot's throat.

"Son, just get us to Salmon Creek, now!" he shouted.

Everyone in the copter was shocked, but slowly the helicopter changed course.

"Salmon Creek it is, you crazy son of a bitch," the pilot said.

Joseph stood in the middle of the dusty road, staring at the oncoming troops. Two attack helicopters hovered over the advancing soldiers as they slowly came his way. Almost a hundred armed men stood behind him spread out, blocking the road. Each man knew that they had no chance of defeating the army, yet they would fight just the same. They would follow Joseph to death itself.

Major Lafferty led his troops and his lieutenant was in direct contact with the helicopter pilots. He prayed that this show of force would finally cause Joseph and his people to negotiate, yet he held out little hope for that.

He stopped a hundred feet from Joseph and brought the loud speaker that he had been carrying up to his lips.

"Joseph, please do not do this. Surrender your people and I will see that you are treated fairly."

Joseph slowly started walking toward him holding his old hunting rifle in his right hand. His men started to follow but he turned, looked at them, shook his head slightly, and they stopped. He walked to within thirty feet of Major Lafferty.

"Go back. There will never be justice for my people."

"Joseph, please," Lafferty was almost in tears trying to find some way to stop what was about to happen.

"Leave our lands."

"I can't," Lafferty replied.

Slowly Joseph knelt down on his right knee, raised his rifle and pointed it at one of the helicopters.

Joseph's men all dropped to the ground and raised their weapons. Lafferty knew he wouldn't survive the first volley.

"Sir, the copters want to fire. What should we do?"

"Nothing, hold your fire!" Major Lafferty screamed, still hoping somehow to stop this.

Joseph aimed at the lead copter and slowly started to squeeze the trigger. His breath seemed to stop and in that instant, just before firing, he heard a faint sound in the distance. He lowered his rifle slightly and looked to his right to see a helicopter racing in from the south, heading directly toward him.

Lafferty saw the helicopter too.

"Who the hell is that?" Lafferty shouted at his lieutenant.

"No idea, sir."

Lafferty turned to his men and held both hands up in the air in a desperate attempt to signal that no one was to fire.

The helicopter descended and then landed right in between Joseph and Major Lafferty. The copter had barely touched down before Paul jumped out, looked around, then ran to Major Lafferty.

"I am Paul Deseno. I'm from the United Nations. This needs to stop now!"

"Thank God," Lafferty said.

Mondo limped out of the forest onto the beach, then stopped and stared at BELWOLF IV. The loggers who had been standing around were so surprised to see him they all stopped whatever they were doing and watched. Leaning on his hiking stick, he walked until he was standing on what was left of the small dock. He looked up at the men on the barge, shifted his weight, and wondered what the hell he was going to say.

By now every logger stared at him. Nobody had any idea who this guy was, but he sure looked beat up. They all wondered if he had anything to do with Tommy, Bud and the radio man leaving earlier today. No matter what, they all knew he had balls to stand before them like he did.

"Listen," Mondo shouted, "three more of your people are dead. We need to stop fighting each other. Nothing is worth it, don't you understand?"

None of the loggers said a word, but each man knew that no amount of money was going to bring any of their friends back from the grave.

"It's got to stop," he shouted again, supporting himself with his hiking stick.

Suddenly Michael rushed to the front of the barge holding a high powered rifle.

"You bastard!" he screamed, and before anybody could react he lowered the barrel and fired, hitting the dock a few inches in front of Mondo. The impact of the bullet blew a large hole in one of the few remaining supporting beams and the dock started to give way. Mondo instinctively pushed himself back but tripped over his hiking stick, and as the dock started to crash around him he looked up and saw Michael cocking another round into the chamber. With that thought he tumbled into the icy water landing on his broken ribs, feeling the pain as the cold took his breath away. Even under water he felt another bullet fly past his head. His broken ribs made it impossible to swim, and as hard as he tried, he couldn't kick himself to the surface.

Michael cocked the rifle again and pointed it to where he could see Mondo struggling under the water. He knew that either way, Mondo was about as good as dead.

No one will ever tell which of the loggers it was, but somebody standing near Michael quietly walked over to him and hit him with a right hand so hard that he crumpled on the deck, dropping the rifle overboard. Three loggers jumped into the water, one of them swam down, grabbed Mondo's shirt collar and dragged him to shore.

Gasping for air Mondo looked up into the eyes of the tough young logger who had just saved his life and couldn't believe the tears that he saw.

"You're right, mister, enough people have already died . . ." he said looking at Mondo, still fighting to hold back his tears.

"Enough of my friends have already died," the logger said softly as he turned away from Mondo, sat on the sand and cried.

* * *

It took Mondo over a month to recover from his injuries. He spent three days in the hospital and countless hours telling the police everything he knew. The logging of the Killiatt Wilderness area was immediately stopped and a government inquest was started to look into the entire issue. The Killiatt had other friends as well, and with pressure from UNESCO and the United States Government, it was on the fast track to becoming a World Heritage Site. It would never be logged.

Chief Yazzi spent two weeks in jail before being released as the police tried to sort out the facts behind the killing of the five loggers. He died at home, his son by his side, two days later. Joseph knew the cancer didn't kill him. It was his father's time to go and greet his ancestors, and nothing could hold him back.

In the end only Leonard Dancing Hawk was charged in the killings. By the time he went to trial the attempted logging of the Killiatt Wilderness Area had become such an embarrassment to the Provincial Government that he would spend less than a year in prison before he was quietly released.

Flick made it back to Montreal and it didn't take him long to find Gloria. She couldn't have been happier when he knocked on her door one evening and asked her out for sushi. They started a wholesale organic food distribution network that made them millionaires in less than five years.

Joseph followed in his father's footsteps, growing in wisdom, and becoming a loved and respected leader of his people.

Michael Jensen never recovered from the head trauma that Mondo inflicted. In less than two years he had lost everything and was living on the streets of Vancouver before he disappeared into the void, never to be seen or heard from again.

The treasure has yet to be revealed to the world. The entire contents of the treasure chamber were carefully removed under the strictest of secrecy, flown out by helicopter and taken to the Smithsonian in Washington D.C. for further study. However, it would never have left Canada without the blessing of the Canadian Government and Chief Joseph, who in his wisdom realized that it was now time for somebody else to care for this precious gift.

Jonathan resigned from teaching and from the museum, and with help from Paul, became one of the many scientists and scholars who started to study this incredible treasure from the ancient past. Jonathan knew that eventually, if no one else did, he would reveal this treasure to the world. It belonged to every person on the planet and he could only hope that somehow, in some mysterious and magical way, this gift from the gods might bring sanity back into an insane world.

Even though there were more than a few years between them, Naomi and Paul became the best of friends, and some think, even lovers.

Mondo seemed at a loss as he healed, but he knew one thing for sure. He certainly wasn't ready to let Dawn walk out of his life again. As a matter of fact they're going sailing this weekend, and the weather looks perfect.

THE END

WILLIAM F. CARLI is a world traveler, adventurer and off-shore sailor. He has a black belt in Taekwondo and also studies Aikido. He and his wife live on a small island in the Pacific Northwest in the summer and an even smaller island in the Caribbean in the winter. Stone Totem is his second novel.

Printed in the United States
154644LV00001B/2/P